A chill shook Meg's bones like empty spools on a thread. Her glasses went foggy as tears welled up. She dug her fingers into the slope and everywhere they were met by roots, roots like long, knotted fingers that were touching her, gripping her. Her scream came easily now, shrill and sharp as broken glass. Her knees and elbows pumped and skidded along the slope. Her line was twisting loose. Then, in a moment of clarity, she yanked the claw hoe of her belt, dug it between the roots, and pulled herself up. Her knees found purchase and somehow shoved her forward. Something snagged her heel and she kicked it free.

And then she was over the crest, running so fast she was nearly on all fours. She could still hear her own screams echoing from that horrible dark slope somewhere behind her . . .

WiZrD

STEVE ZELL

SMP
ST. MARTIN'S PAPERBACKS

WIZRD

Copyright © 1994 by Steve Zell.

ISBN 0-312-95373-9

Printed in the United States of America

St. Martin's Press hardcover edition / February 1994
St. Martin's Paperbacks edition / December 1994

10 9 8 7 6 5 4 3 2 1

To Nina, for being patient, but mostly just for being.

Acknowledgments

M Y thanks to Jennifer Levine and Manuela Wacha for introducing me to St. Martin's Press and to Janine Coughlin for actually opening the door and letting me in; very special thanks to Reagan Arthur for putting it all together and keeping it that way (even without the expensive Macintosh she so richly deserves). I also thank Sedona and Jerome, Arizona, for their part in shaping Piñon Rim, and the people of Tombstone, living or not, who celebrate the spirit of Helldorado every year . . .

Prologue

MICHAEL Buckhorn ran barefoot across the smooth sandstone, the soles of his small feet well-padded and sure. The others had run with him until he'd crossed the dead river into the green valley; now he ran only with the wind.

The ground became cool and soft with pine needles; the floor of the world rose. Soon he would be at the very top of the earth, where the heart of the World Mother was pierced with sorrow.

His grandmother had sung the ancient song, and signs had been revealed to her. He had watched her draw a perfect circle in the sand . . .

Within the circle she drew the tall form of the Spirit of the Under-world. In the belly of the Spirit, she traced another circle, and in that, the form of a sleeping child.

> *It begins with water.*
> *It ends with fire.*
> *Though it ends, it begins again.*
> *The Harvest is gathered.*
> *The Harvest will be scattered in the wind.*
> *This is the Circle of the Harvest.*

Her hands, twisted with age, traveled smoothly across her painting, marking precise points along the way. Two curls of blue sand formed a river. A jagged stroke of black sand became a crow; three wisps of red earth, a sacrificial fire.

"The Spirit of the Underworld stirs in the womb of the

1

*Mother. I have felt the cold rain, and I have heard silence
in the forest as she waits for his song to begin.*

*Michael's grandmother took his hand and poured white
sand into his palm. She guided his hand over the painting
until the white stream broke the circle . . .*

Michael Buckhorn broke from the forest. Where he stood the
rock was bare and bloodred. A deep fissure cut jaggedly
through the heart of the plateau . . .

Where the heart of the World Mother was pierced with sorrow.

The wind gently fanned him. He could hear the waters gush
deep within the fissure. There were no birds singing here, no
squirrels playfully chattering . . .

I have heard silence in the forest as she waits . . .

If he failed, if the Spirit of the Underworld snatched his
spirit, there would be no more birds singing anywhere. He
knew this from his grandmother's songs. But he wouldn't fail.

He dug a spike of braided cornhusks and an old lighter from
his pocket. Fluid leaked from a dent near the lighter's catch,
but that would work to his purpose. He doused the husks with
the oily fluid and walked to the edge of the fissure. He could
feel his grandmother with him; he closed his eyes and saw her.

*Her sight had been taken long ago, but the World Mother
had given her the Power of the Touch in return, and now
the world saw for her. Her eyes were white beneath her lids,
no longer eyes so much as bulbs of white flesh. But Michael
had never feared them. Nor had he ever felt pity for this
woman who seemed to work the dark secrets of the universe
with the same deftness she did her brightly colored sands.*

*"You were chosen to complete the circle," she had said,
"but now you must break it."*

Michael Buckhorn peered into the chasm. The walls of the
great wound were as black as charred wood. The churning
waters far below were angry and white.

Somewhere in that horrible, shadowy place, the Spirit of the

Underworld lay waiting for him. The wind sheared up the canyon walls and he turned away.

He hunched over the lighter to keep it going as he lit his small torch of cornhusks and cloth.

It begins with water. It ends with fire.

Michael Buckhorn emptied the lighter against his shirt. He stretched his arms wide and the wind funneled up around him. He whirled with the wind at the brink of the fissure. The flames licked his sleeve, leapt from the torch, and ran across his arm and shoulders; the hair at the back of his neck was singed.

The circle would be broken. The land would remain at peace.

He chanted the song his grandmother had sung, "The Circle of the Harvest," and he turned faster and faster with the wind.

> *It begins with water.*
> *It ends with fire.*
> *Though it ends, it begins again.*
> *The Harvest is gathered.*
> *The Harvest will be scattered in the wind . . .*

And when the pain consumed him, he plummeted into the great wound.

The waters took Michael Buckhorn away forever.

1

 H E didn't hate northern Arizona. It just wasn't up-state New York.

And the Big House was pretty cool, with its gables and shutters, especially now with the air dewy and still, the dark clouds gathering behind the peaked skylights. Bryce stood on his pedals and coasted the rest of the way down the hill, carefully navigating his wheels along the deeply rutted path. White light cracked the sky, and Bryce counted nine before the shock-wave thundered over the rim. He wheeled the old Schwinn Stingray through the gate and swung himself off, letting the bike glide to a stop on its own behind the rosemary barrel.

Megan's face was pale behind her window as she waved from the second floor. What sunlight there was glinted on those awful glasses. The lenses were too thick for a decent frame; the frame, way too wide for such a small face. He waved back and windmilled his pack across the porch. It smacked the wall with a crack that matched the thunder, and Megan laughed at him through the window, like she always did.

"Honey, please don't do that."

Cathleen appeared at the screen door, looking more weary and bored than scornful. The move hadn't been so easy for her either, and she'd been unpacking boxes for three days straight.

"Sorry."

"And wipe your feet."

"Uh-huh."

He winked to Meg as he hopped the steps and she winked back.

He took another look across the meadow to the forest and the darkening skies beyond, and white light flashed again. He counted five this time. Thunder rumbled and exploded. The low clouds swathed the treetops like angel's hair.

It was going to be a big one.

THE house smelled like a confusion of rain, fresh-baked bread, and linseed oil. Bryce sipped his coffee and stood by the window. He'd never really liked coffee all that much, but hell, he'd be fourteen before the school year ended, he wasn't a little kid anymore. Cathleen hadn't been too thrilled when he'd started drinking it, but his dad was cool about it and she'd given in. Sometimes she'd even offer it now.

Meg had tramped down the stairs to greet him; now she sat cross-legged in the big chair by the fireplace, a *National Geographic* in her lap. She looked up at him over a full-color shot of a caver dwarfed by an immense cavern.

"What's it like?" Two tiny lines crimped the space just above her nose.

"School looks okay. Some of it's pretty new—most of it's ancient."

Rain pelted the windows. Bryce squinted at the forest. The meadow was almost gone now; clouds squatted in the yard. God, this place was strange.

"Is it going to be all right?" Meg's mom asked from the kitchen.

It was a school—it was three buildings and a football field. It was two thousand miles from his friends in New York.

"Yeah, I guess."

It would have to be. He didn't have much say about it, and he could thank Larry Brill for that. Fat, greasy Larry Brill and his song and dance about "the modern freaking Renaissance in Piñon Rim." He owed Larry for that one; Larry, and his father's dry spell.

Meg's mom, the new Mrs. Willems, backed through the kitchen door, balancing a perfectly stacked pyramid of steaming cinnamon rolls on a china plate. That was one thing about her, she could bake all right. She wasn't so bad; it was just that, like northern Arizona wasn't upstate New York, Cathleen Willems wasn't his mom. Not really.

He took a roll and she smiled up at him. He was already two inches taller than she was. Megan was kind of small too, although in the two years he'd known her he hadn't seen much else to connect Meg with her mom. Meg was pretty cool.

Lightning double-flashed the room. Somewhere out there, maybe not so far away, a tree fell. He could hear it ripping through the forest like a broken mast through a deck. Thunder rolled. Sheets of rain slapped the roof. A chill raced through him even though the fire was roaring and the house was warm. It was actually kind of a neat feeling. Electric. Something about to happen in a big way. So he watched the rain and the clouds gobble the forest and imagined something big happening "out there." Judging by what he'd seen of Piñon Rim so far, he'd be using his imagination a lot. It wasn't enough to say that Piñon Rim was dead—that would imply the place had once had a pulse. Cathleen set the plate near the window and stood closer to the fire. As far as his dad's dry spell went, Bryce supposed they were still doing okay.

"Did you see any teachers?" Meg asked. "What are the teachers like?"

"Trolls," he said, "nothing but trolls and ogres. They live in little mounds of mud out by the cafeteria."

Meg's laugh was sort of a happy stutter somewhere between a giggle and a real laugh—more on the giggle side. It was a sound that usually made Bryce laugh too.

"The place is all locked up. Didn't see anyone but a couple little kids on the playground."

"I think the campus is nice, don't you?" If Cathleen stood any closer to the fireplace, she'd be in it.

Campus? *It's a grade school*. He shrugged. It would pass. Saint Andrews back in Niscayuna hadn't been that much to look at either. At least Piñon Rim Elementary had a real football field with real goalposts. The Saint Andrews "field" had been a less than forgiving expanse of blacktop lined with shin-cracking white pickets. The main hall of both schools looked similar: two-story brick jobs with high, pointy roofs to shed snow; both schools had large combination gym/auditorium/cafeterias. PRE also had a brand-spanking-new one-story hall of classrooms. The varnish still smelled fresh on it. Bryce had ridden his bike up to the windows and looked inside. The desks were tiny—had to be for the lower grades. There was, thankfully, no church at Piñon Rim Elementary, so no midday mass.

The land surrounding the two schools could have been from different planets.

The main schoolhouse of Saint Andrews had rested uncomfortably close to the viciously busy Main Street of Niscayuna, which Bryce and his friends had dubbed "The Dog Grinder," a name he'd twice seen justified. PRE was nestled between two giant mounds of red rock covered with some pretty weak-looking pines. There was a decent creek on the other side of the football field, and a thick forest beyond that, the same forest that was melting away just past the backyard.

He described the basic layout for Meg. Her first dad had been a salesman so she was used to changing schools, but it was a new experience for Bryce. His dad had been happy enough in upstate New York before Bryce's mom left. Then came the dry spell, and then his friend Larry Brill came crowing about this magic little slice of heaven called Piñon Rim. Bryce knew his dad was a pretty hot artist. Larry Brill had always been more or less marginal; Brill and New York abandoned each other three years ago. Somehow, he'd wound up here. And maybe there *was* some magic in this place, because he'd been getting a lot of assignments lately. Bryce had to admit Larry's *Rothgar the Warrior* stuff was pretty good.

Across the yard, the tall, dark trees had become grayish, pointy-headed ghosts. Bryce sat on the couch, sipped his coffee, and watched the rain.

The aroma of linseed oil preceded his father's hand on his shoulder, and Bryce felt at home and homesick all at once. Lightning flashed an X ray of the trees, and thunder shook the Big House to its old bones before Bryce had even counted two. The rain had found the old miner's pan that hung on a nail just outside the porch, and the smell of fresh rain and pine needles

7

seeped through every pore of the Big House. Wind rattled the panes and howled beneath the eaves.

"Quite a show, huh?"

Bryce nodded. It was.

"Painting?"

"Cleaning. Sables went stiff on me."

His father took a sip from Bryce's cup and grimaced at the lack of sugar. He handed it back and finished off the cinnamon roll.

"Storms like this are great. Wash the old dead skin away. You get to see what's under all the crud. Tomorrow it'll be a whole different world out there."

Another white-hot flash, and for a flickering moment Bryce saw a laughing wizard in the mist, his dagger-tipped fingers raised, sparking with unearthly power. But it was only the swaying ghost of a tree.

"Good to mix it up, you know?" Trevor slipped an arm around Cathleen's waist and they kissed, and Bryce took a sudden interest in his coffee cup.

Meg had been reading, but now she was staring out the window where Bryce had been looking. Her thick lenses magnified her concentration. Bryce winked, but she didn't wink back. He glanced out the window again but saw only clouds and rain and ghosts of trees.

H A L F a mile from the Big House, Wendell Mackey set about the preparation of Buddy's 7:30 snack as he did every night. One can of Cycle Four (he'd have used Cycle Five if they made it—Buddy was getting on in years), with a little something extra. There was always a little something extra for Buddy. Tonight it was two mean slices of honey-baked ham. Buddy was just over fifteen, which made the dog-year computation somewhere in the ballpark of 105 if you were to believe such things. But his appetite was all pup.

Wendell set his walker to one side. Sometimes the contraption was more nuisance than convenience, and his back was behaving tonight. He followed the bowl along the counter to the door.

It wasn't like Buddy to get caught in the rain. Wendell wasn't worried though. If Buddy'd wound up on the other side of the creek when it swelled, he wouldn't try to cross. He'd just find himself someplace dry and warm and call it a night.

Wendell kept his part of the bargain just the same. He cracked the kitchen door and the cold wet roared in. The small island of dry decking was Buddy's place, protected by a double layer of tar on the roof which Wendell had spread himself. The rest of the overhang leaked and the porch was soaked. Wendell shouldered the door halfway open and slid the bowl next to Buddy's water, which looked clean enough for all the mayhem.

There was nothing but rain and blackness beyond the back steps. He shut the door behind him, shivering the cold away while the rain marched its tin-booted parade across his roof. He looked for Buddy through the kitchen window.

Buddy's a smart old guy. He won't cross if the creek looks angry.

And angry it was. Where it skirted Piñon Rim downstream, Sharpe's Creek thundered. It scooped bloody gouts of mud from the soft shoulders of its banks and rolled satchel-sized boulders along its bed.

Upstream, on a hill not far from the Big House, one of the streams that fed Sharpe's Creek was growing. Above it, the entire hillside was in motion. A thin blanket of needle-covered sod blistered and slid away like dead skin, leaving a jagged scar. Roots gave up stones they'd held for eons, and as the water sheeted down, a whole section of the hillside gave way. Black water gushed from a long-hidden pocket.

The old golden Labrador watched from the shelter of a deadfall. He circled inside his tiny compartment as the taste of sulphur soured the air. There was no relief in any direction. He curled onto his warm spot of earth and waited.

A squirrel skidded down the side of a pine across the wash downstream. Buddy's muscles tensed and his ears pricked up. He made his decision in an instant: The rain was cold and the stream was high—the squirrel got a break tonight. Buddy rested his gray chin on his paws, listening to the crackle of the

9

rain in the high branches and the dull thudding on the sod below.

In a flash he was up again.

A tongue of icy blue light flared suddenly from the hole in the hill. It fanned into the heavens, turning the raindrops to molten silver. Buddy whined and barked as the forest shimmered around him.

The light narrowed to a tight beam. It caught the squirrel full on.

The forest went black except for the ghosts of light in Buddy's eyes.

Gradually, the trees and rocks and the wet bank reappeared. Gradually, he became aware of the squirrel.

The squirrel's tiny head and shoulders popped up over the log. It ducked away, sending the small ferns dancing behind it. Seconds later, it was back. It darted off again, raced into the forest, and returned as Buddy watched.

Buddy woofed out a bark, intrigued and irked by the odd behavior. The squirrel disappeared, returned, and was gone again.

Buddy circled, growling now. He backed to the deepest recesses of his fortress, charged the entrance, and barked again.

The squirrel reappeared at the log, then disappeared into the forest. Heedless of the rain, of Buddy's challenge, it was caught in an endless cycle of activity.

THEIR house had first belonged to a banker named Percival Easton in the boomtown days of Piñon Rim. Built of stone, it was a castle among the small wooden structures that prevailed in the little mining town. It had been a hub of sorts, a watering hole for the town "gentry" as well as home for Easton, his wife, and their two sons. That was a hundred years ago. Until Trevor Willems bought it for a song (actually, two paintings) last spring and had it gutted and fitted for modern times, it had stood vacant, gloomily counting the passing decades with the other less fortunate (and less sturdy) structures that jutted from the surrounding hillsides.

That much Bryce knew. Beyond that, he didn't care. He was here now. He'd been sentenced to spend eighth grade in a school practically a continent away from home and friends— and God only knew how far away from a real city.

The normal course of life as he'd come to know it said you were a little kid through seventh grade. You made your friends and you took your lumps from the big kids and you waited your turn. You were supposed to be top dog in eighth grade. Now Bryce had to start all over again. And next year he'd be a freshman in some Podunk high school somewhere—the lowest of the low all over again.

Bryce pumped the pedals and crested another hill on Sluice Road. The unpaved road was muddy and crosshatched with branches. He'd replaced the Stingray's street tires with a knobby balloon-type the day after they'd moved in. The new tires carried him over the little stuff pretty well, but he had to wheely and stand over a lot of the rougher ground. The storm had been major. He'd seen a lot of trees split down to their roots, their rust-colored insides reduced to sawdust.

He stopped to rest his legs. No hurry. No big plans till Monday, when school started. In the distance, hidden from the road by oak and pine, he could hear Sharpe's Creek churning over the rocks. It had been a peaceful enough mountain stream when he'd ridden out here yesterday.

The cool air tasted of mesquite and fresh earth. It made him feel strong and clean somehow. His legs were sore but it was a good feeling. Getting up these mountain roads took some skill and a lot of strength. It was a feat made all the more remarkable when accomplished atop an ancient street bike with only one gear. But there was a purpose to that: football. He'd rip through the secondaries like they were paper cutouts next season. He'd get a mountain bike someday, but the old Stingray had been his dad's when his dad was a kid, and it was still in pretty cool shape. It didn't take much to keep it going, but if something needed doing they did it together: packing bearings, replacing spokes, whatever it took. Tinkering with the bike was one of the few things that got Trevor out of the studio.

A family of quail scurried onto the road. Bryce laughed at their quick-footed, straight-backed gait: it was as if they were trying to rush and look dignified at the same time. They were no more than halfway across Sluice when a shotgun blast ripped the air.

Bryce's foot slipped and the bike took off on its own. He caught it stiff-legged, and the long handlebars hooked him like an angry bull. Before he knew it, he was tumbling downhill. He took a pedal in the chest and belly flopped in the middle of the road, wheezing. It felt like his lungs had rattled loose.

Not ten feet away two baby quail were tracing erratic circles in the road; they battered the ground with dead wings. A third was little more than a loose clump of feathers and red pulp.

Hoots and hollers and the sound of boots cracking through the forest, then another pounding blast and all the birds vanished in a spray of mud, pine needles, and feathers.

"Whoop! Whoop!"

"Man, they exploded, man! Did you see them freaking explode!"

"Whoop! Whoop!"

Bryce felt Cathleen's hash and eggs rising in his throat. Somehow he kept it all down.

Three boys—two big guys and one little one—crashed into the clearing. A hot flush of anger burned his throat; he pushed the bike away. But cold fear jabbed him deep in the gut when he got a good look at them.

His mouth moved on its own.

"Whoa!" was what he finally blurted out.

The one with the shotgun had swung the barrel Bryce's way and Bryce felt his knees go rubbery. His cheeks burned and he knew they'd gone red.

"Learn to ride a bike."

Mister Shotgun was massive, with greasy jet black hair hanging past his jaw and small black doll eyes. The tallest kid was weasel-thin, his ropy arms twisted from his shirt sleeves like snakes from a tree limb. A big hole in his gums showed where at least two teeth should have been. His hair was crewcut and colorless, the scalp beneath sweaty and pink. The little kid was maybe ten or so, Meg's age, probably Shotgun's brother by the looks of him. It was plain he would grow up just as ugly.

"Yeah. Ride a bike," he said.

Without further ceremony the big ones crashed through a blackberry thicket and thundered toward Sharpe's Creek. The little one spat, then turned and followed them down the hillside. Seconds later, the shotgun pounded the air again, followed by hoots and hollers that rose up and echoed from the creek.

Bryce took a deep breath. His heart thumped. He could still hear them in the distance. His head felt light, and for a moment it seemed he saw himself from somewhere above. He could have taken either of the big ones by himself. But he hadn't tried it. He hadn't done anything.

They had a shotgun. And they'd been together. This place was warped. He was just out riding his stupid bike and somebody pointed a freaking shotgun at him. And those quail! *Geez!* For a moment there was no clearer thought than that.

He swept the Stingray over his head, every muscle twisting beneath his skin.

He nearly threw it.

He set it down. He wouldn't be any better off with a trashed bike.

The heat was still in his face. He hated that. It was such a stupid dead giveaway. If he got scared or mad, his face went red as a freaking fire engine. He stared at the trail of broken, muddied ferns beside the road with a half-crazed urge to go after them.

Finally, he smacked the worst of the sticky reddish mud from his jeans. He rolled up his sweatshirt and gingerly fingered the long red welt rising across his chest. It burned, but the skin wasn't broken. He dropped the shirt and stood staring at the hole in the underbrush.

He didn't feel much like riding into town anymore. But he didn't feel like going back to the Big House either. Ultimately, town won out.

His chest ached, but he was okay. The bike looked as if it had survived, too. He checked the spokes and pulled a handful of needles from the sprockets. Then he climbed on and pumped his way toward Piñon Rim, wondering what to expect next.

P O R T R A I T of Trevor Willems, the artist, in his new studio. That's what Trevor saw in the mirrors lining the west wall of his loft. He hefted a wide roll of cotton duck over his shoulder and shook his head.

What am I doing here?

He rocked the cotton in next to the other canvas spools standing against the row of custom bins he'd installed, then took another coffee break. He clicked on the dimmers and adjusted the banks of lights. Then he clicked them off and let the skylights do their job. He clicked the dimmers again. The lights were a custom job too—honeycombs of alternating fluorescent and incandescent bulbs and tubes. They'd give a decent

14

approximation of daylight all night long. When he really got going time stood still—and now the sun would, too.

When he really got going.

But he hadn't been going for some time now. He'd always have the Mystery series. Those cover designs had won awards and made him a name. The books themselves had survived generally lukewarm reviews to become best sellers, due largely to the eye-catching paintings (set disturbingly off-center) that graced each cover. The same week one of the books landed in the Pans column of *People* magazine, his smiling face and two cover reproductions had appeared in the Bio section.

But that was last fall. He'd submitted the last painting for the series five months before that.

Three industrial-grade easels stood empty at the north end of the room. Calvary before the crucifixion (or was it that moment after?). He cranked up the hospital serving table that had held his brushes, palette, and cleaning jars since his NYU days. Over the years it had doubled as a substitute palette—and looked it. A Pollock masterpiece of thrown color, it was the only thing in the studio that wasn't brand-new and untouched. Except, of course, for Trevor himself.

Soon it would all be touched, would all be unclean and soiled with the grimy afterbirth of creation. It would never be this way again, but that was all part of the process. Creation was a destruction of sorts.

He sipped his coffee and surveyed the situation from his wall-length worktable. Drawers of tubes and jars of every color, brushes of every texture and size, enough canvas and white pine to reconstruct the Pequod.

Everything worked. All was ready.

He just had to come up with an idea. Not even that—a kernel of an idea. That was it.

"Well, that's a wrap." He snapped off the lights and went downstairs.

Cathleen was in the kitchen with the boxes he couldn't touch. His "gifted hands" were notoriously clumsy with glassware. She wasn't unpacking though, she was struggling to raise the window. He could see Meg at the edge of the forest, dressed in her jumpsuit and lantern helmet—the caving suit he'd made for her from Bryce's old G.I. Joe castoffs. She was wrapped head to toe in adjustable army belts bristling with old tools and kitchen utensils. He smiled and shook his head.

"Meg!" Cathleen slapped the window.

"I'll get it."

"Ughh. This thing! It's like a jail window."

"Hold on. You just have to be even with it." He flattened his palms against the frame and gave a little shove. The window popped up.

"Meg! Stay close to the house!"

"Let her go."

"Meg!"

Outside, Meg turned back. The morning sun shot lightning bolts off her glasses. She waved.

"What's up?"

"Nothing. Have fun!" Trevor said.

Cathleen shot him a glance.

"She's got her glasses. Let her go. Meg, you got your strap on? Your glasses strap?"

She nodded broadly. "Yeah."

"See—she's even got 'em strapped on. Have fun, Meg!"

"No further than Slimer!" Cathleen called to Meg.

"Okay!"

Trevor grimaced.

"What's Slimer?"

"The big rock behind the house. She says it looks like something called Slimer from *Ghostbusters*. We made a deal: she can go as far as she wants as long as she can still see the big rock."

"It's a big, beautiful forest, hon. Let her play."

"We don't know what's out there."

"Trees. Squirrels. Running water. Come on, she's not helpless. She's got bad eyes."

"It's more than that."

"No, it isn't."

Cathleen took a deep breath as she glanced out the window. Meg was nowhere to be seen.

Trevor kissed her forehead.

"She's my kid too now."

She smiled. "You just want to mess around."

"That too. Why not? Kids are out playing. We're in playing. The kitchen's ours. Let's christen the island."

3

I T was the last hill on Sluice Road before an easy downhill glide into town and Bryce pushed his legs to the limit. When he made the top he thrust his fists into the air, laughing and gasping at the same time.

"Touchdown! The crowd goes wild."

The jerks with the shotgun had been forgotten—or at least shelved for the time being. He was having too much fun riding the hills.

Piñon Rim was laid out below like one of those rustic towns that model trains run around. Only two streets had anything that looked remotely like businesses on them. Neither was paved; instead they were lined with boardwalks and small buildings with high wooden facades. It could have been the set of *High Noon*. One street looked newer—probably restored. The other was the genuine article. Where they weren't white-washed, the facades had a gray and gnarled look. Beyond that weak town "hub" were rows of houses, some modern and fairly sturdy, some barely clinging to their foundations. The "burbs" of Piñon Rim. They looked like a smile with half the teeth rotted away.

Maybe a half-mile to his right, a peak loomed just north of town, and Bryce could make out a gaping hole near the top, poorly boarded, from which a small section of rusty track jutted. Had to be a mine. He definitely had to check that out.

On a foothill just below the hole was a cemetery that must have been around since the pioneer days. The path into it was paved with white stones; a shorter white path intersected that one near the top, forming a huge white cross. A large rectangle of decaying rubble sat nearby—the ruins of a church?

Bryce stood on his pedals and gave them one hard grind, then coasted down past the intersection and swung up the road to the cemetery. It was a good grade; he had almost enough steam left to make it. Bryce lifted the Stingray over a bank of rocks at the bottom of the path, then jumped back on and pumped his way up the hill.

It was the saddest excuse for a graveyard he'd ever seen. Two neat rows of flat graves ran next to the ruined church; beyond that was nothing but mound after mound of dirt and stones, some marked, some not. It was like they'd given up digging holes after a while and just covered people with rocks. A lot of rocks. As he rode the narrow paths between them, some of the mounds were up to his shoulders. That was due in part to the paths themselves; rain had eroded them quite a bit.

The paths got softer and muddier. He swung off the bike and tried to plant his Nikes on dry rocks, but it was hopeless. They were already covered with gooey red Piñon Rim mud. Trying to keep anything clean here was going to be a hopeless cause. He'd never seen anything like it. The dirt was red, the rocks were red, the mud was red. Was the whole state red?

It was suddenly very quiet.

A gust of wind brought with it a touch of the coming winter and Bryce shivered. Above the cemetery, the open mine looked like a screaming mouth.

You shouldn't be here, he thought.

Why not? He wasn't doing anything. Just checking it out. Just passing through. Quickest way to the mine.

Some of the markers bore brief descriptions: SHOT FOR STEAL-ING. SHOT FOR TRESPASS. HUNG FOR ADULTEROUS ACT.

Hung for adulterous act? That had to be a joke.

Maybe it wasn't. This place was weird.

A pole-and-wire fence marked off the boundaries to his right. Even that had been botched: the fence missed one grave by a good ten feet. That one had its own decrepit wrought-iron fence. He took the next path that headed toward it.

The mound was low; whoever "owned" this was one of the

lucky ones who got buried underground. The little gated fence was filled with dried and broken tumbleweeds. A crumbling stone read simply: ROSE.

Ten feet from the fence.

He felt a clutch inside. Like someone had just reached in and squeezed his heart. Suddenly, he missed his mom. Missed her very much.

Bryce looked back toward town, feeling less interested in the mine now.

He worked his way between the graves, not sure which was the quickest route to the path. Which way had he come? Did it matter? Probably not. He found a fairly dry stretch and rode the bike through. He made two quick turns and hit a dead end. Backtracking, he swung around a particularly high grave and found himself in a clearing. But it wasn't a clearing. It was filled with small graves.

The cold breeze prickled the skin on his neck. No names. No markers.

He pumped the pedals and slalomed back between the tall mounds until he found the fence and followed it out.

H E skidded to a stop at the intersection of the two main streets. Katie Avenue—the street with the new shops—was bogus. He turned up Front Street instead and pedaled alongside the boardwalk. There was a huge wooden facade on the north side of the street. It was so old that the name painted across the front was a barely colored shadow: THE LUCKY SLIPPER.

A real saloon from the Old West. That could be interesting. He was disappointed to find three new wooden signs hanging in the shadows beneath the facade. Apparently, the Lucky Slipper was no more, having been subdivided into the Pizza Wizard, Piñon Rim Drugs, and the Wizard's Palette Art Supplies.

Bryce parked his bike near the steps of the drugstore and locked it. Piñon Rim Drugs took up the center section of the old saloon and still had the bar's big beveled window, now smoky and covered with paper corners and tape marks. Underneath a poster for Ray-Bans were the words FOUNTAIN INSIDE.

Bryce hopped the steps and peered inside, hoping more than the window had been left intact. Pegboard shelves, a lot of displays, racks of post cards. The old fixtures were still there, but the real jackpot was against the back wall—the original bar, with all its brass fittings and stools.

"This *is way* cool."

B R Y C E sat at the bar, where he could see the town's history curling from the wall in sepia-and-gray photos. A man as gray as the photos set a steaming cup of coffee before him. A brown web of fractures radiated from just beneath the handle. Little oil bubbles danced on the coffee's surface.

A yellowed health certificate (somehow the place had rated an "A" at some point in its life) hung just above the coffee machine, next to some framed wanted posters that looked dusty and authentic. In the center of the wall, a large rectangle of black electrician's tape bordered photos of the Lucky Slipper in better days. Above them a banner read: 1ST ANNUAL HELL-DORADO CELEBRATION—1960. PINON RIM HISTORICAL SOCIETY.

"That slab of marble under your elbow's the o-rig-nal bar." The old man held the three syllables he'd allowed the word *original* with dutiful admiration.

A proud gate of gold teeth flashed from his upper bridge.

Bryce lifted his elbows. The marble bartop ran nearly the length of the back wall, supported by a frame of brasswork. The counter was surrounded by rough pine and pegboard shelves stocked with dusty sundries. A particularly sad display of vitamins sat to Bryce's right; he'd take a close look at those expiration dates before he bought anything.

"Real gully washer we had last night."

The old man flashed his gold. Bryce looked up, not sure how to respond.

"The rain did a lot of floodin'," the old man said.

"Oh, yeah. Does it always rain like that?"

"Not a lot, no."

"How old's this place?"

"One hundred and near two years. November 1, 1892, she

was opened . . . not a prouder girl in the West when Piñon Rim was boomin'. Some others maybe come close, but the Slipper was a grand one."

The marble was cool beneath Bryce's forearms. There wasn't a blemish along the length of it—no cigarette scorches, not a water spot—a testimony to the old man's care. But that care seemed to end with the bar itself. The rest of the place was a decaying mess.

"Did they always make bar tops out of marble?"

The old man looked past him to the window, and Bryce turned to see a shiny Jaguar pull up to the hitching post. A darkly handsome woman in a brilliant white T-shirt and jeans just tight enough to highlight a very well kept figure stepped out, a Louis Vuitton bag slung over her shoulder. A wealth of silver and turquoise bracelets on her wrists clacked noisily as she passed the window. From the shade of Coop's Market across the street, two old guys looked up from their game of cards. They smiled toward the window of Piñon Rim Drugs before resuming their game.

The old man gave a nod in return that they couldn't possibly have seen. He made a clucking sort of laugh and winked at Bryce.

"No," the old man answered Bryce's earlier question as though no time had passed. He tipped more coffee into Bryce's cup. "Not likely you'll see a bar top like this one anywhere else. Not anytime soon. This piece of marble came from the Wizard."

Bryce saw the storm again and the illusion, created by the lightning, of a tall man dressed in flowing robes, the glow of brimstone all around. He pictured the man raising a hand as twisted and knotted as a gingerroot above his head and presto, a long slab of marble appearing. Obviously there wasn't a real wizard living in Piñon Rim, Arizona. Then again, most of the stores had *wizard* in their names.

"Who's the Wizard?"

The old man grinned.

"The Wizard Mine, up on Harper's Peak behind the cemet'ry. Was a copper mine before they hit a wall of gold like you never saw. This bar comes from a slab of marble right next to that pocket of gold. One day Piñon Rim was scrapin', next day she was boomin'. Like magic, you know. Folks started calling that mine 'the Wizard.' Name stuck." He extended a hand easily as weathered as the Lucky Slipper. "Bill Jordan. You belong to the Easton place, don't you?"

The old man's hand felt like steel bolts wrapped in old canvas.

"Bryce Willems."

"Seen you ridin' that funny bike round town. Figured you must be part of the new family."

Bryce nodded. It was a little unnerving. Schenectady was a small town, but Piñon Rim was redefining the term.

"Like the house?"

"It's pretty cool, yeah. Have you been there?"

"Long time ago. Been just about everywhere there is 'tween Flag and Prescott one time or other." Bill Jordan tapped a photo just outside the black rectangle on his wall of fame. "This one here's bound to catch your int'rest."

The picture was badly faded and the contrast was poor, but it was clear enough to show a man, a woman, and two sullen, pasty-faced boys, all crisply dressed. They stood before an impressive black coach, probably on their way to church when the picture was snapped. But the main point of interest stood behind all that.

"That's it, isn't it? That's my house."

Bill Jordan nodded.

"The proud group out front, that's the Eastons. The gent in back is Percy. Percy built that big old house you live in with the Wizard's money. Been by the bank on Katie Avenue?"

Bryce shook his head.

"Well, if you ride out that way take a look on the west side. It's a big stone place, like your house. Now it's called the Valley National, but it used to be Easton's Bank and Assay. Katie Street's named after his missus. Was a time Easton owned most of this town."

"Did he own this place?"

Bill Jordan smiled, the gold winked.

"Well, that's a point to argue."

The bell over the door tinkled merrily and two women bustled in. Jordan excused himself, and as he made his way to the far end of the counter, Bryce noticed for the first time that Jordan was crippled.

The right leg of his trousers barely brushed anything inside, and the shoe below it turned at an impossible angle as he swung himself along. It thumped against a canister that hadn't been shoved completely beneath the counter, and he muttered something under his breath. Bryce caught the glint of his eye and looked away, a lump of guilt rising in his throat. Bryce wanted to know what had happened to Jordan's leg, but it probably wasn't cool to ask.

He scanned the wall for other pictures of the Big House and the Easton family. He found one a little farther up the wall. It showed a much older Percival Easton, his wife, and only one boy. Bryce wondered where the other one was. It wasn't as if they had one-touch, sure-shot, any-idiot-can-do-this cameras back then. He probably wasn't taking the picture. This photo was a little better preserved than the first, and Bryce was surprised at how much younger Katie Easton looked than Percy.

Change rattled in the drawer as the cash register rang two sales and Bill Jordan swung himself back. The women bustled out, each with crisp white bags in hand.

"There's two kids in the one shot—"

"Shep, and the little one's Boyd. You're a sharp one; there's a story there—"

A screech of tires made them both glance out the window.

A black Jeep came skidding to a halt just outside Coop's Market. A beefy guy in his late teens, with slicked-back, dirty blond hair and Wayfarers, was screaming at a girl roughly Bryce's age. She locked her bike to a post near the card-playing codgers and ignored him. The guy revved the engine for emphasis. The old men kept playing, but they looked less than pleased with the intrusion.

Bryce couldn't stand the guy already. The girl was another matter entirely: with her round face and her lips like Cupid's, she was closer to Bryce's idea of an angel than any painting he'd seen. Her mouth formed two words, neither of which needed to be heard to be understood, and the beefy Jeep jockey, a flush of desperate anger on his cheeks, spun his charge around, spraying red mud past the trio of shops that had been the Lucky Slipper.

The girl waited long enough to watch him wheel around the next corner, then she simply turned and walked up the steps into Coops, cool and calm as an autumn day.

Bryce laid a dollar on the marble bar top and slid off his stool. His jacket caught on the stool and he nearly lost his balance.

"Do you know who she is?" It was a dumb question. Of course Bill Jordan knew everyone in town, probably everyone 'tween Flag and Prescott . . .

"Connie Bowman. You'd do well to steer clear of that one— and Matt, her boyfriend."

"The guy in the Jeep?" He'd figured that of course, but, man, the guy was probably in college. He thought of Mr. and Mrs. Easton and wondered if that was the way of things in Piñon Rim, Arizona. If it was, it was a world-class bummer of a deal.

Jordan twisted his jaw, his tongue finding a naked spot in his gums. He lay three quarters where Bryce's dollar had been.

"Coffee here's two bits." He winked and slid the change to Bryce.

"Thanks." He was beginning to like the old guy.

B R Y C E clicked slowly through his combination, one eye peeking across the street at the screened doorway that had gobbled up Connie Bowman only moments before. The sun was rising, but the air was still morning-crisp. The streets were a deep sienna, still shiny and wet in places. Red mud pooled beneath the raised walkways on Front Street like creamy puddles of fresh paint.

Bryce gave the dial another twist and eyed the numbers as if they were something new and exciting.

A tinkle of chimes sounded behind him. The two codgers by Coop's were looking his way. People in the stores were probably looking at him too: suspicious eyes, squinting from behind all those bright reflections in the glass. They were probably wondering what the heck this kid was up to taking so long to unlock his bike. Maybe they thought he was scoping the place to steal something. Maybe they thought he was retarded. Maybe he should just walk over to Coop's and buy something, but he'd already made such a big deal about unlocking his stupid bike.

A tap on his shoulder nearly sent him sprawling into the street. He spun around, certain he would find a cop staring down at him. Instead he saw the woman from the Jaguar. She was leaning over the rail.

"Excuse me," she said from behind tortoiseshell Ray-Bans not quite large and dark enough to cover the tiny crinkles at the outer corners of her eyes. Her jewelry clacked against her wrist.

"Could I borrow you for a minute?"

Bryce stole a glance at Coop's, where the two codgers had once again interrupted their game to watch. No Connie.

"Sure." He shrugged.

"Great." She smiled.

The bells from Wizard's Palette chimed and a huge easel with double uprights nosed its way through the doorway, shaking displays and smacking unseen objects inside the shop. Bryce raced over and caught the uprights before they bit a canyon into the boardwalk.

The woman popped her trunk and the man holding the other end of the easel stumbled out, doing a crazy tango with the thing. The man was thin, Bryce thought, then amended that to "delicate." His dark hair was freshly cut and oiled. He was sweating bullets. He sighed with relief as Bryce took enough of the weight to nearly buckle his own knees. How the hell had the guy gotten it this far on his own? Bryce backed all the way up to the railing and propped the uprights against it.

"Hoooo, thaaank you!" the delicate man said, setting down his end and using his hand to wipe beads of sweat from his moustache and forehead.

"Andre, I don't know if this will work."

"Nonsense. It'll fit. I've done this before."

"Not with my trunk, you haven't."

"For god's sake, I've *seen* your trunk, Agnetha!"

Agnetha crossed her arms and leaned over the rail, her long hair shining a brilliant copper where the sun struck it. The V in her T-shirt framed an awesome view, but Bryce tried not to stare.

Andre frowned.

"There's a catch here somewhere; it'll let us slide these two crosspieces together."

"At your end," Bryce said. "I'm pretty sure there's a wing nut on one of the supports."

"That's it, you're right. If it'd been a snake I'd be dead by now." Andre placed his little finger near the bolt.

"My dad has one like this," Bryce said.

Agnetha leaned over the rail, and once again, Bryce fought to master his eyes.

"You're Trevor Willems's son, aren't you?"

Bryce nodded. Being known for something as casual as having moved in across town had been disturbing, but this was different. People all over the country knew his father, and he liked that.

She smiled.

"Do you know him?"

"I'm a fan. The covers he did for that Mystery series are brilliant."

"Thanks."

"Do you paint?"

It was a question he got a lot, and the answer usually brought disappointed looks. Agnetha didn't seem to mind when he shook his head. She simply nodded.

Across Front Street, Connie Bowman skipped down the steps to her bike, a paper bag in hand, and Bryce nearly bolted. Agnetha followed his eyes; a smile flicked up beneath her Ray-Bans.

Connie Bowman leaned over her bicycle, holding a small water bottle and a fistful of metal clips. One of the codgers finally rose to help her attach it and Bryce swallowed hard. He could have done that.

Andre was taking forever to loosen one nut. After a lifetime passed, the crossbars swung free. Bryce took one end and backed down the steps. The load was unwieldy and probably too heavy for him, but he wasn't about to stop. He looked behind him, partly to see where he was going, but mostly to see Connie.

Bryce didn't have a chance to sort out what happened next until he was sitting on his butt in cold mud, and then all he could do was hope there was enough to swallow him whole and kill him fast. It had begun with Connie looking his way—looking at him! At that precise moment, Agnetha had stepped around to help him down the steps. There had been a brief, sweet scent of expensive perfume and the gentle pressure of her against his back. Then his sneaker had missed the step.

The mud saved his tailbone, if not his pants, and he barely felt the heavy oak beams slam into him just after the planet earth broke his fall. He felt something much worse than pain. His red badge of embarrassment flushed into his face even before he turned back to see Connie, and he did that before he did anything else. Yes, she had seen it all! And, worse than that, she'd seen him looking back like a red-faced idiot. The codgers were looking too, and their combined expression cried, "Dweeb!"

Into a street that been utterly devoid of life only moments before, people poured from every doorway on the block. Half a dozen beefy faces circled above him.

"Bite off a little more'n you could chew?"

"Crushed him like a bug!"

Bryce's first impulse was to dart toward his bike. He might have, but Agnetha's grip was firm.

"He's okay, let him be," she said calmly. "I didn't see any of you breaking your necks to help when we needed it."

A large, hairy man in a plaid flannel shirt and a John Deere hat looked as though he might say something, but he didn't. He glanced at Andre, who looked as if he'd just sniffed rotten cabbage, shook his head, and walked away. The others followed.

"Let's finish this up," she said, "then I'll take care of those pants."

28

Bryce nodded, in a blue haze. Connie was gone. The codgers had resumed play. He hoped Jordan had missed it, but he probably hadn't.

They loaded the easel and Andre tied the trunk without a word. The easel stuck out like a ladder on a fire truck, but it seemed secure enough. Suddenly, Andre let out a snort that sounded like a honking goose. Agnetha shot him a glance, then she started laughing. Bryce shook his head. He felt rotten and the mud was caking on his jeans, then he was laughing too.

"Guess it looked pretty funny."

"Guess it did," she said.

"I've got some old Jordache jeans up in my office that'll probably fit," Andre offered.

"That's okay, I don't live that far away."

"Oh, don't be silly. Piñon Rim hasn't got a fashion patrol."

"Take the jeans, Bryce." Agnetha slid the Ray-Bans back on top of her head.

Her eyes were a deep green, lined in gold. Above all, they were smiling. He amended the great figure stuff. Agnetha was just plain beautiful. "I've got something at home that'll even take out red-rock mud. When do you need them?"

It was probably important to say something witty or at least adult just then. Even a day of the week would have been fine. But nothing came out. Instead, his hands fluttered into a vague gesture.

She pulled a pen from her purse and wrote her address on the back of her receipt.

"Tell you what. If you could drop by some afternoon and help me set up this monster, I'll throw in lunch. Such a deal, eh?"

"Okay, ma'am." At least he got that out.

She shot him a glance. "Puh-leeez! Aggie. Agnetha, if you must, but never ma'am."

The chimes jangled and Andre appeared at the door of the Wizard's Palette with a pair of deep indigo jeans with fancy Western stitching. Bryce swallowed hard.

"There's a bathroom upstairs just past the office."

T H E second floor of the Lucky Slipper had been partitioned, drywalled, and painted over. It was too bad. It must have been pretty cool at one time. You could've fit a decent apartment in Andre's office.

Bryce balled up his jeans on the toilet tank and hiked up the Jordache's. They were tight on *him;* what were they like on Andre? Actually, he didn't want to know.

The day wasn't half over and already he'd had a shotgun waved at him by a bunch of jerks and he'd flopped on his butt in front of the girl of his dreams. Now he had to ride home wearing jeans the likes of which he hadn't seen since second grade. He pulled his 501s off the toilet tank and his wallet plopped onto the carpet.

He bent down to get it—a monumental effort in Andre's jeans. When he did, something beneath the sink caught his eye. Where the drywall ended the wood was scorched black.

He scratched it with his fingernail. It had been varnished over.

He bullied his wallet into one of the back pockets and headed downstairs, feeling every step in his groin.

The wall next to the stairway still had the original fleur-de-lys wallpaper and the gas lighting fixtures, now fitted with electric bulbs. Bit by bit Bryce was getting a picture of what the Lucky Slipper must have looked like: there had probably been gaming tables, maybe a small stage where the Pizza Wizard now stood. What had these stairs led to? Hotel rooms? The windows on the second floor weren't there for the view: there were too many small panes to really enjoy looking out.

Andre and Aggie were carrying blocks of clay out to her car. Bryce picked one up and followed them out.

"Did you have a fire up there?"

Andre dropped a block of clay on the floor of the passenger side. He mopped his forehead with a handkerchief.

"That whole second floor was a bordello. It was frequented by cowboys. God only knows what went on there."

"Some of the wood looks burnt."

"A lot of this town actually did go up in smoke," Aggie said.

"The mill down by Sharpe's Creek burned. A lot of the wood they used to reconstruct things came from the mill, so you'll see a lot of scorched wood here and there. I don't think the Lucky Slipper ever burned though. Just a lot of termites—and neglect."

She checked out his pants and grinned. Bryce flushed.

"Do you want a ride?"

He did, but he said no.

4

 T H A T night it was porkchops for supper and Bryce was loving life.

He told them about the Lucky Slipper and Bill Jordan, whom he figured was as much caretaker of the Slipper as shopkeeper of Piñon Rim Drugs; they all agreed they'd have to check out Jordan's old photos of the Eastons and the Big House. Bryce also told them about meeting the woman with the teal Jag and falling on his butt, which was easier to laugh about now. He left out his run-in with the shotgun jerks.

Meg had spent the day exploring the forest out back, looking for caves. Cathleen told her she had better not find one, and if she did, she had better not let Cathleen find her in it. Meg said she wouldn't, but she winked at Bryce when Cathleen wasn't looking, so it didn't count. Meg had been on a spelunking kick ever since they'd gone to Howe Caverns a year ago.

It didn't have the same effect on Bryce. The bizarre formations were pretty cool—the tripe rock and all the organ-pipe stuff—but personally he liked looking at the pictures a whole lot better than being there. The elevator ride down had nearly done him in. He hadn't said anything, but once those walls rose up and swallowed the daylight he'd suffered an awful moment of knowing. It occurred to him then, as it did now, that drowning victims realize at some point they'll never reach the surface again.

Meg tore into a chop and molten fat squirted across her cheek and dribbled down her chin, and she and Bryce broke out laughing so hard they nearly choked.

"Gross!"

She snaked her tongue toward it and Bryce rolled his eyes back.

"You are sick!"

"Meg!" Cathleen swiped at her face with a greasy paper napkin and then left it there when it stuck. Meg continued eating, the napkin still on her cheek.

"That's enough! No apple pie for Megan!" The laugh in Cathleen's voice seriously undercut any hope of authority.

"Last time I eat at this joint." Trevor smiled and sat back. "You two okay for Monday?"

Bryce shrugged.

Meg rocked her head yes while she cleaned her glasses. She blinked and scanned the room without them.

Bryce wondered what she was actually seeing—probably not a whole lot. He'd looked through her glasses once and got a headache for his trouble. She had a disease called retinitis pigmentosa and it wouldn't go away. Meg was pretty, and she had beautiful eyes, a clear ocean blue. But they didn't work.

"What about rides? Are we taking 'em?" asked Trevor.

"Up to them," Cathleen said. "They're signed up for the bus, but I'll drive."

"I'm okay on the bike," Bryce said.

If Cathleen drove Meg, the world would be perfect. The bike was his ticket to freedom. He could hang around after school if he wanted. He pictured himself riding over to Piñon Rim Drugs for coffee or a shake with Connie Bowman. His heart sank when Meg asked to take the bus. She was asking Trevor and Cathleen, but Meg looked at Bryce first. Reluctantly, he nodded. So much for freedom.

"Sure, Honey," Cathleen said.

Trevor looked over at Bryce, but it wasn't necessary.

"I'll ride along," Bryce said. "For a while."

"Until you get used to this place," Trevor said, "it's probably a good idea to stick together."

"You don't have to," Meg piped up. But she didn't exactly peg the sincerity meter.

"I won't do it forever, Nutmeg." He made a squirrel face at her and she laughed. It could be a long winter after all.

S A R A Rojo stared into Clyde's green-eyed face, wishing—willing—the window open. Clyde was her trusty old Amstrad word processor, lately not so trusty: Cervantes had taken to curling up on the keyboard, and it seemed Clyde was allergic to cat hair. He'd taken her through four novels—one during the explosive last years of her marriage to Trevor Willems and one for each year since—all cranked out to the tommy gun rattle of big Clyde's dot matrix. He'd been a faithful friend through it all, but his parts were becoming hard to come by.

A storm brewed outside. Cervantes was curled peacefully on her lap and her iced Evian with a twist sat within easy reach. It was a perfect time to write. The window to that other world should swing out, inspiration should rush in.

Cervantes stretched and hopped onto the desk. He stared Clyde square in the face and walked away bored.

"All right. It seemed like a good idea." She switched Clyde off.

Her own face looked expectantly back at her, the storm clouds rolling across it. It was Bryce she saw in those high cheekbones, dark eyes, and wide-set mouth. But that was all she'd offered him. As strong as those hot-blooded Spanish genes were, she'd given him the looks and kept all the hot blood for herself. If kids came into this world with a program of their own, and she believed now that they did, Bryce had been from the outset, and always would be, Trevor's son. With Trevor's maddeningly even temper. Would Bryce ever be able to fight for himself?

Why did she suddenly think he might have to?

1:20 A.M. Way too late to call.

The first silver threads ripped through the heavens. Sara counted five before the shock wave hit.

5

M E G yankcd the loop of clothesline and a chunk of bark cartwheeled over her shoulder. She plunked herself down on a big boulder that seemed dry enough and removed her glasses. The world went Vaseline. She puffed up her cheeks, blew the bits of bark and dirt off her lenses, and set them back on her nose. Now she was back in the clear world, a world of trees and pinecones and squirrels. She pulled a heap of peanuts from a pocket of her jumpsuit and scattered the load. The squirrels here weren't as bold as the ones back home, but little by little they came.

It was a crisp autumn morning in Caveland, USA. Her mom was on her way to Prescott to shop, and Trevor, who was keeping an eye on her, was already busy stretching canvas in his studio. It was a perfect morning for caving.

Her utility belts were clankingly full: flashlights, a claw hoe for gripping, an ice pick for poking stuff, a small hammer for pounding things if she needed to. The innumerable pockets of her jumpsuit were stuffed as well: rations for her, food for squirrels, zip-lock bags to haul out human waste. She hoped she didn't find any human waste, but the books said you couldn't leave it in any case, so she came prepared. A pocket for everything and everything in its pocket.

The twenty feet of clothesline she'd borrowed from the storage room hadn't found a home in any of those pockets though. She coiled it between her thumb and elbow and strapped it to a utility belt. The rope kept catching on things and was a pain to carry, but if she did find a cave it'd come in handy in case she had to make a pit descent. You never knew when you might have to.

The compass told her she was still heading steady south by southeast of Slimer. She checked her time. She'd been going this way for ten minutes. She made a note, zipped the compass into its designated pocket, and resumed her quest.

Meg had been out here just about every day since they'd moved. It was her secret new world. Presently, it was hers alone. Bryce would have been welcome in it, but he was still asleep when she'd left this morning. Bryce was a pretty cool big brother, even if he wasn't so much into caving. In Schenectady there had been Barry DeRolf, a kid from school. Barry was kind of a crybaby and had a snotty nose, but he kept up okay. And he never made fun of her glasses.

For now, she explored on her own, and she guessed that was okay. She could pretend things and not worry about anyone going along or not. Today, she was an expert caver on a grant from the National Geographic Society. Arizona was a great wilderness that began just outside the back door of the Big House. There was a cave somewhere in Arizona, and she was going to find it.

She'd gone farther than ever today. She was still holding to the Slimer rule, trying to keep him in sight. Her mission was to find the whitish, crusty stuff they called karst in the caving books. It was made out of limestone, just as caves were. She thought she might have seen some the night of the storm. The clouds had opened up just long enough to show a patch of pure white deep in the forest.

Whatever it was, karst or not, it couldn't be too far from where she was now.

Just ahead the forest floor tipped down into a soupy, mist-filled darkness, then rose up sharply till it was mostly out of sight in the treetops.

The ground got mushy with pine needles and wet leaves, and the sounds of birds and squirrels faded away. Only ten yards from the boulder she'd just left, it was another world entirely. Mist clung to the ferns and mushrooms. The air was cold, damp, and still.

The downward slope quickened her steps. A creek murmured from the milky darkness below. The fading bulk of Slimer would be totally out of view if she kept going. She came to a sliding stop a few feet from an old shattered log. A squirrel standing on it didn't seem to mind; he just peered out into the mist.

The mist was heavier past the log. The ground totally disappeared, and the cold wetness bit right through Meg's caving suit. Her teeth chattered.

Very steep here. If she slipped, at the very least she'd be soaked. Nobody knew where she was. What if she fell and broke a bone or something?

She frowned. She was a caver. Cavers were tough.

She ripped the Velcro on one of her pockets and scooped out the last of the peanuts. She had to walk sideways to the log to keep from sliding, pushing up deep black mounds of needles and leaves as she went. This squirrel was the bravest she'd ever seen. She planted her foot on the log and something like a stack of marbles rolled away from it. The squirrel didn't flinch. She pulled back the ferns near her feet.

The ground was covered with acorns.

''Whoa . . .''

They were heaped against the log, piled five or six deep between the ferns. They were everywhere. She rolled them underfoot and nearly lost her balance when they slipped away like ball bearings. This was one busy squirrel.

''Hey, squirrel! Hey!'' She waved her fistful of peanuts. ''Hey! Try these!''

The squirrel didn't so much as glance her way.

''Hey! Hey, squirrel! These are way better than stupid acorns!''

The log was spongy. She steadied herself against a pine and underhanded the peanuts. One struck the shoulder of the squirrel's outstretched arm and stayed there; another loosened a tuft of fur, leaving a bare white spot on the back of its head.

The flesh on the back of Meg's neck crept up to her scalp.

She'd seen dead things before. But dead things always *looked* dead—or at least asleep. The squirrel had totally fooled her.

She braced herself against the pine and carefully stretched her sneaker toward it. A light tap from her toe sent the squirrel cartwheeling into the mist, no heavier than a cornhusk. A dandelion spray of gray fur followed it down.

"Gross."

She closed her eyes and pinned her arms tightly to her sides, trying to stave off the shudder she knew would come. It did anyway.

Dog Grinder Road back home had given up its share of dead things: not just dogs, but also squirrels, cats, birds, and things too badly mangled to tell. But there was no question they were dead. Once, Barry DeRolf had stepped right into a dead woodchuck. It stunk bad, and there were all sorts of ants and wormy things crawling on it. She tried not to see that woodchuck now, but she couldn't help it. Barry had nearly hurled lunch. There wasn't any smell here but the rain and burning mosquito wood, and there hadn't been any ants or anything on the squirrel.

It had really fooled her. That's what made it pukey. She took a deep breath and reminded herself cavers saw all sorts of gross things. She had to be ready for anything. When the trembling passed she opened her eyes and squinted down the slope.

It looked like one of the storm clouds had fallen in and couldn't get out. Meg hugged the tree, stretching one leg down the slope ahead of her. Her sneaker found solid ground, and little by little she eased more weight onto it. She let go of the pine and slid herself off the fallen log.

She stood unsteadily on the hillside. Pulling a flashlight off her belt, she aimed the beam into the mist's milky heart.

Gray ghosts swirled and danced inside the white column of light. She waved the beam from side to side, panning it across the creek. On the opposite bank was an area of pitch blackness—an opening in the side of the hill!

She'd found her cave!

Meg let out a war whoop that echoed back at her and made her laugh. Her feet slipped a little, but she caught herself.

She knew there was one out here! She *knew* it! Visions of vaulted rooms as big as churches and filled with all the twisted impossibilities she'd seen at Howe made her shout again. She fought to get a better view through the mist.

The hole was star-shaped, with a couple of extra points near the top. It was only a few feet wide; small, but not too small for her. She could see a loose hill of rocks and fresh mud in front of it. As her straining eyes gradually took in more detail, she saw a large, flat stone lying near the entrance and her spirits sank. Someone had cut their initials into it. She could make out the letters W Z. She wasn't the first.

She stepped back onto the log and squished her shoes into it, not sure what to do next. Her disappointment ebbed. So what if she wasn't the first? She didn't find Howe Caverns, either, but it was still pretty cool to look at. And maybe this one went on for miles. There were probably all sorts of formations and passageways that nobody had ever seen. Cavers were still finding new chambers in Carlsbad, weren't they? The most likely scenario—that her cave would end only a few feet from the entrance—crossed her mind, but she was getting too excited to give that more than a moment's thought.

The slope was even steeper a few feet farther down, but she could manage. So she'd be making a descent after all. Cavers tied themselves to something first and that seemed like a good idea.

The tree she'd held onto earlier would do. She stepped back up onto the decaying log, then stopped. Someone had whispered. Her skin started its slow crawl again. The whisper was there, and then it wasn't. A breeze had begun to move the small branches. The treetops swayed hypnotically.

But it wasn't the wind she'd heard.

She heard it again: a voice, but not quite.

Meg froze. The hand that clutched her flashlight was shaking; the disk of light bouncing through the ferns like an epileptic firefly. Behind her, the mist roiled and parted. A cold wind tickled the back of her neck. She opened her mouth to scream, but nothing came out. She barely felt the decaying log give way beneath her heel. Her stomach climbed halfway up her throat. The treetops and a patch of blue sky zoomed up and away as she fell.

Then her whole body was yanked upward, her breath woofed out as she belly flopped against the hillside. An avalanche of wet leaves and pine needles rained down on her face. Something else slid down just after, and when she opened her eyes, she saw that half of the squirrel had come to rest just a few inches from her face. The squirrel's eyes were dry and as wrinkled as black crepe. A broken tooth twisted through the torn crack of its mouth.

She was too terrified to move. A few feet above her, her lifeline—a single loop of clothesline—twisted around a protruding root.

And the dry whisper began again. But this time, it was different. This time, she heard words. But they were so faint that she couldn't make them out. Someone was close, very close behind her. But no one could be. Behind her was empty air.

A chill shook her bones as if they were empty spools on a thread. Her glasses went foggy as tears welled up. She dug her fingers into the slope and everywhere they were met by roots, roots like long, knotted fingers that were touching her, gripping her. Her scream came easily now, shrill and sharp as broken glass. She batted the chunk of squirrel away and saw it scatter across the slope. Her knees and elbows pumped and skidded along the slope. Her line was twisting loose. Then, in a moment of clarity, she yanked the claw hoe off her belt, dug it between the roots, and pulled herself up. Her knees found purchase and somehow shoved her forward. Something snagged her heel and she kicked it free.

And then she was over the crest, running toward the everwatchful Slimer, running so fast she was nearly on all fours. She could still hear her own screams echoing from that horrible dark slope somewhere behind her.

She broke into a meadow filled with light and chirping birds, and the echo cut off. Her breath came in raw pants, her chest ached. She allowed herself one deep breath in this free zone, then she ran on.

The Big House was dark and old and still not quite familiar.

If it wasn't home yet, it would be. And home was a safe place, wasn't it?

She didn't stop running until she was safely in her own backyard.

6

T H A T night, Larry Brill came to dinner.

Cathleen served up something she called "seasoned pork loin on a bed of cabbage." But even though the chops stood like soldiers on parade, it was still porkchops and sauerkraut as far as Bryce was concerned. Porkchops two nights in a row was fine with him.

Larry sat with his fingers laced behind his thick neck, his chair tipped back on its heels. He wore a blue chambray shirt that was probably new but was already splattered with color. He'd gotten to about half the buttons, and the undershirt beneath was similarly spotted with paint. His face had a swollen, abused look. The gray stubble on his chin didn't help. Larry had less hair than Bryce remembered from the last time he'd seen him. What there was of it lay in greasy silver strands across the top of his sunburnt scalp. He winked at Bryce.

"Givin' the girls here a break?"

Bryce thought he meant Cathleen and Meg, although he wasn't sure what sort of break he should be giving them.

"Yeah, I guess. I help out."

"Probably help yourself is more like it. I mean around town. Kitty, you better watch this guy. Place only looks like Sleepy Hollow. Little berg has its share of firecrackers."

It was funny to hear Cathleen called by the nickname she hated most, and Bryce stifled a laugh. She rolled her eyes as she passed a bowl of applesauce to Larry.

"Glad to see life in the sticks hasn't changed you."

"Just the good parts. All the bad stuff's still in one piece."

Larry sat up to the table again and slathered sauce over two chops. He forked up a good chunk of pork and eyed it the way a moray eel might an anchovy; just before he popped it in, he pointed it at Trevor. "Make it up to Sedona yet? By the way, thanks for dressing."

Bryce's dad grinned. He and Larry were both pretty well off, but they usually dressed like bums. Trevor had been up most of the night stretching canvases, and he'd been half the day sizing and sanding them; he was red-eyed from too little sleep and too much coffee. His hair, which had begun to show gray on its own (a development he attributed to Sara), was peppered with gesso.

"Tuesday, around eleven. The light was incredible."

"Clear as Stoli. I swear New York has a different sun. This place grows on you, am I right? That whole section of rock near Coffee Pot is something. Get up to the airport and look back over that valley. Amazing stuff. Of course, that's the tourist view. Real thing is around back."

"That's what I figured."

"Maybe a little lonesome for the common folk, but you live off that crap. Pardon my German, Miss Megan. It keeps slippin' out."

Meg acknowledged Larry with a smile that probably meant his "German" was fine with her, but Bryce could tell she hadn't been listening anyway. She'd been quiet all day. She got that way when she was trying to figure something. She figured a lot for a little kid. Usually it was something Bryce wouldn't give a thought to in a million years—like, Does water swirl down the drain clockwise or counterclockwise in Australia? She figured it went counter in Australia. Bryce refused to let it worry him; he hadn't even noticed water always went down the same way here until she told him. Sometimes she had more brains than a kid needed.

"You in town for good now?" Trevor said.

"Gotta fly back to the Rotten Apple middle of next month. Otherwise I'm here. You start anything yet?"

"You know me."

"Yeah."

Cathleen nodded to Meg and they both left for the kitchen. A moment later the coffee grinder was buzzing away.

"Kitty's turned out to be quite the homemaker," Larry said once she was safely out of earshot.

"Surprised me too."

"Heck of an agent. She totally out of it now?"

"Totally."

"Too bad. How're Megan's eyes?"

Trevor glanced over at Bryce, and Bryce felt that sinking sensation in his gut he always got when they talked about it. Someday Meg would be blind. There was nothing anyone could do. The doctors said it was up to chance, though they all knew the odds were bad. Nobody told Meg that, but she read all the scientific stuff she could get her hands on anyway. She knew what RP was. She never said anything.

"They give her more crap to wear. Doesn't help."

"That's a hell of a thing. If there *is* a God, sometimes he's a royal screwup."

Bryce saw the look in his father's eye. Trevor wasn't a religious man by any means—that was just one of the many points on which he and Sara had routinely fought—still, Bryce could tell the blasphemy had caught him off guard, especially since it concerned Meg. Finally, he smiled and let it go. You let a lot go with Larry.

Larry charged on unaware.

"Well, to change the subject, have you got it yet—little bit of the bug?"

He leaned into the table and peaked his fingers like a chapel roof beneath his chin. Bryce could hear the "modern fucking Renaissance" speech building behind the breakwater. It'd blow any second.

"I've got some ideas."

"That's a start."

The kitchen door swung out and Meg and Cathleen came giggling with trays of tiny blue cups and squares of something kind of earthy-looking on china plates. The result of Cathleen's Prescott shopping junket sat on the counter near the juicer. It

44

was one of those hi-tech coffee machines that look like R2-D2.

"Cappuccino and bread pudding with caramel sauce for dessert," Cathleen announced proudly.

Larry held his wineglass aloft.

"The yuppies colonize Piñon Rim . . ."

T H E bread pudding looked pretty strange, but like everything else Cathleen made, it tasted great.

They'd just started the second round when a car topped the hill on Redman Drive and headlights flashed the mirror in the crystal cabinet. Meg was at the window before anyone else could even think about sliding back from the table.

"Green car," she said.

"Aggie," Bryce said, and Larry did a double take.

"Forget the firecrackers." Larry's leer was pure Nicholson. "This kid's messing with dynamite." He raised a pointed eyebrow at Bryce. "I'm very impressed." But Bryce was already halfway to the door.

"Who's Aggie?" Cathleen said.

"Sculptor, painter—little of this, little of that. She's not bad, not great either. Lotta bucks. Didn't come from scrapin' clay, if you catch my drift."

Bryce opened the door before Aggie rang. She stepped back and laughed. A basket of food and wine hung from one arm.

"Did I pick a bad time?"

Bryce didn't think that was possible.

T H E Y brought their cups into the den. Aggie sipped her cappuccino and nestled into one of the big chairs next to the coffee table. She was wearing a fitted white cashmere top with padded shoulders, and it occurred to Bryce that Cathleen, by no means plain, looked somehow formless and transparent next to Aggie.

Aggie laughed at the "unexpected pleasure" of seeing Larry there, and they traded good-natured insults. In spite of himself, Bryce felt a little jealous.

"It's a tradition I'm trying to start," Aggie said, indicating the basket which now sat between Cathleen and her husband. "A Piñon Rim Welcome Wagon. They're decent people in this town, but Larry'll tell you they're a little standoffish toward newcomers, especially artists."

"Guess you can't blame them," Trevor said.

"Of course not. We're a notoriously hostile breed."

Trevor laughed a relaxed, easy laugh, and Bryce couldn't help but notice a change since Aggie had come in. Trevor settled deep in his favorite chair, feet comfortably parked on the ottoman. His hands, usually so frantic without a brush that he often hid them in his pockets, rested naturally on his lap.

Cathleen, on the other hand, had stiffened.

Megan sat in her chair by the lamp, a million miles away once again. Larry leaned quietly against the wall near the fireplace, apparently content to let Aggie run the show for a while.

"We've only been here a week," Trevor said. "I've been in the studio mostly. Haven't gotten to town much."

"Working a cover?"

"No assignment—this one's just for me."

"Really?" She replaced her cup and saucer on the coffee table, and those green eyes squared directly with Trevor's. "I'd love to see what you've got sketched out . . . I mean, if that's okay."

"There isn't anything to show yet."

"Trevor doesn't *do* sketches." Larry folded his arms across his chest and stifled a belch.

"Really?"

"It's all in his head. He'll go someplace and hang for an hour or two and that's it. A week later it's on the shelves."

"That's amazing."

"That's why we hate him."

It amazed Bryce too. His father never took a sketchbook or lugged a camera to a site the way a lot of artists did. He'd just stay long enough to get the feel and head back to his studio to paint. The process was really something to see. Sometimes Bryce would take in a sandwich, pull up a stool, and watch. His dad would start with moody washes of color, and out of that murky soup, a strange, sometimes terrifying world would begin to evolve. And all the while, Trevor would be looking at absolutely nothing but the canvas in front of him. Larry's estimation of the time it took was a little off though. The last painting Trevor had done for the Mystery series had kept him going a good three months.

"I think your cityscapes are my favorite. I don't know exactly how to describe them."

"Pleasant urban nightmares," Trevor said.

"Well, yes." She sipped her coffee. "That pretty much says it." She laughed. "Pleasant urban nightmares. I like that. You're still working along that line?"

"The same feel—the subject is different. I'm trying to find that dark sort of isolation in nature."

"Larry says you're an artist." Cathleen's voice cut the air like a hot knife.

For a nervous beat there was silence. Larry shifted uneasily. Bryce was sure Larry'd make one of his usual quips, but he didn't.

"She's got a great easel," Bryce said, eager to say something—anything. He realized how stupid it sounded the second it came out.

Aggie laughed.

"I've been known for worse," she said.

"She's talented at what she does," Larry said, throwing in as much innuendo as possible, trying to wring a joke from the situation.

"And what is that exactly?" Cathleen said. There was more where that came from, but that was all Cathleen let herself say. It was enough. It was embarrassing.

"I don't think Aggie came over to be grilled on her credentials," Trevor said. An expression of numb horror crossed his face and Bryce knew exactly what he was thinking: this was pure Sara. His dad used to call Sara "TC," which stood for Top Cat, because she hissed whenever a female invaded her territory.

"It's just that she seems to be so well known . . ."

"I hope that's a compliment." Aggie went on as though it was.

Cool, too cool. Bryce's respect for Aggie flew off the meter.

"Mostly, I sculpt. The easel's for a friend. Bryce rescued me yesterday—I'd never have gotten that monster home without him." She winked at Bryce and he felt his face get hot, but it felt good this time.

"I work mostly in clay, sometimes marble when I'm feeling too ambitious for my own good." Aggie retrieved her cup and sipped. "Actually, I have an ulterior motive for coming by. I have a sort of favor to ask, an invitation really."

Trevor straightened a bit, but he was smiling again. It was a softened variation on his polite but official pose—his Trevor Willems the artist pose. He'd become an important man in the business and was constantly asked for favors, recommendations.

"I chair the Redrock Council for the Fine Arts. If Larry's mentioned that at all, he's probably told you it's a fancy name for folks who like to party."

"News to me if it isn't," Larry said.

"Well, that's part of it. But we're doing serious work, too. We sponsor workshops and we're planning a new gallery on Katie Avenue. If you're at all interested, we'd love to have you join us."

"Well," Trevor Willems the artist said as he poured more steamed milk into his cup. He offered it to Aggie and she declined. Megan and Bryce finished off the sweet white foam. Cathleen seemed to have locked herself in an invisible safe. "Part of the reason I came out here was to get away from all that. I'm frankly a little leery of anything resembling 'The Scene.'"

Aggie nodded.

"I'm a long time out of New York, but I know what you mean. It's different here. We're interested in promoting ourselves, but we've established a relationship with the community. Larry's actually been useful that way—if you can imagine Larry's being useful."

Larry ignored the jibe and bowed deeply.

"I help Aggie with the workshops. Nothing major."

"You never told me about that." Bryce's dad nodded his approval.

"Nothing too special. Couple'a three hours here and there. It's Aggie's enchilada."

"We've found some real talent among the locals. Anyway, the scene here is a lot less self-oriented than it is on the coasts. It really has to be. I wasn't kidding when I said the people here were standoffish.

"Bull, Aggie." Larry had ducked into the kitchen to replace the cup and saucer with a Coors. He popped back out looking infinitely more comfortable. "They're glad to have the frigging business."

"From what I know of this place, I'd think so too," said Trevor.

"A ghost town," Aggie said. "For a long time. But it used to be one of the richest boomtowns in the West. Believe it or not, there's a lot of wounded pride here."

"Ancient history—a hundred years ago."

"In two months it will be exactly that: one hundred years since Piñon Rim folded its tents, so to speak." Her smile was ironic, almost not a smile at all. Clearly she knew how ridiculous it all sounded, but it was just as clear she was serious.

"There can't be anyone left who remembers," Trevor said.

"Very few survived the bust. But—and I don't know how to say this without coming off like some sort of carnival mystic—sometimes a place has a memory."

She set the cup and saucer back on the coffee table and her green eyes flashed. "You must feel a presence of some sort when you choose one site over another. I mean, there's more to it than composition and color, isn't there?"

Trevor nodded. There was a skeptical smile beneath the surface, but it was obvious she'd touched common ground.

"There's a definite presence here, a personality. The people who moved back here feel it. Industry didn't bring them back. There's an energy. This place will boom again—and soon. They know it even if they don't know why. But they're very protective of it, too."

"You talk about 'survivors.' " Trevor smiled. "I'm assuming you mean that in a financial sense. Didn't everybody just leave when the mines tapped out?''

"I'm not great with history. I do know quite a few people actually died.''

Bryce saw himself back in the cemetery, the haphazard, almost frantic arrangement of graves. And all those little ones. . . .

"Lousy sales pitch, Aggie.'' Larry waved his beer. "I think the party stuff was a better tack.

"People here are fine. She's right about the energy though. I'm painting like a maniac now. Maybe it's just the clean air. I don't know.''

"Was there an epidemic of some kind? Bad water? Mining waste?'' Trevor asked.

He was sitting up straight now. Love Canal and Chernobyl might have been long out of the news, but they could never be totally out of mind. Bryce had an image of all that red soil seeping into the collective pores of the townspeople, soil filled with some venomous effluence from the mines. He saw them lurching into the streets like zombies. Welcome to Larry Brill's "freaking Renaissance.''

The crow's-feet darkened at the corners of his father's eyes. The idea that he'd just moved them over some sort of deadly landfill must have passed through everyone's head.

Across the room, Megan was suddenly back in the picture. She watched Aggie with the same sort of cautious wonder she might a new and possibly dangerous animal in the wild.

"More of a mass hysteria from what I've heard. I don't really know how many died or what started it. You have to remember when this was . . . the sort of element that existed here. It was the Wild West. The McClowerys and the Clantons, Billy the Kid and Jesse James—that sort. A tough town. Lawless. There were gunfights, fires, lynchings . . . Like I said, I don't really know the whole of it. I guess you could say Piñon Rim suffered its own urban nightmare. And not a pleasant one.''

That last understatement hung in the air like the Hindenburg attempting one last mooring. Megan, Bryce, and Trevor were all leaning in now. Only Cathleen seemed unaffected.

"Didn't I say this place had everything?" Larry smiled like the Cheshire cat.

"Thanks a lot, Larry." Trevor laughed. Everyone but Cathleen laughed too.

"It's had what they call a rich and colorful past," Aggie said, standing. "Anyway, it's anything but a ghost town now." She shook her head. "I'd better get out of here before I scare you back to New York."

"Not a chance," Larry answered for them.

"Thanks for the cappuccino. And Bryce, thank you for Friday." She kissed his cheek and hugged him as he stood, and he hoped his face wasn't turning red again. She looked over his shoulder at Cathleen. "Your son is an absolute knight in armor." Bryce figured she couldn't know how much of a dig that actually was; for all Aggie knew, Cathleen *was* his mother. Then again, Aggie had been pretty right-on so far.

Trevor helped Aggie into her jacket and Cathleen finally thanked her for the basket.

"If you're at all interested, the council meets the second and last Mondays of the month at Saint Martin's Episcopal. Eight o'clock."

"You've definitely piqued my interest."

"Hope to see you there. Either way, I'd really like to see what you're working on once you get going."

"If we haven't all dropped dead by then, you're more than welcome."

She laughed. "Maybe someone else should chair the Welcome Wagon. Anyway, it's really a great town. A little backward, but it'll grow on you."

Like a poisonous fungus, Bryce thought.

She smiled at him wryly, as if he'd said it out loud, then she turned on her heels and left, her boots echoing woodenly on the porch steps.

Bryce stood at the window and watched until the Jag's taillights disappeared over the hill. He felt a little lonely. She definitely left a vacuum behind.

"Well, that's Aggie Hudson, in case you still need to know."

Larry crushed his empty Coors and Cathleen took it on her way to the kitchen. Trevor followed her in.

"What was all that about?"

"I don't know. I just don't like her."

Larry rolled his eyes.

" W E E E E L L , kiddo, I guess that just about does it for the evening, huh?" Larry clapped Bryce on the back on the way out. He smelled of beer, paint, and sweat. His eyes were watery and red and very tired. For just a second something glimmered in there, something vital and very much alive.

"You're headed for a roller coaster ride, kiddo. Look out, but have a good time. Life's a frigging banquet. That's all I gotta say."

Roller coaster, banquet . . . Larry always had something to say. It didn't seem to matter if you didn't have a clue about what he meant.

The kitchen door closed behind Cathleen and Trevor. Bryce could hear their voices, Cathleen's measured and taught, his father's deep but clipped. It probably wouldn't boil over, but it gave him a bitter sort of déjà vu. He would always love and miss his mother, but he'd never miss the fights.

He tiptoed upstairs, but the steps creaked mournfully despite his efforts. He stopped at Megan's room and poked his head inside.

Meg was surrounded by pillows, *National Geographic*s, and two Ninja Turtles. She flipped quickly through one of the *Geographic*s, dropped it, picked up another and did the same. Her forehead was furrowed. Bryce noticed she'd pushed her bed all the way into one corner of the room.

"Nutmeg."

She looked up at him, removed her glasses, and blinked. For just a second, he saw her as she might be a few years down the line. Without the glasses she was going to be pretty, seriously pretty. But she would never be without the glasses.

"What do you think about all that?" he said.

"Don't know. Pretty weird."

"Yeah. People have been here for a while though. And they're okay."

"Yeah. You figure somebody would've gotten sick by now."

"What're you lookin' at?"

"Cave stuff. Did you know caves whisper?"

Well, there she went again. Another "water in Australia" sort of question.

"Did you know you're crazy?"

"It's true. See?" She held a book open to a cave cross section. There were directional lines drawn through and across it. Next to that was a drawing of a boy blowing across the lip of a bottle.

"If the cave's built just right and there's a crosswind inside, the cave whispers. I've been reading up on it."

"You're a major psycho."

"You know what else I know?"

"They whisper backwards in Australia?"

"No." She giggled that crazy staccato giggle.

"What?"

"Not gonna tell."

"What?"

"Nothing."

"Vell," Bryce said in the best Schwarzenegger he could manage. "Den I'm gonta haff to beat it aut off you." He puffed out his chest and plodded menacingly toward her.

She held out a Ninja Turtle to ward him off and laughed.

"Okay! Okay!"

"Okay, what is it?"

"It's a secret." Her voice was hushed. "Gotta come close." He leaned in close.

"Brrrrryyyyycie loves Aggie! Brrrrrryyyycie loves Aggie!"

"Shut up, pissant!"

He smacked her with a pillow and chucked another one at her on the way out. Then he snapped off her light for good measure. She squealed from the darkness and giggled.

"Brycie loves Aggie! Brycie loves Aggie! Brrrrryyyyycie loves Aggie! Brrrrrryyyyycie loves Aggie!"

* * *

WENDELL Mackey woke to Buddy howling at the window.

He cursed and spat, but it wasn't Buddy he was mad at. It was the potato-masher hand grenade that had landed some twenty feet from him in the south of France. That was forty-five years ago. He wasn't mad at the soldier who'd thrown it. The soldier was only doing his job, Wendell figured, just like Wendell had only done his when he rang a hole through the young German's helmet a heartbeat later. The German was long gone, but the masher had buried a splinter in Wendell's spine that would be with him forever.

It was the rain that got it going this time. He'd been taking the pills that kept the tiny dagger from playing mumblety-peg on his lower back since early yesterday morning. When they didn't take, he'd chased them with Cutty Sark. He usually had Buddy's evening snack laid out by 7:15 or so, but he'd barely made it out of the bedroom in two days.

The howls drilled through Wendell's eardrums like air-raid sirens.

His first attempt at Buddy's name was a cough. The second wasn't much better. Finally, he got it out.

"Buddy! Hold on. Hold on, Bud."

The walker gleamed just out of reach. Damned thing. He hated it. Hated being so dependent upon it.

"I'm coming."

He made a feeble, clawing attempt at it that fell way short. The movement was enough to fire a white-hot bolt of pain from his hip to the base of his skull. There were good days and bad ones, and these last two weren't good.

"Sorry, Buddy." He closed his eyes. Blue paramecia swam in a red sea before him. He tapped off the light.

Blessed absolution. The cloudy sanctuary returned; he whirlpooled down that familiar and very deep well. He was only vaguely aware that, back in this world, Buddy had quit barking.

THREE hours later the slap of the kitchen door closing brought him back.

54

The clouds parted on darkness. Someone was in the house, and where the hell was Buddy?

Someone in the house.

He strained to hear. No footsteps. His mind tossed out a useless fact: he'd lived fifteen years unmolested in this house.

There was always a first time. He'd been lucky.

He could see the dark square of the hamper across the hall, beyond that the small archway that opened into the TV room. And Wendell began to notice disquieting things about his little castle. For starters, someone could stand in that little pocket between the arch and the wall and Wendell would never see him. The window behind the Zenith looked directly into his bedroom. The kitchen, all the way on the other side of the TV room, had its own door to the outside. He couldn't see the kitchen at all from here.

But he wasn't helpless; if someone was in the house he had a surprise for him.

He pulled himself up. The pain was there, growling and waiting, but it didn't pounce. He moved his feet to the side of the bed, shifted his weight smoothly, gave the springs time to adjust. The soles of his feet kissed the worn carpet. Careful.

He listened hard. His hands found the cold chrome of the walker. It shook, but it came to him. Time was all he needed. God give him time.

Both eyes on the doorway, he slid down his shiny chrome spine and knelt.

A 12-gauge double load of Remington buckshot lay under his bed, coiled and ready. He drew it to him.

The kitchen door cracked open once more.

Wendell grinned through his pain, a bleached skull in the moonlight. He wrapped his pillowcase around the walker's crossbar and looped it over the stock.

He was ready now. Sure, come the heck in. Sweat dripped from his chin.

Something slid along the kitchen floor.

Wendell lifted the front of the walker, steadied the shotgun, and moved forward. Another push and he was in the narrow hallway.

Another two pushes and he was past the window in the TV room.

He had him.

Sweat splashed the stock. His back sang like a flock of shrieking angels, his arms vibrated from the strain. The louvered door that screened the kitchen from the TV room was all he saw; it danced at the end of a short dark tunnel. Break into this castle, friend, and you pay the price. You pay the price. He was waiting behind the door, just waiting for Wendell to mosey on in. The pillowcase hung nearly to the floor. The shotgun rattled against the crossbar. Wendell couldn't stop it.

Not a sound from the kitchen.

The window was behind him now. Nobody could have come around without him hearing, or could they? He kept the shotgun trained on the door. His eyes roved toward the TV and the window beyond. He wasn't grinning anymore. He turned his head slowly, carefully. His scalp was tight and cold. The shotgun was bouncing . . . at the corner of the window—

The louvered door moved outward and a double load of buckshot obliterated it. Wendell Mackey flew backward, crashed over his sofa, and crumpled like a broken kite. Plaster and wood chips showered the room and Wendell screamed.

His eardrums rang. Wendell could see the kitchen and the porch beyond clearly through the gaping hole he'd just made. Buddy's bowl sat peacefully on the counter. Why a burglar would move a dog dish was a mystery, but on the counter it was, and Wendell hadn't put it there.

Well, the burglar was gone anyway, probably with a couple dozen pellet holes in the butt. That was just fine with Wendell. His back felt as raw as a broken sapling where the splinter was. He could barely feel his legs at all.

Now you've done it, fool. Now you've laid yourself up good.

But he'd protected his own. The walker had mercifully tumbled nearby. He hooked it with his forearm.

As he flicked on the floor lamp, yellow light filled the den. It made the hole in the door look worse. Only a half-dozen louvers remained. The frame was splintered halfway to the floor. A sharkbite of plaster was chewed out around it and the whole area was dotted with black holes the size of BBs.

He stumped toward the kitchen; his back cried out with every step, but it was better than being paralyzed. And a fall like the one he'd taken could easily have done just that.

He flicked on the kitchen light.

The door to the cabinet that held the canned goods was open, as was the pantry door. Buddy's Purina bag had split down the middle, and the pantry floor was littered with rock-hard beefy chunks. Sawdust, plaster, and shot were everywhere.

A gamey smell wafted in from the outside. He maneuvered the walker to the kitchen door and leaned out to close it, but stopped. There were two full cans of Cycle 4 in the trash.

He reached painfully down to retrieve one and dropped it. It was covered with slimy spit. The white label was punctured by rows of jagged teeth marks.

He pushed the walker onto the porch and his knees nearly failed him. The porch was slick with fresh blood.

Then he saw the bodies.

Squirrels, possum, rabbits. Dozens of them, neatly stacked against the screen. Wendell staggered to the steps and slapped on the floodlights. The backyard was dotted with rows of freshly gouged pits and tiny hills of earth.

Something was moving in the forest. Coming his way. Coming fast. Wendell backed into the kitchen. He slammed the door and slipped the bolt.

Buddy tore into the clearing, pulling up just beyond the floodlights. Wendell could see the flat blue glow of his eyes in the blackness. Then Buddy loped across the meadow, something torn and bloody in his jaws. He bolted up the steps and onto the deck. His huge face, a mass of blood and foamy spit, filled the window, and Wendell fell back against the refrigerator.

Can't depend on you. Can't.

Through his terror and pain came that thought.

Buddy dropped to the deck. He tossed the ruined thing on the shortest stack.

Wendell watched with numb horror as Buddy yanked a possum from the stack nearest the steps, loped to the next available hole in the backyard, and dropped it in. He kicked dirt over it, bounded back up the steps, and scooped up a rabbit; it was still twitching.

"Buddy." It was almost a croak. Buddy looked squarely at him.

Can't depend on you.

It was there again. A single thought, sharp as the devil.

"Oh, my God." Wendell said.

I T was a hot Monday morning.

On Sluice Road, the red clay had dried and flaked like sunburnt skin. Bryce powdered the little curls with his toe as he and Meg waited for the bus. They crunched like potato chips.

"Thanks for taking the bus," she said.

Bryce shrugged.

"S'okay." It wasn't. The bus would be full of screaming little kids. Riding the bus wasn't too cool for an eighth grader.

Meg beamed. It was clear she was pretty excited about school, but Bryce wished she'd eighty-sixed the corrective dark contact lens she wore on her left eye, making it look like one big pupil. The bottle-bottom glasses made her look freaky enough; the lens was Martian city. She didn't have to wear it all the time. If he'd been her, he would've waited until everybody at school knew him, kind of eased into it, seen how the cards played. Not Meg. Meg was gonna slam down the whole deck at once.

The rest of her looked cool. Her brown hair was thick and shiny, and Cathleen had given her a pretty cute bob. She had on an oversized white T-shirt with the sleeves rolled halfway up, a Bon Jovi pin, and a denim skirt with lacy, knee-length red leggings.

No more stupid uniforms for either one of them. He wore jeans.

"No more nuns," she said.

"I was thinking that." They could hear the bus chugging its way toward them from the other side of the hill.

"You still think the teachers are gonna be ogres?"

"No, just the principal. The teachers'll be trolls."

She giggled.

"Do trolls eat people?"

"Just girls. They really like 'em best at eleven years old, though, 'cause they're a little fatter. So you still have one month to live."

"What about boys?"

"Guys are too tough and chewy. Especially eighth graders."

"Have you seen the high school?"

He shook his head.

"Well, maybe they don't have one." She squinted up at him with that screwy left eye. She dropped her voice to her socks. "Maybe in Arizona they just grind you up after eighth grade."

He considered that.

"Na. You become a god here after eighth grade. At least guys do. You'll be dead by then, so you won't."

Her eyes rolled in those frames as she laughed. It was a pretty good one about the high school, Bryce thought. She had him on that one.

The bus nosed its way over the hill. As it rolled up, wheezing and smoking, Bryce's worst fears were realized: it was packed with a zillion hyper little kids.

He glanced back down Redman Drive toward the house. His bike would be leaning against the rosemary barrel.

Megan smiled up at him as the door hissed open. He took her binder and lunchbag, and once again, he wished Meg had left the contact lens at home.

The driver's smile froze midway. Bright light was supposedly part of Meg's problem, but Bryce had no idea why that stupid doctor hadn't just prescribed sunglasses or two dark contacts to kind of even out the look. Obviously, both her eyes were pretty bad. Bryce felt his face get hot. Meg was up the steps in a flash as if she hadn't noticed, but Bryce guessed she had. She was just used to that sort of thing.

Bryce swung up into the cabin. The driver made two quick checks on a clipboard, and the door shrieked closed.

Most of the kids wore crisp new clothes; they held shiny new ring binders on their laps. Half of them had their sticker albums open and were conducting complex trades. They stopped to check out Bryce and Meg. One of the girls smiled up at Bryce and giggled. (An eighth-grade boy on the bus was obviously a big deal.) And Bryce felt himself flush again. There were still empty seats, but some of the kids moved over to make room for them anyway. Bryce took that for a good sign.

During the bumpy ride they met Jimmy Potts, a kid Meg's age who had sleepy eyes and a runny nose, and Cheryl Roberts, who, to Meg's amazement, had three sticker albums. It was all a relief to Bryce because it looked like things might be okay for Meg, which meant he'd be on his own that much sooner.

So, he thought as the old bus chugged up Sluice Road, things would probably be okay at Piñon Rim Elementary.

MEGAN's homeroom was long and narrow with tall windows running along the north side. A counter stacked with books ran the entire length of the wall. A formidable-looking wooden pole with a hook on one end to open the taller windows stood in the corner next to the American flag and the copper sunrise which she took to be Arizona's flag. There was a press along the back wall to hang their coats in bad weather and a big, round clock above the front blackboard.

There was no crucifix.

Jimmy Potts and five others she recognized from the bus were in her class. Jimmy's row stood and waited in line for books. He waved at her, and a fat kid poked him.

After Bryce had left, the familiar curtain of silence had dropped around her. Mostly they stared at her glasses; a few of them had whispered when she walked in. Meg didn't care for that, but that's just how it was.

There was a lot of summer talk. A lot of just plain noise. A kid two rows away was making clucking sounds over and over again while his friend giggled like a lunatic. Whether the teachers were trolls or ogres, they weren't strict.

Except when it came to seat assignments.

Ms. Phillips, her homeroom teacher, had gotten ruffled when Meg asked to sit closer to the front. She'd let her make the change, but made just enough of a deal out of it to punch up the fact Meg was different. It was all Meg needed.

Ms. Phillips, a short, stout woman with black hair that shined blue, now sat reading a *Woman's Day* at the front of the room while a kid named Arnold busily jotted down book numbers as the other kids filed past.

Meg had a headache from the contact lens in her left eye, but she figured she'd better keep it in. Lately her eyes were getting tired a lot.

Her row stood and joined Jimmy's by the window. From there, she could see past the playground to Sharpe's Creek and the forest beyond. The forest was dark and thick. She thought about the whispering cave that lay hidden within it. Even though she knew it only *sounded* like it was talking, it still gave her a chill.

"Bigfoot's gonna kill you, Kevin!" someone hissed. "Bigfoot's gonna kill you, Kevin! Gonna k-k-kill you, Kevin!"

Kevin told him to stop it. There were tears in his voice. The clucking boy had graduated to a low sort of mooing sound, and his friend giggled even louder.

Three girls in front of her were talking about boys from Red Ridge High. (Now she'd have to tell Bryce there was a high school.)

"Save it, Jennifer."

"Oh, did you see his eyes!"

"Wait for Helldorado!"

"Brock goes to Ridge too . . ."

". . . shouldn't go up there, anyway, Marcy . . ."

". . . up to Cross Hill and get wrecked . . ."

"Sooo wasted! Totally wrecked."

"Moooooooooooo! Moooooooooo!"

". . . he just wants to . . ."

"Moooooooooo."

"Wait until Halloween night!"

". . . that's what he wants."

"That's gross!"

"M-M-Moooooooooo!"

"Gonna kill you, Kevin."

62

"Up on Cross Hill, these guys from Ridge . . ."

"Helldorado, man. Cross Hill on Halloween night."

If they'd been speaking a foreign language Meg couldn't have understood less. She took a book from each stack. The books were comfortably worn. Their pasteboard corners poked through the cloth like toes through old socks. The last book, Heflin's *World Geography*, had a big black *38* written on the binding with magic marker. The number had bled to purple along the edges.

"Are you like, bline or somethin'?"

The girl in front of Meg had turned to face her. She had puffy eyes and round, full cheeks. She smelled like soap, and oddly, like tears. She talked lazily.

"No."

"God, Jennifer, you're a genius—Not!" Two other girls in line were giggling. The blond lazy-talker turned back to them.

"Tol' you."

Arnold took down Meg's book numbers as she passed, and when Meg helped him find her name on the list, Ms. Phillips gave her the eye . . . this strange new kid who changed seats.

Ms. Phillips gave Meg the creeps.

"Bigfoot's gonna kill you, Kevin."

Meg sat down at her desk and stared at the worn covers of her books. Slowly the morning passed.

T H E teachers at PRE didn't waste time. By the end of second period, Bryce already had homework. A small stack of books had grown beneath his desk. He didn't care. The gold chain had him mesmerized.

He could only see small parts of Connie Bowman at any one time. Sometimes it was just her soft brown curls, sometimes the side of her face too. Every now and then, the girl in the next row and the guy across from her would lean forward, and then Bryce could see more. Connie wore a man's white shirt with blue pinstripes, a blue silk vest, and a white skirt that showed a smooth tan from the middle of her thighs on down to her sandals.

But it was the chain that had him.

It winked just above her right ankle, a thin gold chain with a single round charm on it. It spoke to him somehow, conjuring feelings for which he could supply no image. Finally, an image did come, a crazy one, and he couldn't help wondering how hard—or how easy—it might be to snap a chain like that in his hand.

When the bell rang Bryce nearly jumped out of his skin.

The others spilled into the hall. Bryce was closer to the door than most, but he took his time. He piled the books on his desktop carefully, one on top of the next until Connie was even with his aisle. Then he fell in line next to her.

She was smaller than he'd thought. That was okay. He caught a scent of sandalwood and sweet soap. It was the closest he'd been to her, and his lungs felt like they'd shrunk to the size of peanuts. His head felt light. She looked up at him then, and maybe she recognized him from the other day, maybe she didn't. He hoped she didn't. Someone called her name and she looked away.

He couldn't remember if he'd smiled at her or not. He didn't think he had, and that was probably best.

He juggled his lunch and his lock on his books and moved away from the main current of bodies. There was a fifteen-minute break, a good time to check out his locker. Lockers were a new experience.

Connie was at the end of the pack, near the stairwell. He wanted to run over and introduce himself, but he didn't. Best to let her make the first move.

Like that's gonna happen. He watched her descend till she disappeared in the pack.

Bryce glanced out the window to see where they were all going. A steel window had opened in the wall of the cafeteria and an older man and two kids were busily selling junk food.

He swung his locker open and shut a couple times. An old sticker inside had been partially removed and freshly painted over. He could still see the PiL logo underneath. Otherwise it looked okay. He checked the lock and wrote the combination on a scrap of paper. When he put it in his wallet, he saw the receipt with Aggie's address and phone number on it. He felt a curious twinge of guilt thinking about Aggie after thinking so hard about Connie. It passed. He put his books in the locker, retrieved a Granny Smith apple and a napkin from his lunch-bag, and tossed the rest of his lunch into the locker. Well, that was pretty cool. He could keep a lot of stuff in there.

He took a great, snapping bite out of the apple. He could like this place.

8

W H E N lunch hour came around it was definitely not cafeteria weather. The sun was so bright the hills glowed red and gold; the sky was a deep aquamarine.

Bryce poked his head inside the cafeteria anyway. A million kids. A steady clamor of sliding plastic trays and silverware. The building smelled sweet and slightly rancid, the same as the cafeteria at Saint Andrews—probably the same as cafeterias everywhere. He didn't see Meg so he headed out to the football field.

A pipe oozed milky sludge from the kitchen into a sudsy mudhole. He steered well clear of that and sat in the grass. A little girl in jeans skipped past him, tossing a white ball in the air and chanting a sort of Sesame Street rap she composed on the fly. On every fourth beat the ball rose high into the air, the rap stopped, and she stuck her tongue out like Michael Jordan waiting for the ball to come down. It made Bryce laugh, but she was concentrating so hard she didn't seem to notice.

Cathleen had packed a whopper of an Italian submarine and, stop the presses, one of her famous cinnamon rolls. She was definitely trying.

Bryce took care of half the sub and the sweet roll in record time. Fat, dumb, and happy, he rested his head against the cool stone wall and closed his eyes. The mountain air was sweet with pine. The sun seemed gentler now than it had this morning.

When he opened his eyes again, about twenty guys had gotten together on the field. Two of them broke off from the others and headed his way.

"You wanna play British Bulldog?"

The first kid was tall and dark-skinned. His hair was straight and black. He wore reflector sunglasses with searing green rubber stems and a matching tie string. The second kid was short and stocky, with a crew cut, a kind of a pig nose, and a mess of freckles.

"Yeah, sure," Bryce said, slapping the dirt from his jeans as he stood. He had no clue what British Bulldog was.

"All right, who's gonna be the bulldog?" the dark kid said.

The stocky kid raised his hand and spat.

"I'll go."

"Chuck's the bulldog."

That fit. Chuck sort of looked like a bulldog.

Chuck the bulldog walked across the field and stood at the near hashmark.

Bryce watched from the sideline with the rest.

"Okay." Chuck spat on his hands, rubbed it in, and wiped his hands on his pants. Then he screamed, "British Bull-daaaawg!"

The whole crowd broke across the field, howling like madmen.

Bryce loped along somewhere near the middle of the group. Chuck bounced from side to side like a mongoose, then he barreled straight into them. A kid running next to Bryce folded in midair with a great "Woof," Chuck's shoulder in his stomach. The two of them hit the ground, rolled to their feet, and sacked two more kids.

What the hell kind of game is this? Bryce ran faster.

He pulled up with the survivors on the other side of the field. The dark kid had gotten there first.

"Got the hang?" The dark kid smiled.

"Yeah. Got the hang." Bryce said, getting his wind.

"Last one up wins. Get ready."

There were now four bulldogs in the middle.

"British Bulldaaaawg!" they screamed.

Bryce teed off this time. He passed them before they could close ranks. When he looked back, nearly half the others were

67

either sprawled on the ground or being dragged down from behind.

Somehow, the dark kid had gotten to the other side ahead of him again.

"Pretty fast," the dark kid said, barely winded.

Bryce could do little more than nod. His legs had always been pretty good to him, but this kid wasn't human. Bryce's lunch had started to tie a pretty good knot in his stomach. Finally he said, "You do track?"

"I run." The others plodded up. "This is where it gets good." The dark kid turned, ready to go. Then he said, "Crud."

Three more boys, big ones, were walking toward them up the dirt path from the cafeteria. Bryce felt his scalp tighten. The kid who'd blown the quail away and his white-haired friend with the missing teeth were two of the newcomers.

They looked at Bryce and smiled. The third kid was tall and lanky. His right eye was focused on another planet.

"We wanna play," Shotgun announced.

Some of the other guys looked at the fast kid. They didn't make a sound, but it was plain he was in charge and they wanted him to say no.

"Free world," he said and shrugged. And then the call to battle roared from the center of the field.

"British Bulldaaaaawg!"

Bryce bolted again, but the bulldogs were ready for him this time. It didn't matter. He turned on the afterburners, dodged and weaved. A narrow lane opened and Bryce charged through it. One kid planted himself at the other end of the lane, his shoulder down. Bryce met that shoulder with his own and sent the kid reeling. He high-stepped away as hands swept at his ankles. He kept pumping until he'd crossed the line on the other side. In the corner of his eye he saw the three newcomers go down in one big, easy clump. He bent over and took two deep breaths, grabbing his knees for support. But it was a heady feeling just the same.

Even the dark kid was panting this time. There was a whole string of kids on the ground in his wake. Three others tramped across the line behind them.

A horde of bulldogs gathered in the center of the field.

"Jesus," Bryce said. The odds didn't look so good. His shoulder stung a little and his stomach was threatening an all-out cramp.

The dark kid smiled.

"Some fun now, huh?" He spat. "Those three are buttheads. They'll all go for one of us. It's why they all went down at once like babies." He spat again.

A foaming pool of red mud had formed near his sneakers. "Big one's real strong, but slow. They're all mean."

"British Bulldaaaawg!"

It was like running through oncoming highway traffic. The one saving grace was that there were so many bulldogs coming at once they tripped each other up. Bryce hurdled over one rolling body, crashed into another, and saw two more go down.

He kept his feet and kept going. He tried to run straight away from the three newcomers, but escaping the other bulldogs turned him their way. The white-haired kid caught his foot. Bryce whipped his leg and spun free, and the kid with the walleye wrapped him up, but he wasn't trying to pull Bryce down so much as hold him steady. Bryce had a quick, terrifying glimpse of Shotgun chugging straight for him, big as a house, his fist clenched and high. There was a sharp *crack* and the walleye's hands went slack. Bryce lunged free just as Shotgun left his feet. The fast kid jolted by, shaking his stinging forearm, and Shotgun crashed to the ground with teeth-rattling force. Three more bulldogs went for Bryce. He and the fast kid both went down as another kid crossed the sideline, hooting, his arms raised in triumph.

Five yards back from where Bryce sat, catching his breath, the kid who'd grabbed him was sitting more or less upright. His head lolled from side to side. A mouse was already rising beneath his bad eye.

"No fair!" Shotgun was on his feet. "You cheated, Cody!"

"Was in my way, Bigfoot. Dude was in my way." The dark kid rose to his feet.

Bigfoot spat.

Bryce stood. He was getting that lightheaded feeling again.

Something about to happen, probably bad and certainly dangerous. The heat began to well up.

The friend of Bigfoot's who could still stand got up.

Bigfoot looked squarely at Bryce. The meaning of that look wasn't lost on Bryce. Bigfoot was afraid of Cody. But sometime, somewhere, Bryce would be alone, and Bigfoot and his friends would be waiting. Bigfoot turned and the white-haired kid helped the other one, still lost in the stars, to his feet. The three of them hobbled away, mumbling.

"Who is that idiot?"

"Bigfoot. Well, Johnny Blackfoot. We call him Bigfoot 'cause he's an ugly butthole. Don't say it to his face though."

"You did."

"S'okay if I do. Same tribe."

"You're Indians?"

"Apache-Navajo."

"That's cool."

Cody shook his head like Bryce was crazy, but Bryce thought it was pretty cool that Cody was an Indian, especially an Apache. Apaches were supposed to be pretty fierce.

"What grade are they?"

"Hard to say."

"Don't they go here?"

"Walker and Tyler do. Walker's the one with the crazy eye." Cody put his hand next to his temple and flicked his pinkie out to the side. "They're both supposed to be in seventh, but they're in sixth. Bigfoot's been held back a couple times; he should be in high school." Cody smiled. "They're all dumb mothers."

He held out his hand for Bryce to slap, which Bryce did. The stocky kid trotted up to them.

"I'm Cody Muledeer and this squirrely mess is Chuck Weaver."

"Bryce Willems."

"Dudes." Chuck slapped their hands. "You from back East?"

"New York."

"Thought so. Got the sound. You run a streak, man. Almost fast as my man, the Mule."

"You tackle good."

The bell rang, just as piercing and unwelcome as the one at Saint Andrews.

"Could you get my ball?" It was the little girl in jeans who'd been rapping before. "Could you get it?"

"Yeah, sure," Bryce said. "Where is it?"

"Down there, in the creek."

The storm had covered everything down there—boulders, tree trunks, vines—in a thick layer of red clay. Chock up one more pair of jeans and Nikes. Bryce picked his way down the bank. Cody held back.

"Second bell's gonna ring," Cody said.

"Go ahead. I got it."

The ball, smeared with red clay but otherwise no worse for the wear, sat in a pool of red-tinted water behind a snarl of muddy branches.

Bryce stretched one leg over the water and planted his foot firmly on the tangle. As he bent out over the pool, his heart crawled up his throat.

Inches from the surface, two wide, silvery eyes stared up at him. No more than a finger's length from the ball, a small hand lay between the twisted branches. Had the boy in the water been living, he might have been reaching for the ball himself.

Bryce's head seemed to float ten feet above the water. The second bell rang and then he heard his own scream like a high horn blast from somewhere far away.

His arms pinwheeled as he stepped away and nearly lost his balance completely.

The girl saw it too. She shrieked. Cody's head appeared over the bank, his jaw dropped.

"Get Mrs. Curtis! Someone's drowned!"

More faces popped over the bank; the screams came in waves.

"Get the little kids away! Come on! Get 'em away!"

The big kids herded the little ones as the teachers came running.

Bryce searched the tiny frightened faces for Meg's.

Cody ran down to the water's edge.

"You okay?"

"Yeah." At least he could breathe now. He took one more look at the face in the water. Strands of long hair waved over it with the current. "I gotta find my sister."

Connie stood on the bank. For a second, their eyes met. Then he was scrambling up the bank. He didn't see Meg anywhere.

M E G sipped her milk and walked by the rows of lockers outside Bryce's homeroom. One of these lockers was his; if she were a year older she'd have one too, probably right next to it. She wished she were older.

The building wasn't well lit and the sunlight from the window at the end of the hall erased everything around it. The building was old and it had a moldy, bookish smell to it. It was creepy. The happy chaos of an entire school at play echoed up the stairs and through the windows.

Meg headed back.

A ball rolled past her foot and she nearly hit the ceiling. She hadn't seen anyone.

"Hello?"

She tried to focus on the shadow around the window; it doubled and grew comet tails. She dumped her carton and started downstairs. If someone wanted to play tricks, she didn't want any part of it.

The ball rested on the first step. It was old leather, scaly and cracked, and poorly stitched.

From the dark recesses of the hall a throat was cleared. A small voice said, "Kin I have my ball, please?"

Now she really had the creeps. A little boy was silhouetted in the harsh whiteness of the window.

"Kin I have my ball, please?"

Retrieving it was an automatic gesture—politeness before fear. She underhanded it to him. It made a dirty, grating sound when it struck the floor and rolled.

He disappeared in the shadows below the window.

"I'm Meg," she said.

The school bell wailed through the empty halls.

"See you," she said. She hurried downstairs.

The boys here were weird. Like the one who made those clucking noises and his giggling friend, and the other kid torturing Kevin with the Bigfoot stories. She was starting to miss Saint Andrews.

The second bell rang before she pushed the doors open. Outside, the sunlight made her temples pound.

Everybody was running toward the playing field. She'd never seen such disrespect for rules.

Two boys ran right past her.

"Dead kid in the creek!" one of them crowed over his shoulder with a lift in his voice that said she'd be crazy to miss something like that. Her insides dropped like hot candle wax to the pavement. She didn't see Bryce anywhere. Meg stared at the wave of running bodies without a single rational thought. Suddenly, she was running too.

She stopped at the end of the courtyard.

The boy from the hallway stood near the blacktop, his dirty leather ball in hand.

Kids ran right by him like he wasn't there. A breeze Megan couldn't feel caught his hair, carried it away from his pale blue eyes. He wore shapeless gray coveralls that were too short. His brown leather shoes had high tops like basketball sneakers. She wondered what kind of mom would dress a kid like that. The way he looked at her was scary. She felt sick to her stomach, like being in a car going too fast down a steep hill. Obviously he knew some kind of shortcut—a Titan missile couldn't have gotten him here that quick.

"What do you want?" she said. She was sure she was going to throw up.

Ms. Phillips looked the way Megan felt as she swung herself around the corner, puffing, red-faced, and sweaty. A lock of blue-black hair bounced over her eyes. She was surrounded by dozens of wide-eyed kids. Some of them were crying. Most were just excited.

"Did you see the dead dude?" A blond kid with spiky hair danced just ahead of the rest.

"I was right on top of him, man!" Another one ran up to the front.

"That was *gross!*"

"Dude bit it bigtime!"

"Bigtime!"

"Homerooms! Now!" Ms. Phillips was doing her best to herd an unruly flock. There were too many. A bald man with a big gut swung out of the teachers' lounge, a messy napkin still tucked into his shirt.

"What the hell is going on, Hilde?"

"Help me get them in! A boy's drowned!"

"Oh God!" The man threw the door open wide; it cracked against the wall like a gunshot. "A kid's drowned! Call the sheriff!"

Half a dozen teachers skidded through the open doorway.

"Homerooms!" they shouted.

A boy had drowned, Bryce was nowhere to be seen, and there was this weird kid with his stupid clothes and his stupid ball. Meg felt limp. Ms. Phillips snatched her arm, guiding her back the other way.

The tremble in her hands brought Meg back.

"Who drowned?" Meg wailed.

"I don't know. Everyone to homerooms!"

That was worse. If it had been someone who'd gone here awhile, Ms. Phillips would have known the kid's name. *But it couldn't be Bryce.* Bryce was too big to drown in a stupid creek. Meg craned her neck to look back toward the field. The smaller kids formed crazy, chaotic lines, the kind ants form when their trails get stomped. Some of the bigger kids were just now making their way into the courtyard. Bryce wasn't with them.

"I need *everyone* back in their homerooms!" Ms. Phillips shouted.

There was nowhere to go but forward. Meg walked sideways as the crowd jostled her along. The boy with the ball stood and watched. Bryce blew past him into the courtyard and Meg hopped with relief. Bryce skidded to a stop when he saw her and waved. His face was red from running, but he was okay.

She got one more glance just before being herded into her classroom.

The boy with the ball was gone.

T H E big man in the khaki uniform introduced himself as Sheriff Tom Gordon.

Trevor invited him inside and Gordon turned nearly sideways to get his shoulders through their door. He carried his hat in his hand and apologized for the intrusion.

"Always liked this place. It's the best of the old ones." He spoke softly, but his voice could have come from the bottom of a huge oak barrel. "Lotta people just tear 'em down and put up those stuccoed monsters, those yuppie jobs."

He looked a little sheepish when Cathleen offered him a cappuccino.

"That'd be nice but no, thank you. I don't want to take your time. I just stopped by to see how your young man here's doing."

Bryce's hand nearly disappeared in Sheriff Gordon's big mitt as he shook it.

"Kinda tough to see something like that."

"S'okay." It wasn't. He'd come way too close to touching that small, clay-covered hand.

They'd let everybody out after a thankfully brief assembly in the auditorium. Principal Curtis had announced that counselors would be available to speak to all students with "questions or concerns about the incident."

The entire ride home Bryce had told and retold the story of finding the Indian boy. And it hadn't ended once he'd gotten back to the Big House.

"He was a Navajo boy from the Yavapai Reservation, I expect," Sheriff Gordon said. "Been in the water a few days, probably since the rain last Friday. Navajo keep to themselves . . . don't usually file Missing Persons right away."

"Where's the reservation?"

" 'Bout five miles northeast."

"He floated for five miles?" Trevor said.

Sheriff Gordon nodded.

"Most likely. The ones from the reservation pretty much stay put. They don't feel protected unless they're on Navajo land."

"Do you know Cody Muledeer?" Bryce asked.

"Good kid."

"He doesn't live on the reservation."

"They don't all follow the traditions. Cody's folks left a few years back. I guess you've met Johnny Blackfoot, too?"

Bryce nodded.

"Well, that one's trouble."

And that was an understatement.

"It's awful about the boy," Cathleen said.

The big man shook his head. Clearly, the find had shaken him as well.

"Flash floods . . . well, they're deathtraps is all you can say. A good rain turns these washes into rivers in no time. Haven't had much rain this summer, and that was a big one Friday. Doesn't take a lot when the ground isn't ready for it." He looked squarely at Bryce. His eyes were older than the rest of him somehow; he couldn't have been much past forty. His handshake had been a crusher, and the muscles of his upper arms showed through the khaki shirt, as did the beginnings of a decent paunch over his belt.

"It's kind of like saying 'it's a dry heat' when it's one-twenty in the shade, but drownings aren't common here. Kid's who grow up in the Redrock area know to stay away from the washes when it looks like rain. And you need to know that too. Stay on high ground when it clouds up. If it rains and getting home means crossing a wash, stay put—even if it means getting a little wet. Indian kids are pretty keen on that point."

"You think he might have been pushed?" Trevor leaned away from the fireplace and massaged the back of his neck with one hand.

"Well, it's hard to figure. I'm sure he knew better. Kids are kids; they horse around."

Megan clumped down the stairway and Sheriff Gordon did the slightest take when he saw her. As she trotted the rest of the way down, Bryce was glad to see she'd aced the dark contact.

"This is Megan," Cathleen said. "She'll be eleven in October."

"Two grown-up women in the same house. That sounds dangerous." He winked at Meg and shook her hand. "Pleased to meet you, Miss Megan. Tom Gordon."

"Bryce isn't in trouble?" she asked and the sheriff smiled.

"Not even a little bit. He just had a rough day. You okay?"

"She didn't see him," Bryce said.

Tom Gordon nodded.

"How was school?"

"Good. Some of the boys are weird though."

"How's that?"

"They just are. I don't know. And some of them dress funny."

"Like on MTV?"

"No. Like 'Young Riders.' "

The idea that Meg thought Piñon Rim kids dressed like kids in a Western struck Cathleen and Trevor as pretty funny. They both laughed; the sheriff coughed into his fist. Bryce hadn't noticed anything more Old West on the playground than a few pairs of jeans that weren't stonewashed.

Sometimes Meg was bizarre.

"Well, I'll let you enjoy your afternoon." He handed a card to each. "The office is on Katie Avenue, right across the street from the Redrock Cafe if you want to drop by."

Bryce watched from the big window as Gordon tramped down the steps and squeezed himself into the copper-colored Chevy. Gordon waved as he cranked up the V-eight. Then he backed onto Redman and headed over the hill.

Meg was halfway up the stairs.

"Nut, who was dressed like a Young Rider?"

She took the last three steps in one hop and leaned over the rail.

"You know, that kid with the overalls and the funny shoes." She shook her head impatiently when he didn't remember.

77

"He was playing catch. You know, you nearly ran him over just before you saw me."

He shrugged. He'd been looking so hard for Meg he'd probably have missed Jabba the Hut.

9

SHERIFF Tom Gordon watched a falling star dust the northern sky. The view was ever so slightly impaired by the reflection of Daryl Strawberry checking his swing in the window of Ned Hartley's Gold Dust Tavern.

Ned's was the best bar in town—maybe in the whole Redrock area. Ned had a satellite dish the size of Montana mounted out back; he could pick up jai alai on Mars if the event were televised. But tonight Tom Gordon wasn't interested in sports.

"Refill?"

"Yeah, sure."

Ned's wife, Nancy, tended bar. She was just as bony and wrinkled as Ned, with hair the color and texture of cracked straw. She flipped up a tumbler, socked in a measure of Jack Daniel's, and laid it down so close to the last two water rings that you could measure the distance between them in microns.

The facade of the Lucky Slipper was a black cutout against the blue-purple sky. Harper's Peak jutted into the heavens.

Tom thought he'd seen a light up there on Harper's, near the entrance to the Wizard mine. The mine and the old cemetery beneath it were favorite hangouts for the local hooligans. The sheriff's department made routine sweeps of the area, mostly on Friday nights. The mine was fenced in and boarded up, but you couldn't keep kids out when they had the urge. He knew that from experience. Most people got misty-eyed about the back of some old Chevy or Buick when they talked "first time" experiences. Gordon had done the dirty deed right there on Harper's Peak with Sheila Carruthers on homecoming night.

But the mine was dangerous. Most kids here had sense enough to stay within a few yards of the entrance. But there were always the muleheaded few who had to push it and go deeper. Three had dropped out of sight. The Piñon Rim Historical Society saved the mine from a permanent wall. They saw some beauty in it, he supposed, but when it came right down to it, drained of its gold, the Wizard was just an ugly, unhealing wound in the side of the earth.

But that was *Sheriff* Tom Gordon talking. Red Ridge High all-around jock Tom Gordon had liked the view all right that night with Sheila. She'd gone on to graduate with the first co-ed class at Notre Dame. That was the last he'd heard.

He took a long, warming sip. A few cars lined up on Katie Avenue indicated that the Redrock Art Council was in full swing. Just enough Mercs and Beamers (and, of course, Aggie Hudson's Jag) to sour the Old West flavor of the town. But it would never go away completely. As much as the facades looked like cutouts, Piñon Rim was no candy movie set. Piñon Rim was the Old West, always would be, and it didn't matter how many shiny new cars prowled its streets. It had real ghosts. If you couldn't see them, you felt them.

Christ. What got him running down this track? A light up on Harper's Peak, a light that probably hadn't been there in the first place.

Nancy smiled, her eyes automatically checking the level in his glass.

Well, it had been a decent enough diversion. The closest thing to a run of pleasant thoughts since he'd pulled that broken little body from Sharpe's Creek.

But that body was why he wasn't drinking Jack Daniel's and watching the sky from his porch. Klu MacPherson would be coming up the boardwalk any minute. Klu had left for the Yavapai Reservation just after one o'clock, and, if there were a God in all that wild blue yonder, Klu would have some answers. Gordon needed answers right now.

The kid had been little more than a bag of splintered bones. Considering how far he'd come, you could expect that. But there were blisters on his torso; remnants of clothing they'd found upstream were charred.

A baseball bat cracked at Chavez Ravine and two octogenarians at the bar howled as a powder blue figure bolted for home plate across the window. The somber face of Deputy MacPherson appeared behind a late throw to the plate, and Gordon carried his drink to their booth.

Klu MacPherson was tall, dark, and powerfully built. The Scottish name was one of those unintentional jokes parents are somehow oblivious to; Klu's looks heavily favored his Navajo mother.

Nancy set an Evian with a twist on the table even before the booth finished creaking from their combined weight.

"His name is Michael Buckhorn. Turned ten in August. Parents both dead. Lived with his grandmother. She's sort of a holy woman."

"Ritual?"

"Human sacrifice isn't exactly part of the Navajo tradition."

"Ten-year-old boy could be a lot of trouble for an old woman. Any history of abuse?"

"None. I spoke to half a dozen families. The two were inseparable."

"Well, something separated them. When did she see him last?"

"She never did." MacPherson drained the glass in two long gulps. "The old woman's blind—a childhood illness."

Tom Gordon crunched back into the booth; he rubbed a calloused palm against his forehead.

The ever-efficient Nancy collected Klu's empty glass.

"Want something stronger?" she asked.

"Thanks, I believe I will. Same as Tom."

"Jack, rocks. You got it. Still working yours?"

"I'm fine, thanks."

Her butt swayed as she walked back behind the bar. At least her butt wasn't bony, Gordon thought. *Definitely* feeling the liquor. He'd nurse this last one.

"Some kids playing near Verde Creek were the last to see him. They were racing and they all stopped running where the reservation ends, but they say Michael Buckhorn just kept going."

"When was that?"

"Friday morning, before the rain."

"And somebody picked him up?"

"That's what I think."

"Could be anyone, from just about anywhere. Whole area's full of tourists and New Agers planting medicine wheels from here to Sedona."

Thousands of latter-day hippies were constantly scouring the area, looking for "vortexes" and arranging rocks into large circles they believed were "prayer focal points." They'd been at it since 1987, when the Mayan calendar ended. They were annoying at best.

Nancy set the Jack Daniel's in front of Klu; he sipped it slowly, letting the fire ease down his throat. Klu hadn't enjoyed going back to the reservation. Many of his friends were still there, but he rarely went back. When he did, it was nearly always for something bad. He hated even thinking about what he said next.

"Possible sex crime?"

Gordon shook his head.

"There's always that. No evidence so far. Hard to say what gets people off these days though. The lab's run some preliminaries on what's left of the clothes. They found traces of lighter fluid . . . just about the most common you can buy.

"Maybe"—Gordon clicked his glass against the polyure-thaned pine table—"just maybe, he set *himself* on fire. You know, an accident? He finds a cigarette lighter someone threw out and starts to play with it. The fluid gets on him. It lights and *boom!* His shirt's on fire. He dives for the creek, maybe hits his head on the way in."

"Possible."

"I'd like to think that's how it was. I'd like to think there isn't some pervert roaming free in a hundred square miles of good cover, waiting to pick off little kids in the height of tourist season."

"What if there is?"

Gordon stared at his drink.

"We have bits of clothing and we have a body. There's lighter fluid on the clothing, burns on the body, but no evidence of a perp. It could have been an accident."

"I don't think it happened that way," MacPherson said.

Sheriff Gordon leaned back; he could still see the window from his position in the booth. A group of people tramped up the steps to the Wizard's Palette. Class was apparently out and reconvening at Andre Tomasi's place for after-hours aperitifs—or whatever it was those artist types had or did. Gordon recognized Aggie Hudson right off. Even at this distance her shape was hard to miss. The Bowman girl was right there at her elbow. Now *that* was a dynamic duo.

"Alright, neither do I. So what do we have? Can we establish a point of entry? Verde Creek doesn't feed Sharpe's, does it?"

"Not aboveground, but it might below. It runs under the sandstone in places. There's a Navajo belief that only one river runs beneath the land. But I don't think he went in at Verde Creek. The other kids say that he crossed and disappeared into the forest, not that he was running alongside the creek."

"Okay, so what's the closest water starting from where he ran off?"

"We'll have to check our Geological Survey maps. John Anaweh's made some pretty good maps of his own. He'll drop them by tomorrow."

Tom Gordon grunted. Anaweh was a hawkish, acerbic man who wore his silvery hair in a shoulder-length ponytail. Tall and angular, he was not so much skinny as sun-dried, as though anything unnecessary had evaporated away. Klu and Anaweh had been friends since Klu was a kid. Gordon had never cared for the man.

"I'll check the survey maps when I get back," Klu continued.

"Let Phillips do it. File your report and knock off for the night. We'll get a fresh start—"

The shriek of skidding wheels cut him off. The two men were out of their booth before the crunch. And the crunch was a good one. The tavern shuddered from the impact. A patrol siren blasted the cool night air as they cleared the doorway.

Wendell Mackey had decided to pay Ned's tavern a visit. He was halfway up the pine stairway. The only problem was Wendell had never left his truck.

The sheriff department's Ranger skidded up behind him, cherries blazing. The siren mooed mournfully and died.

From across the street, the Redrock Art Council poured out to see the ruckus.

Tammy and Ron Coop had left the cash register unattended at their market to watch from the boardwalk. Bill Jordan's spectral face appeared at the window above Piñon Rim Drugs. The Pizza Wizard had already closed. Gordon thanked God for Piñon Rim's lack of night life: tourists usually left for Sedona or Prescott before the sun went down. The streets were nearly empty.

Wendell's Dodge Ram bucked at an ungodly angle, and so did the boardwalk. The bumper had taken out one of its main supports. The engine gunned.

"Please turn your engine off!" The bullhorn amplified the voice of Deputy Pat Phillips.

Klu reached in the cab of Wendell's truck and flicked off the ignition. The resulting silence was tomblike, suffocating, as if the background hum of nature had been switched off as well. Piñon Rim's ghosts had stopped to listen. The Ranger's blue-and-whites arced off stunned and expectant faces.

The silence was shattered by a throaty laugh that made the hair on the back of Tom Gordon's neck stand on end.

Whites showed all around Wendell Mackey's eyes as he sat straight up in the driver's seat. Blood trickled from his nose, slipped around his mouth, and dripped down to his sweat-stained undershirt.

"I got the smartest dog in the whole world!"

The lights flashed blue to white.

"The smartest dog—"

Deputy Phillips stood, feet spread, behind his open door with the window rolled down. One hand hovered over his unsnapped Beretta.

"Holy doughnut, Pat. Turn the light off," Gordon said. "And if you draw that gun I swear I'll make you eat it."

". . . in the whole world!"

Phillips killed the flashers. His bulging Adam's apple yo-yoed in his collar.

Andre's party had reconvened around the truck. Wendell turned, blubbering, to each face.

"B-Buddy can talk! My dog, Buddy, he can talk!"

Gordon looked to the skies for guidance. Klu tried the door on the passenger side, which had frozen shut on impact. He got it on the second pull. Phillips thrust his head into the cab. The smell of rancid booze was overwhelming.

"Okay, old man, let's sleep this off in the tank."

"Ease off, Pat," Gordon said. "Show's over, everybody! Show's over."

The window above Piñon Rim Drugs went black, and Bill Jordan's pale face hovered there for a moment, then disappeared. Gordon was gratified to see the Coops had returned to their market.

Those artists were another story altogether.

Aggie Hudson stood next to Klu. The Bowman girl hovered at the edge of the light, a look of ethereal detachment on her face as she watched. In spite of himself and the circumstances, Gordon felt a stirring down below. He felt suddenly guilty and stupid when he realized what his body was trying to tell him.

What was she now—thirteen, fourteen? He made a mental note to bust her boyfriend Matt Connors's butt good if he ever caught the two of them up on Harper's Peak.

"Aggie, do us a favor and take the party back across the street."

She nodded, but first she leaned into the cab. MacPherson had his hand over the old man's nose.

"Is it broken?" she asked.

"Feels okay. It's just a good bump. He'll be fine. Lean back and breathe in through your nose, Wendell."

"Wendell, what did you mean about the dog?"

"Aggie." Tom Gordon sounded tired, but threatening nevertheless. She gave him a "just a second" look, which he was obviously in no mood for, and leaned in farther.

Wendell's eyes rolled Aggie's way. Here was a sympathetic ear at last.

"Smartest dog in the world. He makes his own dinner. Hell, *he talks to me. He really does.*"

"I'm asking, Aggie."

She shook her head and pulled out. Tom was patient, but she'd pushed the envelope.

"Back to Andre's for brandy, everybody."

Connie Bowman watched the truck till Aggie was even with her. Her eyes flashed up to Gordon and that strange, not-of-this-earth look that seemed to be a permanent fixture on her face took on just a hint of a smile. Gordon acknowledged her with a professional (very professional, he hoped) nod. Nevertheless, he felt that warm embarrassment again. Then she turned on her heels and walked at Aggie's side back to the boardwalk; the others followed.

Mother hen and chicks.

Sheriff Gordon leaned into the cab and spoke very slowly.

"You're gonna have to pay for the damage, Wendell, you understand? You're never going to drink when you're taking your medication, are you? And you're never, *ever* gonna drive under the influence. Am I right?"

Wendell blinked and his whole body jerked. He looked around wide-eyed, like someone coming out of a very bad nightmare. It was finally beginning to sink in.

"You understand me, Wendell? This is serious. I don't want you to think it isn't. You could have taken somebody out just as easy as you snapped this post. You take your medication—you don't drive. You drink—you don't drive."

Wendell's jaw dropped open and he swallowed.

"Bu—"

"I don't want to hear it, Wendell. And if your dog talks, you definitely don't drive."

Wendell's mouth snapped shut. He nodded.

"He's on my way," Klu said. "I can drop him home."

"Okay." Gordon turned to Phillips, who stood cadet-straigh

at the Ranger's open door. "Get Jack Peters on the horn. He'll need the tow and crane. Tell him there's structural damage to the walkway outside Ned's. Probably need a whole crew to shore it up."

Klu MacPherson backed the other half of the department's "fleet" up to the cab, got out, and practically lifted Mackey into the car.

"I'll bring the report on Michael Buckhorn tomorrow."

Gordon nodded. "You okay with Wendell?"

Klu slid back into the driver's seat and buckled up.

"No problem," he said.

"All right. See you tomorrow."

They rolled away down Front Street, the copper Caprice flashing like a new penny as it passed through the streetlamp halos. Klu waved as he turned onto Katie Avenue.

For no reason at all, a shiver ran down Sheriff Gordon's spine. He would think of that moment often. It was the last time he saw Klu MacPherson alive.

"D I D J A ever see something that was dead, but it really fooled you?"

"What?" Bryce had heard Meg's question all right, but his head was a million miles away—or at least as far as Santa Fe. He closed *The Lost City*, his mom's first novel. It was a story about modern-day pirates and treasure. He'd read it five times. It was told in the first person and Carla, the protagonist, was so much like his mom it was as if she was right there talking to him. He hadn't picked it up in over a year. He'd called the little house in Santa Fe just after the sheriff left, but his mom's message tape was full. He couldn't even leave a message.

"Okay if I come in?"

"No. Get the heck out!" He tossed a pillow Meg's way. She snatched it out of the air, plumped it over the desk chair, and sat.

"How do you mean 'fooled'?"

"Like you think it's alive. I mean, it looks so alive that you think it's watching you, but then you touch it and it's dead. The Indian boy looked dead, didn't he?"

"Like a fish on ice." Bryce regretted the image right after he'd come up with it. It was too close to the truth. The dead kid's eyes had been filmy and silver, just like those of the big fish at the market. For a second Bryce saw himself stretching out over the water, reaching for the ball with absolutely no idea what was lying underneath.

"I saw a squirrel out in the woods that looked real. I mean it looked alive—it *was* real. But it was so gross. I was gonna feed it, and it just kind of fell apart."

"That's sick."

"And it had a ton of acorns around it, like it'd been collecting 'em for years."

"Is it still there?"

"Some of it may be. I saw it Saturday"—she glanced out toward the hall, then she whispered—"when I found the cave."

"*You found a cave!* Why didn't you wrap it and tell me for Christmas?"

"I was gonna tell you, but you looked occupied."

"Preoccupied."

"Yeah."

"I've been thinking about things."

Meg raised an eyebrow, then mouthed Aggie's name.

"I swear I'll smack you."

Meg giggled.

"I got scared, so I didn't go in. I thought somebody was there—whispering—but I remembered something about that from a book, and I looked it up."

"I was wondering where that came from."

"The squirrel scared me. I really thought it was alive and everything. And then I fell."

"Meg. Write me a memo. You gotta tell me when stuff happens, okay?"

"Okay."

"Where is it?"

"Not too far. Twelve minutes from Slimer."

Outside Bryce's window, the trees were already purpling from the sunset. He saw the big pool of red water behind the deadfall, a white ball turning lazily on its surface. A shiver raced through him. No way he was going into the forest tonight.

"Show me after school tomorrow, okay?"

"Okay." Meg threw his pillow back. She was so excited she practically flew into the hall. She stopped at the door.

"You know . . ." Something of cosmic importance seemed ripe to burst from her. She did a little dance to reign it in. Then she shook her head. "Nothing."

"What?"

She took a deep breath, and the words all tumbled out at once.

"When they said someone drowned, they didn't know who it was. They didn't know—and I couldn't find you. I don't know. I got really scared. I guess it's stupid. Good night."

She was out the door and down the hall before he could say a word. He shut off the light and sat, slack-jawed, blown away by information overload.

He lay back and stared up at the ceiling. She'd found her cave. Man, he'd hated that one in New York. But he couldn't let her go alone. She looked up to him. He hadn't known how much until just now.

He closed his eyes and he was plunging down that elevator at Howe Caverns, his lungs racing up his throat.

He opened them again. The rectangle of moonlight on his ceiling was blue—blue and far away, the way the sky looks from the bottom of a swimming pool.

That's what it's like. That's what it's like when you drown.

He fell into a fitful, restless sleep.

10

I T was a windy September morning and red dust devils rocked the station wagon as Tom Gordon drove the twisting three miles to town. They'd laughed when he bought the old wagon two years ago. It wasn't like he had a house full of brats to lug around.

A yawn nearly pitched him into the shoulder. He'd thrown down a cup of scalding black tar to get himself going, but his heart hadn't revved up yet. He never came close to sleeping last night; he kept seeing that awful package Sharpe's Creek had delivered. Murder just didn't happen here.

A roadrunner whizzed across the road, a lizard still struggling in its beak; Gordon dutifully slowed till it passed. He was just picking up speed again when a huge pair of wings blotted out his windshield. The *thump* sent a numb wave through him.

He slammed the brakes. A dust devil whirled the feathers away, but a token clot of down remained, dead center on his windshield.

An owl, he was sure of that.

What the heck was an owl doing flying around this time of day?

He pulled over with the somber intention of finishing off the poor devil if it looked too broken to mend. Feathers decorated the scrub alongside the road in tufts as thick as Christmas flocking. It was gone.

But where? It couldn't have flown off naked. And judging by the downy stuff floating around, naked it would have to be.

Gordon toweled off his windshield and let the wiper remove

the last traces. The owl must have flown off somehow, but most likely to die.

And that made him think about the Indian boy, though he didn't want to, so he started thinking about the station wagon again. When he was little, the family car had been a big old hulking station wagon; his folks said they'd bought it before he'd been conceived—just in case.

That got him thinking about Sheila Carruthers again. What would her kids be like?

H I T T I N G the owl set the tone for Gordon's day.

He noticed two things right off as he turned in behind the office: he'd beat Klu in for the second time in five years, and John Anaweh's Blazer was here.

He parked where Patrol 1 would normally be and cut the engine. As he reached for the empty cup in his coffee caddy, a cold wave of dread crawled over him.

Through the windows he saw Trish breaking out a roll of Styrofoam cups at the coffee urn. Just past her, Klu's empty chair was turned toward him. For just a heartbeat, he was sure he'd seen Klu sitting there.

Tom dropped the cup in the trash as he walked up the back steps. Pat's desk was empty too, but Pat was on graveyard today and Wednesday.

"Sheriff Anaweh's here," Trish announced.

"Has Klu called in?"

Trish shook her head.

"Call him at home. If you don't get an answer right away, call Wendell Mackey and ask him what time Klu left last night. Better yet, just buzz me when you get either one of 'em on the line."

He walked to his office without waiting for a response, absently rubbing his palms. He'd felt a strange tingling there, like the phantom itch of an amputated limb.

John Anaweh turned his unblinking eyes Gordon's way. Gordon didn't bother extending a hand—John didn't "do" handshakes. The maps were already laid out on his desk.

"Good morning."

"Morning."

"I've circled the most likely places Michael Buckhorn would have entered the water." He indicated three registration hash-marks in a triangle to one side.

"These marks correspond with the U.S. Geological Survey maps."

Gordon was about to say he'd go over the maps with Klu later, but the double beep from his phone cut him off. He picked it up without missing a beat.

"No luck from either line, Tom."

Gordon felt a stitch in his chest. Anaweh looked up.

"Okay, Trish, thanks. I'm heading up the hill to Mackey's place. Keep the lines open."

Anaweh was at the door before Gordon hung up the phone.

т о м Gordon's thoughts were tangled as he jounced along the twisting road.

Five years in the department and Klu MacPherson had never called in sick—let alone not called in at all.

Maybe Mackey had talked Klu into a shot or two. Gordon tried to force the image of Wendell and Klu passed out on the floor of Mackey's kitchen. It was a ridiculous image: a field mouse couldn't get drunk on the amount of booze Klu consumed in a year.

John Anaweh rode beside him, with his braided silver ponytail and his trademark bowie knife strapped to his chest. Anaweh, who would have looked more natural standing outside a tobacco shop than riding shotgun in a patrol car. Why had he allowed it? Anaweh's jurisdiction ended at Verde Creek.

He couldn't find it in himself to stop him—not when it concerned his friend Klu. But that wasn't the full picture: as "out there" as Gordon thought the guy was, he had a gut feeling that, whatever might take place next, Anaweh could be a good man to have around.

"You ever use that thing?" Gordon said, cocking his chin toward the knife.

"Sometimes."

"What about your gun?"

Anaweh looked straight ahead, his eyes focused somewhere beyond. Gordon had the eerie feeling he was looking through the forest and right into Mackey's home, though that was impossible from the road.

"Not yet."

He slowed as they approached the turn-in to Mackey's place. Gordon felt that tingling, crawling sensation in his skin.

"You smell that?" Anaweh's eyes squared with Gordon's and narrowed. It hit Gordon a second later—a warm, porkish smell, faint but noticeable. A boiling lump of acid popped somewhere at the base of Gordon's throat.

The whitewashed house appeared through the pines. The wind died down for a moment and now the smell was so strong that Gordon's eyes watered. And there was something else—a steady drone that seemed to come from nowhere and everywhere at the same time. Anaweh motioned for him to stop.

An ancient oak stood to the right of the path, its broad leaves a mass of brilliant reds and golds. The trunk was plastered with flies.

Jutting from the ferns at its base was a large man's shoe. *Department issue.*

Anaweh slipped out as they rolled to a stop. He made a circling motion with his hand. Seconds later, he had disappeared among the trees.

Gordon unhooked the two-way and nearly dropped it. His hand seemed to have lost all feeling. He gripped the receiver hard and clicked it twice.

"Sheriff?" Trish's voice was professional, but with an edge on it now.

"Trish, wake Pat up. Get him down here."

The radio clicked off. Anaweh intended to circle around to the back of the house. Gordon would give him some time.

The radio crackled back to life.

"He's on his way."

He replaced the mike and stepped out, the ground somehow unsteady beneath his feet, as though he'd just touched land after a long, rolling sea voyage. His eyes roved from the tree

93

trunk to the rear of the house and back again. He groped for his handkerchief, cupping it over his nose and mouth.

Flies rose in waves, raising the pitch and volume of the buzzing to nauseating heights as he approached the tree. Each wave challenged him briefly before returning to the tree.

To do what, exactly?

He drew his gun. His hand tingled, feeling oddly disconnected from him.

The yard was covered with tiny mounds and pits like some virulent geologic rash. Gordon crouched near the tree and scanned the windows of the house (each one an eye sighting a rifle, he'd been taught), then he nudged the shoe with his foot. Horseflies swarmed; one bit him below the collar. He crushed it. The shoe made a ripping sound as it tore loose. It was soaked through with blood.

Klu was dead.

Mackey should have spent the night in the tank, but Gordon had let him go. He'd let Klu drive him back here. But he couldn't have known. Mackey had never been violent.

Another horsefly nailed him, but he barely felt it. He released the safety and aimed the gun at the side window. Then he slid around the tree and brought the gun to bear on the porch window. Anaweh should be in place.

From here the yard was completely in view.

Graves. Hundreds of little graves. A patch of fur was visible from a nearby mound. *God, let them all be animals.* But he couldn't help seeing Michael Buckhorn, couldn't help thinking . . .

Gordon felt his breakfast rising in his throat. How long had Mackey been up to this? Even with a strong back it would take weeks to dig all these holes. He couldn't have done it by himself. But who helped him?

No movement from the house. No movement anywhere. Just the steady, molasses-thick drone of the flies.

"Wendell! This is Sheriff Tom Gordon! Come out on the porch now!"

Nothing.

The screen door slapped its frame as a dust devil spun into

the porch, and Gordon nearly pulled the trigger. Beads of cold sweat broke from his forehead. Panes rattled in their frames, the wind howled.

"Wendell. Come out the back door! I'm not going to tell you again!"

There was only the wind screaming in the branches. Even the droning of the flies had died.

Laughter pealed across the meadow. Another dust devil flung dirt and flies through the air like meteorites, and Gordon had to duck behind the tree to save his eyes until it passed.

He could see two windows: one on the porch and the other alongside the house. That left an area near the raised porch blind to anyone in the house. But there was a break in the paneling beneath the deck. Someone could be hiding there.

He tossed the handkerchief and the wind carried it away. Damn the stink, he needed both hands.

He dashed to the next tree. He could probably make the blind spot under the porch from here, but it would be a dangerously long run with no cover.

Anaweh should be on the other side of the house, ready to make his move. Still, the smart play would be to wait where they were until backup arrived.

Something shattered near the front of the house, and Gordon cursed under his breath. Time had run out.

Gordon bolted for the blind spot, painfully aware of how slow he was. The eyes of the house bore down upon his huge, lumbering form. He slid up to the paneling under the porch and swung, gun first, into the hole for a look.

Old lawn chairs and rusting gardening tools.

Okay.

He concentrated on getting one good long breath. His hat hadn't made the dash. A gust of wind rolled it between the graves, then dropped it into an empty one.

And the laughter began again.

He crawled to the stairway and hoisted himself up. The entire floor of the deck was covered with blood and globs of putrefying flesh. He trained his gun on the porch window. The stairs creaked as first one, then another, took his weight. He reached the top of the porch and slowly pulled the screen door open.

There was a quick movement at the porch window. Then the entire window blew out in a white flash. He managed to pump two slugs through it as he reeled off the steps. Someone inside the house shrieked, as Gordon slammed into the soft earth.

He spat out two blazing pellets of buckshot with a rash of blood. His left arm was numb. He fired again and the slug pounded something metal inside. He rolled out of the line of fire, and Klu stared back at him from the fresh red earth, his eyes and mouth filled with horseflies.

Gordon retched as he stumbled to his feet. He pushed himself up the stairs, hearing no sound now but the angry rush of blood in his ears.

He kicked the door in. Glass littered the kitchen floor; more glass and fresh blood had been splattered across the counter. One of his slugs had ripped a good-sized tear in the icebox. With any luck at all Mackey was carrying the other two with him.

The door to the next room was shattered; barely a frame still stood. He kept his gun aimed at its center as he walked. Suddenly, all he saw were gaping jaws and long teeth. His shot went high. He slammed backward through the kitchen; the gun flew from his hand as he crashed out onto the porch.

A huge dog had his left forearm in its jaws. He swung everything he had into the punch. The body of the dog flattened against the railing with a sickening crunch. It tumbled down the steps in pieces.

''You killed my dog!''

Wendell appeared in the doorway, a wide grin on his face. There was a ragged gap in the muscle of his left upper arm where Gordon's slug had bitten through. He cradled a shotgun. Gordon skidded backward on his heels as the barrel swung his way.

There was a loud, ringing pop, and Wendell's neck sprayed the doorway a brilliant crimson. Wendell rocked backward. A hand reached from the darkness, yanking the shotgun up. It discharged with a deafening blast, punching a skylight through the porch awning. Mackey toppled into the kitchen, dead.

Anaweh secured the shotgun and holstered his revolver.

"Nice firs' shot," Gordon said, barely able to spare the breath. The left side of his face felt the size of a basketball. The dog had been long dead. Mummified. Mackey must have thrown it, but for a moment he was sure he'd felt real strength in its jaws. But it had happened so fast.

"Lucky," Anaweh said. He looked past Gordon to Klu's body and his eyes lost all their light. He said nothing more.

11

M E G and Bryce walked the edge of the ravine just upstream of the cave. When Bryce saw the star-shaped hole in the hill, he quit snapping his bubble gum. His long whistle was much more dramatic than it needed to be.

"You sure that's a cave? Maybe it's a rat hole."

Meg frowned. She didn't like her cave slighted. Since Bryce found the Indian boy they'd paid him a lot of attention at school. He'd been acting a little cocky.

"It's a cave. I could get in there okay, but we'll have to dig it out for you."

Bryce balanced the army spade on his shoulder and snapped a gooey pink bubble.

"I got nothing else going. How do we get down there in one piece?"

"I tried there and it wasn't too good."

Bryce nearly sucked his gum down his throat when he saw where she was pointing.

"Whoa," he said.

Without the mist she could see it was at least a twenty-foot drop to the riverbed. It gave her a weird feeling, bordering on nausea.

"It was all foggy then. I couldn't see."

"Guess not."

The stream gurgled below. The light was still good. Bryce looked up and down the ridge. There were some decent-sized boulders against the cliff downstream, and a couple of fallen trees they could use as ladders.

"This is the log where I saw the squirrel."

Bryce kicked it and sent a million-dollar jackpot of acorns clattering down the hillside. The sound echoed back from downstream.

"That's pretty wild."

"It must have taken him forever."

"Couldn'ta been just one squirrel. You found the First Federal Acorn Bank here. That was a guard you saw." Bryce pointed his toe at a small ring of gray-white fur on the incline below the log. "That all that's left of him?"

"Most of him went over the side."

Bryce nodded.

"Heads up." He swung the spade and underhanded it toward the cave. It flipped once and stuck near the entrance.

There was a lot of fern and blackberry to pick through, and they made a wide detour around a leafy patch that looked suspiciously like poison oak. When they got to the boulders, things didn't look a whole lot better. It was a short enough jump from the bank to the closest one—but a long drop to the rocks if they missed.

Bryce went first. He slid when he hit the boulder, but caught himself with room to spare.

Meg bit down hard and jumped. She made it easily, but it was good having Bryce there to catch her just the same. The fallen trees offered enough support to climb down, but the dead branches were sappy and mostly just got in the way. Eventually, they made it to the creek bed.

They hopped rocks to the other side and raced along the bank to the cave. Bryce got there first, but Megan gave him a good run.

She screwed up her nose. There was something sour in the air.

"Smells like rotten eggs."

Bryce nodded and pointed his chin at the cave.

"Might be something dead in there."

Below the entrance, deep marks showed where the fresh soil had been gouged by padded feet. Large, muddy prints were visible on some of the nearby rocks.

They looked at each other.

"Coyote?" Bryce suggested.

"Maybe a wolf."

"Could be. Probably just a big dog, though. There's houses not too far from here."

Meg nodded. Whatever it was wouldn't stop her.

Red mud covered the rock that bore the letters *WZ*. Groaning, Bryce and Meg dragged it into the stream. In a few seconds the smooth surface was nearly clean, but the red soil remaining in the scratches spelled:

WiZrD.

"Someone was trying to spell *Wizard*. I thought it was someone's initials."

Bryce shook his head. "Half the town is named Wizard something. The Wizard's that old mine above the graveyard." He spit out his gum and rolled it into the pebbles beneath his foot. "You know what I bet this is? I bet this is a back entrance to the mine! There's probably gold in there!"

"I don't know. The mine's all the way over by school. Do you know where the school is from here?"

Bryce scanned up and down the riverbed. They were at the center of a giant S curve. After the bend it was all trees and rock both ways. The sun was no help; it had already past whatever horizon there was. He shook his head.

"I've got no idea. This probably runs into Sharpe's Creek. It might even *be* Sharpe's Creek for all I know."

Meg shrugged.

"It isn't the mine. It's a real cave. I *know* it is."

"It might be. It might be a real cave. Just 'cause it leads to a mine doesn't mean it isn't. This might be a gold mine! We could be rich. You could buy a cave."

"Your friend Aggie—she said the gold was gone."

"Maybe it is, maybe it isn't. Maybe whoever scratched up that rock knew more than everybody else." He snatched up the spade and unscrewed the catch. The blade swung up and he set it. He wedged it beneath the stone.

"I say we keep it to ourselves."

"What are you doing?"

100

"Getting rid of the evidence."

Muscles roped up beneath his T-shirt. The stone stood at attention, and then flopped over on its face with a splash that threw icy water on them both.

"Well, me bucko. Find the buried treasure, says I."

"A pirate's life for us." Meg grinned.

"You got it. That's the 'tude." Bryce pulled off his T-shirt and folded it neatly over a rock that was covered with muddy footprints anyway. Meg laughed, but Bryce didn't seem to care.

He tossed a heaping spadeful of red soil toward the stream. The hole was too small for both of them to work. Megan watched impatiently.

Things could be worse than having your own gold mine, but she wished it would open up to huge caverns like Howe or Carlsbad, not a framework of rotting wood braces. Not knowing was driving her crazy. Swinging spade or not, she was barely able to keep from running up to the entrance and digging it out with her bare hands. The blade hissed into the soft soil; the muscles of Bryce's back and arms twisted like pythons as he worked. She wished she could grow to be that strong.

With each cut of the blade the entrance widened. Little by little, the star grew into a rough oval. Soon the oval was an archway big enough for them both to crawl through, and Bryce began shoveling away the soil that hadn't made it to the stream. Much of it swirled away as quickly as it went in.

They covered the rest of the soil with stones.

Meg sprinted toward the cave, but Bryce caught her by her utility belt and pulled her back.

"Wait a sec . . . one more thing."

"What? Let's do it!"

"Gotta do it right. We still have a big hole everybody can see. Did you bring a knife?"

"Bryce, I wanna see!"

"Hold your hogs! You got one?"

"Yeah," Meg ripped open a pocket on the thigh of her jumpsuit. "How big?"

"Good size."

She changed her mind and ripped one on her hip. She flicked an eight-inch blade into place.

"Where'd you get that?"

"I sent away."

Bryce nodded, eyeing her warily. She had easily a dozen pockets in that jumpsuit. God knew what else she'd sent away for.

He harvested an armload of vines and they anchored them over the entrance with rocks. Megan pulled out two small flashlights and handed one to Bryce.

"Now?"

"Now!"

They dove for the hole and poked their heads in.

Disks of white from their flashlights stretched and widened along the stone surfaces. The floor tipped down and away beneath them. The walls were narrow but solid-looking, as was the ceiling. There were no wolves or coyotes or bears yet, but the cave curved away ten yards in and there was no telling what might be waiting beyond.

"Hey!" Bryce yelled to the far walls, and the echoes rang back, metallic and wet, vibrating like a Jew's Harp. "Hey! Anything inside?" He grinned back at Meg and they both hollered. "Any beasties?"

"Hey, Wolf! You in there?"

"Any yippie-yie coy-otes!"

They listened until the echoes died and the only sounds were their own breathing and the peaceful babble of the creek behind them.

Megan let out a war whoop as she slid down inside.

"Careful!"

Bryce slid down behind her.

There was room to stand up straight, but the walls—wet and clammy—were so close that Megan could touch both sides with her fingers stretched out. It was cold, but she wasn't going to let that stop her. Bryce held the knife out to her; she put the flashlight in her teeth and wrapped both hands around the knife handle. It felt warm in her hand, secure. But she didn't know what she'd do if a wolf came around that bend. She didn't think she could stick a knife in something. Then again, if a wolf really did come around that bend . . .

The floor angled down, and though they were moving down with it, Megan felt as if she were floating. She was exploring—really exploring now—not pretending at all. And Bryce was with her.

Their lights twitched on the back wall, stretched along it, and made the curve before they did. She wondered what those little ovals of light saw from there. Limestone castles? A pack of wolves? Her breath was getting shallower, louder. And she heard water dripping. Something splashed her nose and she jumped. She looked up and the light moved with her. The ceiling was covered with little droplets. Bryce nodded. He had his light in his mouth now too, and as he grinned at her, a line of drool spilled out the corner of his mouth. He laughed and nearly choked.

"Gross," she said, then nearly did the same thing.

They were only a few steps from the bend now. Bryce clamped down hard on the light and squeezed the spade in his hands. He tapped Meg on the shoulder and hissed, "Count of three."

She nodded.

Bryce lifted his chin and dropped it once, then twice—"Three!"

They ran to the bend, their weapons thrust before them.

Five yards ahead the cave ended in a pool of black water.

"Oh, man . . . ," Megan muttered.

Bryce tested the pool with the spade. As far as he could reach, the water was only a few inches deep.

"Well. It's still a pretty neat cave," he said. "I mean, you could use it for club meetings or something, like in that *Dead Poets* movie."

Meg folded her knife and dropped it back in its pocket. She took a deep breath. Club meetings were the last thing she wanted for her cave.

Bryce thought she might cry. Instead, she shook her head. "Damn."

He reached over and hugged her, then he pinched her ear.

"Oww!"

"Come on, Megwort—it's only your first one! I think it's pretty cool. How many people find caves anyway?"

"I dunno. Just, I dunno."

"Come on, it's getting dark out there anyway."

Meg trudged along at his side as they made their way back to the entrance.

"I guess it's okay," she said finally. "I mean, for my first one."

"It's better than okay—it's awesome. It's a totally awesome cave."

But as they climbed out, Bryce felt a swell of relief. He didn't like it in there. Didn't like it at all.

They dropped the vines back over the entrance.

"Why do you think someone wrote on the rock?" Meg asked.

"Prob'ly like I said about a club. I don't know. It looked like a little kid must have scratched it in there . . . somebody who couldn't spell." Bryce folded the spade back onto its handle and locked it. "Maybe some kids playing miners or something. Heads up." He took a short run and swung the spade into the air. It cracked against a tree above the ravine and dropped next to the squirrel log. Acorns cascaded down the bank.

They walked back in the purpling dusk. Meg looked back. The entrance was well hidden now. But how did all that water get in there? Did the creek really get that high? Could all that water have seeped through the walls? Maybe. It wasn't deep, at least not where Bryce had tested it.

Bryce had gotten ahead of her. When she realized how quickly he was walking, it suddenly occurred to her that he was scared. And that made her scared. It made her think about something that had been in the back of her mind ever since they'd crossed the meadow, something that had struck her the first day:

"You notice how there aren't any birds singing down here?" she asked.

He'd noticed. At first there had been a constant chatter in the trees above them. He couldn't remember when or where it had stopped—somewhere above the ridge. There were no fish in the wide, shadowy pools they passed either.

But there had been those pawprints.

"I dunno. It's late, maybe they're sleeping." Bryce shrugged. It was lame and it wasn't the point, but Meg didn't challenge it, and that was just as well.

He started to look back toward the cave but then didn't. Instead he hopped the stones and crossed the stream faster than he needed to, anxious to be back over the ridge again, back where, late or not, the birds were probably singing.

12

I T was a windy noontime in October, three weeks after Bryce had found the Indian boy. He walked the school grounds with his lunchbag, restless and bored. Cody was home with the flu, and without him British Bulldog just didn't happen.

The Indian boy had given Bryce some notoriety at Piñon Rim Elementary, which Bryce hadn't minded a bit. People still talked about it, but the story of Wendell Mackey, Piñon Rim's "Wolfman," had eclipsed everything else.

Apparently Mackey had trapped a load of animals in the woods, ate what he could, and buried the rest in his backyard for leftovers. No problem there until he went for bigger game. He killed a deputy and buried him back there, too. Chuck said that when they found the deputy, his liver and one leg had been eaten off, but Cody didn't believe him. Bill Jordan agreed with Cody, but he thought the whole thing was pretty sick anyway. Bryce wasn't sure what to think. If Bryce saw the sheriff again, he figured he'd ask him.

Although it wasn't exactly national headline material, it had made the *National Enquirer*. Chuck had brought one in to show the class and Coop's was sold out of them the next day. At last Piñon Rim was on the map.

Bryce munched his sandwich while he walked, holding it in the bag to keep the dust and sand out. He'd never seen the wind this bad. It was probably stupid to be out in it, but it was kind of cool too. Everybody was eating indoors. The cafeteria was packed and noisy, and as far as Bryce was concerned, the wind was easier to deal with.

He still hadn't gone over to Aggie's for his pants. Meg was cool on the bus now, so he biked to school. He could ride by any day. Any day at all. He just had to get up the nerve to do it. Just had to be the *right* time. It wasn't like he was scared of Aggie or anything.

Meg was back on her cave kick again. He wished she'd give it up, do normal stuff, and make some friends. He hung out with Cody and Chuck, and everybody knew who he was after the Indian boy. Meg hadn't been so lucky. The glasses had worked their ugly magic once again; the girls he'd see her with once in a while weren't exactly prime. And none of them was interested in the same stuff she was. *Nobody* was. Bryce thought about being inside that stupid cave with its slimy walls and that dead smell. Meg was going back there after school today, and he'd agreed to meet her by the squirrel log. But he really didn't want to.

A smoky cloud of red dust exploded right in front of him, and the sun became a perfect Halloween moon. Halloween was only a couple weeks away. Bryce wasn't sure what he'd be this year, maybe something from one of the 2s *(Terminator 2* or *Batman 2)*. Maybe the T-1000. He could always cop out and be Dick Tracy again—he still had the trenchcoat and hat. Meg hadn't said what she was planning.

Meg's birthday was coming up. She'd be eleven in a week. He didn't have a present yet.

His windbreaker snapped like a flag in a storm. The wind howled.

Suddenly it all stopped.

Bryce was at the edge of the playground, which was separated from the forest by Sharpe's Creek. He'd wound up at the spot where he'd seen the Indian boy.

The creek was a trickle now, and though the dam of dead branches was still there, not much water was behind it.

He finished off the sandwich and climbed down the bank. A burst of wind rippled the pool. Bryce shuddered. He pictured the white ball bobbing casually along the surface.

"That's right where he was."

Bryce's heart packed up his soul and went south.

It was Connie Bowman!

His heart quickly made up the beats it had lost.

She stood above him at the edge of the bank, her hands deep in the pockets of a threadbare denim jacket. Her eyes squared with his, and his heart stopped beating again. She looked over him to the pool.

The thin gold chain sparkled on her ankle. Her skirt rippled in the breeze like the surface of the water, and she didn't make a move to catch it. Bryce saw the tiniest half-moon scar high up on the inside of her right thigh. He looked quickly back at the pool. A warm flush burned his cheeks. His chest ached. He'd had the most amazingly vivid mental picture of her totally naked.

The flagpole rang a warning from the courtyard as a powerful gust snapped the chain against it.

"Okay if I come down?"

He nodded, unable to look her in the eye—not after the picture he'd just seen. A breeze carried the scent of sweet soap and sandalwood.

"Yeah, he was right next to those branches."

"And you almost touched him."

"Almost."

"Were you scared?"

Bryce swallowed hard. She was standing so close to him he could feel the warmth from her skin.

"Nah." He amended that: "Not really."

She nodded. They stood together watching the ever-changing surface of the pool. But Bryce wasn't seeing anything but Connie. *Don't blow it . . . don't blow it.* He'd almost given up on her. She'd never even said hi before.

"I don't think I'd be scared. But I don't know. Pretty wild." She shook her head. "You're name's Bryce, isn't it?"

She knew his name! *Brainiac—it's not like they don't call roll every day.* Still, it felt like a big deal.

"Yeah."

"I'm Connie."

"Good to meet you," he said.

"Yeah."

108

He almost reached out to shake her hand, but he wasn't sure that was the right thing to do. She kept her hands in her pockets, so he did too. The corner of her mouth lifted as if something had struck her funny, but not funny enough to bloom into a full smile.

"See you," she said, and walked back up the bank. She turned back at the top, and Bryce hoped she hadn't caught him looking. If she had she didn't show it. Instead, she said, "You're from New York."

"Yeah."

She nodded.

"You doing anything after school?"

He shook his head no, not quite sure if he should believe his ears.

"Wanna get a Coke, or something?"

"Yeah. Sure." Bryce was suddenly reduced to monosyllables, happy even to get those out.

"I've gotta pick up a couple things after Civics. We'll hook at the bike racks—you've got a bike, right?"

"Yeah."

"Okay. See you."

He tried not to stare. His head and neck were on fire; he hoped his face wasn't bright red, but it probably was. When she was gone he flattened against the bank and took a deep breath.

"Whoa," he said. "Whoa!"

T H E birds weren't singing. And it wasn't late, it was just after four. But Meg didn't care about the birds. More than anything, she was disappointed. Bryce would have been here by now if he meant to come at all. She wanted Bryce to see this.

She'd read up on it and she was sure the water in the cave wasn't an ending at all: it was a doorway—what the books called a *sump*. The books said that sumps could lead to miles of hidden chambers.

When Bryce had tested the water, he'd leaned out as far as he could without getting his feet wet. He couldn't reach the far wall—and that's where the doorway would be.

Meg was wearing her waterproof moonboots today, and she had an old car antenna which she could telescope out to about four feet. She should be able to wade out far enough to touch the back wall with the antenna. If the pool turned out to be shallow all the way back, then so be it—she'd give up on this cave. But she had a feeling, a strong feeling, she wouldn't have to.

Their camouflage job had been pretty good. She could see the entrance from the squirrel log, but she doubted she'd notice if she weren't looking for it.

She didn't have a lot of time, barely enough to get down there and check before it got dark. The shadows were already pretty long. She couldn't wait.

Then she heard them: boys. They hooted and cursed as they ran. The sound was barbaric and jarring after so much silence. Meg couldn't tell how many there were.

She picked her way quickly through the thick blackberry and ferns. The sooner she got down to the creek the better. She didn't want them finding her cave.

One of the boys passed within a few yards of her up the ridge.

He ran, huffing, between the trees, a tall, skinny wreck of a boy with white hair and whiter skin. His shirt, torn and muddy, flopped away from his shoulder as he ran. The others stampeded after him like bulls through the brush.

"You're dead, Peters!"

"Ooooo, mommy's boy!"

"You better run, you baby!"

He hadn't seen her. She crouched in the ferns and hoped the rest would go by as well.

"Bust his butt!"

The next one ran past, sweating and puffing. He was thick as a cow, with close-cropped black hair and brown skin. His voice was hoarse from shouting. She'd seen him before at school, but she didn't know his name.

"Gonna kill you, Peters!" he screamed with a murderous certainty that sent a shudder through Meg.

Two others broke into the clearing. She recognized the tall

one, Walker, because of his crazy eye. The little one was from her homeroom: Warren Blackfoot, but the other kids called him Wart. The cowlike boy who was about to commit murder on Peters had to be Wart's brother, the bully her classmates called Bigfoot.

"Hey!" Wart called. Her veins ran ice water.

Wart pulled up and Walker ran right over him. They flopped out of sight in the ferns. Walker jumped up and screamed at Wart, who was shrieking.

Bigfoot swung around a small pine and stopped himself. When he saw her, his eyes got huge.

"Hey, it's Bottleface. The Martian."

She started to run, but Walker caught her by the arm and spun her so hard that her shoulder nearly popped. Her glasses flipped up on her forehead.

"Let me go! I didn't do anything to you!"

Bigfoot said, "She doesn't look like a Martian without the Coke bottles."

"My brother's gonna kill you if you don't let go."

"Let her go," Bigfoot ordered.

Her captor lifted her up high, then dropped her. Meg barely kept her feet.

Bigfoot's face was in hers. He smelled like old sweat. Before she could make a break for it, he pinned her arm behind her back.

"I was just kidding," he said. "Nice boots . . . You like being a Martian?"

"Yeah, you like being a freak?" Walker said.

One of his eyes stared at her, the other stared off into the treetops. His lips were too short to cover his wide, crooked teeth. Wart stood to one side, whimpering about being kneed in the back during the collision with Walker.

Meg tried to say something, but the muscles in her jaw were all tied up. She was terrified and angry at the same time. She wished Bryce were here. Bryce could take care of these guys.

She pulled away from Bigfoot with all her might and only succeeded in hurting her arm and pushing herself backward

111

into his legs. When she did that, she noticed something hard there and felt nauseated, because she knew what *that* was.

"Oh yeah, do it again." Bigfoot laughed, and the laugh made her stomach turn once again. "Man, you gotta lotta pockets in this thing. Whatcha got in there? Huh? Whatcha got?"

Meg had a terrifying thought that he'd find one of her knives and use it on her, but his fingers were going nowhere near her pockets.

"Hey, man, what are you doing?" One of Walker's eyes rolled.

"Nothin!" he hissed. "So who's your brother, Martian?"

"He—" Her jaws locked tight.

"Who is it?" He wrapped his arms around her and squeezed so hard she could barely breathe. His breath on her neck was hot and foul. She was sure she would vomit. Tears welled and she could barely see.

"He's big . . . *bigger than you*—"

"No he isn't," Wart said, between his sobs. "He's that Bryce kid."

If Megan got out of this she would kill Wart. She knew that right now.

"That butthead?" For a moment Bigfoot eased up, actually thought about it. Then he tightened his grip. "Okay, that's great, that's even better."

The white-headed kid they'd been chasing poked his head sheepishly from behind a tree. Her capture was apparently grounds for a temporary truce.

"Peters! Let's see you prove you're not a girl," Bigfoot sneered.

"Man, they'll send you back to Fort Grant if you do that," Walker said.

"What you gonna do? Tell? She's not gonna tell." He had her pinned with one arm. He slid his free hand down, right past her biggest knife.

"You're not gonna tell," he hissed in her ear. Her stomach churned. "You're not gonna say nothing!"

She swung her leg up and tried to heelkick him, but he was

too quick. He squeezed her so hard she saw stars, and that thing of his seemed to grow even harder.

"Don't even think about doing that again," he hissed. "Come on, Peters, you wimp!"

Peters started haltingly down the ridge. Walker was doing an agitated figure eight in the ferns, as if first one foot, then the other had been nailed to the ground. He was about to say something, then changed his mind.

"My brother . . . brother's gonna kill you . . ." Her voice was a sob. She knew what they wanted to do, she'd read about it. Mostly she knew it was bad, very bad. And it would hurt.

"M-my broth—"

"Your brother's not here, Martian. But mine is, and he's hurt 'cause of you. Come here, Warren."

His brother obeyed.

"Go ahead and let her have it in the gut, come on."

Wart started to shake his head no and Bigfoot spat. The yellow wad landed on a fern near Wart's foot and slid down a branch like a dying slug. Something hot and bitter rose in Meg's throat.

"Come on, you little wuss, give her one in the gut."

Wart gave her a sort of pawing tap, and she jumped out of reflex.

Bigfoot slid his arms up, giving Wart a better shot at her stomach. He locked up her legs with his. There was nowhere to go.

"Hit her."

"I can't!"

"Hit her!"

"Okay!"

He let loose with a punch that made the little wind Meg still had sail out. She groaned and fought for a breath. The forest spun. Her whole body cramped up.

"Good job."

Bigfoot let go of her, meaning to shove her to Peters, but she bolted like a scared rabbit.

"Get her!" Bigfoot wailed.

She ripped open a pocket on her thigh. She had the handle

in her hand when Peters caught her shoulder. She spun and the blade locked in place. His other hand lashed out and for a frozen moment he held it there as if nothing had happened. Then his eyes were saucers. His palm opened and a red stream pumped over his forearm.

"She cut me! Oh God! She cut me!"

Bigfoot bellowed and dove for her, but she was out of reach and running hard. Peters screamed like a girl. The others pounded through the brush behind her. They'd kill her for sure if they caught her now. She'd cut him bad.

She thrust her hands high in the air and ran straight through a patch of poison oak; the rest of her was well protected. They followed her in—and they'd be sorry for it later. When she got to the boulders she jumped the chasm without a thought. The moonboots slowed her down, but they saved her feet as she scuffed her way between the boulders and down the dead trees. Behind her, one of them chickened out before the jump, and another one slammed into him. She heard a sound like two sides of beef colliding and a scream. Rocks slid into the creekbed.

"Oww! Oh, God!"

One of them was moaning. She hoped he was dying.

She kicked off the moonboots on the other side of the creek. The pebbles bit her feet, but her whole body had gone numb somehow. If pain had left, her other senses had risen to amazing heights. She saw every rock, every vine. The pine smelled stronger than incense, the babble of water was thunder. The boys splashed through the creek as she rounded the bend.

Screams and sobs echoed against the rocks. Meg pulled up one of the dead vines she and Bryce had left for camouflage and brushed it through the sand behind her as she ran to the cave. She leapt in, closed the vines, and flopped onto her stomach. She slid down till her feet touched the floor.

If they found her she was dead.

M O U T H S gaped as Bryce rode into town next to Connie Bowman.

Bill Jordan raised an eyebrow but greeted them cordially

114

He'd set out a Coke and Bryce's usual asphalt black coffee before they'd even sat down. He didn't seem to mind eighty-sixing the Coke when Connie asked for coffee too.

The rest of Piñon Rim Elementary was flying by on bikes or racing down the boardwalk to Pizza Wizard or Coop's. Every now and then someone would pause by the window to stare at them. Bryce didn't mind. He'd just won the lottery.

The little bells inside the door jangled as an older woman pushed her way inside, a small boy in tow. She saw Connie and looked as if she'd forgotten what she came in for.

"Hi, Mrs. Henley. Hi, Nathan."

"Hello, Connie," the woman said, a little too slowly.

" 'Nee," the little boy said.

Bill Jordan swung himself down the counter to the pharmacy, and Bryce tried not to look at his leg. Connie sipped her coffee and leaned against the counter, curls falling loosely around her face.

"I don't come in here too much. I usually end up at Pizza Wizard, but this is cool. I like the pictures."

Bryce nodded. Was she really sitting there next to him? It was like holding a snowflake, she could be gone any second. Connie looked straight ahead at Bill Jordan's Wall of Fame.

"My house is up there," Bryce said, pointing at a grouping outside the black tape.

"Which one?"

"The Easton place."

She nodded. "That one's got some radical ghosts."

"You believe in that stuff?"

Connie sipped her coffee without answering.

"You know, it's a lot better with cream and sugar." She plunked a fistful of sugar packets between them, scooped up two, and tore both at once. She offered him one. When he shook his head she dumped the contents of both in her cup, then added cream.

"You don't believe in ghosts?"

He shook his head.

"You picked a great place to live then."

"My dad came here to paint . . . We came with him."

"An artist . . ."

"Yeah. I guess people here don't like artists too much."

"Doesn't bother me. I paint a little, but mostly I make jewelry."

"Did you make that?"

She followed his eyes down to the gold chain on her ankle.

"No. That's from a friend."

She held out her wrist. A silver chain held half a dozen delicate star shapes encased in circles.

"I made these."

Bryce was genuinely impressed. Whatever they were supposed to be, they were pretty intense.

"They're talismans." She raised her eyebrows. "Magic."

"You're really good."

She sipped her coffee and looked back at the wall of pictures, and Bryce got the weird feeling he'd offended her somehow. If he had—and he had no idea how—it wore off quickly enough. She turned back. Her dark eyes had grown even darker somehow. She smiled.

"What did you feel like when you saw the boy in the water?"

That threw him. He was feeling too good to think about the Indian boy now. For weeks he had seen the kid whenever he closed his eyes. But now Connie wanted to know, so he didn't have a choice; if she asked how it felt to eat his own intestines he'd grab a fork.

"I dunno." He saw the ball bobbing in the water again, heard that high-pitched wail, saw the clay-covered hand reaching, almost touching his own hand. "I guess I was . . . surprised."

"That's all?"

He had no idea what she was looking for. He had a horrible, sinking feeling he was failing some major exam. He searched her eyes for an answer, but they were flat, unreadable.

"Grossed out?" he tried.

That clearly wasn't it. She sipped her coffee and straightened.

He grasped a thread.

"So, do *you* believe in ghosts?"

"Yeah. Might as well in Piñon Rim. More people underground here than above it."

"Have you seen one?"

Her eyes sparkled.

"Check out the picture over the blender."

The caption read: UPSTAIRS AT THE LUCKY SLIPPER.

The photo showed two dour male patrons seated in over-
stuffed chairs, tended by three of the Lucky Slipper's working
girls. The girls, probably scantily dressed for that time but
overdressed since Madonna, stood rigidly beside them. Only
one girl was smiling.

Bryce had seen the picture before. He'd sat here a dozen
times, but he couldn't believe he'd missed that cherubic face.

"It's you!"

He had an unsettling feeling of the world shifting. Beneath
that sensation was the most terrific feeling of longing he'd ever
known.

She laughed.

"Could be. You never know in Piñon Rim."

"Who is it really?"

Suddenly the whole building throbbed with a raucous rap
beat. A Jeep had skidded to a stop across two parking spaces
out front, music blaring from its oversized speakers. Matt's
sunglasses stared at them through the big window. Bryce
stared back. He was really beginning to hate that jerk.

"I dunno. What do you think?" She scooped her books from
the counter and smiled. "See you."

She slid off the stool and reached into her bag, but Bryce
shook his head.

"I got it."

"Thanks."

"Can I see you again . . . I mean, can we get coffee or
something?"

She turned around, her hand on the doorknob.

"Sure."

Her bike was quickly attached to the Jeep's rack and Matt
Connors whisked her away. Bryce ran to the window, nearly

taking Mrs. Henley and Nathan with him. He watched the Jeep disappear around the corner. Connie never looked back.

Mrs. Henley uttered something about the thoughtlessness of young men as she left. Bryce barely heard it and couldn't have cared less anyway.

Bill Jordan had already cleared Connie's cup and the empty sugar packets. It was like she'd never been there at all. Bryce hadn't felt so suddenly empty since he'd watched his mom drive away three winters ago.

The other Connie Bowman smiled from the picture over the coffeepot.

"Who is that—the smiling girl?"

Jordan didn't even glance over his shoulder.

"Yeah, she's a Bowman too. Rose."

Bryce thought of the lonely grave just outside Cross Hill Cemetery. The little fence stuffed with broken tumbleweeds.

As if he'd read Bryce's mind, Bill Jordan told him, "Some graves were dug because of that Little Miss, I'll tell you. And this one's following in her footsteps by the looks'a things."

"What did Rose do?"

"I'd waste a lot of breath answerin' that, and it won't change anything, will it?" He flashed that brilliant gold bridge.

"I wanna know. That graveyard is so screwed up. I thought they just missed hers when they put up the fence."

"They didn't miss nothin'. Fence was there way before Rose."

The chimes jangled and three small girls came flying in like Tasmanian devils. They screeched orders for vanilla Cokes from halfway across the shop. Jordan obliged.

"Why'd they bury her outside? Did she kill someone?"

The girls bounded up to the counter and Bryce moved down for them. They smiled at him and giggled.

Jordan wiped the vanilla dispenser and hung the towel over his shoulder.

"No. Rosie didn't kill no one. Not like you might with a knife or a gun, anyway. You know what a catalyst is?"

Bryce shook his head.

"That's something that makes things happen. It don't d

nothin' by itself, but just 'cause it's there, well, things that'd never happen by themselves suddenly do. That's what Rose was.''

"A cattle-list?"

"Town was booming. Percy Easton, he had it all in his good hands. The Wizard was pumping the purest ore you ever seen. Rose Bowman came"—he leaned in so the girls wouldn't hear—"and it all turned to crud.''

"Is that when all the little kids died?"

Jordan squinted, cocking his head.

"You know, all the little graves?"

"Well. Doctoring wasn't like it is now. Something like the diphtheria or the cholera'd hit, and the little ones didn't always make it. Can't blame every death on Rose, I guess.'' He tapped another photo on his wall. "This one you can say for a fact. This one's Rose all the way.''

The photo was cracked, practically crumbling off the wall. It showed a team of plumed horses drawing a black, glass-sided coach up Cross Hill. The paths were lined with mourners. The caption read: PERCY EASTON'S LAST RIDE.

"She killed the guy that lived in our house!"

"In a fashion.''

"Wow!" It made Connie even more mysterious and cool. He glanced up at the big clock over the bar, and for the first time since he'd seen Connie at Sharpe's Creek he thought about Meg.

It was past five! He was screwed.

"Oh, man! I gotta go."

Bryce slapped his money on the counter and whipped out the door to his bike. He didn't want to go back inside the cave, but he didn't want Meg going in there alone, either. Maybe she'd just gone home when he didn't show up. Right. Who was he kidding?

His stomach churned while he worked his lock. He had to straighten up and take a deep breath. Sweat broke over his eyes. *God, what now?* He yanked the lock and it didn't budge. He'd messed up the numbers. He ran through them again and got it, swung himself onto the seat, and nearly lost his balance.

Man, you are totally fogged. There was a pulsing in his temples, a deep, unfocused pain.

He pumped the pedals hard and blasted away. By the time he'd made the first hill on Sluice Road his heart was racing and his chest ached. He had to coast and take a long, deep breath. His stomach felt like it had been pumped up with cold foam.

He pushed himself on, rocketed over the hill. Half a mile ahead, a group of kids on bikes crested a hill. As the last one dropped out of sight behind it, the head and shoulders of someone walking his way came slowly into view. He descended the next dip and picked up speed for the coming hill. He was burning up. He coasted into the next trough. Thank God he was almost home. A bathroom was all he wanted now. Meg was going to have to stay out of trouble on her own. Sweat ran down his forehead and he squeezed his his eyes shut briefly.

When he opened them he saw an old Indian woman walking toward him.

He pedaled painfully up the hill. When he reached the top, the Indian woman was right in front of him. He swerved around her. His balance was failing, he nearly fell.

She screamed and the sound rang in his head in a wet, metallic way. *The way everything sounds in that cave.* His head spun from the effort of turning back.

"Go!" she screamed. "Stop her!"

Every hair on his body stood up. His feet slid off the pedals and found them again. There was nothing but white beneath her eyelids.

"There's no time! Stop her!"

"What?" *She didn't say that.* Bryce wasn't sure what he was hearing anymore.

"She's with him now!"

His insides scrambled. For a second there was nothing at all, as though his soul had shattered on the hardpan like an old bulb. He saw every crevice, every twist in the old woman's face as if it were inches from his; he saw those terrible snow-white eyes.

In a flash, he saw Megan standing in the darkness at the

water's edge. She was not alone. Someone—something—she couldn't see was there with her; it waited, watching her from the bottom of the pool.

Connie or not, how could he have let Meg go back there alone? He saw the dead Indian boy again. What if that wasn't an accident? The kid had been about Meg's age.

And then he was slamming down the pedals. His body was burning itself up, but that didn't matter.

M E G A N hugged the slanting floor and prayed the camouflage was enough. She could easily see between the dried and shrinking vines and she could hear everything.

Bigfoot and Wart had stormed right past, but they'd double back when they saw there wasn't anyplace for her to go around the bend—and they'd look more carefully when they did. Walker had limped up soon after Wart and Bigfoot, and now he sat not ten yards from the cave. He'd chosen the same mud-stained rock Bryce had used to hold his T-shirt before he'd shoveled out the entrance. She wished Bryce were here now.

Walker was moaning. Syrupy red blood pooled and dripped from wide strawberries on his forearms. His jeans were torn and filthy and his face was scraped from the fall he must have taken near the boulders downstream.

He'd been lucky: the fall could have killed him. Should have.

Her heart fluttered, her throat felt raw and dry. She could hear Bigfoot and Wart. What she couldn't tell was which direction they were going. Most likely it was back this way. She swallowed hard. She'd lost her biggest knife in the scramble down to the creek. For all she knew, they had it. Slowly, she peeled open a Velcro flap with her thumbnail, hoping the kid outside wouldn't hear the telltale rip over his own moans and the sound of the creek. She peeked at the boy as the handle filled her hand. He was standing now, his head canted like a dog listening for its master. The splashing and shouts were closer now—Bigfoot and Wart were coming back. She was trapped.

Her breaths were coming fast and shallow; her head felt light. She opened the blade and held it out toward the entrance as she backed deeper inside. Remembering that dull, knuckling sensation of the blade cutting to the bones of the boy's hand, she nearly dropped the knife. Whatever happened, she wasn't sure she could take that sensation again.

She heard shoes crunching in the gravel near the creek as she slowly felt her way to the back of the cave. Maybe they wouldn't come in. If they did, maybe they wouldn't go all the way around the curve. *Sure they would*. She slid her hand along the cold, wet stone. She was shaking.

"She's somewhere around. No way she got that far upstream. No way she climbed up the bank."

Bigfoot's words were spadefuls of dirt filling her grave. She closed her eyes and tears trickled out the corners. Her legs and arms were vibrating like hot, bare wires. She had a crazy urge to run straight out the front of the cave and give up. She'd done that once when she and Bryce had been playing hide-and-seek in the house on Baker Avenue in Schenectady. She'd gotten scared. She hated hiding, wasn't good at it, either. But this time it wouldn't be a matter of being tagged. They meant to kill her. There was a familiar unwelcome pressure in her bladder— now she had to pee too.

"I didn't see nothin'," Walker said.

"Yer half-blind. What difference does it make if *you* didn't see nothin'?"

"I can see, and I didn't see nothin'."

"Hey, Martian! We got your Martian boots! And we got your knife too! I wanna give 'em back! Quit hidin' and we'll give 'em back! We'll show ya how to use a knife, you mutant!"

"Let's get out of here. I don't feel good."

"You're a wuss!"

"I think my arm's broke."

"Go home, wussy!"

Water splashed. They were either throwing rocks in the creek or chasing one another through it.

"Martian! I've got your knife!"

Megan backed around the corner. She sank to her knees and

covered her face with her arms. The tears came freely now. She should have listened to her mom and never let Slimer out of sight. She would be back home with her mom right now, and Trevor. And why wasn't Bryce here?

"Martian!"

"Somethin's itchin' me."

"So scratch it."

"Oww! Oww! It hurts!"

"Crap! Poison oak! Oh, you are dead, Martian! You are freaking dead!"

Megan smiled in spite of herself.

Sunlight struck the back wall and she flattened against the other side, clutching the knife so tightly her knuckles popped. A single shadow slid across the wall and then the light went out. There were footsteps inside the cave.

They would really kill her now!

She started the Lord's Prayer in her head but couldn't remember the words. Bigfoot was stalking her, coming in for the kill. She closed her eyes and pictured him hulking toward her, big as a grizzly bear, a demented grin as wide and broken as a jack-o-lantern's, and her own knife craned over his head, ready to scythe down into her. She remembered "Give us this day our daily bread" and she started over again, but none of it made any sense. "Forgive us our trespasses . . . Kingdom come, thy will be done . . ."

The footsteps stopped and Megan quit breathing. The cold water lapped at her bare feet and she stifled a cry. Something struck the ground near the entrance of the cave. She heard it roll slowly down the stony incline toward the back wall. She opened her eyes and nearly jumped out of her skin when it came to a rest at her knees.

That scary little kid! This was *his* cave!

It all made sense then. She really did hear whispering that first day. It was the boy with the ball. He was the one who'd carved *WiZrd* in the rock.

At least it wasn't Bigfoot.

But how did he make it past them? Had they sent him in to get her? She edged her way around the bend. The little boy stood near the entrance, silhouetted by the filtered daylight. He'd give her away, if he hadn't already.

"Missy, kin I have my ball, please?"

"They'll hear you!" she hissed.

He looked over his shoulder, then back at her.

"My ball. Kin I have it, missy?"

She shushed him and quickly fetched it.

When she turned back he was standing at the wall looking toward the entrance.

"Don't run up on me like that," she whispered and held the knife up. "How did you get past those guys?" He was pale, almost to the point of glowing.

"Missy? Kin I have it?"

"Are you braindead? Can you maybe whisper?"

She underhanded the ball to him and he tossed it back. She was so frustrated she wanted to scream.

"I don't wanna play catch. I wanna get out of here!" She set the ball down.

Outside she heard footsteps again. Rocks struck wood, struck other rocks. Bigfoot was pitching stones at every piece of cover he could find, trying to flush her out. One cracked against a manzanita branch near the entrance and Megan jumped.

"How did you get in without them seeing you?"

The boy stared at the ball at her feet and she wanted to strangle him. He looked up. His eyes were blank.

"Swim some?"

She nodded.

He walked past her to the pool. The smell of mildew and old dust in his clothes almost made her sneeze. He stepped in without so much as untying a shoelace. Two steps from the wall, he sank up to his neck. His mouth smiled, though his eyes didn't.

"Yer welcome to come."

A rock whizzed through the vines outside and clattered across the limestone floor of the cave. Bigfoot would notice that all right. A second later, another stone skipped through.

She heard Bigfoot say, "What the—?" She didn't need another invitation.

She hadn't come dressed to swim—just to wade in to the top of her moonboots, which were probably hacked to pieces somewhere outside. The jumpsuit was going to be heavy once it got wet, but there wasn't a chance she was going to take it off with Bigfoot chasing her and the little creepy kid waiting on the other side of the sump. Besides, the kid had gone in with all his clothes on.

She removed her glasses and secured them in one of her Velcro pockets. It was too dark to see much anyway. She folded the knife and stuffed it away too.

She slid into the water feet first. It was cold, really cold. She could only see a whitish blur where the little kid's face was, then he disappeared beneath the surface. She slid herself farther in. The water soaked up to her waist and she started to get used to it. Near the back wall she felt the floor drop away. Behind her, Bigfoot was kicking away the blackberry and manzanita. This was it.

She took the biggest, deepest breath she could and sank.

The water folded a cold blanket of silence over her head. The jumpsuit dragged her down. It was deep—much deeper than she'd thought—but her feet touched solid rock. She pushed off and glided forward. The opening had better come soon; she didn't have all that much air left.

She thrust her arms and fingers out, but there was nothing in any direction. Some of her air bubbled out. She opened her eyes to total blackness. She had no idea which way to go. There had to be an air pocket somewhere above her: the boy had to breathe. She turned. She didn't know which way was forward or back anymore. She wasn't even sure which way was up.

Holding her hands to her sides, she let herself glide back to the bottom. Okay, that's *down*. She pushed off the bottom and shot straight up—until her palms hit rock. There was no air pocket above her. No air anywhere. She kicked her legs. Her lungs ached. She screamed out the last of her air in bubbles and something snatched her wrist, yanking her forward and up.

Her eyes opened to a blue light. The light filled them.

125

There was something out there. Something moving toward her. It was too bright; her eyes stung, but she couldn't close them. She couldn't even blink.

And then she didn't want to.

B R Y C E pumped across the yard and jumped off the Stingray. His head pounded as he jolted onto the deck. The bike struck the porch and flopped to the ground behind him. Cathleen met him at the door.

"Is Meg back?" Bryce panted.

"She went to meet you. *Where is she?*"

Cathleen yanked off the silly lace apron with one clean jerk and threw the screen door open wide. Her eyes were huge. Trevor tramped down the stairway behind her. Bryce jumped off the porch, barely finding his feet when he landed. He yelled over his shoulder. "The creek! She's down by the creek!"

No time for explanations. The Indian woman was screaming in his head, berating him as he ran. His legs felt rubbery and weak, but they carried him forward. He could hear his father's voice and Cathleen's in a quick exchange, and then the porch drummed with his father's footsteps.

Bryce wanted to throw up. His stomach did fishtails. He ran as hard as he could, but that was painfully slow. He felt poisoned. His father caught up at the edge of the forest. Trevor was a tall, athletic man; still, Bryce had never seen him move so fast. Trevor pointed ahead, indicating Bryce should keep going.

"What's the trouble?"

"I don't know! I don't know . . . We gotta find her."

His father nodded. He glanced over at Bryce and his expression flared from concern to alarm.

"You okay?"

"I dunno. Caught something."

"You gonna make it?"

"Yeah."

The wind was cold against his face, but Bryce was on fire. His clothes were drenched with the oily sweat that dripped from his forehead, stinging his eyes. He wasn't sure he could make it to the creek, and even if he did, he wasn't sure he could find the place in time. He wouldn't by himself. But with his father beside him he'd entered an invisible zone of protection, as though his own fading strength didn't seem to matter. Together they'd find Meg and she'd be okay—everything would.

It wasn't dark yet, but it would be soon. As they crossed the meadow before the high ridge, the rasp of their breathing and the crunch of their footfalls were the only sounds the forest had to offer.

Nothing's alive.

Bryce pushed that thought as far back as he could, slapping the trees for balance as he ran. He was flying; he could barely feel the ground beneath him.

Where had that Indian woman come from and how did she know Meg? Of course, she couldn't have. She was just a crazy old blind woman; she hadn't said Meg's name. She was throwing out a meaningless rap, just crazy talk. Bryce had seen a crazy lady once in Scotia, shuffling through the frozen, cardboard wasteland of an alley, saying the same weird stuff over and over again. He'd stopped when he thought she was talking to him. Then he'd realized she wasn't talking to anyone.

The Indian woman must have been like that. If Bryce hadn't felt so sick and so guilty, maybe he wouldn't have listened to her at all.

How did she get there?

Who would drive a crazy blind woman that far from town and just leave her? There weren't any houses on that stretch of Sluice Road. It wasn't like she'd just stepped out her front door and waved at him.

How and why? The only answer was the one he didn't want, the one that said, crazy or not, she meant to be right where she was, and her message was for *him.* But that was impossible.

"Luff."

His father's voice came as if through a wall of wet gauze. Bryce realized he was telling him to run to the left, and then he saw her too.

Through the ferns they could make out Meg's jumpsuit, a ball of gray rags. The low, wet ferns whipped Bryce's ankles

127

and slowed him down, making those last few yards an eternity. When they were close enough to see Meg's face, Bryce's heart sank. Her skin was white as a doll's, nearly translucent, and she didn't move when his father dropped to his knees beside her.

Her clothes were wet and her hair had kinked and fallen around her face in torrents of deep brown strands. In a scary way she was beautiful, Bryce thought, the way mannequins can be beautiful.

"Meg!" Trevor pinched her arm. "She's ice-cold."

He pulled off her jumpsuit and replaced it with his smock. He wrapped her in his sweater. Her eyes opened then, and Bryce let out the breath he hadn't even known he'd been holding. Meg pulled her arms from the wraps and folded them around Trevor's neck. Trevor squeezed her and it seemed ten years rolled off his face. He wheezed as he picked her up—and the years rolled back. It had been a long, uphill run.

"Tired" was all Meg said before her eyes closed again.

There was fire in Bryce's lungs. Meg and his dad doubled in front of him.

"Okay, hon, we're taking you home," Trevor said. "Where are your glasses and shoes?"

"Shoes'r gone," she said sleepily. "Glasses in my cave suit."

Bryce was about to collapse. All he could think of was how happy he was that Meg still had her glasses, because her spares were even uglier. Yeah. That was great. She had her glasses.

"All right." Trevor gave a quick look around, just in case her shoes might turn up. His eyes settled on the shadows past the ridge, where the peaceful gurgle of water provided the forest with its one and only sound.

"What was she doing down there?"

"There's a cave. It's got water in it. She wanted to explore it." His head ached. "I was supposed to meet her."

And it isn't the first time . . .

His father nodded and coughed. He coughed again, a deep lung-rattler that made him wince. Then he started walking back, Megan cradled in his arms.

Blinking open, Meg's eyes lolled lazily toward Bryce and locked there. For a moment, he had the eerie sensation that it was his mother, Sara, and not his ten-year-old stepsister, staring at him.

"Can't depend on you," she said dreamily, and drifted away again.

A sledgehammer couldn't have done worse damage. Bryce was staggered, his jaw dropped.

"She's asleep, she doesn't even see you." His father glanced back at him. "Can you get us home? I'm not sure where I'm going."

Bryce checked their direction. Not only were the trees doubling before his eyes, but tears were making the whole picture mist around the edges. *It was his fault.* Whatever had happened—*and so many things could have.* He pretended to wipe the sweat from his forehead, but his palms just happened to find the wet spots at the corner of his eyes while they were there. Just over the treetops he could see the tip of Slimer's bald head, now actually two wavering tips. It was the direction his father had started in, anyway.

"We're all right goin' this way."

"Good enough."

"Did you see him?" Megan said from her dreams.

"Who, hon?" Trevor fought back the cough that was creeping up his throat.

"The Wizard . . . Did you see the Wizard?"

M O R N I N G Sun was far from home. She fingered her prayer beads and listened to the Song of the Wind. Soon after Michael's sacrifice she had felt a strange, backward current beneath the Wind's true course. That current was very strong now.

She had not foreseen the coming of another.

She had sung the Songs of the Ancient Ones, the Anasazi, and listened to the Wind for an answer. The Wind told her of the girl. The Anasazi alone understood the Circle of the Harvest. They sang of only one channel through which the Spirit

129

of the Underworld could exist. This turn of the Great Wheel had produced a second.

The boy was long on his way. Still she heard the labors of his breathing, the wisp of tires over packed earth. If he failed, as Morning Sun had failed, the circle would remain unbroken. The Harvest, the sickness, would begin. She could not teach an outsider to understand as she had taught Michael to understand. If the Spirit claimed the girl, only the love she still held for this boy could save them. And even that love, in all its bittersweet innocence, had a dark, ruinous side.

Passion fueled the Spirit and turned the Great Wheel.

The forces of the Wind fought her as she walked. She had traveled a great distance, guided by the same magic that carried her colored sands to their unseen targets. Now she was an old woman far from familiar paths, sightless and alone.

The wind dropped sharply away. She swung her cane in a wide arc. The cane found nothing in any direction.

"Who's there?"

The marrow of her bones turned to ice. A cloud of poison was rising from the bowels of the earth. The earth was shifting, writhing, tearing loose layer upon impacted layer of decay. The wind swirled up around her. It moaned.

"You've had your Sacrifice! *Sleep in the earth!*"

The wind tugged her cane. She sliced through it.

A terrible power surged through. Fiery explosions of light. The ground swelled beneath her feet, the wind spun faster.

"Leave her in peace!"

The road dropped beneath her, the air grew thin. A warm breeze tugged her skirts. Her feet touched nothing and yet she did not fall. Her eyes were thrown open.

She floated over a great valley, over rivers of gold, pure as the sun, and fields of corn stretching to the sunrise. A desert painted green with life.

Far below, a brave rode bareback between the tall rows, his hands stretched to the sky, as he sang his good fortune. A city had been hewn from the mountains.

A beautiful young woman drew a wide circle in the red

130

earth. Morning Sun felt the sun that warmed the girl's face, tasted the sweet green essence of new growth around her.

A shadow slowly crossed the valley; its fingers stretched through the fields, pulsing with dark life. Lightning shattered the sky and rain began to fall. High above the valley floor the rain turned to snow.

The brave's song wavered, thinned, and then soared until it became a cry of war. He carried a lance. His horse's eyes became wild and milky blue, its stomach bloated; lather ran in soapy gray rivers between its ribs. The brave's skin hung from his bones in leathery nets of veins, and his long black hair had fallen from his scalp. All that remained were a few, whiplike strands of coarse silver. His bony fingers clutched the lance like talons and his jaw swung freely as he tramped the snow-covered fields, raking the dying stalks to either side.

Oily smoke fouled the air. Scores fled, screaming, from their burning homes.

The young girl was thrown to the frozen earth. Her face left bloodred circlets on the ice.

Morning Sun screamed, but all she could hear was the anguished cries from the doomed city and the shrieking of the girl.

A creature raised a stone high above the girl's head and turned toward Morning Sun. His was a face unfinished, blank but for white knobs of flesh where eyes no longer mattered, and a black cavern for its mouth. He gaped at her, a grim parody of a human smile. He brought the stone down and the screaming stopped.

The city vanished. All vanished. There was only desert.

A trickle near the stony red mountains became a river. Hogans appeared, crops sprang up around them. Women spun cloth and ground corn. Craftsmen busied themselves behind potter's wheels. Huge domes of kiln-dried earth were erected and quickly overfilled with corn. Silver and gold were fashioned into necklaces, woven into clothing. Men and women were naked as infants beneath their jewelry and yet barely a patch of smooth red skin could be seen.

The skies grew dark. Rain fell in gouts, turned to snow. Bracelets dropped from withered wrists like rotten fruit and lay in heaps, quickly joined by their owners. Fires bloomed between the bodies. A cloying, sweet scent billowed up with the smoke.

The river sank into the earth and red mud swept over the valley.

The process began again. Another city emerged and fell, and another. Again and again cities rose and prospered; again and again they were ravaged and laid waste.

She closed her eyes and still the deadly cycle continued before her:

> Though it ends it begins again.
> The Harvest is gathered.
> The Harvest will be scattered in the wind.

The world was black again. She welcomed her blindness like an old friend. The air was calm. She had returned.

But her age and foolishness had cost precious time. The union had taken place. The girl must be destroyed, and she could not leave it to the boy. The Spirit of the Wind had led her to him, and now it must take her into town. She had to warn them.

Someone, *something*, stood before her. She swept the space with her cane. She cried out as the cane was torn from her hands.

It whispered through the air. Her hands were too slow to rise. White-hot pain scorched her ear to ear. She fell back, her hands clawing empty air. The second blow shattered the thin bowl of her skull like fine china.

She tumbled bonelessly over the side of the road. An echoing slide of rock cascaded toward the creek. Her cane whickered out into the cool evening sky; cracked against a tree trunk, and disappeared among the ferns. Then there was only the babbling of the water.

F O U R miles away, a burst of wind threw open the door of a small earthen hut. Cold, invisible fingers sent wisps of colored sand snaking across the floor. The door slapped its frame twice and shut for good. By then, the large blue circle on the center of the floor was complete.

13

BRYCE was drained. Cody's flu had found him too. He'd spent the first hour stumbling between his bed and the toilet. Thankfully, the double-end geyser action had passed, but his thermostat was totally on the fritz. Five minutes ago he'd been freezing; now he was sweating bullets. More than anything, he felt weak.

The cures were nearly as bad as the illness: Tiger Balm fanned cold flame into his joints and chest, and a throat-welding-hot cup of ginger tea dared him from the nightstand. He closed his eyes and found that his lids had become hot pennies, so he opened them and stared at the blue cracks in the ceiling.

Cathleen and his dad were arguing in their bedroom, really going at it. The way they never had . . . the way Trevor and Sara *always* had. Bryce figured prominently in the conversation.

Can't say you didn't bring it on.

He'd blown it once right after Meg and Cathleen had moved in. He'd gone skating with his friends after school that day. No big deal. He did that a lot. Except that Meg was staying late to work on her project for the Saint Andrews Science Fair. It wasn't until the lights came on in the park that he remembered he was supposed to wait and walk her home. He'd totally blanked. By the time he'd run back to school Meg had already walked the mile and a half back home alone in the dark. Meg was okay, but Cathleen was not impressed. It was a lousy way to start.

Tonight, they'd found Cathleen pacing at the edge of the meadow as if the treeline were an impenetrable barrier. There was no "A mistake was made here, but let's go on" in the icy glare she gave him, and certainly no "Bryce, you look terrible—I didn't realize how sick you were!" in her voice. Tonight, he understood clearly that any ground he'd made up with her had been lost.

What did he expect? He screwed up. He screwed up royal.

The worst thing was he'd let Meg down. Why did she look up to him in the first place? It wasn't anything he'd done. She just did.

Their bedroom door slammed, cutting the debate to a dull, hypnotic murmur.

When he felt better maybe he'd run away. Bryce pictured himself walking resolutely to the Greyhound station, his suitcase stuffed with nothing more than a pair of jeans, a couple of shirts, and some underwear. He'd take enough money to get by for a few days. Then he'd jump off that bus and his mom would be waiting. He'd be the son of Sara Rojo instead of the son of Trevor Willems.

There was only one thing wrong with the whole scene, something that wasn't written in his mom's letters or scrawled on her book jackets, but was there just the same: he might not be welcome in her house, either.

He'd called right after he'd gone to bed. She wasn't home. She was never home.

The voices seeped through his floor like a deadly gas. His stomach did a slow barrel roll and he retched dryly at the pail beside his bed. Even his intestines wanted to take a hike. He had a teary, feverish sort of laugh at that, then he thought he heard the Indian woman again and that gave him the shakes.

His pillow was soaked with sweat, but he crushed it around his ears anyway. He closed his eyes, tried to think about Connie, and just before he drifted away, he saw Rose Bowman smiling through the haze of a hundred years past.

VOICES.

Bryce's eyes opened on blue moonlight.

The digital clock on his radio glowed a red 2:00. He didn't remember the dream, though he remembered having one. He

134

woke feeling as if something very cold and very ugly had passed nearby.

The voices were still coming through the walls. He couldn't believe they were still at it. Must be going for the gold medal. He closed his eyes and drifted.

Too high.

He opened his eyes. The voices were too high, not grown-up voices.

It was Meg's voice.

But then it wasn't.

Bryce stared at the blank spot on the wall just above the chest of drawers, right under his poster of Dave Meggett of the New York Giants. The headboard of Meg's bed would be just about there. That's where the voices were coming from, not downstairs. Meg and a little boy. Whispering.

He couldn't make out the words.

He imagined himself pulling the covers from his bed, walking to the door, turning the knob.

He saw himself doing these things, but he never left his bed. He couldn't.

The skin on the back of his neck puckered into gooseflesh.

He went on lying in his ice-cold sweat, staring at that blank spot on the wall, while Megan, who hadn't once brought anyone home from school, played with some kid in her room in the middle of the night. He kept staring, and they kept playing. There was a muffled *thump* and a long, lazy, grating sound, like a ball rolling over hardwood. Meg giggled.

Bryce closed his eyes and little by little the fear grew dull and misty. He slept.

T R E V O R Willems sat cross-legged on his workbench, the white beards at the ankles of his blue jeans muddy from the woods. His smock was still damp and his sweater now hung from an empty easel like a thick growth of brown moss. He sipped his coffee and contemplated the naked canvas in front of him. It was the same canvas, in the same stage of undress, he'd been contemplating each day and most nights since he'd been here. Why he figured tonight might be different from any other he didn't know.

Hope springs eternal.

Trevor had felt something in Piñon Rim that first time he'd flown in with Larry—an energy, something he couldn't place. But things had soured back home, and Arizona was fresh, new. Maybe that's all it was. He'd been looking for a fresh start and could have found one in Portland or Seattle or Outer Mongolia as easily as Piñon Rim. He'd just thrown the dart and Larry had guided it here. Nothing more than that. If there really had been a Renaissance going on in Piñon Rim, it had passed him by.

He absently squeezed out a couple inches of burnt sienna, doused it with turpentine and a couple taps of linseed oil, and swished his favorite Grumbacher filbert through the glop till it looked a little like sun tea. He daubed the canvas without any real purpose, wet a larger brush with pure turp, and pulled through the marks he'd just made.

The flat, wet planes that rose from the sanded gesso looked like the red-rock cliffs he'd seen that first day near Sedona.

Cathleen was in a raging fit. The worst of it was, before this, things had been looking up between her and Bryce. Now that was blown. Not that Trevor faulted Cathleen's concern for Meg. As independent as Meg seemed, without her glasses she really was blind. But it wasn't Bryce's job to parent Meg—it was theirs.

Still, that wasn't the heart of the matter. The real fight wasn't about Bryce leaving Meg on her own. That had just flipped up the lid and let the steam blow through. It was really about these blank canvases.

He'd blown a lot of money on the move. He'd turned down assignments for "artistic reasons." Christ, who did he think he was? He'd be just one more out-of-work, starving artist pretty soon. Cathleen knew it. They weren't kids. They had a family.

He stood back and sipped his coffee. He daubed on more color.

The cliffs had taken on a haunting sadness. They seemed to stretch a thousand miles in each direction. In the midground, half a world away, snow drifted through a slate-colored sky.

The floor of the valley below had become a desert. But it was more than that: there was just enough green to give you the feeling it wasn't quite dead yet. It was *becoming* a desert. He had captured the final dynamic moment of growth in a failing ecosystem.

This was something. And he wasn't even tired.

He'd totally lost track of time. How long had he been painting?

What the hell, he'd make more coffee and keep going. He started toward the Mr. Coffee on the far end of the workbench and stopped. The pot was nearly full. There was no clock in his studio by design. Who needed that kind of pressure? When he really got into a project—felt that dynamo wheel of creation in his hands—Mr. Coffee was his chronometer, the ebb and flow of jet fuel out of that pot the only measure of time that mattered. Getting a good wash on canvas was a six- to twelve-cup job. A pot more before the really meaty painting started. This couldn't still be the first pot?

He turned slowly toward the canvas, half-afraid it had regained its original chalk-white nakedness behind him. His breath whistled out through clenched teeth. The washes were a blueprint for a masterpiece. His eyes drifted up to the skylights for one more quick confirmation of the time. The sky was black, as it had been when he started.

But he'd been a beggar too long to get choosy about success. He stirred a spoonful of sugar into his cup and picked up his brush.

The canvas was too small. His idea was a big idea. It needed space. He looked to the neat racks of one-by-fours on the far wall. He had stacks of them and enough canvas to start a circus. Trading his brush for a hammer, he moved the easels and the instrument table out of the way. He stuck some nails between his lips.

He'd do right by Cathleen. Set it all straight. And he'd have a talk with Meg about wandering off on her own like that. He'd make it up to Bryce too. But not right now. Right now he had stretchers to build and canvas to size. Then he had paint to slather over the whole thing. Was there a better feeling than that? He pulled out some good straight wood and braced it. No. He guessed there wasn't a better feeling anywhere.

B R Y C E woke to the slam of the screen door.

With great effort, he pulled himself up to watch Meg run across the meadow. She ran all the way up Redman to the bus stop. She was early, but that didn't seem to matter.

At least she hadn't caught this thing—and there was no chance now of catching it from him. The sickroom was off limits for Meg. Although she *did* sneak in once, with an extra piece of her birthday cake. He slept through her party.

A litter of comics and sports magazines decorated the bed and floor. Cathleen had kept up with it for a while. The first couple days, no matter where they'd wound up during the day, they magically found their way to piles separated by size, if not content, by morning.

Bryce closed his eyes, and for a moment he actually slept, then woke as if no time had passed. That's how it had been for the better part of a week.

It was the weirdest sort of flu he'd ever had. He didn't feel sick anymore, just tired. Very tired. The nights were the worst. Nights took forever. His dreams weren't even like dreams: he'd drift, half-awake, from one dreary episode to the next, usually winding up more exhausted than he'd been to start with.

He hadn't told anyone about the voices. He knew he was dreaming it, and it was a little kid thing to be scared of dreams, like being afraid of the dark.

He was definitely falling behind in school, even though Meg brought his homework. He couldn't concentrate.

His desk was littered with half-done homework and envelopes. He owed letters to everyone he knew, Sara included, but he didn't feel like writing. He didn't feel like doing anything. Freaking flu.

He closed his eyes and drifted.

s o o h h Zweeeeet . . . Briiizoooaaaawaaake . . .

"This is so sweet. You have company. Bryce, are you awake?"

138

He was now.

Cathleen's head drifted in from the hallway and floated like a tethered balloon. The longer he slept, the weirder things seemed on the return trip. He'd caught the "company" part.

Connie stepped in past Cathleen's balloon head, a foil-covered plate in her hands, and suddenly the world came into diamond-sharp focus. He knew he looked like crud.

"She's baked cookies. Isn't that sweet?"

"Hi." Her eyes traveled across the wasteland of comics and magazines. She smiled.

"Guess this is the sickroom."

"Connie. Hi." She was wearing black bicycle shorts and a baggy T-shirt with the sleeves rolled back to show a lemon lining. Her long hair was pulled into a thick ponytail except for a few curls that had judiciously fallen to either side of her angel face. She had on white LA Gear shoes with two sets of strings, one white and one lemon to go with the shirt. Two matching metal loops sparkled from her right ear.

"Is there anything I can get either of you?"

"Not for me, thanks," said Connie.

Bryce shook his head. "I'm fine."

The balloon head disappeared, but not before Cathleen had winked at Bryce, a gesture so un-Cathleen he almost laughed. She obviously approved and he wasn't sure what to make of that.

"You look . . . really coordinated."

"You look really sick."

Connie pulled the chair from his desk, stacked the magazines neatly on top of his bureau—in front of the talking wall—and sat. Bryce felt like a total wimp for being too weak to move the chair himself.

"The room's not usually like this." That probably sounded even more lame to her than it did to him.

"Yeah, right." She rolled her eyes.

"No, really. I'm neat when I'm not sick."

"I'm sure. Try one of these. I'm not too good at baking. You're a guinea pig." She handed him the plate and a little box wrapped in black tissue paper decorated with blue stars and moons. "See if you can keep them off the floor."

"What is this?"

"Open it."

He balanced the plate atop a pile of magazines on his night stand.

It was like he'd died and gone to the good place—except that his throat and chest still ached. He just wished he could think of something cool to say. He had the weirdest feeling with Connie, like she were sculpted of ice and if he wasn't careful she'd just melt away. He couldn't believe she'd baked for him. And now this. He unwrapped the package. A silver dragon with a single twinkling green eye stared up at him.

"That's radical."

"Will you wear it?"

"Yeah!"

"Great!" She turned her fanny-pack around and pulled out a silver chain and handed it to him. He looped it through an eyelet on the dragon's back and snapped it around his neck. It felt cold and foreign there at first, but it warmed up right away. He held it to the light and moved it back and forth. The eye threw green fire.

"It's too cool. You made this?"

"Uh-huh. The tail was tough. The eye's a real emerald."

"Whoa, thanks."

He slid out a cookie and tried it. It was ginger, like the gallons of "tea" Cathleen had forced down him.

"It's good." He had to fight the choke reflex from his raw throat.

"I think I overcooked them a little. They're kind of hard."

"No, they're great. Thanks."

She sat back, obviously pleased.

"Bigfoot was suspended."

"Did he murder somebody?"

"Just some crows. He and Peters were feeding them Alka Seltzer by the cafeteria."

"What does that do?"

"Makes them explode inside. I guess they can't belch."

"No way."

"Yeah, they were flopping around and getting blood all over the courtyard. Pretty gross."

It was so sick he started laughing. Then he coughed so hard he saw stars.

"I'm sorry—" Connie began.

He waved her off and grabbed a tissue.

"No, it's okay. Listen, what about this Helldorado thing on Halloween? Cody says it's pretty cool."

"The one cool thing they do here. There's a costume dance at school, then everybody heads up to Front Street. They rope it off—no cars. They have booths for hot cider and cocoa, games and stuff. Everybody stays up all night." She shook her head and her ponytail bobbed. "I hope they do it this year."

He was stunned.

"Why wouldn't they?"

"Everybody's sick. You know they canceled football this week and they might drop the rest of the season."

He shook his head.

"No. I didn't know. Cody never said anything." And that was weird. He'd talked to Cody every day since he'd caught it.

"I'm home 'cause my dad called me in sick. He didn't want me to catch it."

Bryce looked at the clock for the first time since she'd come in. It was still early.

"He must be a cool dad."

"He just likes a slave around when he's drunk."

Bryce looked for some sign of humor in her expression. There wasn't any. Stunned twice in one conversation.

"Meg didn't tell me how bad it was."

"It's just a flu, but everybody's got it. It'll get me sooner or later. I might as well rest up."

For no reason, or maybe it was the cookie dust in his throat, he started coughing. Connie waved her arms to ward off the germs.

"Time to go."

He nodded through a cough.

"Thanks for all this," he managed to say.

She turned back at his doorway.

"It's got a spell on it, you know."

His face must have had "no clue" written all over it.

"The dragon . . . you're under my spell now." Her eyebrows climbed to giddy heights, and she was gone.

H E wondered, as he heard her say good-bye to Cathleen, if he really were under some sort of spell. Maybe—but the magic had started way before the dragon. He watched from his window as she cruised her bike onto Redman. Finally she disappeared over the hill. He remembered Matt at the drugstore: staring at him through those dark glasses like some huge, hungry locust. Was she going over to Matt's now? Probably. He wished she weren't. He deeply wished that.

He took another sip of Cathleen's ginger-lemon concoction and dialed Cody's number.

"Road-Kill Disposal. You truck 'em, we chuck 'em."

Well, Cody was sounding better.

"That's the stupidest one so far."

"Gimme a break—I'm sick."

He recognized the synth music from Space Harrier in the background.

"You won't believe who just left my bedroom."

"Wait . . . uh, two legs or four?"

"Connie Bowman."

"No!"

"Girl's hot for me."

"In your dreams. She musta' got lost looking for my place."

"Step aside, Matt Connors."

"Only steppin' Matt Connors's gonna do is all over your face. You're in deep do-do."

"Connors is history . . . excuse me . . ." His throat tickled. He sipped more tea. "Connie said they might can the rest of the football games."

"What?"

"It's like the whole school's sick. She said they might not even do Helldorado this year. Jason didn't say anything?"

"Nada. Coach prob'ly told him to tell me, and he forgot. Lil

142

twerp's been in another world. I think he's coming down with it. Not like I was gonna suit up for the games, but I'm feelin' pretty good. That's news though. Lil' bro's 'sposed to bring me my news.''

"Meg didn't tell me either.''

"Oh, these kids today! No respect. If he doesn't come home sick, I'll have to pound him. Hey, gotta go. I just hit level eight on Space Harrier!''

"Later.''

Bryce lay back and stared at all the little cracks and swirls in the ceiling, then his eyes went fuzzy. Maybe it wasn't a big deal. But if there were enough people sick to drop football games and maybe even a town institution like that Helldorado thing . . .

Were the teachers sick too? Or was it just the kids? He saw the Indian boy and all those little graves on Cross Hill.

Doctoring wasn't like it is now . . . the little ones didn't always make it.

He felt tired. Very tired. He closed his eyes and didn't wake up until it was time to watch Meg run to the bus stop again.

J O H N Anaweh stood at the top of the earth and stared into its wounded heart.

The cigarette lighter and the charred remnants of a weaved torch he'd found nearby, were Zip-locked and tucked safely in the pockets of his jacket. The waters below were loud and hungry, maybe hungrier now that young Michael Buckhorn's suicide had rendered the boy unworthy.

Anaweh kneaded his aching temples. He withdrew a small plastic bottle from his shoulder pouch and knelt at the edge of the cliff, his joints protesting the effort more than they should.

He wasn't so old as he felt right now, not nearly old enough to have seen the Harvest his own grandmother had sung of, and he couldn't find himself truly believing in it. But her words had left a mark inside that the years could not erase.

Klu had borne such a mark: he had been raised Catholic. He had quit his church by his sixteenth birthday; even so, Anaweh had seen his friend as a grown man wince at harsh references

143

to the names Jesus and Mary, had seen him touch his fingers to his forehead, heart, and shoulders. He'd even seen him genuflect before an altar at the wedding of David Antawnna, who had taken a Catholic bride. When John Anaweh later asked his friend what he had been doing, Klu had shrugged and smiled like a child caught in a mischievous act. He called it the "sign of the cross."

The Circle of the Harvest held no more purpose in Anaweh's adult life than the sign of the cross had in Klu's. If Anaweh truly believed his grandmother's songs, he would have to believe young Michael was the last taken of that Harvest.

Or the first taken of a new one.

Morning Sun, the blind woman, had taken these songs to heart and passed her belief on to the boy. Now she had disappeared. When John Anaweh found her—and he would find her if he had to cover the entire reservation on foot—she would be charged with the murder of Michael Buckhorn.

The icy breezes were gaining strength; a few hopeful snowflakes had settled on the ground. These would soon vanish, but before the month was over enough would fall to cover this plateau and the red lands beneath it. A harsh winter was coming. He felt it in his bones.

Anaweh blew warmth into his stiffening fingers. He chose a small pebble and a length of fringe he'd broken from his sleeve, and sealed them in a bottle with a note to Sheriff Gordon. Then he dropped the bottle through the clouds below. He closed his eyes. Silently, he touched his fingers to his forehead, his heart, and his shoulders.

14

T O M Gordon finished his business and washed his hands. They were saving Yavapai County's precious pennies by keeping the heaters off in the johns. His breath fogged the mirror. Maybe a little mist on the mirror wasn't such a bad thing, considering. He forced a smile; the flesh of his face gingerly obeyed. Funny what you took for granted.

He stared at the stippled pattern on his left cheek, the tattoo of ash-colored dots Trish had taken to calling his "Queequeg starter kit." A couple of the larger dots, where two of Wendell Mackey's buckshot pellets had smashed through to demolish a molar, were still scabbed over, a suture protruding from each like an insect antenna. Inside his cheek were two little bubbles of flesh he'd probably be chewing for the rest of his life. At least he was getting some feeling back, and some control. He didn't want to look like Droopy Dog the rest of his life. Not that there was so much to smile about.

He shouldered open the door and slid his coat off the hook near the entryway. A spanking new sign greeted him: HANG 'EM HIGH OR HANG 'EM LOW—BUT HANG 'EM HERE!

Pat Phillips looked up briefly from another poster he was lettering and smiled.

What would this one be? OUR AIM IS TO KEEP THIS WASHROOM CLEAN—YOUR AIM WILL HELP? No, this time it was something to do with the copy machine.

He'd known Pat Phillips since Pat was a snot-nosed third grader. Pat had always been one of those pale, too-good-to-their-momma boys. Somewhere along the line he'd found Jesus. Now he was finding art. Gordon shrugged and stepped into the cold dusk air, just past a bee-you-tee-ful, hand-lettered poster that read: THANKS FOR THE VISIT!

A ROSY cloud lined with gold hung over the Wizard mine. In the foothills, raw-pine skeletons of new homes were popping up like mushrooms. It occurred to Gordon that all those wooden cages presented more construction than ever in Piñon Rim. It also occurred to him the contractors had better move quickly to flesh out those bones. He'd worked some construction—enough to know raw wood didn't fare well in the snow. And snow would be coming. He could feel it, could smell it in the cold breezes.

And there was something else in the air, a sense of anticipation, of movement maybe. He couldn't put a finger on it. As high up as Piñon Rim was, it was really the floor of a basin, girdled all around by mountains of red rock. Protected. Isolated. Whenever his mind wandered lately, he found himself looking at the mountains, as if something was out there just beyond those bell-shaped behemoths. Something heading this way.

It was people. People moving in. *Staying*. It wasn't just the occasional snowbird who'd missed the turnoff for Sedona. *Arizona Highways* was partly responsible: the magazine had run two spreads featuring the Redrock area this year—one just on Piñon Rim.

Well, that was good . . . good for the town, he guessed. A pain in the butt for him, though. More people meant more mayhem. More New Agers. He'd broken up five more frigging prayer wheels in the acres of scrub between Front Street and Cross Hill this week. Those New Agers would flee their graffiti-ridden cities and drive hundreds of miles to rearrange the rocks and basically do the same crud they hated to the high desert. He'd love to catch them at it just once. He'd give them a frigging "harmonic convergence" they wouldn't forget. He made a mental note to check with Sedona and Oak Creek to see if it was getting worse there too. Maybe he could put Pat Phillips's budding art talents to work, have him draw up a special poster to distribute through the whole Redrock area—

one of those big red circles with the slash running through a crystal: NO FRIGGIN' NEW AGERS!

A line of well-dressed folks stood outside the Redrock Cafe. Two doors down, the old Piñon Rim Livery, its facade replaced by the biggest darn window he'd ever seen, was gussied up for an opening. Man, what was happening to this place?

They'd gotten that design through the building code (which stated clearly that all construction on the first three blocks of Katie Avenue and Front Street must retain the "Western character" of Piñon Rim) in a sort of novel way: they'd left the inside pretty much intact—complete with hayloft and stalls—which they used as a working studio/meeting hall and showcases, respectively. So now it was sort of a cross section of a livery stable (never mind all those objects-do-art springing up from the floors like odd trees in a mutated forest).

Artists.

He'd wound up outside Ned's. His wagon was parked back the other way, behind the station, but lately, more often than not, he wound up here after hours.

Three burly jerks he didn't recognize bulled their way through Ned's door and practically wound up on top of him. One stopped, stared stupidly at his strangely scarred face, then fixed a bleary red eye on his badge and grunted an apology. The other two plowed ahead, oblivious, and the curious one followed them—after taking one more not-too-sly glance. Tom shook his head. Such reactions were becoming common, but more often they came from children.

It was noisy inside. A ball game blared from the set, but Gordon could only hear the commentary through tiny cracks in the general melee. Ned's wife offered a harried smile. Two other waitresses raced between the tables, trays in hand; neither face was familiar. A barstool emptied and Tom hauled his butt onto it. The Jack Daniel's was maybe two beats later than usual; busy as a one-legged tap dancer, Nancy was still a pro. She winked at him between squirts of soda.

He took a deep, stinging gulp and watched two cars jockey for one space. They'd be pouring foundations for concrete parking structures soon. Boomtown, Piñon Rim. A practical consideration hit close to home. He'd already penned his manpower forecast for the new year. He hadn't upped the department's warm body count in five years. But without Klu . . .

Hell, just a heavy tourist season. It would all be over when the snow hit. He kicked back the rest of his drink. There was an angry exchange as the second car momentarily blocked the first, then drove off in a huff of gravel and dust.

Pat could handle the overflow—if the endless stream of posters didn't drive Gordon crazy. He waved off a second drink. He was restless, nervous, and the endless chatter around him wasn't helping matters. He collected his hat; a moment later he was back on the walkway.

There had been a message from John Anaweh, who was somewhere on the Yavapai Reservation following a lead in the Buckhorn case. Anaweh had asked him to look for a sealed plastic bottle near where the boy was found in Sharpe's Creek. Anaweh thought he'd found the boy's original point of entry—a river that sunk underground not far from the reservation. Gordon hadn't seen anything out there today, and the chances of finding one bottle were slim, but he'd check again tomorrow. Why not? He'd run out of ideas, and the Navajo weren't talking. They still hadn't reported Buckhorn missing.

A small crowd had gathered at the retooled livery. He headed back that way. If nothing else the walk would put him closer to his wagon and home.

His boots crunched the cinders and red earth as he stepped off the walkway. It was a healthy feeling somehow, earthy, like roots in good soil. It would be a shame to pave it. But they'd be voting on that soon. Cars were parked in every conceivable nook and cranny along Katie, and more nosed along the fringes like pilot fish picking out carrion. Why not tack on a Traffic Division to the manpower report? No problem. He was passing some nice cars, Mercs and Beamers. He smiled at the deep layer of red dust they'd already accumulated. Try getting that off your soft-tops.

The sun was done for and the moon was a shiny silver dollar in the sky. Gordon stood across the street from the livery and blew a plume of frosty white breath. Elegant couples wrapped in more waste-the-species fur than he'd ever seen passed him on either side. So this was an "opening."

The gallery's huge window revealed a regular ant farm of activity. Corks popped and champagne poured. Lights flashed. Thin, tuxedo-clad men with bizarre haircuts and busy hands rushed up and down the stairways, waving at framed monstrosities and chunks of twisted, moldy-looking metal on white pedestals. Well-kept women twisted and dipped and laughed. Where the hell was he—LA? New York? He glanced up the street at Cross Hill to get his bearings. Yeah, he was still in Piñon Rim. The white cross was painfully evident. Probably a lot of backflips going on up there right now. He shook his head. As he took one last glance at the ant farm before heading back to his car (and a reality he could understand), he saw Aggie Hudson in the eye of the storm. She'd never looked better—and that was saying a lot. She wore a deeply cut, dangerously tight black gown that was worth a closer look, but he held his ground.

Artists.

"Tom. View's a lot better across the street."

It was Larry Brill, looking so toasted and haggard that, for a moment, there was almost a blur in front of Gordon's face, as if his last picture of Larry had superimposed itself over this new one—and not quite matched. Brill was a well-meaning but slightly obnoxious man whom Gordon had nonetheless grown to like. He'd moved in no more than a year ago, but he'd already gained a sort of "local character" status.

"Come on in and swill down some of the good stuff. Lotta great broads bustin' out all over. There's even some decent art."

"Thanks. Just checking out the commotion."

"Yeah, quite a party! Just wish we'd designed a couple more toilets in there, if you catch my drift."

Gordon made a quick extrapolation. Brill had come from somewhere behind the buildings on this side of Katie, probably the sheriff's station. The picture of what had really caught Brill's drift wasn't a pretty one.

"Don't even think about drivin' tonight."

Brill stuck his wrists together, shook his head, and arched a gray eyebrow halfway up his balding head. Gordon thought of Nicholson on a bad night maybe ten years down the line. He amended that to fifteen.

"Enjoy your party, Larry."

"Intend to, Tom, intend to. Sure you don't wanna stroll over?"

"Yeah. Take it easy."

"Only way I do. Regards to Aggie?"

"Yeah."

"You got it."

Gordon felt a gentle sort of burn as Brill banked toward the gallery and Aggie Hudson. As awful as that little jerk looked, he'd always have an inside track on someone like Aggie that Gordon never would.

Brill turned on his heels and saluted, and as he did, a white shirttail popped through his unzipped fly. Gordon smiled, feeling slightly avenged for Brill's unauthorized use of county property. He watched Brill's jauntily sloshed progress into the gallery.

Connie Bowman appeared in the loft. Her white dress left her maybe a little underdressed against the black gowns, but from where Gordon stood she looked like a jewel on velvet. That one was born to break hearts.

Downstairs, Larry Brill's unzipped reentrance was stopping the show. A laugh burst from Gordon's throat like a cannonball, surprising even him. He laughed again. It felt good. He didn't stop until he was back at his car with a hot stitch in his side. He buckled up and adjusted the rearview, taking one last incredulous look at the opening. Then he headed for home, his eyes firmly on the horizon.

15

B R Y C E threw back the covers, a breath away from a scream, and listened. In his dream he'd been hiking the misty, fern-tangled bed of Sharpe's Creek with Connie Bowman.

Their laughter echoed through the stony canyon. They skipped stones and talked about crazy stuff. Her bracelets jingled as they walked, the circle of gold on her ankle flaring in the sunlight. He slipped his arm around her waist . . . and then they were in his room. It was nighttime. She was saying it was okay to be there and she was giggling, but he was sure his dad and Cathleen would hear. He said she'd have to whisper if she was going to stay, but she went on talking and giggling. Then he realized it wasn't her voice at all. It was the voice of a little boy.

Now Bryce was wide awake.

Blue light washed through the window. There must have been a billion stars and a moon the size of Hulk Hogan out there, but he didn't see any of that. His eyes were riveted to that blank spot just above his dresser.

His sheets were soaked, but he wasn't cold. The fever pounded hot blood through his temples. He stared at the wall and the wall moved away; the room stretched out, becoming a narrow corridor. His head thumped, his ears popped, and the room shrank. The distortion gave a sense of nauseatingly slow and rolling motion.

He heard a voice (Meg's?); her words were clipped and whispered. *She knew he heard her.* A heartbeat went by and another voice answered.

Bryce slid the sheet from between his teeth—only now realizing he'd been chewing it. This was ridiculous. He was going to get an answer once and for all. If he really heard voices, all it meant was Meg had some kid over to play. That wasn't scary—just weird. Most likely, he wasn't hearing voices at all. Houses made all sorts of noises all by themselves. Especially big old houses like this one.

Then he heard the ball again, that ball rolling across the floor, and goose bumps raced across his back and arms. That was worse than the whispering. The voices were atmospheric, almost not there at all; he could almost believe they were his imagination or the wind or a combination of normal things. But the ball hitting the floor and rolling—that was exactly what he thought it was.

Bryce swung his legs over the side, his stupid childhood fears of a monster under the bed rising to the fore. He closed his eyes and gritted his teeth. His feet felt swollen and numb against the rug. He barely felt the knob in his fingers, but it turned somehow and then he was standing in the hall.

Devils of light and shadow danced across the walls and ceiling. He allowed himself one quick glance over the balcony. The den below looked canyon-deep. The same wolf's head andirons that looked so cool during the day were casting evil, wavering shadows now as the embers flared up behind them.

He listened hard for the voices, but all he heard was the thump of his own heartbeat.

Meg's door was just past the top of the stairway. He imagined the door in the horror film *The Haunting*. Monstrously ornate, with hidden faces, it was a door that seemed to hiss and breathe, barely able to contain some powerful force on the other side.

Bryce heard her voice clearly this time, and every hair from the back of his hand to his scalp stood straight. He pushed the door open.

Meg said, "A boy. It's just a boy!"

A small boy in gray overalls sat on the floor. The ball rolled from the door back to the boy. He stared blankly up at Bryce with flat, gray eyes.

Meg sat at the side of her bed. Her body was long, way too long, and her nightshirt pulled tightly against . . . God, she couldn't be growing breasts! But her eyes—they weren't eyes at all—each one was a million needles of blue light.

"Just a boy" was all he heard Meg say. His own scream blotted out everything else.

Bryce sat bolt upright; the room, *his room*, was filled with morning light. A phantom echo of his scream rang in his ears. His heart thumped so hard and fast his chest ached. His covers were on the floor.

Downstairs, the screen door slammed. There were quick footsteps on the porch.

He pushed himself off the bed and stood at the window.

Megan bolted across the meadow to the road, her backpack flopping as she ran. She hit the road in full stride.

He watched her disappear over the hill on Redman.

The grass in the meadow was frozen and white, and Megan's shoes had left a trail of green triangles across the yard. He stared at that trail with so many thoughts crowding his head that the net result was a white blank. He lay back on his bed and stared at the ceiling. When he stopped shaking, he called Cody.

M A R I E T T E Henley's boy wasn't about to catch any flu. She'd rather see her angel held back a grade than be sick. She'd had enough of that Marjorie Banks from the elementary school and her phone calls. Nathan would be seen in class when the flu had seen fit to leave the classrooms—and not a minute before. She had lectured her little man vigorously about germs. Germs were *everywhere*. Tracked in by everyone. And, as pretty as his newest friend was, visitors were out.

To tell the truth, Mariette had found the brazen little girl who had taken to following her Nathan home downright eerie. She knew nothing about her. Mariette had never met her parents. For now at least, that girl was not allowed inside their home.

And home Nathan Henley stayed. Home and alone and safe.

At least, that had been Mariette's intention.

* * *

153

NATHAN Henley stood by the outflow pipe near the cafeteria, well out of sight of the classrooms. He wore bright red mittens, the kind with the string that runs from one jacket sleeve through the other, a red wool cap pulled down around his ears, and a blue Gore-Tex ski jacket. It was sixty degrees Fahrenheit and sunny, but his mother always stressed you didn't take chances with the weather, or with germs. They were lessons he could recite in his sleep, and he wasn't far from sleep now. As he waited for the girl with the pretty face, Nathan was running on the human equivalent of autopilot.

Slipping out of the house had been easy. Another lesson Mariette Henley had etched deep in young Nathan's subconscious was that the two hours after lunchtime were nap time—hers as well as his. At precisely 12:15 every day the lights went quietly out for Mariette, and somewhere between 2:15 and 2:30 the lights came quietly back on. Daytime sleep had never quite worked for Nathan. But he'd learned to be quiet during that time. Very quiet. If Mariette Henley hadn't allowed modern chemistry to set her own quiet time, she might have realized her angel was wide awake. Nathan knew there were pills that made mommy stop and pills that made mommy go.

An icy breeze wafted the smell of stale milk directly in Nathan's face, and the relays in his head popped and crackled to life. Suddenly, he was standing next to the cafeteria building by that gross pipe. Then, *pop!* He was gone. His mitten motored up to his face on snot-removal detail, tapped his lip where a gooey yellow trail was forming, and descended slowly back to his side, pulling a shiny, wet string with it.

Nathan had done his own experiments with modern chemistry. It seemed that warm fluids dissolved those pills . . . warm fluids like the Sweet Dreams tea she drank right after lunch. The lights wouldn't be coming on for Mariette Henley ever again, quietly or otherwise.

A bell rang somewhere in another world, loud enough to tickle the relays but not to trip them. Moments later, the girl with the pretty face appeared.

Mariette Henley hadn't liked the girl with the pretty face.

The girl smiled as she came toward him. Her skin was white

as snow, and she had the most beautiful eyes he had ever seen.

She wiped his nose with a tissue, then she kissed his forehead and he felt happy inside. The boy with the ball was with her today. She squeezed Nathan's hands and told him to go with the boy. Nathan didn't like the boy with the ball so much. He didn't want to go, but he would do anything for her. Anything at all.

"C O D Y went in?"

"Yes. Cody is feeling very strong today. My Jason is sick now."

The flu was making the rounds fast, but at least it wasn't lethal. Of course, he and Cody were both older. There was still no telling what it was going to do to little kids like Jason and Meg.

"And you? You are better?"

"A lot better, thanks, Mrs. Muledeer. I think I'm gonna go in too."

Bryce had no intention of "going in." But when he'd hung up, he dressed for school anyway.

Meg's door was open and he popped his head in. Same old room. Full of caving books and magazines. But what did he expect? A leather ball, a little boy with dead, gray eyes. Was he crazy?

He was still woozy. On the way downstairs he stole a glance at the fireplace and the stupid andirons with the wolf heads, and nearly lost his balance. They were just chunks of black iron, same as always.

Oh, God.

His dad was in the kitchen with Cathleen. They both looked up. His dad must have been at it all night. His face was haggard and drawn. But his eyes were happy. He must have hooked into one again.

"Feel great," Bryce said. "I'm going to school today." He'd said that way too fast.

"What?" they said in tandem.

He headed for the door, fast.

"I'm okay."

"You can't just—"

"He knows if he's up to it. He can always come back."

His dad was great. And it made Bryce feel like a total toad for lying. He didn't give them a chance to take it back. He jumped down the steps and nearly fell.

H I S strength wasn't back by a long shot, and he had no endurance at all. It took forever to top the hills. He had to stop and rest on each one.

He had names for most of them now: Big and Little Dipper, K2. The hill he was heading for now was Splash Mountain— there was usually water at the bottom of it. It was on top of Splash Mountain he'd seen the Indian woman. Crazy or not, he wished he'd see her now. If she couldn't tell him what his nightmares meant, at least she could tell him what *she* meant. She hadn't said "Megan" exactly, or "Stop Meg from going into the cave," but she'd said enough. She hadn't appeared there by accident. Maybe she knew how the Indian boy came to drown in the creek. The sheriff said it was probably an accident, but he also said Indian kids knew better than to play in the washes when the rain came. It didn't make sense.

He wished Cody hadn't gone in today. Cody might have a clue about her. But that's how it was.

He pulled to the shoulder on top of Splash Mountain to let a VW go by and his nose screwed up from a sudden, foul assault. Something rotten was in the blackberry thicket near the shoulder.

A good drop there, rocks and trees below, and a tortuous path down to Sharpe's Creek. Maybe a deer got hit by a car and went over the side. He checked the skies for the circling buzzards that he'd come to recognize as flying markers for such natural calamities here and found none.

And that was weird too. Before he got sick he usually saw quail and *always* saw other kinds of birds flying around. He hadn't seen any since he'd left the house. He remembered that dead quiet near Meg's cave. It was quiet everywhere now.

He was just being stupid. What did he think was going on—a wildlife conspiracy? Everyone was getting sick. Maybe animals were getting sick too. Could birds catch a flu? He corrected that earlier thought: *everyone* wasn't getting sick. As far as he knew, it was only kids. And maybe animals.

He thought of all those little graves on Cross Hill.

Sometimes a place has a memory.

Where had he heard that? Aggie had said it when she was over. And that gave him a destination, something he didn't have when he started out today. He couldn't just waltz into town since he was already late for school, technically AWOL. Jordan probably wouldn't mind, but the drugstore was near the sheriff's office. God knew what the truancy situation was here. He didn't know Aggie all that well, but he was pretty sure she'd give a rat's butt about him missing class. She'd said she didn't know all the details about the life and times of Piñon Rim, but she knew more than *he* did.

He coaxed his bike over the crest of the hill. The right time to visit was finally here.

A G G I E Hudson's home jutted from a hill on one of the original subdivisions of boomtown Piñon Rim. The streets here were paved, and though some of the original wood-slat homes remained, most were fairly new, stucco or brick. Bryce wasn't sure what to make of the resulting mix.

Aggie had stemmed the decay around her own house by knocking down those on either side. Hers recalled what Sheriff Gordon said about "stuccoed monsters." The main structure was a jumble of pink stucco slabs embedded with turquoise tile. Above the rough lumber deck, a window of dramatic proportions looked out over the valley. The lower half of another window stared through the first, a lidded eye raised partway to the heavens.

The eye followed Bryce as he pushed his way up the street. It reminded him of a book called *Kama Sutra,* which Jamie Wills had snuck into Saint Andrews once. The women in the book had eyes like that. The book had some pretty radical pictures, and remembering them made his cheeks and neck start to burn again.

157

Bryce glided off the road. A ribbon of white smoke curled from the chimney, lacing the air with mesquite.

He stopped at the gate and had a sudden urge to ride away. *She invited you over.* What was he scared of?

The Stingray waited patiently, ready for whatever course he wanted to take. Just leaning there was fine with the Stingray; a spin out of here would be great too.

Bryce took a deep breath and opened the gate. He'd come this far. The walkway was lined on one side with juniper bushes and upended railroad ties. The ties supported copper wind-chimes, each in the shape of a different farm animal. Bryce gave them all a tap as he passed. They made a barnyard full of odd, happy sounds.

From the deck he could see the entire valley in panorama, the reds and the greens of the mountains fire-bright against the slate sky. From here, the cross on Cross Hill was nearly perfect.

He pressed the doorbell. Deep, churchlike tones echoed inside the house. He leaned out over the deck; one of the Stingray's handlebars protruded beyond the gate.

Through thick circles of turquoise glass in the wall, he saw a pink-and-white form approaching. When Aggie opened the door dressed in a short, white robe spattered with fresh clay, his jaw nearly dropped to his waist.

"Bryce, come in!"

She kissed his forehead and the sirens went off. It was going to be a twelve-alarmer and there wasn't a thing he could do about it.

"I just made coffee. If you're brave enough to try a cup, you're welcome." He nodded, not trusting himself to say anything until he was completely sure he remembered how to speak. He followed her through the tiled entryway. Pedestals holding all manner of oddly shaped bronze and clay forms lined the sunken den. One piece near the fireplace caught his eye: it was a female form, unmistakably Aggie's, nude except for a necklace of silver-and-turquoise squash blossoms. He looked away, but then his eyes went back to Aggie and he wasn't sure he should be looking there, either. Every curve of her seemed to meet another curve more interesting than the first, and the robe did nothing to hide any of them.

"Sorry about the outfit." She smiled. "I think it's easier to work the clay if I don't feel all bound up."

She reached high into a cupboard and Bryce's heart nearly squeezed through his ribs. He supposed he'd dreamed about her enough to expect the sort of sensory overload he was feeling right now. But nothing could have prepared him for it. He was sure his face and neck were as red as everything else in her kitchen. How was he going to talk history with her? He surreptitiously yanked his shirttails down over his jeans, which were suddenly tight.

"By the way, I did manage to get the easel up, but it's a monster. I could use some help moving it."

"Sure." His first word. He'd managed it.

She fished out a cup, filled it with steaming coffee, and handed it to him.

"Cream or anything?"

"Black is great."

"Come on back, I'll show you." She unplugged the pot and carried it with her.

Walking was tough. Keeping his head straight was tougher. He was trying to think about Piñon Rim as she led him down the hall, but man, she had great legs.

It was a good-sized studio, but not as big as his dad's. And it wasn't as well lit. In fact, it was kind of dark and shadowy. She had some spotlights trained on a stage big enough for human models. There were a few paintings and several large lumps of clay in various stages of development, all wrapped in plastic and towels. The forms beneath those towels were unmistakably female.

He must have been staring, because that same half-smile she'd had just before he fell crossed her face.

"Maybe if we could move the easel a little closer to the workbench. I pretty much set it up right where I dragged it in."

She leaned in to pull the easel with him, and it was a fight to look away.

"Did you ditch school to see me? I'm honored."

He tripped but caught himself. Now he knew he was bright red.

"Uhh—"

"I'm just kidding. Is this a special day or something?"

He could lie to Cathleen; he could even lie to his dad. Why couldn't he lie to her?

"No. I did ditch."

"Oh." She looked surprised but shook her head. "Don't worry. I'd be the last to snitch. But is that such a great idea?"

"I dunno. Actually, I wanted to talk to you. I mean, you know a lot about this place, the history and stuff."

She stood behind the easel, looked toward the stage, and walked the easel a few inches to the right. She poured herself a cup of coffee, then leaned back against the workbench.

"What I know probably isn't worth ditching for, but fire away. How's your coffee?"

He took a sip and nodded. "It's great." So was the view. He had to remind himself what he came for.

"Help yourself."

She set the pot next to a box of sand with an electric cord. Bryce noticed a lot of tiny wax sculptures scattered nearby.

"What's that?"

"A soldering tray. It's for making jewelry."

"You do that too?"

"Not like Connie. She's good. She uses that thing more than I do."

That took him aback. Connie's name was the last thing he'd expected to hear.

"She comes over here a lot? You're friends?"

"Uh-huh."

He held up a small wax dragon with a broken tail, then slipped the medallion out of his shirt to show Aggie.

"She likes you. She spent a lot of time on that."

It made his head spin. He almost didn't catch the sadness in her voice. Almost.

"I don't think Mr. Jordan likes Connie. He said people died because of Rose Bowman and Connie's just like her."

160

Aggie sipped her coffee. "Ah . . . you're interested in *that* history."

"No. I mean, I wanna know all of it. But what's the deal?"

"First off. Bill Jordan just doesn't want you to get hurt. It's not that he doesn't like her. It's hard not to like Connie. But sometimes she has a way of . . . letting people down. It's not her fault."

Bryce almost felt the wind from that one flying over his head. You either liked someone or you didn't, and if you let someone down, it was your fault.

"I don't get it."

"You want to know about history. Well, it isn't on another planet. It's here and we're part of it—it's always going on. *We're history.*" Aggie smiled. "See, you didn't really ditch today. You're taking Philosophy and History at Hudson Elementary."

Bryce shook his head.

"People really think she's bad because of what Rose Bowman did?"

She nodded. "The Bowmans haven't fared too well."

"But that was a hundred years ago."

"What you really mean is *it's history,* ancient history at that."

"Yeah." He was catching on, although it didn't completely make sense to him. "And history doesn't go away."

"Uh-huh."

"Why don't they move?"

"That's the million-dollar question. My two-cent answer is: I don't know. Except that it isn't easy to leave a situation you're used to—even if it's bad. It's destiny, I guess. Some people are destined to play the goat. And I doubt a man like her father would be any more welcome somewhere else."

"Is he an alcoholic?"

"That sounds almost glamorous. At best, he's a drunk. At worst . . ." She shook her head. "I don't even know the worst, and if I did, I wouldn't say. You're going to go away thinking I've trashed Connie, and I don't mean to do that. She's a special kid. She has a heck of a lot to deal with."

"So what's the deal with Rose Bowman? Did she kill the guy that ran the town?"

"In a sense she did. You'd have to go down to the Historical Society for the whole story. I can give you the short form."

He nodded.

"The way I understand it, once they hit gold the town broke up into two camps: a really Puritanical one, like the fundamentalist Christians today, and another—just as fanatical—hedonistic one, lushes basically. Percy Easton was one of the town elders, the unappointed mayor. He pretty much kept the two sides from tearing each other, and the town, apart.

"Rose worked at the Lucky Slipper. She was one of the 'soiled doves,' and a very hot dove at that. The Slipper was owned by a despicable man named Ben Cole. He was in love with Rose, like half the male population of Piñon Rim. Unfortunately, Easton fell for her too—"

"But he had a family."

Aggie laughed.

"I don't mean this in a bad way at all, but sometimes I forget you're in grade school."

Bryce turned red.

"Take my word for it—it happens. The story is: it finally came to a duel."

"So Cole shot Easton?"

"That's the story. After that scandal, the Puritanical side pretty much took over, which isn't to say things got better. In fact, I think you could make a good case for saying their taking over was what really destroyed Piñon Rim. That is, of course, my own hedonistic point of view."

"And everyone blamed Rose Bowman."

"The 'liberal' side blamed her for Easton's death, as well as the religious backlash it sparked, and the self-righteous made her a symbol for everything bad about the town. Sort of a no-win any way you look at it."

"And then the Wizard ran out of gold."

"About the same time."

"Was there a plague or a flu or anything like that? Something that might hit little kids harder than grown-ups?"

"That's a strange one. What makes you ask?"

"Everybody's been sick at school, and there's a lot of little graves on Cross Hill."

"Well . . ."

He half-expected her to say "Doctoring wasn't like it is now"; instead, she shook her head.

"Flus come and go. They can be serious though. I don't recall any stories about a lot of kids dying from one here. You might be able to find something about it over at the Historical Society. Medical records or something. They're in the same building as the library, just off Katie on Woolcrest."

That wouldn't be hard to find. It was a little closer than he wanted to get to the sheriff's office, but it would be his next stop.

Bryce wasn't sure how to put his next question. He didn't even know what he was asking.

"Was there anything more than that?"

"In what way?"

"I dunno. Anything spooky . . . Indian legends?"

"You're really into this stuff."

"I'm . . . doing a report on it."

"For school."

He nodded. Now he'd lied to Aggie. The lies were getting easier. The fact he was a little proud of it was probably a sign of some deep-rooted sickness. He wasn't even sure why he was doing it.

"Well, it was a ghost town, so there're the usual ghost stories. I tend to put it all on a par with Elvis sightings, and I'm usually a sucker for that stuff."

"What about the Wizard? Did you ever hear anyone say they'd seen one?"

She laughed. "That's just the name they gave the mine. Finding gold in a copper mine was like magic to them.

"Tourists swear they've seen Rose Bowman or Percival Easton, or heard things near the mine. But there is no Wizard."

T H E Piñon Rim Historical Society took up two rooms in what was once a decent-sized house and was now a pitifully small library. The old woman at the front desk had bitten his "report for school" story, although he probably could have been Satan for all she cared as long as he paid the fifty-cent "donation." So at least he felt okay being here.

The walls were hung with pictures of Boomtown, Piñon Rim as a bustling, if small, metropolis. In the tiny historical reading room, there were a few paper-cover "histories" and some photo books. Some of the original newspapers were preserved under glass.

Bryce sat at a small desk and flipped through one of the photo books. He'd come for clues—to find the real history of the place—but it was Rose Bowman he kept looking for. God, women were amazing. His thoughts kept drifting back to Aggie in that robe. Leaving hadn't been easy. *This is important: pay attention.*

He found a couple shots of Rose with Ben Cole. Cole had a thin moustache and practically no lips. His eyes were small. To Bryce, he was basically an ugly guy, but he'd probably been a real Rhett Butler to Boomtown, Piñon Rim. He stopped at a full-page reproduction of the "Upstairs at the Lucky Slipper" shot. It might have been taken from the original tintype or shot directly from Bill Jordan's photo some time and many cracks ago. It was quite a bit clearer than Jordan's.

Still the same old Rose smiling away in the middle of everything. What had gone on a century ago in those upstairs rooms?

He imagined the whole scene in motion: the man on the left twisting his walrus moustache with one hand, discreetly stroking the thigh of the girl on his left with the other, while he tried to look nonchalant; behind Rose, the two ladies trying to be rigid for the camera; the men on the right, obviously tipsy at this point, trying to look dignified and probably wondering (too late) how dignified they'd feel once their likenesses were forever frozen, part and parcel of the infamous "Upstairs of the Lucky Slipper" shot.

Only Rose looked comfortable. She wasn't trying to do or be anything. She simply smiled at Bryce; and old and faded as the photo was, the promise in that smile was clear. Sitting here a hundred years after the smoke had cleared from that flash, Bryce could feel the fire engines rev in his cheeks. His eyes traveled down her form. Whalebone-and-satin underthings, so clumsy on the others, only accented the smooth lines of her body. Her arms and calves were bare, and at her ankle . . .

"Whoa!"

He glanced up at the old woman at the front door. Yes, she was staring at him.

He looked back at the photo. It might have been a scratch on the original, but it wasn't: the line was too perfect and there was a shadow beneath it. Rose Bowman wore an ankle bracelet like Connie's! He could even make out a little bubble shape on the chain where the little heart would be. It gave him a chill. He would almost bet Rose's bloomers hid a small, crescent-shaped scar on her inner thigh.

Maybe it shouldn't have surprised him. Connie probably saw pictures like this every day of her life. If she really did identify with her infamous great-aunt, it would be no problem for her to make a bracelet like Rose's. Except she didn't make that one. She'd said it was a gift from a friend.

He flipped through for a better picture of Rose's legs and couldn't find one. But another thought came to him while he searched: the bracelet had come from Aggie. But given the town's obvious dislike of her infamous great-aunt, why would Aggie want Connie to look any more like Rose than she already did?

M A R G E Wilkinson kneaded her forehead, leaving a shiny skin of soap there.

She hadn't liked the idea of Brad playing football. Teenage bodies weren't equipped for the abuse. (She'd seen enough injuries in pro ball to doubt any bodies were equipped for it.) But Dan and Brad had put up a united front. They'd begged like puppies for her to let Brad play for Red Ridge. She'd relented on the condition that father and son work together to pack some muscle on her boy first.

But these weights were abominable. They showed up in the worst possible places and they were impossible to remove. But this one was the worst. Brad had propped a barbell on end and leaned it near the top of the garage stairs. The flat disk on top said 30 and there was a similar one on the other end of the bar as well. The bar itself probably added ten more pounds. Lord, how had he even managed to set it there? There was no way she could move it.

Best not even to touch it.

She'd give them hell for it tonight. From now on, all weights would be corralled in the garage or all bets were off.

She pulled a clean dish towel from the linen closet and made a mental note to avoid the whole stairway area until the menace was removed.

Her kitchen was so dark sometimes. It was actually brighter in the hallway. Their next house would have a kitchen facing east, so at least her mornings would be bright. She adjusted the angle in her blinds for the most possible light and clicked the lights on.

How could Mariette Henley stand having her drapes shut all day? Marge shook some Bon Ami in a skillet and set aside the crusty mess to soak. The Henley household was directly across the narrow street from hers. Mariette was a strange bird—a little too God-fearing for Marge's taste. And didn't she just smother that little boy of hers? Lately Marge had been amazed to see Nathan actually coming and going on his own. That was a major breakthrough. Maybe Mariette was loosening up a bit. With that flu going around, it was a miracle she let him out at all.

Marge rinsed the rest of the plates and silverware, then bracketed them in the dishwasher. She snapped on the dial and the washer hissed into action. The Henley household faced her with its strangely closed eyes.

She wondered if Mariette had caught the flu herself. That would explain the curtains: with a fever burning sometimes light could just split your head in two. If that was the case, Marge had been a terrible neighbor. Mariette could have been wasting away sick in there for days.

Just then the Henleys' front door popped opened and little Nathan emerged, earflaps down, jacket zipped, and mittens dangling. She'd seen him go in not thirty minutes before while she was loading the dryer. Probably running errands for his sick mom. The window was cold as she rapped between the louvers to get his attention.

He unlatched the front gate and started toward town. Marge rapped harder.

"He's in his own world," she muttered.

She unhooked the blinds and swung them away. She pushed the window up and called his name, but Nathan continued on.

Even the simplest things could be a trial sometimes.

Marge toweled her hands dry and untied her apron. It was time to be a neighbor.

16

TREVOR's brush skimmed the huge canvas, hardly seeming to touch it. He whistled along to Buffalo Springfield's *Mister Soul*, not aware that he was whistling, barely aware of anything. He'd hooked into one again and he was lost in it. He no longer saw a painting: he saw cornfields and deserts, sheer red cliffs and green plateaus. The skies were blue and clear, and yet there was a darkness coming, gray clouds on the horizon.

"Trevor!"

He had no idea how long Cathleen had been at the door, only that she was really banging away at it now and her voice had an edge to it.

"Trevor, open up!"

His first impulse was to hide, a kid with one hand in the cookie jar. What he was doing felt so good it had to bad. He might have smiled at the notion except that he was annoyed, really annoyed. And his temples were throbbing.

"Trevor! Turn off the music and open up!"

He snapped off the music. His first steps toward the door were angry. He took a deep breath and cooled down somewhat before he twisted the knob. He opened the door a crack. Cathleen stood in the hallway, a hammer and screwdriver in one hand.

"Storm windows," she said.

"What?"

"It's time to put the storm windows up."

He wanted to choke her.

"It's been great outside." Of course, that wasn't the point.

168

You couldn't put them up in a blizzard. But for Pete's sake, the leaves had only just turned.

She looked around him. He stepped into the hall, shutting the door before she could see. Normally, he liked her to watch his work progress, but this one was special. He really wanted this one to be a surprise.

If she was upset with his cover-up, she didn't show it. She was too involved in her little project.

"It's getting cold. If it snows here anything like it rains, we're going to be in trouble. Come on, some fresh air will do you good."

CATHLEEN, ever the pushy agent, strolled into Bryce's room to check Trevor's progress.

"Do I *have* to do this now?" he mouthed through the window.

Trevor balanced the load and wiped the sweat off his fore-head with his Yankees cap. He was freezing in the shadows, burning up in the sun. Hauling these antique monsters up the ladder was hard work. Next spring he'd buy modern aluminum ones. With all the improvements they'd made, he'd never given storm windows a thought. He had found these beasts piled up behind the studio, in what remained of the attic. Good thing too, the last thing he wanted to do today was drive all the way to Babbitt's Lumber in Oak Creek.

She raised the window and leaned out to kiss him.

"Oooo, you're salty."

"You taste like cinnamon."

"I brought you a present."

She popped a Coors and traded it for his coffee mug. He guzzled half the can in one long gulp.

"That's the ticket."

"And yes—you have to."

He'd done thirteen windows. He'd asked her on each one. Just to annoy her.

"If it snows anything like it rains . . . ," she threatened darkly.

"All right. Thank you. Very nice. We'll go with the lady's

intuition." One thing he'd learned in two marriages: if you bet against a woman's intuition, right or wrong, you paid for the impertinence.

"For somebody famous, you're a real putz sometimes."

"Check with the pastor. I think you can go to Hell for saying *putz.*"

"Too late to save me." She kissed him again. "I've already slept with a married man."

She shut the window and mouthed another kiss. Trevor shook his head. He was glad the kids weren't around to hear that last bit. He had, in fact, slept with Cathleen before the divorce. It was way after Sara had bailed out (emotionally, at least); the marriage was long gone by then. Still, it didn't exactly fit the image that model parents were supposed to build.

He hoisted the monstrosity in place and locked the catches. His shoulders were killing him.

Bryce down, just Meg's room to go; then a shower, maybe a rubdown from Cathleen, and back to work.

If you could call it work.

Painting had never been so easy. *Nothing* had ever been so easy. He planned less than most artists he knew, but finding that groove between thought and action and having the dream appear in oil without sweating the mechanics of it was rare, to say the least. And he'd definitely found the groove now. He'd plugged into a total alpha state. Maybe Larry was right and all that New Age bull wasn't just hype. It might be that some places really did channel energy. He chugged the rest of the beer on his way down the ladder, almost missing the last step.

He was already buzzed. He couldn't wait to get back into the studio.

He walked the ladder over to Meg's window. Two squirrels chased each other over the power lines and skittered across the roof. He'd always liked watching them play. I should have brought some peanuts out, he thought.

Back to the task at hand . . .

As a kid, he'd always hated storm windows. They'd made him feel trapped, and these clunkers were every bit as heavy and clumsy as the old ones he remembered, designed way before families thought about little things like fire-escape routes. He hauled the last clumsy beast up the ladder. He shouldn't have chugged that beer. His legs felt like washed-out shock absorbers.

He reached Meg's window—no Cathleen. That was a surprise. Then he heard the screen door slap.

"Ready for another beer?"

"I'm fine, thanks."

He didn't want to get too looped to paint. He was really sweating now. And one catch on Meg's window wasn't cooperating. Rusted tight. It had to happen—couldn't do a job without at least one hitch. He put one foot on the roof for leverage.

Something went *thump* behind the peak of the roof. Another *thump* quickly followed, then another. He gingerly shifted more weight to the roof and raised his head over the gable. There was a mad scraping as two more squirrels practically flew off Meg's big Slimer rock behind the house and hit the roof. They dashed across the peak and disappeared over the side of the house. They were moving so fast it was almost scary.

A beer popped on the porch below him and the swing shifted.

"How's it going?"

"Good. Just about done."

He gave the frame a good rap with the side of his fist, then gave it another one, harder this time. He got a splinter for his efforts. His balance wavered.

"Whoa!"

"Are you okay?"

"Fine. Just a splinter."

"I'll get the Neosporin."

"It's okay."

He heard them before he saw them: half a dozen squirrels were high-wiring the power lines at warp speed. They chattered, practically screamed at each other. His first feeling was amazement. The precariousness of his own situation caught up

171

to him a split second later, when they hit the roof next to him practically at once.

They were not playing.

One smacked the ladder, went off its feet, and tumbled. Then, faster than Trevor's eyes could focus, the one behind bit it, not a playful nip but a real, ripping bite. The next one did the same. The first one limped screeching and bleeding after them.

Trevor lost his balance. The storm window slid away, struck the eave, and shattered in midair. Somehow he managed to catch the gable. He hugged it for dear life as the ladder screaked along the edge and caught the porch awning.

He stood on the roof, suddenly stone sober.

A litter of blood and fur marked their path.

"What happened!"

"I slipped. I'm okay."

Was he? A spasm shot through his shoulders. He bent, and pulled the ladder straight. One storm window to replace. It could have been a lot worse. Stupid to just let go like that, but . . .

"Oh my God!"

Cathleen's voice brought the spasm back. Across the meadow, dozens of squirrels had broken from the forest. They dashed across the yard.

"Close the door!"

He didn't need to tell her twice. The door slammed behind her. Another wave tore out of the woods; they ran and tumbled and fought, chattered and screeched. Their speed was frightening. A dozen more hit the lines to the house and came rocketing toward the roof.

Once more Trevor found himself dangerously out of position. It struck him that he was facing bodily injury for performing a simple household chore, one he hadn't cared to do in the first place. But there was no time to ponder ironies. They had to be rabid. By the time he made it down the ladder, he'd be up to his ankles in them . . . and Cathleen had probably locked the door behind her.

More flew off Slimer. They didn't seem to care where they

172

went or what they crashed into, and they bit everything that got in their way.

He palmed Megan's window. It came up a little, then it came up a lot. Cathleen was inside helping to raise it. He put his foot around, but there wasn't enough ledge there. He could break his neck trying it. The squirrels hit the roof.

"Close it! The attic! Go to the attic!"

For a moment, all he saw were black button eyes.

One bit through his jeans. He jerked his foot away, kicking the squirming thing into the others. A mad skirmish broke out.

The attic windows had metal frames. And they were locked down tight. He pounded them. The squirrels swarmed around him.

Cathleen frantically spun the catch handle. The window opened out. Somehow, he squeezed through and shut it.

In another minute, the squirrels were gone.

Cathleen and Trevor gaped out the attic window.

"I have no idea," he said finally in response to the question she hadn't asked.

C H U C K was still sick. Classes had been more like study halls. It was boring.

Cody trotted toward the field. He'd had his lunch during the first break and now he just wanted to do some laps. He was feeling pretty good, but he'd have to work to get his speed back. He broke into a sprint at the end of the courtyard. He heard his name before he'd gone ten yards.

"Down here, by the creek."

Bryce was the last person he'd expected to see.

"What's up?"

It was the first time Cody had actually seen him since he'd been sick. Bryce looked like he'd seen a ghost.

"You gotta come with me to the drugstore. You gotta see something."

Cody shrugged. "Sure."

"We have to go back this way—I'm AWOL."

"Okay." He looked quickly around. No teachers. He trotted over to him. "Little sis is looking hot."

"What?"

"Meg. She looks cute—you know."

Apparently Bryce didn't. He stared at him.

"Without the glasses . . . she's a babe without the glasses."

C O D Y had even described her clothes: blue skirt, pink leggings, black shoes, a pink T-shirt with the *Billboard* magazine insignia, a black-on-blue Gore-Tex ski jacket.

"So she's wearing contacts? What's the deal?"

"They don't make contacts for what she's got—except the stupid dark kind."

Piñon Rim Drugs was empty except for Jordan and a woman buying hair dye. Jordan waved as they came in. Bryce slid onto the stool closest to all the photos, and Cody grabbed the next one.

"So she got better. Don't worry. Be happy."

Bryce shook his head.

"It doesn't get better. I dunno, man, something's weird with her. Something's goin' on."

"She's growing up."

"Gimme a break. She's ten years old. Scratch that—eleven."

"See, practically a grown woman. So what's the deal? What am I supposed to see?"

"Last night I had a nightmare about her."

"So?"

"It was so freaking real. I dreamed there was some kid in her room with her."

"She's growing up real fast."

"I'm serious."

"It was a dream—kinky, maybe—but a dream."

"It's more than that. When I was really sick I swear I heard voices coming from her room in the middle of the night."

"That flu was bad news. I thought I heard all kinds of stuff."

"Like what?"

"Just stuff. Crazy stuff. It's the fever, man. So what?"

"The day I found that kid in the water, Meg said some weird boy had bothered her at school. She said he was wearing Old

West clothes. Things were pretty intense that day. I forgot about it until I saw *him*."

"Saw who?"

Bryce pointed to one of the pictures of the Big House on Jordan's wall.

"Boyd Easton."

"What?"

"That's who was in her room. In the dream, I thought Meg was saying, 'It's just a boy,' like she was saying it was no big deal to have a boy in her room. I didn't connect it until I saw his picture again over at the Historical Society today. She was saying, 'Boyd. It's just Boyd.' "

"Knock, knock, Bryce! You're talking about a dream. You've seen this picture before, your sis said she saw a kid at school wearing Old West clothes. You filled in the rest. Call me Sigmund. That's ninety bucks for the Dream Ream."

Jordan slid black coffee to Bryce and a Coke to Cody.

"How are you men doin' today?"

"We're cool," Cody said.

"What do you know about Boyd Easton?" Bryce asked Jordan. "You told me once there was a story."

"That was a sad case. Boyd wandered off, lost himself, died out in the desert. His older brother there, Shep"—Jordan tapped the photo—"Shep never got over it. Wound up dead himself."

"How did he die?"

"Drowned in Sharpe's Creek, not far from where you found the Buckhorn boy."

"Was the Lucky Slipper ever rebuilt or restored or anything?"

Jordan looked wounded. Cody looked like Bryce had just pulled one into left field.

"Well, if you can call the magazine racks in here a rebuild—or the pizza oven next door. It's what's underneath's what counts, and the Slipper here's the genuine article."

"What about upstairs?"

Jordan laughed.

175

"Well, the brothel's gone, so it's a mite lonelier up there. There's just my place now, and Mr. Tomasi's next door."

"But the outside . . . that's the way it was?"

"The way it *is*. Never been no need to change it."

" s o what was all that about?"

Bryce shook his head. He pulled a thin yellow paperback from his pocket. It was one of those Historical Society cheap print jobs.

"Well, he said the same stuff they say here: Boyd Easton got lost and died. Shep never got over it and ended up drowning. The Lucky Slipper is the same as it always was, if you don' count the fact that it's three separate stores now. And they don't mention a flu or anything, but there must have been one."

Cody skimmed his palm over his head and made a sound like a rocket passing. Bryce crossed the street, looked back at the drugstore, then moved a few steps closer to Katie Avenue. Cody followed him.

"I've gotta get back. What's the deal?"

"You know who Aggie Hudson is?"

Cody leered. "Who doesn't?"

"She came over one night and said a lot of stuff about how screwed up Boomtown Piñon Rim used to be."

"Connie Bowman *and* Aggie Hudson—are you *all* studs in New York?"

Bryce felt himself go a little red.

"I think she wanted to see my dad."

"Okay, you're half a stud. Yeah, when dinosaurs ruled the earth, this town was rockin'."

"She said Piñon Rim *had a memory*. I didn't get it then, but I think I do now."

"You're running off, man. What's to get?"

"I saw a little kid last night who died a hundred years ago— *kid who used to live in my house*."

"You *dreamed* you saw a kid last night."

"His brother drowned in Sharpe's Creek. A hundred year

later I find a kid drowned in Sharpe's Creek. And everybody's been sick, right?''

"Yeah."

"But not *everybody*—just kids. Teachers aren't sick. My folks didn't get it, did yours?"

"No."

"Back when this place was booming, *a lot of kids died at once*. But they don't mention it in the historical pamphlets at all. And if you ask any grown-ups about it, they sort of shrug it off, like kids always died in those days."

"I think a lot of them did."

"*But not all at once.*"

"What makes you think they all died at once?"

"A whole bunch of them are buried together."

"Oh, man. On Cross Hill?"

Bryce nodded.

"That's the 'Kiddie Section.' They did that on purpose. You know, just put the kids together. They planned it that way. Most of 'em don't have markers, so they could have died years apart."

"No way! Look at that place. I mean, there's no plan at all after the second row. It's like they just dragged bodies up there wherever they found room, but then, right in the middle, there's a whole bunch of kid graves."

Cody didn't say anything right away. He looked suddenly thoughtful behind his trademark shades. He shook his head.

"Nobody's died from this thing."

"Maybe the *real* flu hasn't hit yet."

Cody grimaced. Clearly he was trying to imagine how a "real flu" would compare to the one he'd just had.

"And there's something weird about the Lucky Slipper too. A lot of the town burned, right? If you ask any grown-ups about it, they say the Lucky Slipper got through it intact. The history books all say the same thing. But look."

Bryce opened the pamphlet to a photo taken close to where they stood, in front of Ned's Gold Dust Tavern. The Lucky Slipper was in plain view, and Harper's Peak loomed behind it. There was a blurry, angled line at the top edge of the photo.

"Look at the second-floor windows in the picture."

Cody looked and shrugged.

"Now look across the street."

At first Cody just shook his head, then he moved his sunglasses up and looked again. His eyes narrowed.

"The windows are bigger now. That's not a big deal though. So they put new windows in."

"Look again. That's what I thought too, at first."

Cody shook his head.

"Look at Harper's Peak over the facade. Look at the mine. In the photo you can just make out the top of the entrance."

"Yeah." Cody looked back at the picture, then across the street and beyond to Harper's Peak. He nodded. "You can see more of it from here."

"You can see the top of the water pump now. Which means either Harper's Peak grew, or the windows are the same size *and the facade is smaller.*"

"We're probably not right where the camera was."

"No, but we're real close. See the gray stripe at the top of the photograph? That's the awning from the boardwalk just behind us, so the camera's perspective was *higher* than ours. We should see even less of the mine from here."

"No way." Cody whistled. It was like one of those trick drawings that hid one image in another one: like the girl at the vanity who turns into a skull, or the young girl with the hat who turns into an old woman with a scarf. Once you saw it, you couldn't miss it.

"What's the big deal? So it burned down and they rebuilt it. Why don't they just say so?"

"Maybe they don't know. I mean, nobody's old enough to remember. The stuff at the Historical Society is all based on old newspapers and stories written by people that are dead now. They talk about the mill and the rest of the town getting smoked, but they make a point of saying the Lucky Slipper made it through."

"But why would the boomtown people lie?"

"I dunno." Bryce shook his head. "I think something real *bad* must have happened in there."

"Like what?"

"Don't know."

"I gotta get back. Bell's gonna ring any second."

"Wait up. I gotta ask you something."

Cody turned back, but the engine was running. He bounced on his toes.

"Ask away."

"I keep thinking about that little kid in the water. Are there any Indian things going on here? I mean like legends or stories."

Cody had flipped his glasses back down. His face was unreadable.

"Nothing important, man. Bell's gonna ring."

C O D Y trotted into the courtyard ahead of the second bell. A commotion had broken out by the kids' hall. Two small boys were shoving each other.

"I saw her first!"

"She's my girl!"

First love at nine. It was sort of cute. Some of their friends were cheering them on, others filed toward the classrooms. A few just stood and watched. Cody took a quick look around. No teachers in sight. He trotted over.

"Come on, chill!"

And then one of the blows connected, *really* connected. The sound echoed in the courtyard. The other kid reeled and screamed.

It was no longer cute.

Before Cody could make a move the other kid was on top of the screaming one. The scream choked off.

"Chill!"

Cody fought to pry the kid's hands off the other one's throat. Their faces were bright red. The downed kid's eyes were wide as plates. Suddenly, Cody felt his own wind go. He'd been mulekicked.

"Little—"

"What's going on here!"

Teachers at last.

Cody put his hands up and shook his head.

"Cody!"

He bent at the waist and caught a breath.

"Tryin' . . . to keep the little dudes . . . from killin' each other, Mr. Perkins."

Megan stood just outside a nearby classroom.

She beamed at him, a totally winning smile.

17

SHERIFF Gordon didn't hear the fracas across the playground as he stepped sideways down the slope to Sharpe's Creek. All he could hear were the mounds of red dirt and loose rock sliding ahead of him, and all he could think of was how much he disliked it down here.

The tangle of wood was dry and white now. The small pool behind it held only minnows and water sprites, but he couldn't be here and not see Michael Buckhorn's silvery eyes staring up through the icy water.

A swirling wind moaned in the forest, fanned the surface, and shattered it. Gordon zipped his jacket and anchored one foot on the deadfall. A white bottle bobbed behind the net John Anaweh had stretched across the channel. Gordon yanked it free. He couldn't shake the water from his hand fast enough.

The plastic sides were nearly opaque, but he could make out a small, dark stone and a short length of what looked like leather fringe pressed against the side. He pulled himself back onto dry land, unscrewed the cap, and shook the contents into his palm. A scrap of folded white paper slid out with the rest.

> *Please deliver to Thomas Gordon, Yavapai County Sheriff, Piñon Rim.*
> *Bottle released at Dugan's Point, known to Navajo as Place where the Heart of the World was Broken. Seeking Michael Buckhorn's grandmother, Morning Sun. Believe she is perp. Contact Daniel Whitefeather on Yavapai Reservation, re: "Circle of the Harvest."—Anaweh*

181

Gordon dropped the leather fringe and the stone back in the bottle and stuffed it into his jacket.

He coughed into his hand. Dugan's Point was a good six miles away. He had a sudden, horrible image of Michael Buckhorn's final swim.

The walkie-talkie on his belt beeped and Gordon checked in.

Trish's voice echoed over the quiet of Sharpe's Creek. When she'd finished, Gordon bit his lip.

Two women had been found dead right across the street from each other. One was an overdose; the other one had been crushed under a set of barbells.

What was happening to this town?

J O H N Anaweh slid out of his pack and sat beside the deafening cascade. He stretched some relief into his shoulders and back and finished off another tasteless nutrition bar. The sheer walls of the canyon were black against the slate sky. It had taken nearly two days to reach the mouth of the cave, and night was falling again. Somewhere above these falls, Michael Buckhorn had stood for the last time.

The boy's death was only a sad footnote to what had brought him here. Anaweh no longer sought Morning Sun for the murder of her grandson; he believed she too was dead.

If he failed here, many more would die.

Anaweh's eyelids flickered; soon he slept, but it was a troubled, restless sleep. The dream returned, as it had each night since he'd visited the hogan of Morning Sun and seen the painting in the sand. Again her hand was suspended before him, the stream of white streaking unerringly from it to the symbol on the floor. The symbol was not Navajo, nor was it Anasazi. It was a symbol from a people long before, a race that had never known the warmth of the sun. He watched, as he had over and over again, unable to move, unable to close his eyes as she completed the Circle of the Harvest before him.

As the last grains of sand fell, the air grew cold.

All was white. All was still.

Fields of dry, broken stalks were covered with snow. He passed silently between the rows. Countless braves stood nearly hidden by th stalks, their faces painted, weapons raised. Frozen monuments to war.

The vision was gone, but the dream remained. Once again he stood in the hogan of Morning Sun. The fist that hovered before him was his own. He opened it slowly. He held a gold medallion . . .

Anaweh woke to the thunder of the waterfall and searing white daylight. The mouth of the cave gaped behind the white water. The cave of the Spirit.

He checked his weapons and food, and clicked on the bright halogen lantern. It was time to begin.

T H E Y ate in silence, just the three of them. Trevor hadn't left the studio since he'd finished the storm windows.

Megan had her glasses on. Bryce didn't ask.

He'd spent the rest of his day at Sharpe's Creek reading the pamphlets he'd taken from the Historical Society. The stories were the same. Nothing about a fire at the Lucky Slipper.

"So how was school?"

It was the sound of Cathleen's voice, not the question, that startled him. Her voice sounded hollow somehow, forced. He'd been ready for the question. The best answer was the simplest one.

"Okay. No big deal."

Meg went on eating without a hint anything was up. Maybe she hadn't noticed he wasn't there today.

"May I be excused?"

Cathleen nodded.

He took a glass of milk upstairs.

Buffalo Springfield was playing through the studio door. He knocked lightly, then louder when he got no response.

"Dad?"

Still nothing. He gave it a couple good raps.

"Dad!"

That stupid "I've fallen and I can't get up!" ad flashed through Bryce's head.

"Dad, it's me! Are you okay?"

Suddenly, Stephen Stills was singing twice as loud.

It was such an unlikely message that it took a second to register.

He turned the stereo up! He knows it's me and he turned up the freaking music!

It stung him hard. A mix of embarrassment, amazement, and pain. He'd never been shut out of his dad's studio before. The picture he had now was not of Trevor, but of Sara. Not the hug before she'd left, not the smile and that last sad wave from her car: *it was Sara the moment after, when she'd turned forward again, her eyes riveted no longer on him but on the long road ahead.*

He made it to his room and shut the door before a single tear slipped out.

That was all that came.

He hit the memory button and listened to the phone dial his mom. When it rang once and picked up he knew she wasn't there. He listened to her voice anyway. He hung up on the tone.

A knock on his door startled him.

"Come in."

Meg shut the door behind her.

"I know you weren't there today."

He nodded.

"Where'd you go?"

"Hung out by the creek, mostly."

"By the cave?"

"No. Along Sluice."

She seemed to decide that was okay. Her voice was measured, with none of its usual bounce. She should have been teasing him, maybe threatening to tell; instead, it was a little bit like being grilled by an adult—or at least a big sister.

"If something was up, you'd tell me. Right?" he asked.

Her eyes brightened. He thought she might even giggle, but he had no idea what was funny.

"Sure. Things are cool."

"How come—"

The phone rang. He grabbed it hoping it was Sara. It was Cody.

"Dude."

"Dude."

Meg was out the door.

The call couldn't have come at a worse time. He wanted to ask about her glasses. Timing was everything.

"What's up?" Bryce asked.

"You doin' anything tomorrow?"

The days he'd missed had totally thrown him, but the fact that "tomorrow" was Saturday finally sank in.

"Open."

"Come over. I have something about this place, an 'Indian thing.' "

Bryce felt a tingling. He remembered breaking the "bar barrier" on the swingset when he was ten. It was the first time he'd actually swung higher than the bar that held the chains and seat. There was a moment of total freedom, and with it came a feeling of absolute terror. In that moment, with the sudden slacking of those chains, his entire connection with the planet earth had ceased to exist. He could have flown off into the few puffball clouds that seemed so incredibly, so suddenly near—or been dashed to pieces against the concrete wall he knew very well was only a few short feet behind him.

Bryce leaned over the phone.

"What is it?"

"Can't talk now. Come over when you get up."

B R Y C E couldn't keep his eyes shut. And when sleep finally did come, he was only vaguely aware that it had and that he was dreaming. It was a good dream, though: he was with Connie in a meadow near Sharpe's Creek. They lay in tall grass and the sunlight was warm on their faces. The water found its way downstream with a contented purr.

She kissed him full on the mouth. He'd only felt that once before, and it was nothing like this. She pulled slowly away. There was something different, but he couldn't place what it was. The ground beneath them was like a warm, soft blanket. Then they were in the water, suspended in a great warm pool. The water reflected turquoise diamonds off the stone walls high above them. Connie smiled, but not her usual, sort of sad one. This smile was full and happy. He could feel her all around him. She was pulling him gently down.

And then he realized what was wrong with this picture. Most of their clothes sat on a rock near the water's edge: his dungarees *and her satin-and-whalebone underthings*. It wasn't Connie at all. *It was Rose kissing him, Rose Bowman wrapping her arms even more tightly around him.*

They were no longer in the creek.

The water reflected turquoise diamonds off the pool deck and the diving board high above them. The water closed over their heads. She pulled him deeper. He couldn't break her grip. The surface of the water was a sheet of liquid silver above them, broken only by a single form: the Indian boy floated overhead. He stared down at Bryce with silvery, dead eyes.

The last of Bryce's air blew out in bubbles of mercury. He'd never make it. *He was going to drown.* He pushed, pushed with all his strength.

An explosion turned the water to flame . . .

Bryce woke to a phantom scream.

It echoed in the wide, dark halls of his imagination as he stared straight up at the ceiling, too petrified to move. His heart beat like the wings of a frightened bird.

18

BRYCE held the comfortably worn Duke football in both hands. He took two steps back, checked the oak to his left, pump-faked the Douglas fir, and let the ball fly toward the streaking form of Cody Muledeer. Cody hauled it in at the forest's edge and spiked it. It bounced over his head, glanced off a pine and he caught it again.

Cody had tossed him the ball as soon as he'd walked into the yard. Football wasn't exactly prime on Bryce's mind, but he was starting to realize Cody had certain rituals. If he wasn't ready to talk about something, Bryce would just have to wait. Playing catch was Cody's way of settling into things first.

Playing catch wasn't so bad, anyway. It was the first "normal" sort of thing Bryce had done since he got sick. It sort of made him *feel* normal again. Maybe the world (or Piñon Rim's tiny corner of it) wasn't such a strange place after all. A game of two-on-one would have been better, but Chuck was still getting the sweats. His mom wouldn't let him out of the house.

Cody's yard was even longer than Bryce's. It was a perfect practice field. Bryce stretched out and snagged a pass on his fingertips. He was feeling a lot stronger now. He'd lost some weight with the flu, but he'd lift weights over the summer, bulk up a bit, and play for Red Ridge next year.

Cody trotted toward him and broke for the porch. The throw slipped wide, skidded off Cody's fingers, and wreaked football havoc on the flower pots sitting on the deck.

Cody's mom palmed up the kitchen window. Bryce could hear something sizzling on the stove behind her, and his stomach reminded him he'd run out before breakfast this morning.

"You two rest for a while. Have some cocoa."

Cody's teeth flashed beneath the ever-present rubber sunglasses.

"Works for me. Wanna go in?"

"Yeah, sure."

Cody's mom was cool. She made great hot chocolate and didn't even use a packet or anything. But the best thing was her fried bread with honey. Bryce's stomach growled like an old bear as he wiped his Jordans on the mat. Cody snagged the cocoa and a basket of fresh fried bread, then headed toward the den.

Cody's little brother, Jason, was stretched out on the couch wrapped in a blanket. A half-ton peak of wadded-up tissues rose from the floor between the couch and the wastebasket. "Sesame Street" blared from the TV.

"Sickroom," Cody said, and veered off down the stairway toward the rec room.

Jason sneezed and his tired hand came up with a tissue just in time to have it blown out of his fingers. Bryce knew exactly how he felt.

" 'eye, Bryce."

"Jason."

" 'ow's Neggin?"

"She's doin' okay."

"Teller zed 'eye."

"Yeah, I will."

That was good anyway. At least Meg was making friends. *And not all of them were dead kids.*

Out of all the bad dreams he'd had, that was probably the worst. Although last night's feature was running a close second.

The Muledeer rec room was pretty intense. The house wasn't very big, but it did have a basement and the Big House didn't. Cody's dad had put in a full-size pool table and foosball. The best thing was the big-screen TV, equipped with both Nintendo *and* Sega. Cody loaded up the Nintendo with Super Mario Brothers. He had the barrel of the lightgun stuck through a belt loop at his waist and the fried bread in his teeth. He clicked on

188

the set with his remote and handed the basket to Bryce. Bryce took a plump, warm one shiny with honey and butter, grabbed a wad of napkins, and set the basket on the floor.

"Marios? Duck Hunt?"

"Go for the ducks."

"Awesome. You got it. Gonna be anything for Halloween?"

"I dunno. Maybe Madonna."

"Too obvious."

The first round started and Cody flipped the gun to Bryce, who blasted the first duck as its beak hit the screen. He pretty much had the ducks figured.

"Maybe the T-1000 from '12 when he's all silver—if I can figure out how to do it."

"Do something with a lot of clothes. It's usually pretty cold here on Halloween." Cody smiled. "Of course, it always gets hot up on Cross Hill—quacker at three o'clock."

He had this game down. A millisecond later the duck appeared and Bryce blasted it.

"You really *make out* at the cemetery?"

"It's the hang—creamed that one!"

"Duckmeat!"

"It's a Helldorado Days tradition: Halloween night, if you're cool at all—and we are—you end up on Cross Hill with a girl and mess around. If you're totally cool, you go all the way up to the Wizard, but there's usually Red Ridge buttfaces up there, so the cemetery's safer."

"Cemetery's gross."

"On Halloween it's a happening place, dude. And if Connie Bowman said she'd only do it on fresh cowpies, you'd look for a pasture, am I right? Believe me, graves make chicks horny."

"No way."

"Way."

"And they just let everybody go up there and mess around?"

"They tell you not to go, but they don't stop you if you're cool. You know, you can't be upfront. You gotta sneak out of the Helldorado stuff in town. But once you're on the hill, with all those mounds and paths, you can duck down and nobody sees you. It's cool."

"Connie says they might cancel Helldorado, anyway."

"Ooo, 'Connie says!' " Cody made a kissy-face. "They can't. It's the only thing this town's got going."

"So what're you gonna be?"

"A famous Apache warrior: an ancestor of mine, Big Chief Running Nose."

Bryce coughed and a storm of fried bread shot through the air. Cody dodged the fusillade and ended up on his butt next to the pool table.

"Gross!"

"Man, you're lucky I didn't spray hot chocolate!"

Bryce was laughing, but it felt like a tribe of hot ants were running through his sinuses. He blew his nose in a napkin and tossed it toward a wastebasket near the TV. He missed by a good foot. Cody kicked it away.

"You're pathetic!"

Bryce missed the next three ducks in a row, and Cody blew him away on the round.

Cody pushed up his glasses with the gun barrel. "Did she really bring you cookies?"

"Yeah."

"Man." The glasses dropped.

"And she also"—Bryce pulled the chain from his shirt collar and the dragon flashed its green eye—"made me this."

"Whoooooa!"

"It's a real emerald."

"She's hot for your dog, Bud. Better take out Matt Connors insurance."

"He's old news."

"He's also huge and a total butthead."

Bryce ripped off another chunk of bread and honey and washed it down with hot chocolate. His sinuses were itching now. Hell of a place to scratch. Big Chief Running Nose was still picking off ducks and picking up points on the round.

There was a crucifix on the wall. It was one of the old kind, a real wooden cross and a Jesus made out of painted plaster.

"How come you guys don't have Indian stuff around?"

"Feathers and dolls?" He raised his palm to his shoulder. "Hihowaya? Hihowaya?"

"I dunno. I think it's pretty cool. I guess I'd have the stuff around."

"Man, I am destroying you on the ducks." Cody handed the gun over. "For one thing, that 'stuff' you're talking about is religious, and we're Catholic. My dad says it's time to live in this century."

Bryce wasn't sure what Catholicism had to do with this century, but he let it go. He racked up six ducks in a row, in a mindlessly rhythmic way. He was trying to understand. He thought being an Indian was cool and he wasn't sure if Cody did or didn't.

"Which brings us to why I asked you here."

Bryce wasn't sure he wanted to know anymore. He'd been having a good time. He'd been able to stuff all the darkness away for the first time in days.

Cody set the gun down and closed the door.

"First off, my folks don't even like this stuff mentioned in the house, so be cool."

Bryce nodded. "So what's wrong with this place?"

"Besides being in the middle of Bumwater, Nowhere, probably nothing. But there *is* a legend. *An old wives' tale*. My grandfather doesn't quite qualify in that department, but when I was a kid he used to say stuff."

"Are we on Navajo burial grounds?"

"No. Although a lot of us supposedly died here—and a lot of Anasazi before that. Did you ever hear of them, the Anasazi?"

Bryce shook his head.

"Their name means 'Ancient Ones.' They were here way before the Navajo, and they were really advanced, like the Egyptians. They disappeared and nobody knows why. At least, no white people do. My grandfather said something underground here took them away—a Spirit. He used to scare me with that stuff when I was a little kid. Tried to keep my folks from moving off the reservation with it. He says the reservation's the only safe place. My folks think he's crazy. They don't talk to him anymore."

"What do you think?"

"When you're five or six and you hear that stuff it has to scare you a little. My folks say that kind of talk sets the Navajo back a hundred years. They say it's cavemen calling Halley's comet an angry god."

"How come no white people talk about it?"

"Most Navajo don't. And it's not like the whites and the Navajo spent the last couple centuries sitting around campfires swapping ghost stories."

"So most people here really don't know anything about it?"

Cody shook his head. "What's to know? It's a stupid fairy tale."

"Can we talk to your grandfather?"

"No phone. We'd need wheels—and I don't mean bikes. He lives way back in the mountains. There's hardly even roads there. Don't even *think* I'm asking my folks to drive."

Bryce thought about his dad locking him out of the studio. No help there. Bryce was pretty sure he could drive the Trailblazer if he snuck it out, but that was probably all it would take to send Cathleen over the top.

"Can you remember anything else?"

"Not much. The thing that made me bring it up in the first place is that he said it was something that happened over and over again. A *cycle* or a *circle* or something. When you said that stuff about Cross Hill and the flu, I started thinking about it. Maybe all those kids *did* die at once. Maybe there really *was* a flu or something a hundred years ago like the one we had. Maybe a hundred years before that too. I don't know. My grandfather always had a lot of stories, but I never thought he was crazy.

Bryce shook his head. "I don't know what it has to do with torching the Lucky Slipper though."

"And why make it smaller?"

"I think I got that figured," Bryce said. "The lumber mill was one of the first places to burn down, right? Aggie said the town got taken over by religious people after Easton died. I there wasn't much wood, the last thing they'd want to do would be waste it on some stupid facade for a whorehouse."

"But why rebuild it in the first place?"

"That's why I think something bad happened in there. It had to be so bad they didn't want anybody to know."

"But everybody in town had to know it burned down."

"That's what makes it so scary. They *had* to know it did. But the stuff that's written down—it all makes a point of saying it didn't. The whole town lied."

B R Y C E felt better with the cold, fresh wind on his face, his hands firmly gripping the Stingray.

But *better* was a relative term. He really wanted to ride back to Cody's place and start the morning all over again.

Cody had chores, and Bryce wasn't sure what they could do next anyway. He'd stopped at the library to see what they had about the Anasazi, but the whole Indian section was checked out. All five books of it. He'd have to go to Prescott and use the library there.

No problem. Two years from now he could drive anywhere he wanted to.

Maybe it was just as well. It seemed like the more he found out about Piñon Rim, the worse he felt. Helldorado was coming. Good times. But he was living in a town that boomed once and then blew up big time, a town that died with a secret.

The scary thing was that it might not have ended there. It was easy to believe the stuff Aggie said about history just going on and on. Especially when one of the main players in that first big soap opera was here now, in the form of Connie Bowman.

And there was that Indian kid he found. And Cody's fairy tale. *And there were those dreams.*

He should forget it, all of it. At least for a while. He had homework up the kazoo.

My grandfather said something underground here took them away—a Spirit.

He pumped the pedals, driving them until their own momentum made them spin faster than his feet could go. He rocketed over the next hill, actually floated in space the way he had years ago on that swing, disconnected from the earth and all its bothersome physical laws. And the same reality that hit him as a small child struck now with a razor-edged clarity:

You are not in control here. You could die here.

His back tire didn't strike home till he was halfway down the other side of the hill. Somehow he kept the front wheel straight. He skidded to a stop.

There was no need to push himself, no need to go that fast. He pedaled in a wide, slow circle and studied the raw crescent his back tire had gouged in the hardpan. If he'd slipped, the hurt would have been serious. No skinned elbows and knees here—this would have been a neck-snapper, a skull-cracker.

God, there really was a legend about this place.

Up ahead a Corolla was getting set to overtake an old truck. Bryce swung right and waited till they passed him. Dust and pebbles peppered him as the Corolla chugged by. The truck rumbled slowly on, a gray Indian man gripping the wheel like it was salvation.

He topped the next hill. The road would be flat for a while, then there would be another quick drop—Big Dipper—and following that was Splash Mountain.

He pumped up the speed and coasted down Big Dipper, wishing he'd see the Indian woman ambling over Splash Mountain again. She had to know more about the legend.

A whole civilization had disappeared: a powerful one, like the Egyptians. People bragged that Piñon Rim had been prosperous once. The fact it was a ghost town right after seemed to whiz right over their heads.

It boomed *and busted*, just like the Anasazis had.

It's booming again.

Sometimes a place has a memory.

He pulled far left as he climbed, giving a U-Haul truck a wide berth. It wasn't exactly gridlock, but he'd never seen so much traffic on Sluice. He stopped at the summit of Splash Mountain.

Sluice Road was a bright red gash through the pine-covered hills. An icy breeze brought the scent of rain from the mountains beyond. The lower sky was a deep Payne's gray. It could snow. But the idea of snow right here and now didn't carry the same homey associations it had back in upstate New York and Bryce didn't know why.

The old woman had stood just a few feet from here.

He slowly circled the spot where she'd been. He closed his eyes . . .

Stop her!

He saw her eyes: sightless snow-white bulbs beneath the fleshy folds of her lids.

He saw himself down at Sharpe's Creek his first day of school, saw his own hand reaching for a snow-white ball in the water.

The ball bobbed near the branches, yawing slowly. And as the bottom of the ball rolled upward, it came up smeared with blood.

It floated in a river of blood.

His shoulders tremored and a high-pitched cry jerked out of him. He looked around quickly and satisfied himself that no one else had heard him screech like a girl. His hands were shaking. He gripped the handlebars and the shaking stopped.

Man, why even think about this crazy stuff? It's a day in the country. Everything's fine. Life is good.

He stopped circling and straddled the bike. He took a deep breath and winced; the smell up here was even worse now. He scooter-stepped closer to the edge.

It was a tug-of-war between an overpowering stench and a thirteen-year-old's curiosity. The shoulder jutted out over the cliff, leaving a treacherous, vine-covered outcropping of loose rock and broken earth. He stretched as far as he could without tumbling over the edge, but still couldn't see the source of that awful smell. Vertigo and the ripe odor were making his head light. Sharpe's Creek babbled far below. He inched himself closer. Some of the blackberry vines above the outcropping had been sheared off. It was something big. Had to be a deer.

Bryce was aware of the vibration of the earth almost before he heard the Jeep bearing down on him. He dropped his bike and dove to the ground. The cold hardpan socked the breath clean out of him. As the Jeep's rear wheel passed within inches of his handlebars, he covered his face and shut his eyes to the flying pebbles and dust.

He fought for breath. When he finally got one, there was so much dust in it that he coughed most of the air out. The Jeep skidded, caught itself, and drove on. And laughter went with it. Then the music started up—a pounding rap beat.

Matt Connors flicked a silver can far out into the forest as his Jeep topped the next hill. The can echoed tinnily against the rocks.

Bryce's hand jutted into the vines over the side and he yanked it away. He rolled back onto the road. His temples pounded. His face and neck were on fire and he knew they were bright red. He stood so fast his feet nearly left the ground. His right forearm was tender along the bone, but the heavy denim jacket had protected him from anything worse.

He would kill Matt Connors. It was as clear and simple as that. He didn't care how much bigger and older Matt was. When he found Matt, Bryce would kill him.

He yanked the Stingray up by its handlebars. The fall had gouged a jagged red scar across the seat. He pounced on it and slammed the pedals down, all of his fears forgotten.

T H E dust had barely settled behind him when a single snowflake drifted down from high above the valley. A breeze wheeled it up and around and swirled it back toward the red earth below. It danced without purpose or direction, carried by the Song of the Wind across the bald rock of the mountains and over the spires of tall pines. It drifted over Sluice Road, over the blackberry thicket, and settled only inches from where Bryce's hand had been. It rested on the shattered cheekbone of the Indian woman.

One white eye, now as flat and dry as paper, stared past the snowflake to the heavens. The other was gone now, victim to the harvester ants that were marching evenly from her open mouth into the black ravine that split her forehead. The flake melted and trickled down, momentarily blocking the trail of the ants. The ants tapped impatiently up and down its watery length until it vanished in the warming sun.

The Harvest began again.

19

"YOU'RE doin' no such thing as killin'."

Bill Jordan's eyes held a grip on Bryce that was nearly as tight as the one he held on his prized marble countertop.

Bryce swallowed hard. He must have frightened the old man with his *High Noon* declarations on the forthcoming demise of Matt Connors. Jordan had the look of someone scared into anger. In retrospect, Bryce realized that he had probably looked ridiculous.

He'd smeared rubber halfway down Front Street and plodded up the steps like a drunken ape. Once inside he'd shouted something brilliantly prophetic like, "Connors's gonna die! Gonna freaking kill him! You seen Connors?" Then the old man's eyes had locked on him in an icy half nelson, and Bryce felt his wheels spin in empty air. Jordan had taken him at his word, and that was just scary enough to knock Bryce off-balance.

"I'm buyin' coffee," Jordan said. "You sit down and drink it. Take a minute to think, then you tell me what brought the whistlin' Furies down on Mr. Connors."

Bryce's foot tapped the hardwood floor; he stopped it with some effort. He opened his mouth to say something but couldn't manage a coherent thought, let alone find words to express one, so he closed his mouth.

The coffee was poured.

"Drink it."

Jordan swung himself around, and something in that near-empty pant leg followed him to the big silver containers near the fountain. He lifted the sleeve on the one marked VANILLA, then hauled up a jug that, but for the brackish fluid beading the sides, looked suspiciously like a bleach bottle.

Jordan topped off the container and dropped the sleeve neatly back in place. It made a hollow, final sound like a falling casket lid.

Bryce took a big, hot sip from the heavy mug. The coffee tasted like early Sunday mornings. There should have been bread toasting, eggs frying. His right forearm throbbed where he'd slapped the hardpan, and he switched hands to keep it from banging the countertop. He still wanted Connors, but the raw heat had vanished. The full-tilt ride into town was a bit much to ask of a body still recovering from a flu. He felt like a juiced orange.

"Nearly ran me over in that freaking black Jeep. He tried to kill me."

The old man eyed him darkly.

"That I don't like to hear. Not at all. But I can tell you, was a time they'd hang a man for stealing another man's horse, and that was a legal hangin', not a lynchin'. Now a woman, and especially one like Miss Bowman, well, that's a piece of prop'ty men are like to kill for."

"It's not like he owns her."

"True enough. But sometimes a man gets to *feeling* that way, if a woman lets him."

The doorbells jingled merrily and two old women in flowered dresses bustled in. A van pulled up to the walkway and spilled a family into the street. In front of Coop's, the codgers were at their never-ending game. Near them, the new section of walkway where Piñon Rim's own Wolfman had once parked his Dodge Ram still looked just that—new. It would probably never blend in.

A truck loaded with tied cornstalks and some of the biggest pumpkins Bryce had ever seen stopped in the middle of the street, and two men in coveralls began unloading. A car swerved past them, honking. Apparently Helldorado was on after all. But Piñon Rim's newly acquired traffic was making decorating for it a dangerous proposition.

"Morning, Eva. Morning, Bev. How's that cheatin' husband of yours?"

They giggled cheery good-mornings.

"Parker say's he's ready to take your money whenever you get the itch to play, Bill Jordan."

"Maybe Monday night."

"I'll tell Parker."

"Bill, you have any of that nasal spray? My sinuses are just tighter than a drum."

"Over by them eyewashes. But read the label on it, hon, just three days and not a minute more. Don't you get hooked."

The van family peered through the window like a curious spider with ten bright eyes, decided it was looking into a drugstore after all (despite the Lucky Slipper facade), and moved on.

Bryce sipped his coffee as Jordan tended to the ladies. Jordan had thrown everything back on Connie. Aggie'd said some people were destined to play the goat. She was supposed to be Connie's friend, but if she did give Connie that bracelet she wasn't helping much. It wasn't fair.

Rose Bowman smiled at him from Jordan's Wall of Fame.

Bryce leaned over the bar, his dream about Rose suddenly fresh in his head again.

He jumped a little when Jordan passed behind him.

"Someday they're gonna close me up for a porno-graffer 'cause of that picture. Beats me what it is."

Jordan tipped the pot over Bryce's cup and topped it without so much as a glance. He shook his head at the photo.

"She's got it all right. Some women have it. Most don't. Some that do, don't know it. *But those that have it—and use it—they're a rare and scary breed.* They're deadly for men and for other women too."

Bryce frowned. The "scary" part had zipped over his head. Freddy Krueger was scary. Girls were just . . . He didn't know, exactly.

"You say Matt tried to run you down. Now that's a serious thing. That's a police sort of thing. And you takin' it right back at him. Well now, that's just gonna make it worse. More'n likely, you start a fight. You gonna get your butt kicked 'cause he's a lot bigger and meaner than you are.''

Bryce's hackles rose at that, and the old man changed his tack.

''All right, let's say you take him. Let's say things get outta hand. Let's say you do just what you said and kill him. You think you'll get the girl and walk together into blazing glory? All you'll get's a trip to Fort Grant, where you'll spend your life learnin' how to be a *real* thug. Killin' one kills two. Nobody wins. Nobody's right after.''

It wouldn't get that far. Bryce wasn't really going to kill Matt Connors, but he was definitely going to hurt him. He didn't care how big or mean Matt was.

''He came right at me.''

''Like I said, that's not somethin' I like t' hear. This town went an awful long stretch without talk of killin'. Then that little Navajo boy drowned, and now a deputy's gone too. And who knows who or what they'll find before they're through digging up crazy Mackey's rosebeds.''

''What's that got to do with Matt trying to run me over?'' Jordan was running off the track.

The old man squinted at a dull spot on the bar, toweled it briefly, and shook his head.

''Nothing.'' Then he qualified that. ''Probably nothing. Someday you should visit the li'bry, browse through the history this place . . .''

It was exactly what Bryce didn't want to hear. He felt unsettled again, as though the world were spinning just slightly off its axis.

''Better yet, take a walk up Cross Hill and check the markers. Take a look at some of the reasons the good people of Piñon Rim were sent to heaven.'' Jordan frowned. His voice dropped nearly to a whisper. ''Was a time killin' was more pop'lar here than the movies are now. Was a time it looked like this place wanted to kill itself.''

It gave Bryce the chills. It was Cody talking about the Anasazi all over again, and the way Jordan said it was like the way you talked in an empty church or near a grave: careful not so much because *someone* might be listening, as because some all-powerful or otherwise unmentionable *thing* might be.

"Did you ever hear a Navajo legend about something living underground here—an evil spirit or something?"

Jordan laughed.

"Cody tell you that? Guess you can't stand behind this counter long as I have without hearing 'em all. That's a new one."

"His grandfather told him about it. Cody said he's not the only one who believes it."

"Well. One thing you need to know before you get yourself all spooked is that the Navajo are proud people. They didn't just decide the reservation was the place to go and move there. They were put there by the whites. I'm not proud'a that. It's a terrible thing. But you have to know their grandfolks've come up with all sorts'a fancy reasons to stay put.

"Only two evils ever lived here, and only one of 'em lived underground: that was *gold,* and that particular evil up and left." Two more cars whizzed by outside. Jordan shook his head.

"Other one's that soiled dove you've been lustin' after." He winked.

Rose Bowman had obviously been looked upon as something much worse than a prostitute, and now, a hundred years later, Connie bore the stigma. It was unreal. It was stupid. But Jordan was serious. His "soiled dove" reference brought up something else that had bothered Bryce ever since he'd been well enough to leave the house.

"What about the birds?"

Jordan squinted.

"I mean, shouldn't there be more birds around? Even when it gets really cold in New York you see birds—just different ones. I haven't seen any since I got sick, and it's not even that cold yet."

"I wouldn't worry too much what birds are thinking. Birds hear there's more bugs down the road, that's where they're gonna go."

Bryce laughed at that. He guessed it was true enough.

"Piñon Rim was a good enough place to live when copper was all the mines gave up. It wasn't a wealthy town, but folks made an honest living for themselves. Then Harper's mine tapped gold and the *magic* happened. Harper's became the Wizard and life here got sweet. Maybe too sweet."

Jordan topped off Bryce's coffee and poured himself a cup. Then he set a crate on end and sat.

"That brought more people in, some good but most not. A different kind of people, the sort that don't *build* a town so much as live off it. Women like Rose.

"Piñon Rim got to be a different sort of place then. A small town with the nastiness of a big city. You know, Front Street wasn't the main road back then. Front Street was what you call a red-light district 'cause of the lanterns the soiled doves hung outside their windows to lure their prey. The main road was Katie Avenue, and you can see all that's left of Boomtown Piñon Rim on Katie: the bank, mostly rebuilt, and the sheriff's station, totally rebuilt except for the front door. The rest all burned."

"How did the fire start?"

"The last big one could've been set by anyone—or everyone. There were lots'a little ones before it. But there was always enough clear heads to put 'em out. With the last one . . . that just didn't happen."

"People just watched it burn?"

"Helped out is more the way it went, I guess. Things were sour by then. Public hangin's was pretty common. Normal hangin's first—for horse-stealing, rustling—just a lot of 'em was all.

"Then hangin's got to be a little too routine. People was gettin' hung for bein' adult'rous or lewd. The law got bent around in a big way once the good people of Piñon Rim got the taste a blood in 'em. And the law was there mostly to satisfy it. It got so that law finally went straight out the window. The out-and-out lynchin' started, and then the gunfights. Gunfights over trampled gardens, spilled groceries. A man got his head blown clean off for bein' drunk on Katie Avenue. One postmaster, he was blasted near in two 'cause a package was torn in the

202

mail. Swear to God. You can read the markers on Cross Hill."

"You say that Rose was the catalyst, that she got Percy Easton killed. But what was Easton doing messing around?"

"From what they say, he never did. Oh, he loved Rose all right, but not that way. He wanted to save her."

"They never . . . you know, did it?"

"That's what they say."

"And you believe that?"

Jordan nodded. "Easton was a town elder and one of the few decent Christian folk. Now, I believe in Christ myself, but the more corrupt the town got, the crazier the Christians got. Pretty soon one was bad as the other. In the end it was an out-and-out war."

"Because of Rose Bowman. And you think Connie's just as bad."

The old man smiled and shook his head.

"I can say with some degree 'a cert'nty you'll learn a few tough lessons about women with that one."

"You talk like she's the devil or something."

The doorbells jangled, and had Connie been standing in the doorway, Bryce might have imagined horns jutting up through her curls.

But it wasn't Connie. It was just a little boy in a jacket and mittens.

He regarded them blankly.

"Can I get a 'nilla Coke?"

"Think I can handle that. Come on in and set yourself down."

N A T H A N Henley sat at the counter at Piñon Rim Drugs and waited as Bill Jordan prepared his vanilla Coke. A big kid sat two stools away. Nearby, a pot slowly filled with scalding black coffee. The big kid sipped from his cup, his eyes practically nailed to the pictures on Mr. Jordan's wall.

Jordan turned back to Nathan. The old man's face was very close to his own, and Nathan could see every wrinkle and every ugly white hair on it.

"You want one shot or two, Nate?"

For a moment the relays crackled to life again. He'd always liked being called Nate, and Mr. Jordan was the only one who did. His mother made everyone call him Nathan. Of course, she wouldn't anymore. He smiled up at Mr. Jordan.

"Two."

The relays fizzled, went dark.

The old man showed his back. The pot was halfway full. Jordan pushed the vanilla tap twice. A dark and oily liquid swirled over the ice. The soft-drink machine whizzed the glass full of cola, and Jordan turned back to set it on the counter. The old man wasn't clean. The wrinkles and hairs on his face were gross. They were probably teaming with robust germs, 'crobes, and ba'teria.

"Like I said, she's a catalyst," the old man said. "She might not do anything directly, but things'll happen. Hurtful things."

The boy shook his head and muttered something about Connie Bowman, and that tripped another switch somewhere inside Nathan. Nathan liked Connie. Connie was pretty. She always said hi when she saw him. He sipped the vanilla Coke. The taste nearly brought him up to the surface. And then he couldn't remember how he'd come to be at the drugstore. His body jerked as if he'd slipped in a dream, and the older boy looked at him sort of funny. Then Nathan slipped far, far below the surface. Back into the darkness, into the spreading anger that was starting to boil up like some black witches' brew.

The boy and Mr. Jordan went on talking. Nathan didn't like the chatter. It hurt his head. Or maybe it was the ba'teria hurting him. Maybe it was those robust germs on Old Man Jordan's face. Maybe the germs were after him.

Nathan could see the cause of his hurt now. They crawled around the side of Jordan's head from the leathery folds of his neck. Blue and red, the size of gorged wood ticks, the germs and 'crobes and ba'teria fell like gumdrops from the old man's greasy hair down into his shirt collar.

The pot, now nearly full of steaming, germ-boiling coffee, was less than an arm's length away. Again, Jordan turned his back to him.

Jordan moved back to the vanilla dispenser a few feet from

where Nathan sat. Jordan wiped the big silver cylinder. The red and blue germs had topped the old man's collar and were racing down his back now. Some dropped to the floor, others sped down his shirt sleeve. Several became mired in the vanilla near the spout of the dispenser. The old man toweled them away with the sugary excess.

"What about Easton's wife?" the boy said. "I mean, didn't she know?"

The steaming pot was inches from Nathan's fingers. The back of the old man's head hovered less than two feet away. His microbe-covered neck was exposed.

"Sure she did. Katie Easton was a strong woman. In fact, there's a story about Katie . . ."

The older boy was still staring at a picture behind the counter. Nathan's hand darted toward the pot.

The door chimes jangled, and Nathan's hand slid off the handle. Coffee sloshed over the side of the pot and sizzled on the hot plate. His elbow toppled his vanilla Coke as he yanked his hand back. A protoplasmic arm of dark, fizzing liquid and ice snaked along the marble countertop. Jordan spun, towel in hand, and fell.

An acrid plume of smoke rose from the coffee machine. Nathan was off the stool in a heartbeat. He was halfway down the walkway, snaking through tourists, before the chimes quit jangling.

" W H A T the hell was that about? Damn this leg!" Jordan's towel fizzed as he raised the pot and quickly mopped the hot plate.

Bryce had made a dive over the counter when he saw Jordan slip, but he was too late to help him. There was a nasty welt rising over Jordan's right eye, but otherwise he looked okay.

"I just saw him reach for the pot," Bryce said. "He did it so quick. It was like . . . I don't know."

Bryce dropped a wad of napkins on the counter. They went dark immediately, like sheets soaking blood.

"Don't know what the heck he'd wanna do that for."

"I think he was gonna throw it."

"Oh heck. There isn't an ounce of mischief in that one. He's a timid little guy. More likely he thought it was gonna overflow, probably just wanted to stop it. God knows what little kids think sometimes. He's probably scared right now 'cause he made a mess."

Bryce lifted the sopping mass of napkins, and Jordan held a trash bag open. He plopped it in.

"Are you okay?"

"I'd be better with two good stems beneath me."

He was smiling so Bryce did too, but it didn't feel right.

"Okay. I'm gonna take off."

"Forget that hocus-pocus Indian hogwash and have yourself a great day. Hey, you've never been to a Helldorado Days celebration before, so you've got yourself a treat coming Halloween night." He dropped his voice again.

"Don't get caught." He winked. "Best way out is back of the Haunted House, but don't tell anyone I said so."

Bryce shook his head. Jordan was definitely one of a kind.

"Thanks."

"And do what I said about Matt Connors. With no wolfmen runnin' loose, Tom Gordon's sittin' on that fat butt'a his with nothin' to do. Gordon's gotta earn his keep like everybody else."

"I'll tell him."

Bryce had no such intention as he walked quickly out into the fresh air. Maybe Jordan knew that, maybe he didn't. Bryce didn't care. Right now he just wanted to get on his bike and ride.

There was more traffic, pedestrian and otherwise, than he'd ever seen. Through the window at Coop's he'd seen an actual line at the register. The Pizza Wizard was full and it wasn't just kids from school.

More trucks full of Halloween paraphernalia were parked along the street. A banner proclaiming WELCOME TO HELLDORADO DAYS! was being hoisted over the intersection of Front Street and Katie Avenue.

The sounds were good. Laughter, music. Families calling

their various members together. People were happy. But things weren't exactly right, were they?

He glanced over his shoulder at Coop's. The codgers were there, but they weren't playing. They were staring at the tourists, who were staring at them and taking pictures from a distance as if the codgers were caged wildlife.

They feel it too.

Bryce wanted to ride over and talk to them. It would almost be a relief to know that maybe not everybody in town shared Bill Jordan's optimism. *Because something is wrong here.* And it wasn't Rose Bowman's doing this time. And there wasn't any gold rolling out of the Wizard. For just a second, when that little boy's sudden motion in the drugstore had caught his attention, Bryce had seen something much worse than mischief in the kid's eyes. For a split second, he thought he'd seen a monster.

In the end, he didn't talk to the codgers and he didn't see Gordon, either. He just kept going, because getting out of town was suddenly important, the way breaking through that silvery blue surface was more important than lifting the last penny off a swimming pool floor.

There were people on Cross Hill taking pictures and nosing around the markers. Not one of them was taking any notice at all of the grave just east of the fence. One hundred years later and Rose Bowman was still an outcast.

Tourists climbed the narrow path up to the Wizard. From where Bryce was, they looked like ants lazily picking at the corpse of a larger insect, the better parts of which had already been scavenged.

At the juncture of Katie and Sluice, he passed a group of little kids heading into town. They looked blankly up at him and said nothing as he passed. He rode by and didn't look back.

He was afraid they'd be staring.

E V E N in the lean times, Trevor's work had never been like this.

As an artist, he'd always known there was a wellspring inside him. He'd tapped it before, but never bared it.

There was a good reason for this: that wellspring had a lot to deal with. The same essence that captured light and shadow, transforming life into art, also told the legs to walk, the body to feed itself. So it was seldom tapped for long periods, because doing so was dangerous—dangerous for the mortal, physical self that raised families, found work, and paid bills.

His talent was no greater than it had been, but now the fear was gone. He hadn't tapped the well with a spigot, he'd ripped it wide with an axe and drenched himself in the floodwaters.

He stood in them now. His hands had never been so closely linked to his heart and eyes and mind. He thought it, and the brushes made it real.

His eyes blurred. He stood back, closing them for a moment. That was all the rest the mortal coil would get. Refreshed, he began again. And so what if those hands that held the brushes showed more odd ridges and lumpy veins now than they had yesterday? Creation was destruction, hadn't he always said so? Marble was worried and chipped into sculptures; stones were crushed for their pigments, trees rended for the wood and turpentine that became his paintings.

And there had never been a painting quite like this one.

T H E fire was burning at Aggie's house. A round puff of gray-white smoke lay above the roof like a fat housecat.

Bryce parked his bike at the gate and walked up the juniper-bordered path. He could hear piano music playing softly inside. Once on the porch, he took a deep breath. He couldn't help feeling that Aggie knew more than she'd let on. But that wasn't the only reason he was here.

It was the second reason that made it hard to ring the bell: Aggie would come to the door, probably dressed in nothing but that robe again. He really just wanted to see Aggie. Needed to see her. He pressed the bell and watched through the turquoise circles.

A door closed inside, and then her pink-and-white form danced in the glass.

Sure enough, she had the robe on.

"Bryce. I was wondering when you'd remember your pants."

He hadn't given them a thought.

"You caught me in formal attire once again. I'm doing double duty today. We're taking turns modeling," she said as they crossed the den.

His eyes landed on her nude statue. He shouldn't be here.

"How's that report coming?"

He swallowed hard.

"Good, it's coming along good."

Her smile said she saw right through him. He hoped his face wasn't blazing. She didn't seem to care anyway.

"There's coffee in the studio. Grab a cup in the kitchen if you'd like. Middle cupboard."

It finally dawned on him she'd said she was modeling. Andre must be here. His hopes deflated.

"I don't want to interrupt. I mean, you know, if you're doing something."

"You're welcome to watch—if you promise to be a gentleman, that is. You're used to having models around, right?"

He nodded, maybe too broadly. This could actually be very cool.

"Yeah, sure. Dad has models over all the time." That was only a partial lie. His dad used live models from time to time, but Bryce wasn't allowed in the studio if they weren't dressed. *And that's what she was talking about, wasn't it?* And this wouldn't be like seeing some model he didn't know. *This would be Aggie.* This day was turning out totally unreal.

She brushed by him in the hall. Linseed oil mixed with the earthy aroma of clay and another, sweeter scent—honeysuckle.

"Let me find your jeans and I'll be right back."

Aggie disappeared somewhere in the house.

He found a cup and nearly dropped it.

The piano music was coming from the studio. Liz Story. His dad played her while he painted sometimes, when he wasn't playing Buffalo Springfield. Bryce ambled toward the sound, somewhat dazed.

The door had opened just a crack. He pushed it gently and the music grew louder. His jaw went slack as he swung the door the rest of the way.

The modeling stage was occupied.

"Hi, Bryce."

Connie sat among the wooden blocks. Her lips smiled at him, but her eyes were focused ten miles beyond. A cigarette dangled from her hand. She was nude.

He almost fell backward into the hall. When he found his legs beneath him, he turned and bolted out the front door.

T H E R E were no stars outside his window, just an even blue-gray sky.

Bryce nudged the letter across his desk with his pen. He'd been writing to his mom for two hours. Every fear and disappointment from the day they'd arrived was in that letter, from Bigfoot and the shotgun all the way to Aggie and Connie. He'd gone from sensory overload to shock. Now he felt like they'd scooped out the gray stuff and lined his skull with dry cotton.

He pushed himself away from the desk and checked the hall.

White light spilled from beneath the studio door. He tried the door, but it was locked.

"Dad?"

Stephen Stills was all he heard from the other side. He gave up without a fight this time. Meg's door was closed. There was a time he wouldn't have thought twice about knocking. It was this town that was weird, not Meg. It should have been he and Meg against Piñon Rim. But it didn't feel that way.

Cathleen had been up a little while ago. He'd heard her cleaning up in the kitchen, but outside of Stephen Stills, there wasn't a sound from anywhere in the house.

He'd tried his mom's number twice without luck. It was pretty late for her to be out, and all the raw and twisted feelings inside him twisted a little tighter at that.

Bryce went back to his room and threw the letter in his wastebasket. A minute later, he pulled it out.

He looked at the spot on the wall where he had heard voices.

Joe Montana smiled from the *Sports Illustrated* cover he'd tacked over it.

Shutting his door, Bryce turned out the light and stared at the gray light filtering through the frosted window. He never wanted to see Connie again. Bill Jordan was right. Connie and her screwy Aunt Rose were bad news. *Aggie too.*

He wished he was back in New York.

More than anything, he wished his mom would call.

20

T H E Y ' D really done a job on the cafeteria.

Spooky effects thumped, creaked, and shrieked from twin Marshall stacks at the far end. On a stage behind the stacks, Freddy Krueger jockeyed records and growled a monster rap, flicking strobe lights when thunder boomed. The stage held half a dozen barrel-sized jack-o'-lanterns. Dozens of smaller lit and smiling jacks were parked on tables from one end of the cafeteria to the other. The whole place smelled of roasting pumpkin.

A tent of orange and black streamers climbed high into the rafters, where a revolving mirrored ball skimmed bright orange UFOs along the walls and across the painted faces below. Ghouls and goblins dangled from the halfcourt hoops. A tall, blow-up Dracula floated above the main doorway, his arms raised to snatch unwary victims.

Near the kitchen, a huge papier mâché wizard in flowing star-covered robes held a threatening, dagger-fingered hand above the crowd. Two gigantic cauldrons squatted beneath him. A witch with a face full of warts and a carrot nose—with that stiff posture, it had to be Principal Curtis—stirred them with a large wooden spoon. She cackled as she ladled out hot chocolate and cider to a crowd of giggling little kids who gingerly held their cups out to her. The only other teacher Bryce could easily recognize, even behind the hockey mask, was his algebra teacher, Mr. Perkins. Perkins was the only teacher massive enough to carry off Jason Voorhees, although Bryce was pretty sure the real Jason never had a beer belly—even near the start of the series, when there was more Jason to be scared of.

Bryce's metallic Terminator hadn't happened, so he'd pulled out the trenchcoat and hat and opted for Dick Tracy. It wasn't the greatest, but he'd seen two flattops already, so he didn't feel like a total loser.

Cody and Chuck were dancing with a black cat and a ghost near the stage. He laughed at Cody, who really had dressed like an Indian chief with a full headdress and warpaint, an effect somewhat destroyed by his dark sunglasses. Bryce had no idea how Cody could see. Chuck's blond hair had been spiked up with something shiny and gross enough to be Vaseline. The crude, uneven black circles he'd painted around his eyes were already running from the sweat. Bryce wasn't sure what the hell Chuck was supposed to be.

"Call me Richard!" Cody yelled. The black cat waved and shimmied, and Bryce could see the cat was Peggy Schroeder, whom Cody had supposedly felt up once. The ghost was draped head-to-toe in sheets, but it was definitely Cathy Hintze's voice that called his name. Bryce flicked the hood up over her head. Her eyes and cheeks were black with greasy makeup. She blew him a kiss.

"Back off, man!" Chuck said.

"What the heck are you?"

"Bart Simpson!"

It was a stretch.

Peggy rubbed up against Bryce, catlike, and he could feel himself go red. There was a light but definite smell of alcohol mixed with green Life Savers.

"Hiiiii . . . Dick," she purred with every bit as much raunchy emphasis on the name as Madonna doing Breathless Mahoney. "Aren'tya gonna 'rest me?"

Cody pulled up his beaded vest. On the T-shirt beneath he'd very deftly drawn what, at first glance, looked like a nose with legs and running shoes.

"Whoa!"

"Did you see Cindy Westman? She's Axl Rose!"

"Yeah," Chuck said, "but she wussed out. She's wearing a body suit."

"No guts at all," Peggy said.

"It's hot in here." Cathy flipped her hood back.

Freddy Krueger switched to MC Hammer's "Pray," and Chuck and Peggy mimicked all the moves.

Bryce stepped out of the way. Everyone else was dancing. The flu was over. Life in Piñon Rim was back to normal. He didn't see Connie. He couldn't remember wanting to see someone and not wanting to see someone so bad at the same time.

"If you're looking for Bowman, she's not here." Cody spun on his heels. "We're gonna get something to drink—you guys want?"

They shouted their orders over the stomping bass, and Cody and Bryce cut across the dance floor.

"They won't let Matt in," Cody said. "No Matt, no Connie." His shrug meant it wasn't a great loss. He slipped between a pretty decent Phantom of the Opera and a girl named Janice-something who was dressed in silver lamé with antennas like some sort of alien, and Bryce followed. "They're probably at Helldorado already."

"Yeah."

"Forget her, kimosabe. Babe's bad news."

"Yeah."

"But what do I know?"

"Jack. You know jack. You're a freaking dipshit. What's up with Jason?"

"He's okay. He's a Ninja Turtle—Raphael, Leonardo, I don't know which one."

"I don't think it matters."

"You kidding? It's religion to those freaks."

The best Axl Rose Bryce could imagine passed right in front of them, and Cody slapped her butt. That drew a disapproving look from a tall scarecrow standing against the near wall.

"Axl!"

"Running Nose, my man!" Cody and Cindy slapped palms, and Cindy Westman slugged Bryce's shoulder. "Tracy! Tracy!

214

Tracy!'' She was a big girl and nearly knocked him off his feet. ''Gotta go.''

She snaked off through the crowd.

''That was frightening.''

''She's for real.''

They stepped in behind a bunch of little kids at the cauldrons. The wizard loomed over them. Whoever built the Wizard had left his eyes white, and Bryce tried hard not to see that blind Indian woman in them. It gave him a chill anyway. The spotlights flared and the wizard's eyes glowed a burnt orange. When Bryce turned away, two blue dots followed everything he looked at.

''Anyway, Jason's okay. He had the flu, but he's over it now.''

Cody had dropped his sunglasses over his eyes again. Bryce tried to see past them, but it was too dark.

''How's little sis?''

''Meg's okay.''

Cody nodded.

''Is she here?''

''Somewhere.''

They'd ridden all the way from the Big House in silence. After Cathleen had dropped them off, Meg had split to be with the little kids. That shouldn't have seemed strange, but it did. Bryce wasn't certain where the magical line was drawn, but he was pretty sure Meg had crossed it. Meg wasn't a little kid anymore.

Principal Curtis cackled a greeting and praised the wholesomeness of their costumes as she measured out their drinks. Apparently Axl Rose hadn't set well with the faculty. (Bryce would have given ten bucks for Cody to flip up his vest just then.) They thanked her and somehow managed to juggle the cups back through the dancers without spilling too much.

Bryce looked for Meg's lantern helmet in the crowd—she'd dressed as a caver, to the surprise of no one—as he danced first with Cathy, then Peggy. But he never did see it.

He wondered what Connie and Matt were doing, even though he knew that was a bad idea.

She'd been totally naked that day at Aggie's.

He hadn't talked to her since. The weird thing was *totally naked* was exactly how he'd wanted to see her from the git-go. *But not like that.* Not there with Aggie. Models got naked all the time. Maybe it was the way she'd looked at him, the way she hadn't tried to cover up or anything. Like she knew he'd be there or she didn't care anyway.

He was an idiot. He should have just sat back and enjoyed the view.

Cody and Chuck were having a great time. The scarecrow, who had revealed himself as Mr. Regis, the world history teacher, had come by twice with warnings about their "manner of dancing." Bryce could see him now, throwing an icy scarecrow stare Cindy Westman's way. Peggy and Chuck were getting pretty chummy now. Cody and Cathy were doing some sort of bump thing, practically knocking each other over. He guessed the scarecrow would be back.

Bryce found his cup under a chair near the door and let the last chocolate dregs slide down his throat. It had already gone cold, but it tasted okay. A particularly frigid blast of air hit him as two kids pushed their way in, and Bryce was glad for the lined trenchcoat.

Still no sign of Meg. He hadn't seen Jason, either.

"You wanna dance?"

It was Janice-something.

"Sure." He crushed the cup and pitched it at a huge rubber wastecan that was already overflowing. Freddy Krueger flicked the strobe and the whole room went into stop-motion. Across the room, the wizard's eyes flashed.

Cody flipped him a thumbs-up.

Janice turned out to be a great dancer. After their first dance he quit looking for Meg and Connie altogether. Two more and he was actually enjoying himself. Piñon Rim and its eternal woes began to slip away into the depths where yesterday's dreams go. It was the first dance of the year and he was in eighth grade. Top of the heap.

They joined up with the others after two more dances and

another hot chocolate. Then the thunder roared, the mirrored ball stopped, and the lights flashed.

"Boys and ghouls!" Freddy growled. "Prepare to follow the lights. *It's Helldorado time!*"

The cafeteria roared with hoots and whistles. Billy Idol's craggy voice boomed, "Rock the cradle of love!" Anticipation was hot and sharp as a buzz-saw blade as they danced their last dance.

"*H E L L! Do-ra-do!*"

The cheer exploded around them. Nobody wasted the chance to swear in front of grown-ups with impunity. As they marched toward town, the kids at the vanguard threw their hands high into the air, dropped them, and turned to watch the wave progress. It carried all the way through the stragglers and that prompted more laughter, hoots, and shouts.

"Hell! Do-ra-do!"

It had turned cold, really cold, but nobody cared. The warnings about snow hadn't fallen on deaf ears, and it was funny to see ghouls and goblins and all sorts of oddities too bizarre to identify tramping along in fluorescent ski jackets and boots. They bunched together for warmth. Chuck was definitely taking advantage of that situation. From the corner of his eye Bryce could see Chuck's ski glove clenched firmly over the left breast of Peggy's jacket. Bryce walked arm in arm with Janice, Cathy with Cody, who had his glasses up over his headdress. Cody was watching Chuck with interest. He glanced Bryce's way and they both laughed. There was no way Chuck could be getting anything through all that goose down.

"What's so funny?" Janice squealed.

"Nothing," Cody said, and Bryce echoed him, then they started laughing so hard Bryce's stomach hurt.

"Hell! Do-ra-do!"

Bryce felt like lightning ready to flash. Ever since he'd gotten sick, everything had seemed so off and so serious. *This was freaking great.* He threw back his head and howled and laughed and even went so far as to squeeze Janice. He felt even higher when she returned the hug.

Their breath cast smoky plumes into the night. The path was lined with flickering orange pumpkins all the way to Front Street. Dumpling-thick clouds rimmed with moonlight floated above the wide valley, and here and there moonbeams broke through, streaking the odd, bell-shaped peaks behind town with blue fire. Colored lights flooded the streets, and the irregular, blocky facades along Front Street and Katie Avenue looked like the toothy maw of a gigantic, glowing jack-o'-lantern.

On Cross Hill a single floodlight staked above the paths made the white cross flare eerily. As they passed below, something flashed in the blackness beyond the floodlight and Bryce strained to look.

"Pretty weird, isn't it?" Janice's face was inches away, but she still had to shout to be heard.

"Do people really go up there Halloween night?"

She rolled her eyes.

"After they check out Front Street."

"Hey, *it's the thing*," Cody said. "Don't even *think* you're wussin' out."

"After a while the chaperones'll thin out," Chuck said. "Past their bedtime."

"I think it's gross," Cathy said from beneath her hood. "I mean the graves are real. They don't bury people there anymore, but they used to."

"I like the Wizard better," Peggy hollered back at them.

"It's a hike."

"Yeah, but you can always find someone from Red Ridge at Helldorado. They drive up the back."

"Yeah. You can always get a ride," Janice said.

Bryce was blown away. Every now and then during a dance at Saint Andrews (if no one was looking) you might get to cop a feel. But it was rare. He'd never imagined a world where the whole process would be organized. Public school was great.

They trotted down the hill and trudged up a steeper one. It was a saddle in the road he liked to whiz up and down on the Stingray. It was strange walking it, watching the town yawn slowly open above them. He got that image of Piñon Rim as a jack-o'-lantern again, its jaw swinging wide to swallow them all. Suddenly a feeling of dread hit him so cold and absolute that, for just a second, his muscles froze.

He was jerked forward by the others and nearly fell. They were under the banner he'd watched the workman hauling up last Friday at the intersection of Front and Katie: WELCOME TO HELLDORADO DAYS!

Above it was another banner with a depiction of a wizard just like the one in the cafeteria. This one's eyes were white too. It made him think of his dreamwalk to Meg's room, of seeing Meg almost grown up, just sitting there with little, dead Boyd Easton.

Her eyes were glowing . . .

Janice and Cody were laughing, trying to pull him along. He stopped and other kids piled right into them; they all nearly fell. *The laughter and hoots around him distorted, until they seemed to knit into one long and blood-curdling scream.*

"I gotta find my sister."

"She's okay. The place is lousy with faculty," Cody said.

"You guys go ahead."

They pulled off to the side and let the crowd go on.

"You all right?"

"Yeah. I haven't seen her all night. I mean she's just a kid."

Cody's sunglasses were back in place.

"There's two hundred kids here. They're all fine."

"Let him go," Janice said. "If you're worried about her you should find her. See the Haunted House back there?"

Front Street was totally decked out. Huge jack-o'-lanterns burned at odd intervals above the walkways, sending ghoulish shadows across the facades. Scarecrows stood at each post on the walkways, surrounded by stalks of Indian corn. The streets had been roped off to all but foot traffic, and gaming tables and refreshment stands sat in the middle of the road, manned by Old West gunslingers and saloon belles. Soiled doves stood on the roof of the boardwalk and solicited their wares. Screaming kids in colorful costumes and jackets ran back and forth between the stands, dragging bags of candy half their size.

At the far end of Front Street, a huge new facade had been erected. Ghosts with cowboy hats and blazing six-guns battled one another from the second story. A gigantic wizard with pointed hat and white, sightless eyes had been painted across the front. The wizard's gaping mouth was the entrance and kids were already massing around it. Janice pointed at the house.

"That's where we'll be. If you don't see us, wait out front; we usually go through it two or three times. It's pretty radical."

Bryce nodded. Cody mumbled that he should let Meg fend for herself. Chuck and Peggy were oblivious. Cathy was already halfway up the street getting a cup of hot chocolate.

Bryce felt stupid as he watched them go. Meg had been getting along pretty well. There had to be a rule chiseled in stone somewhere that said he wasn't allowed to have a good time. Why was he worried? Cathleen wasn't worried. She'd seen Meg run off with the little kids and she had just waved and driven off.

He watched the kids go by, but he didn't see a freaking lantern helmet anywhere. He'd been feeling good, better than he had since they'd moved here. Why did he have to shepherd Meg? Meg finally had friends at school. That was good. He'd had those nightmares when he was sick, but they didn't mean anything except that the fever was high. Kids laughed as they ran past. Everyone was having a great time.

But that scream . . .

Kids were screaming all through town, but this had been different. The white cross blazed up on Cross Hill. He watched the Haunted House gobble up his friends. Why didn't the Wizard have eyes?

The last of the stragglers passed him. He'd missed her. She must have left the dance early and walked to town with the other kids. He looked up Front Street, then back toward the school, and wondered what to do next.

"Problems?"

It was Mr. Perkins, alias Jason Voorhees.

"Have you seen my sister, Megan Willems?"

"Little dark-haired girl, dressed like a miner?"

"Yeah, something like that."

220

"She left with the first troupe. I haven't seen her since then, but hold on. Fred!"

Mr. Joyal, dressed as Batman, waved from across the street. He trotted up, much more pigeon-toed and knock-kneed than Bryce remembered Batman being.

"You seen the Willems girl? Miner?"

"Caver," Bryce corrected.

"Hardhat with the light? Cute kid. Yeah. Hi, Bryce."

"Hi, Mr. Joyal."

"Your sister's been in and out of the Haunted House a couple times. Haven't seen her for a while, though. She'll turn up. Whataya think, Hank? We got it pretty well covered."

"Haven't lost one yet. We'll keep an eye out."

"Thanks. If you see her, let her know I'm looking, okay?"

"You got it. Hank, you see that Niners' game?"

"Hell, without Montana . . ."

Well, that was that. She'd left early. No big deal. No worries. He looked back over his shoulder as he trotted toward the Haunted House, his yellow trenchcoat flapping behind him. It was sort of fun watching Batman and Jason Voorhees discuss football.

He almost didn't see the little kids on the walkway. They were Meg's age, maybe younger. While everyone else laughed and screamed and ran from booth to booth, they stood at the end of the boardwalk and watched, their faces hidden behind Ninja Turtles and Dracula and Snow White.

T H E shrieks were deafening.

By the end of their third run through the Haunted House, Cody's headdress had been plucked down to two broken feathers and Janice had only one antenna. Bryce's hat was crushed beyond recognition, but he didn't care. It was too much fun running, half-rolling over the mattress-covered floors, trying to keep away from the ghouls.

The dining room was the best. It had a long table set with all manner of meaty fare: plates full of hands and feet (two or three actually moving), an arm on a bed of cockroaches and weeds. A waiter with an open gash running from his right ear to his left collarbone lifted two casserole warmers, revealing a screaming head beneath each. Other ghouls dressed like cooks scuttled about carrying various gruesomely prepared body parts. Others, wielding humongous pieces of cutlery, chased the kids toward a blood-spattered door marked DEVIL's KITCHEN. The kitchen was a long, dark room where rubbery, wet unimaginables hung at face level from the ceiling. The Devil's Kitchen was Janice's least favorite part of the Haunted House, and she screamed bloody murder as they pushed her through.

Outside, they plopped themselves down on bales of straw. Screams came in waves from inside, the dark *thump-thump* of the heart beat through the canvas walls.

"Too cool!"

"Do it again?"

"God, take a break! I gotta rest!"

Cody lay full-length across a bale. "Anybody hungry?"

"Yeah, right."

"No—really. I could eat something."

"Pizza?" Chuck suggested.

"You're sick."

"Red, meaty, sausage pizza?"

"That's way gross."

"Pizza Wizard's open. They just take the sign down for Helldorado."

"God, there's a million things to eat out here," Cathy said. "Why pizza tonight?"

"Yeah. I could go for some of that fried bread." Janice plopped herself down on a pile of straw next to the bale where Bryce sat. She blew a puff of white frost into the air.

"They got cake and stuff at that booth by Ned's."

"Anybody thirsty?" Peggy said quietly. "Bryce?"

"Yeah, what the heck, I'll have some."

"Twist the arm. Twist the arm."

"Follow me."

They crept into the shadows past the walkway and darted into the alley behind Coop's. They hurried by a place that smelled like the cafeteria outflow pipe and hid upwind by a stairway.

The sky was a moonless, charcoal gray. The smell of fried bread and hot pumpkin from Front Street mingled with the scent of evergreen, and there was another scent coming through, a scent something like new rain and yet something all its own. Bryce knew it would snow before the night was over.

Peggy looked up and down the alley, satisfied herself the chaperones were elsewhere, and unzipped a black boda bag from the lining of her jacket. She took a sip, munched a Life Saver, and handed the bottle to Bryce. Whatever it was tasted awful, and the traces of sweet synthetic fruit around the mouthpiece didn't help. But it was warming. He'd had wine before, and occasionally his dad had let him sip beer, but this was a lot stronger. He took another, longer drink and held out the bottle, but Peggy stepped back into the darkness beneath the stairs.

"Come here," she said.

He did, and she pressed herself tightly against him.

He'd been wrong about Chuck before: you really could feel breasts through a down jacket.

She kissed him full and very wet on the lips. Then something happened he'd only heard about before. Her tongue slid into his mouth. It was sweet and warm and maybe just a little too strange to get totally excited over, but he felt a definite rush.

"Whoa," he said, when it was over.

"Don't you like it?"

He guessed he did. She felt good, but the whole thing was so weird. He kissed her back, clumsily, without the tongue thing, and she giggled.

"Sorry," he said. His head felt like it was floating off by itself.

"It's okay."

She squeezed him and kissed him again. Then she released him and they headed out of the alley.

So that was sex. Well, that was all right. That could be fun.

Chuck was sitting on a straw bale choking down a wedge of pizza as they swung back onto Front Street. Cathy and Cody were just coming back with cake and hot chocolate. Janice stopped eating her fried bread and stomped her foot when she saw them. Cody and Chuck broke into hysterics.

"*Peggy!*" Janice's broken antenna bobbed angrily.

"Mr. Smooth!" Cody said. He made a "safe" sign with his cake.

Bryce wiped his face and his hand came away covered with black cat paint.

"God, Janice, have a cow why don't you." Peggy sat next to Chuck, who offered her a chunk of his pizza, which she said was gross and pushed away.

Cody handed Bryce a square of cake. It was the best darn piece of chocolate cake with orange icing and chocolate sprinkles that Bryce had ever tasted, and he told them all so.

"No more boda for Bryce," Cathy said, and they all laughed.

Peggy tossed Bryce a Life Saver. It bounced off his chest and onto a straw bale. Just as he popped it into his mouth, Freddy Krueger walked around the back of the Haunted House.

"Hi, Mr. Hicks," Peggy said, and the others followed suit. Peggy's hand made a nervous sweep up her jacket where the boda bag was hidden.

"Hi, kids. Just wanted to let you know some of the chaperones are going home. We'll need you to keep an eye on the little people."

"No problem," Cody said.

"Under control," Peggy said.

"Great. Well, you all have a Happy Halloween!"

"Thanks, Mr. Hicks."

"Happy Halloween!"

"Happy Helldorado!"

He left and Janice giggled.

"That was close."

Another group tumbled out, screaming and laughing.

"Hi, Peggy!" one of them said. It was Cindy Parker, dressed like a Pepsi can.

The guy with her had on a musketeer outfit that must have been rented. He was an older guy, probably from Red Ridge. Bryce didn't recognize him.

"Chuckie, great costume!" the Red Ridge guy said, then added, "Not!"

"Willis, you're so *amaaaazingly* cool," Chuck returned. "Not!"

Cody twisted off his last feather and held it at arm's length. He brought it to his nose and back again. "Well, what now?" he asked.

"Check out the games?" Janice said.

"It's the usual stuff. I say we hit Cross Hill." Chuck crushed his paper plate and smoked it into a nearby trash barrel.

Janice glanced at Bryce. "Bryce hasn't seen the rest of it."

Bryce was looking past her, staring into the lights or beyond.

"Earth to Bryce. Time to land," Peggy teased.

Whatever was in Peggy's magic bag had hit a long fly ball. For a second, Bryce had seen himself sitting and staring off, just the way they had. He'd totally zoned out.

"What?"

They all laughed.

"All right, don't ask Bryce," Peggy said. "*I* say one last blast through the Haunted House and then split for the boneyard."

"I'm open," Bryce said.

"Glad we settled that," Cody said.

They jumped to their feet at once, forming an impromptu huddle inside the bales.

"One! Last! *Time!*"

They broke huddle and raced around to the front of the Haunted House. Janice pulled Bryce along behind her.

They gathered at the wizard's mouth and waited for another group to make it through the first room. Then they plunged in.

It was as if someone had cranked up all the levels. Screams were louder. So was the *thump-thump* of the heartbeat. They ran faster, the ghouls ran faster, the terrified laughter and the music rose, pumped to concert pitch.

Bryce lost his balance and fell flat on his face in the Polka-Dot Room. The floor was covered with wrestling mats on top of what must have been partially inflated inner tubes. Black lights strobed the walls and ceiling, which were painted Day-Glo orange and green and covered with a zillion black dots of every size. The ghouls who chased them had painted faces and wore body suits dotted to match the walls. You could hardly see them at all. They were just hands and arms that seemed to appear from nowhere. Janice screeched and made a grab for Bryce as he tried, unsuccessfully, to roll to his feet. Then she was rushed away by more polka-dot-covered creatures. Bryce was laughing and screaming so hard he was practically in tears. Every time he gained a little purchase, the ghouls would bump him just enough to floor him. The strobe lights had him totally disoriented. His stomach started to roll.

Oh God, don't lose it. Don't get sick now.

Another group of kids was already rushing through. He was still tumbling out of control, and the ghouls were laughing now too. Finally, one actually tried to help him up and they both went down. He was starting to feel like a total fool, but he couldn't stop laughing and he really was starting to feel nauseated. His head was spinning from the strobe. And then, through the movieola flashes, *he saw Connie.* True to form, she was dressed in Old West bordello getup like her beloved Aunt Rose. She smiled as their eyes met, but at least she wasn't laughing at him. And, best of all, Matt Connors wasn't with her.

Just that quick, she was gone.

Bryce made it to his feet, stumbled toward the doorway, and missed.

He was on solid ground but in total darkness. He'd missed the door and gone right through one of the canvas walls. The screams and the laughter and the music were all around him. He was between rooms, in one of the tunnels the ghouls used to get from chamber to chamber. In a way, it was a relief. He'd been in that polka-dot place with the freaking strobe light way too long. He took a moment to let his stomach settle.

A light crackled to life. Connie was standing right in front of him.

"God!"

The light went out.

"You scared . . ."

226

She opened a flap of canvas and light spilled out as she stepped into the next room.

His heart raced. Goose bumps flared over his entire body. She was getting back at him for running away. But she didn't have to scare him like that. He followed her, frightened and angry.

Bloody waiters carried their ghoulish entrées around the tables filled with glistening gore. They were in the dining room. Kids screamed and ran, chased by the cooks with their outrageous knives. Connie walked on through as if it was a stroll in the park. Two cooks ran at Bryce and he sidestepped and ducked them both. It wasn't scary *or* funny anymore. All he wanted to do was catch up with Connie and ask her what the big idea was. Another cook came at him and Bryce spun off.

Connie stopped and knelt by the door where a girl sat among the meat and mannequin parts that were apparently part of today's menu. Like Connie, she was dressed in saloon belle clothes, but she was soaked with blood. One arm ended in a mangled, bloody mass just below her elbow. They'd gone all out to make it look real. The rubber organs and assorted mannequin parts on the tables looked totally weak by contrast, but kids rushed by the girl like it was no big thing. Connie put her arms around the girl, and Bryce grabbed her shoulder. Connie turned quickly. Her dress was torn and black with soot, and now it was covered with blood too. She stared at him, wide-eyed, as if he were from another planet. Then she screamed.

It was a scream from the pit of the soul, as if every breath a person takes in a lifetime, every sigh and laugh and cry had been twisted into one agonized wail. And from wherever you go when shock takes you away, Bryce realized that *he'd heard that scream before*. He'd heard it tonight while walking into town, only it had been far away then.

And he'd heard it in his dream.

Bryce had the sensation of falling, of watching himself drop down a bottomless well. Something stopped him.

"Come on, man. We've been out there forever! Babes are gonna split."

It was Cody and Chuck. They pushed him through the

Devil's Kitchen, with its hanging garden of grisly dark fruit, and out into the cold night air.

"What was that all about?"

"Had to get you, man. Thought they ate you or something."

"No, I mean, Connie screaming. Why did she scream?"

"Didn't hear her," Cody said.

He looked at Chuck. Chuck shrugged. "Didn't even see her."

"You guys are full of it. I'm still shaking." He was. And he knew why, but somewhere in his head a steel door had slammed shut before he could peek around the corner and see the answer full on.

"Who cares? We gotta book if we're gonna do this thing." Cody pointed a broken feather toward the floodlights at the end of the boardwalk. You couldn't see a foot past them. "We're in a good place to make a break—if we don't all go at once. You get by that light and nobody's gonna know about it."

Hadn't Bill Jordan said so? Good old Bill Jordan. Bryce kept his eye on the Haunted House exit. Another group of kids came shrieking out. Connie wasn't one of them.

Janice stood next to Bryce.

"Okay. Here's the way it goes," Cody said. "Nobody can see us here behind the Haunted House, but there's about fifteen feet or so between the end of the house and those lights that's totally open. The old farts on the Slipper are lookouts, and you know they're gonna be looking this way most the time because it's the best way out."

"One thing we got going is that they're playing up the gun-fights and the soiled dove thing," Chuck said.

"Yeah, and the other thing is they basically don't care—if we're not totally obvious."

"What about going the other way? You know, toward town, and circling back?" Janice said.

"You can do that too. They're not gonna stop you from going home. If you go one street over you can get past the lights, but it takes a while."

"And they can see you from the top of the Lucky Slipper."

"They might."

"I say go for the lights."

"We need a lookout."

"I'll do it," Peggy said.

"Too obvious. If *you* do it they'll know exactly what we're doing."

"Up yours."

"Janice, you do it, okay?"

She looked at Bryce, but he wasn't sure what she wanted.

"Okay. I'll do this when it looks good." She flicked two fingers toward the lights.

"Great. Everybody go all the way to the bottom of the wash behind the Slipper, and don't stand by the lights or the walkway or we'll all get caught."

Janice drifted toward the end of the boardwalk, near the spot where Peggy had first slipped away with Bryce. She leaned against a post and pulled her antenna the rest of the way off. She pretended to mend it while she watched the rooftops.

Another group came screaming out of the Haunted House, and as they trotted toward the Pizza Wizard, Janice signaled. Chuck and Peggy were first. When they passed the lights it was as if they'd dropped off the end of the earth.

Cathy went on the next signal. She slipped and nearly fell in a flutter of sheets, and it was a miracle she got away at all. Cody smacked his forehead with his palm. Once she'd disappeared behind the lights, he laughed and muttered something in Navajo. He flipped his sunglasses back.

"You wanna go next?"

"Go for it."

Another group poured out the back of the Haunted House. Janice signaled, and Cody sprinted past the lights so fast it made Bryce's floating head spin as well. He watched Janice from a slightly unstable three-point stance.

"Hi, Bryce."

It was Connie. She wasn't dressed like Rose Bowman.

She wore a medieval white headdress with a huge blue jewel in the center. Charms and talismans hung from her wrists and throat. He guessed she was supposed to be some sort of sorceress, maybe Morgana or something. Every hair on his body was standing on end. He saw himself in his dream, thinking he'd

229

been making out with Connie and all the while kissing Rose. Then that steel door slammed again and the connection shut down completely. It didn't happen. *He never saw Rose Bowman in the Haunted House.* He never saw anyone.

Connie, *not Rose*, was draped all over Matt Connors. She was the best part of his costume, which consisted of Levi's and an expensive-looking green-and-black ski jacket. A Cheerios box with a knife handle sticking out hung from a belt that was slung over his shoulder: cereal killer, ha-ha. Probably thought that up all by himself too. Without his sunglasses, his eyes were close together and small, like one of those English bull-terriers. Bryce's first impulse was to put his fist between them. Then Connie put her arms around Matt's neck and kissed him, and Bryce felt something tear loose inside.

Janice was signaling frantically; her foot was poised, ready to stomp. Bryce took off for the lights, very aware of the cold, dull slap of the silver dragon on his breastbone as he ran. He didn't look back till he'd passed the lights, and when he did, it was as if through a damp and heavy fog. Connie and Matt were gone.

"A T least the snakes won't come out." Chuck remarked.

They huddled together as they walked, cold but undaunted. Behind them, Piñon Rim was still laughing and playing music and glowing pumpkin orange. The great white namesake of Cross Hill rose dead ahead.

This is crazy. They were actually hiking to a cemetery through the tangled scrub north of town. They were doing this close to midnight under the dull glow of an overcast sky. A gentle snow was falling. It wasn't sticking yet, but it would. To Bryce's right, Cody hummed softly as they walked, probably not aware that he was.

They were walking to a graveyard. The same one where Rose Bowman was buried.

Yea, though I walk through the Valley of Death . . .

Rose Bowman, whom he'd just seen walking through the Helldorado Haunted House. No. *He hadn't seen that.* His mind clamped shut once again. *But he had seen Connie reach up and kiss*

Matt right there in front of him. And there was no steel door to swing shut on that one. That was his heart, not his mind. There were worse things than fear.

They weren't the only ones making the trek to Cross Hill. Bryce could make out other small groups off to either side. They all took care to stay clear of the floodlight.

Bryce walked in silence, letting himself by hypnotized by the dull, anesthetic mechanics of walking. It would work for a while, but then he'd see Connie's arms wrapped around Matt's neck. He didn't even want to know how long that image of Connie would be with him. He had a vague idea it might be forever.

The ground sloped upward. Above them, the dark monuments and rectangular mounds of Cross Hill Cemetery rose through the scrub like the bombed-out ruins of some forbidden city. The Wizard loomed over all, its crudely boarded mouth still seeming to cry out.

Chuck lifted a strand of barbed wire that had *tetanus* written all over it, and Bryce stepped into the ancient graveyard. As soon as his foot touched the other side, he felt a chill that had nothing at all to do with the falling temperature.

This was no garden-green, exquisitely manicured monument to peace and tranquility. If the facades on Front Street were a nostalgic snapshot of better times, the wretchedly preserved Cross Hill Cemetery was the grimmest possible reminder of the worst.

They stood among the haphazard and violent arrangement of rock-pile graves, some of which were "protected" by wicked-looking wrought-iron fences, now badly bent and rusted. *This place gets girls hot?* It looked bad enough in daylight, when you saw the whole picture as overwhelmingly bleak. But the shadowless glow at night made you focus in on subtleties right there next to you: the way a lot of mounds had eroded, leaving frightening gaps; the tufts of whip grass and sage that had taken root; and the small, suspicious-looking tunnels near them.

"What snakes?" Bryce found himself saying, suddenly remembering Chuck's comment.

"Rattlesnakes, coral snakes," Chuck said. "It's too cold now. They won't bother us."

"Good deal."

"Almost there," Cody said.

Snow frosted the tops of the markers. Janice's eyes were wide and transparent in the moonlight. She almost hadn't made it. She had chickened out and gone the long way, and Cody didn't want to wait. Bryce felt the gentle weight of her hand sliding over his hip and a dull electric charge seemed to buzz there. It felt good. He concentrated on that feeling.

Their footsteps were padded, muffled, as they threaded their way down the dirt paths. He could still hear shouts and laughter from town. Someone in the valley below had brought a radio and began randomly flicking through stations.

They came to a place where runoff had gouged the trails particularly deep, and the mounds were arranged around it like the walls of a fort.

"Ta Da!"

They passed around Peggy's boda bag.

A shriek knifed through the frozen air. It choked off, gurgled, and the lingering echo returned from all sides. They froze, then turned in different directions. Bryce felt the skin over his temples draw tight as drumheads. The scream might have been far off, but the night air made it seem close.

"What is that?"

"Somebody's coming," Cody said. A split second later Bryce heard it too. Heavy footsteps down in the valley between Cross Hill and the town.

Branches snapped and something howled, a sound that was somewhere between a hyena laugh and the squeal of a pig.

"It's a joke. Somebody's screwing around. Tryin' to scare us," Chuck said.

"No," Cody said shaking his head.

The howl started again, sharpening into a cry so childlike and helpless it ripped the night apart.

"God," Janice said. "Oh, God!"

They ran down the pathways back to the fence, and Chuck threw his hand out like a hound on point.

Below them, a black, hulking figure broke into the clearing, its arms swinging as if to ward off an attacker. It stumbled, picked itself up, and ran forward, mindless of the brush and cactus tearing at it as it ran. It bleated like a wounded animal.

"Bigfoot," Chuck said, "it's fucking Bigfoot!"

Cody jumped the wire and caromed sideways down the hill and into the valley. Bryce was following him before he knew it.

The ground was slippery with snow; he slid and heard the trenchcoat shred as it dragged behind him. His breath puffed white, and his throat and lungs ached from the cold. Snowflakes drifted peacefully around him.

Cody practically flew when he hit level ground. When Bryce hit, his legs went out and he rolled. Something stabbed his arm, but he barely felt it. He got up and ran after Cody. He could hear the others tramping up behind him.

"Aaaaagh!" Bigfoot clasped one hand over his face. He swept the other in front of him in a wide arc. Black fluid dripped between his fingers.

He stood in the clearing now, but he had no way of knowing it.

Cody stopped and Bryce pulled up next to him. Other kids still on their way to Cross Hill had made it before them; they stood wide-eyed, terrified, in a rough circle that shifted away each time Johnny Blackfoot lurched forward.

Chaperones came running, flashlights in hand, littering masks and costume parts behind them. The sheriff's Ranger roared down Katie Avenue, sirens wailing and flashers blazing. It lurched toward them over the luminaries and bounced into the valley. Mr. Perkins and Mr. Hicks were the first adults to arrive, and the circle of kids parted to let them through.

"Johnny, take it easy. Let us see," Mr. Perkins said.

"Nooooo!" Johnny Blackfoot screamed, and then his scream disintegrated into tiny childlike sobs.

"Let us help."

"Where's my little brother! Where's Warren!"

"We'll find him. Sit down and take your hands away. Dan, get that light over here!"

"Get my daddy! I want my daddy!"

Mr. Hicks touched his shoulder and Bigfoot shook him off. "Stay away! It hurts!"

Parents quickly collected their own. The siren and flashes died as the Ranger rolled up and flooded the area with a harsh white light. Sheriff Gordon and a deputy jumped out.

Gordon's face was ashen and drawn tight, the face of a man expecting the worst. To Bryce, he looked nothing like the gentle giant who'd come to reassure him after the Indian boy died. There were horrible pockmarks on the left side of his face, made even worse in the shadows cast by the floodlights.

"Johnny, put your hand down. Let us have a look at it," Gordon said.

Johnny's hand shook like a thousand volts were pumping through it. Slowly, Mr. Hicks guided it away. Bryce wished he hadn't.

"Oh God," Hicks said.

Mr. Perkins turned away. A spasm shot through his hand, and the flashlight clattered to the rocks at his feet and went out. Blood rushed down Johnny's cheeks. But for the torn meat of his lids jiggling hideously loose from his skull, his eyesockets were empty.

"How bad is it? How bad is it!" Johnny wailed. *"How bad is it?"*

Janice broke from the growing knot of onlookers and ran toward the lighted path. Hicks chased her. He wouldn't catch her.

Gordon pressed a folded towel to Johnny's face. Blood soaked right through it, so he wrapped two more around Johnny's head and taped them. He was still asking how bad it was when they strapped him into the Ranger and drove him away. Nobody told him.

Someone finally had sense enough to call the kids together. If anyone said they shouldn't have been out here in the first place, Bryce didn't hear it.

The snow peacefully filled the torn black earth where Bigfoot had stood.

Cathy and Peggy were gone. Cody and Chuck sat on a boulder next to a pathetic-looking pine. Bryce joined them. He couldn't stop staring at that dark patch of earth slowly filling in with snow.

Gordon remained behind, speaking into a walkie-talkie. Despite the chaperones' efforts, there were still stragglers.

Cody had his sunglasses on again. At this point, Bryce figured Cody couldn't see much more than light on the snow, but that was probably enough.

"He's tough . . . ," Chuck said, and his voice trailed off. He scraped a gash in the snow and dirt with his heel. "I'd've been in shock for sure."

"He was in shock," Cody said. "He was running in shock."

"If that happened to me, I'd wanna die." Chuck's jaw was set, his words slurred as if his lips were swollen. His face was as white as the snow. "Maybe I'd kill myself right there."

Something flashed in the darkness along the broken trail Bigfoot had made, and Bryce could see someone walking toward them. As he watched, the light flashed again.

"Saguaro cactus could take out an eye," Chuck said. "Maybe he ran into a saguaro."

"Saguaro—hell, something scooped his eyes clean out," Cody said. "Wasn't a stupid cactus."

"Any of you see his little brother out there?" It was Sheriff Gordon. He looked at Bryce and a sad half-smile of recognition flickered over his strained face.

"Didn't see either one of them till just now," Bryce said.

Cody and Chuck nodded. Cody pushed his sunglasses back up onto his featherless headdress.

"Looks like he was at the Helldorado early on." Gordon shook his head. "Nobody's seen him since. I'm gonna put a search team together with the parents here."

"Can we help?"

"Best thing you could do is help the chaperones get the little ones together. Party's over for tonight. I don't want you wandering around the desert. I know you've all had problems with Johnny, but somebody's out here who'll do that sort of thing to a kid—*any* kid. I'd as soon you all just went home." His walkie-talkie snapped to life and he turned away as he spoke into it.

A gust of wind swirled the snow at their feet. It was falling harder now.

"I'm freezin'," Chuck said. "I think I'm gonna take off. See you guys." He looked like he might throw up or faint as he hurried off.

"I gotta find Meg," Bryce said. "If anything happens to her . . ."

The chaperones were going hoarse calling the little kids together. Cody and Bryce trotted over to them.

"Your sis looks okay to me."

Bryce was relieved to see Meg standing off in the shadows with some little kids. It was odd though: he'd always thought of her as being so small, but he saw now that she was the tallest of the group. She was with the kids he'd seen watching Helldorado from the walkway on Front Street. Except for the jackets and boots, they were still in full costume, masks and all.

"Hey, Jason. What're you doin' out here?" Cody said.

A Ninja Turtle turned at the sound of Cody's voice. He looked back at Meg. She smiled and said something, and the turtle turned back.

"Jason! Yeah, I'm talking to you. What are you doin' out here?"

"He's okay," Meg said. "He's with me."

Cody glanced over at Bryce as if to say, Did I hear that right? Bryce shook his head; he didn't know what to say. Meg smiled at them, and the moonlight glinted off the mirrored lantern on her helmet. Suddenly, a huge, cold worm seemed to be twisting in Bryce's gut.

It was Meg he'd seen a minute ago walking toward them from the desert. It was her lantern he'd seen flash up on Cross Hill right after they'd left the dance.

The wind howled, and the snow kept falling, getting thicker every minute.

"Where are your glasses?" Bryce's mouth was dry. His tongue felt swollen. It was barely more than a whisper.

"I see a lot better at night. You know that."

236

Bryce shook his head. "No. I didn't . . . That's good."

"Uh-huh."

She walked up and hugged him, and Bryce straightened. Her jacket was open. He felt a soft, unsettling pressure on his chest. She kissed him and smiled.

Cody watched them, dumbstruck, Jason suddenly forgotten.

"Everyone stays with the group." It was Coach Wilkens. He waved them toward the others. "No one goes back up the hill tonight. It's either Helldorado or home. We have rides for anyone who needs them."

Meg walked happily at Bryce's side, but when they joined the crowd she was gone. He didn't try to find her.

21

H E could have been flying. He couldn't feel his feet beneath him as he ran into the valley. The snow had stopped falling. The only motion anywhere was the pumping of his legs.

His shoes glided over the snow, the trees and boulders passing by with impossible quickness. He sprang up the white cobbled trail on Cross Hill without effort. Black horses snorted white-hot steam, dipped their plumed heads, and accused him with their eyes as he passed the hearse and its tragically tiny cargo. Reverend Carroll stood straight as a spire outside the church doors. His eyes were ice blue.

Shep ran on through the cemetery's two neat rows of graves. Soon the need for order would be eclipsed by one of urgency.

One small grave yawned open before him, a mound of displaced soil and charred wood beside it. The fire had burned day and night to soften the frozen earth.

He passed the grave quickly, taking care to keep his eyes away from that terrible blackness. He vaulted the fence.

The Wizard loomed above the treetops. He'd seen his brother there, at the entrance, silently watching the tragic charade below.

The ground rose steeply and Shep pumped his legs harder, the breath freezing on his lips.

And he saw him again.

Boyd stood at the mouth of the Wizard, his new coveralls torn and dirty. He held the leather ball Shep had stitched for him from a worn-out vest. Boyd watched as Shep struggled toward him up the hillside; then he turned away. Shep yelled

238

for him to wait, but by the time he'd crested the rise, his brother was gone.

The ball thumped against the side of the cave and rolled inside.

Shep wheeled from the entrance. Below, on Cross Hill, the mourners stood silently, their heads bowed, as two men lowered the tiny casket into the frozen earth. Shep watched in horror, unable to speak, as one face turned slowly up to his . . .

T H E back door slapped its frame and Bryce sat up straight. His bedroom was filled with a strange white light. His heart hammered in his chest. He was soaked in sweat despite the freezing cold. He wasn't sick this time.

As tired as he'd been, sleep hadn't come easily. When he'd finally shut out the events of last night, the violence of the wind had kept him awake. When he'd drifted off at last, the dream had begun.

The storm window was glazed with spiky crystals on the outside, and the inner pane was foggy. Bryce stared out through the blinding crystalline whiteness. He could just make out a plow chugging its way over the hill toward Sluice, leaving a red gash in the snow as it went. Everything in the forest and yard was white.

Everything but Meg.

Meg was bundled in her cobalt blue down jacket. She was halfway across the yard, heading for the forest.

Bryce pulled his ski pants over his pajamas and stepped into his boots. He grabbed his jacket and zipped it as he ran downstairs. Cathleen was sipping a cappuccino, with the Style section of the *Arizona Republic* spread out on the coffee table.

"Where's Meg going?"

She glanced up from her paper.

"To play in the snow." There was a bite in Cathleen's tone that made it clear she'd been annoyed by his. "What's wrong?"

"I wanted to make a snowman. Thought she might wanna help."

"That's nice," Cathleen said.

"Did she have her glasses on?"

"Of course she did. Why?"

"I saw a pair upstairs and thought I'd bring 'em in case she, you know, ran out without 'em."

"She'd never make it out the back door. *You know that.*"

"So you didn't really see her?"

"She ran right by me, but you know how she's been."

"Yeah."

"Have some breakfast."

"That's okay, thanks."

He turned on his heels, ran back upstairs to his room, and shut the door. He dialed Cody's number and hung on as the phone rang and rang in his ear.

There was a loud *thump* as Cody's receiver hit the floor.

"Hello?"

"Cody, it's me. You go up to Cross Hill a lot, right?"

"Yeah. Why?"

"Get dressed and meet me there."

"What's going on?"

"Just do it. And don't tell Jason where you're going."

"Jason's outta here before I get up anyway. How you gonna get there? It's a ways for you."

"My bike."

"You're crazy. Snowed hard, man."

"See you."

"Bye."

It *was* crazy. How crazy was apparent to him after he'd shouldered the bike across the yard. The snow was over a foot deep in places, and though it had stopped for now, the sky looked like it wasn't nearly finished. He pushed the Stingray over the bank and let it slide down the other side on its own. He climbed over and rested while he surveyed the road.

It didn't look good. The plow had cut through all right, but it was a bad road even on good days, and all the bumps and potholes had left pockets of ice and snow everywhere. He'd ridden over ice before, but it was a chancy proposition even on the relatively flat streets of Schenectady and Niscayuna. Over these hills it might be suicide.

He jumped up and down on the road. The footing wasn't bad. The roughness of the surface, frozen as it was, might even help. It was the smooth ice that would kill him, the kind he was sure to see at the bottom of Splash Mountain.

He mounted up and circled, getting a feel for it. The dream was fading, but it had planted an awful seed. He didn't want to think about it, didn't want to think about where he was going and what he had to do.

Meg's trail led straight from the porch deep into the forest.

He took a deep breath. Then he pumped the pedals and started up the first hill.

"DANIEL Whitefeather?"

Tom Gordon stood before the earthen hut, his back to the rising sun. Today Whitefeather's hogan looked more like an igloo, but the weather had been kind to the Yavapai Navajo Reservation: the snow was patchy and thin, the droppings of a freak winter storm that would probably burn off by noon. Piñon Rim, on the other hand, was pretty well socked in.

"Come in, Sheriff."

Gordon unzipped his jacket as he entered, surprised at the heat inside.

"I'm Whitefeather. And you've found a bottle."

Gordon nodded. He was beginning to feel like the butt of a joke he didn't get. He'd spent the night freezing his butt off in a fruitless search of the desert north of town during the worst snow he'd ever seen. Johnny Blackfoot had gone into shock after surgery and stayed there. And if his worthless old man had any idea where Warren might be, he wasn't telling.

Gordon's patience had packed and left.

"How I can reach Anaweh?"

"There is no way to reach him."

Gordon was stunned and his face didn't hide it. The crud had hit that great, cosmic fan. The Blackfoot boys were only the latest in a string of tragedies. A week hadn't passed since Mariette Henley and Marge Wilkinson had been found dead in their own homes. Henley's suddenly orphaned son was missing as well. Gordon's town, the population of which barely filled the bleachers at the Red Ridge gymnasium, had been the site of five questionable fatalities in just over a month. There had been six aggravated assaults in the past week.

"What's so damned important—"

"That he would risk his life for you?" Whitefeather's eyes locked on his own. "I can't speak for John Anaweh's respect for police procedure, but I do know his respect for you and your people."

"What's this about 'risking his life'?"

"Anaweh is on a mission."

"Where?"

The old man shook his head and handed a woven pouch to Gordon. "This is from Anaweh and it's for your eyes alone. I don't know what it contains."

"Do you know how I can find a woman named Morning Sun?"

"By making peace with your God."

"She's dead?"

"She was old and blind. She left the protection of the reservation two weeks ago."

Gordon felt like he'd been cracked on the skull with a sack of bricks. With Anaweh gone, Michael Buckhorn's grandmother was the only lead he had. He was wasting his time. He thanked Whitefeather for inviting him in. He had started to stuff the pouch away when a circle embroidered on it reminded him why he was here.

"I don't mean to be abrupt. I'm having some trouble with all this."

Whitefeather nodded for him to go on.

"John mentioned a Circle of the Harvest. What can you tell me about that?"

"Some might call it 'The Great Red Hope,' I suppose, although I don't share their cynicism." A smile bent the innumerable lines of his face.

"It goes back thousands of years, long before the Navajo. One of the very few Anasazi songs to survive. The Circle of the

Harvest is a cycle of planting and reaping, of birth, death, and rebirth. The song speaks of bountiful crops which are later 'scattered in the wind.'

"It's something farmers chanted to make the crops grow?"

"Yes. That was its purpose. Its meaning is that prosperity and destruction are bound together, one turn of the same great wheel. Literally, it could apply to the Anasazi themselves."

"From what I know, the Anasazi just packed up and left."

"Prospered and vanished. The belief among my people is that we are descendants of an underground race. There is no direct link between the Navajo and the Anasazi; still, we have a common thread in our legends. The Anasazi believed a Spirit dwelled beneath the land. They built underground temples—kivas—to worship it, possibly to appease it. Many believe the Anasazi were destroyed, perhaps by that Spirit."

"A few thousand years ago," Gordon said.

"The song states, 'Though it ends, it begins again.' A circle never ends, Sheriff. Some believe the life and death of the Anasazi culture was only one turn of the Great Wheel."

"After I found the bottle, I looked through every book on the Navajo and Anasazi I could get my hands on. I never read anything about this."

"The trade between our cultures has rarely been one of ideas, has it?" There was no bitterness in the old man's tone, only irony in his smile. "Very few Navajo know the song, and those who do see it mainly as a story for children. I know for a fact Morning Sun took it very seriously."

"Why would she kill her grandson?"

"She wouldn't. She would have passed on her belief and left it to the boy to do as he must."

"She wanted him to kill himself?" Gordon was shocked. "He was ten years old."

"For one who truly believes, one life would seem a small price to pay for that of an entire civilization."

"But why the boy?"

"Morning Sun may have believed Michael was the Chosen One."

Gordon shook his head. Whitefeather waited patiently for his attention.

"According to the legend, as the Spirit grows old and weakens, it chooses a successor: a child through whom it channels its remaining power. Once chosen, this child, and the people of this child, prosper. The earth bears fruit.

"But as the cycle draws to a close, there is a terrible shift. The Spirit draws the life-force it has created back to itself, to the child now *within* it.

"If the child were to die before the Spirit is reborn, the Circle would be broken."

"So if there *was* anything to this, it's over."

"If Michael was the Chosen One. But if the Circle of the Harvest truly exists, as some believe it must, it has continued unbroken for countless generations. The child would provide an obvious weakness. It's not unreasonable to believe the Spirit would conceal its true choice, perhaps by diverting attention to another."

Gordon mopped the sweat from his forehead. It was getting uncomfortably warm. He shook his head.

"You think Michael Buckhorn was a decoy?"

"If the Circle exists, it's possible."

"And if he was?"

"One could see the past of your Piñon Rim as a Great Harvest and scattering of sorts; like the passing of the Anasazi, just one turn of the Great Wheel. It may be time for another turn."

"John Anaweh believes all this?"

"John Anaweh is the worst kind of skeptic: he believes, yet remains skeptical enough to believe he can stop it. Whatever John has given you, I would inspect it soon." Whitefeather seemed amused.

Gordon wasn't. He stuffed away the packet and zipped his jacket. Anaweh had gone off the deep end for a children's story. And Gordon had just spent the morning running right after him.

Still, he turned back once again.

"If there's something to it, what would I see?"

"Life patterns would repeat as the cycle repeats. Find what

244

you can about the Piñon Rim of old. No doubt you'll see human excess; the Spirit thrives on life. Be watchful of those with unusually strong life-force: children, adults with strong desires or abilities. The Spirit gives tenfold and takes ten times what it gives."

"In English. What does it do to people?"

"The worst thing imaginable." He smiled. "It gives them what they want."

J O H N Anaweh pulled himself through the crevice and stood, feeling each of his fifty years in his back. He'd crossed the last hundred yards on his belly while the underground river thundered an arm's length away. For nearly a day the roaring water had been his only companion. Then the droning had begun.

Up ahead, the river plummeted through a large fissure in the cave floor. Water droplets flared through his lantern beam like sparks from a welding torch.

The drone grew louder.

A galaxy of sparks caromed off the walls; one struck his face. He crushed it and held it up to the light: a cricket, pure white and eyeless.

The narrow tunnel opened out onto a cavernous chamber. Crickets poured through, swirling into its depths. Far below, thick limestone formations mushroomed from a lake, some as wide across as three men standing shoulder to shoulder. He worked his way carefully down, the drone of the crickets fading at last.

Something pale streaked through the pool. Within seconds, a dozen nearly transparent creatures lined the water's edge, some finger-small, others two or three feet long. They shoved one another mindlessly and nosed along the wall, following the vibrations of his footsteps. He slid his bow from the pack, snapping it together as he walked.

He would be crossing the chamber waist-deep in freezing water, surrounded by these eel creatures.

As cold and treacherous as his entry at Dugan's Point had been, it was an oasis of hospitality compared to any place he'd found since. It had been the last natural light he'd seen.

Something protruding from one of the yellow-white stalagmites caught his eye. The end was almost a perfect triangle. An arrow. It jutted from the formation, nearly a thumb's width of its shaft visible within the translucent stone. High above, water dripped from calcite draperies with agonizing slowness. How many centuries had passed to cover that arrow? And why had it been used? To fend off these eel creatures, as he might?

Anaweh touched his bow to the water. The creature closest twisted up to it, tapped it, and swam off. The others followed suit. He broke the surface a few feet away, and they repeated the action. Their mouths were tiny, toothless. Farther up, two crickets hit the water and disappeared without so much as a splash from the eel creatures.

He collapsed his bow, replaced it carefully in his pack, and slipped into the icy water. The eels buffeted him and swam off, returned and bumped him again.

He waded between the formations, the sound of the river growing louder. The constant buffeting of the eel creatures was beginning to whittle at his nerves. And then his lantern caught something strange in a pillar only a few feet away. He trained the beam on it:

Entombed within were the petrified remains of a brave; the shaft of an arrow protruded from his chest. Anaweh moved the beam from one pillar to the next.

Formation after formation, sightless eyes stared from the translucent yellow stone; hands grasped mortal wounds, clutched weapons.

A war party no doubt sent on the same mission that now drove Anaweh, and their last war had been waged on each other.

W I T H its famous crossing paths stamped in clean white snow, Cross Hill looked like some huge, embossed sympathy card. Sunlight flared in every direction, and Bryce wished he'd grabbed his shades on the way out. Cody waved from his perch on a grave halfway up the hill, but Bryce could barely see him.

The cold bit through his torn pants as he leaned his bike against the snowbank and stretched his legs. He'd fallen twice on Sluice and his knees felt tired and sore as he traced Cody's packed footprints.

When he finally made it, Cody handed over fried bread wrapped in paper towels, and a thermal blanket. It was a gift from Heaven. He poured Bryce a cup of brackish-looking fluid from his Thermos, twisted on the lid, and dumped it in his pack.

"Hot chocolate. I threw in a little coffee for you."

Bryce wolfed down the bread and chased it with the chocolate-coffee. He felt some of his strength return.

"What are we doing here?" Cody said.

"How well do you know this place?"

Cody glanced around.

"Like turds know flies. It's not like it changes. What are we looking for?"

Bryce had to wait for a good breath. As weird as thinking it had been, saying it out loud was worse.

"A fresh grave," he said.

T H E Y passed between the stones like ghosts. The cemetery looked worse now than it had last night. Snow had painted its own deathly quiet creepiness over the place. Whitewashed, Harper's Peak assumed the size of Everest; the entrance to the Wizard, black and empty where the boards had slipped, looked more than ever like a screaming mouth.

Cody stopped, leaned through one of the fences, and brushed the snow from a gravestone. Then he looked toward town, got new bearings, and started walking again.

Where Bryce could easily reach the markers he brushed away the snow himself. The markers that read LYNCHED BY MOB or HUNG FOR ADULTEROUS ACT no longer seemed oddly amusing. They passed the Kiddie's Section, and a shiver walked cold fingers down Bryce's spine. The next jumble of adult graves included two KILLED IN CLEAN FIGHT. In one ragged grouping of eight, every stone read BURNED IN WILDFIRE. Two names in that group, Lilleth Trenton and Del MacKenna, clicked in Bryce's mind.

"Are there any Trentons or MacKennas at school?"

247

The sound of his own voice breaking the silence was a blasphemy; it sent the little fingers racing.

Cody said he didn't think so. But if Bryce hadn't heard the names at PRE, he had no idea how he knew them.

He passed two more HUNG FOR STEALING.

"Didn't anybody just die?"

"One back there." Cody pointed to a marker that might have been an angel once. "That was a lady named Louise Dalmaine. Hers doesn't say how she went, but she was sixty—pretty old for back then. There're a couple other ones: John VanHorst—we're just about to him—his says OLD AGE and Wes Johansen's does too, but that's about it. Piñon Rim was a pretty ornery place."

Bryce cleared a SHOT FOR ADULTEROUS ACT. The next was simply LYNCHED.

Cody muttered something under his breath in Navajo, and Bryce stopped dead in his tracks. His heart raced.

"That one," Cody said. He glanced at Bryce, then pointed to a snow-covered mound near the north fence. "That one's new."

M O S T of his dream had faded, but he remembered plumed horses in front of a church, the tiny casket in a glass-sided hearse, a feeling of running—almost flying—through the cemetery. He glanced up at the mouth of the Wizard. Had something moved near the entrance? He blinked and squinted. Nothing but white snow.

The new grave looked no different from the rest. It was a roughly rectangular mound of snow-covered rocks marked by a heavy stone cross.

But there was a difference. A cold pocket of air seemed to form around Bryce's heart.

"That can't be new. It's got a marker."

"Yeah," Cody said, "but that's what gives it away. Look around. Except for the big one on the side, there's only three crosses on this whole hill. It's tablets or angels if they're marked at all. That's what threw me before." Cody checked his bearings once more and then pointed back the way they had come.

"This cross belongs over there, next to John VanHorst. The writing's broken off, but it's his wife's." He reached over the grave and Bryce's heart skipped a beat: he'd had a quick, horrible image of a hand seizing Cody's wrist through the snow.

Cody brushed the snow away. The cross was blank, the face of it long since eroded away.

"That was dumb," Cody said. "Everybody knows whose cross this is. Would've been better if they hadn't marked the grave at all."

But it was a Catholic thing to do: you bury someone, you put up a cross. The cold pocket was growing around Bryce's heart.

"How could someone have carried it this far?" Bryce heard himself say. It sounded like someone else's voice, coming from far away.

"Couldn't be one person. Take a few big guys to get it up here."

Bryce nodded. He could almost believe it was a prank after all, a bunch of jerks from Red Ridge being cute. Almost.

"Yeah, that's definitely Mrs. VanHorst's. It's a pretty good job otherwise, the grave looks real. It's a good joke. How did you know?"

Bryce reached through the snow, found the edges of a big stone, and pulled.

Cody practically leapt at him. "Don't wreck it—it's cool!"

"No, it isn't." Bryce bit his lip and felt a coppery, acid taste in his throat. The stone was wedged tight; he rocked it till it came free and the two stones above it slid away. *"It's real."*

Cody yanked back his hand as if a snake had bitten it.

"Help me," Bryce said. "Come on!"

Cody reached haltingly into the snow, but when he touched a stone he jerked his hand back again and the snakebit look returned to his face.

"Come on!" Bryce took hold of a wide, flat stone, braced his feet against the mound, and pulled. It barely moved. "Cody!"

249

Cody found the other side. They backed it away and a whole section of the new grave crumbled.

"Wait!" Cody said. He sat back in the snow.

Bryce squinted into the shadows; his eyes were killing him, and his throat clicked dryly. He tugged another stone.

"Leave it alone," Cody said. "Just leave it."

Bryce yanked and a small landslide of smaller stones poured out. They left bright red pocks in the snow.

A small, blue hand jutted from the hole they'd left, its palm matted with red ice and dirt.

"Oh, man," Cody whispered. His mouth hung open. A tear had caught between his cheek and the rim of his sunglasses.

Bryce's eyes fogged; he blinked them clear. He reached toward the little hand, meaning to push it back in. His own hand hovered there, unable to obey that order. Finally it did. The fingers were so frozen and so stiff that the cold bit right through Bryce's glove when he touched them.

"What are you doing? We can't . . . j-just . . ." Cody stammered.

"Help me put these rocks back."

"Okay. Okay. We'll put the rocks back and go tell someone."

"We can't tell *anybody*!" Bryce wedged in more rocks. "I need time. I've gotta think."

"Oh man, it's not cool to just leave him."

Bryce's jaw was set, and Cody realized he had every intention of doing just that.

"What if somebody saw us? I mean, somebody could just look up here and see us."

Bryce looked back toward town. It was true, there were people in the streets, and he and Cody weren't exactly hidden. But he had to chance it.

"Come on, help me."

Something moved in the corner of Bryce's eye. He scanned the grounds and the short stretch of trees beyond: nothing. The sky was darkening, ready to drop another load. They replaced the bigger stones and stuffed the others around them, then packed snow over the hole.

250

"It doesn't look good."

"It's gonna snow again. That'll cover it."

"We gotta tell."

"What are we gonna say? They'll think *we* did it. We were up here last night! Cody, you gotta promise you won't tell anybody."

"Let's go!"

"Promise!"

"Okay! I promise! We gotta get out of here!"

"Where are the Easton graves?"

"Oh man. I'm gonna throw up!"

"Come on, show me."

Cody pointed toward the only two neat rows in the entire cemetery. Instead of massive mounds there were depressions in the snow in front of them.

"There's one at the end of the second row. The rest are scattered around. Let's get outta here. I'm sick, man."

Bryce headed toward the one in the second row; it seemed miles away. He trotted, then ran. Soon he lost the feel of his feet beneath him. *He had the sensation of flying. He could see the old church as it once had been, its tall white spire knifing the slate sky; he saw the hearse drawn by black, plumed stallions; he smelled the charred remains of the gravediggers' fire.*

He stood before the last decently executed grave in the cemetery. As he stepped over it, his foot sank briefly and caught on the other side. He brushed the snow away.

IN LOVING MEMORY

BOYD EVERETT EASTON

1883–1894

LOST TO US

FOUND BY GOD

The last neatly executed grave on Cross Hill. The last one they had time for. And it belonged to Meg's new little friend, Boyd.

"Let's get the hell out."

Bryce nodded.

* * *

"I DON'T get this. I don't get any of it."

"My eyes are killing me."

"Put these on." Cody handed Bryce his sunglasses and blinked at the whiteness.

Finally, Bryce could see the plane of the sky meeting the plane of the land. There were trees and clouds; everything was mostly white but in sharp relief.

"You got any money on you?" Cody said.

"Five bucks."

"We can pick shades up in town for that. You can go blind out here when it's like this."

"Let's walk."

"I gotta get my bike."

"Leave it. We gotta talk."

They started walking toward town. The debris of spent luminaries pulverized by snowplows littered the banks. The Helldorado banners flew over Piñon Rim. The air still reeked of roasted pumpkin. The snow began falling steadily again.

"Man, this didn't happen," Cody said. "Why did you call me? How did you know?"

"I had a nightmare about it."

Cody shook his head, as if that might dislodge the morning from his memory. He grimaced.

"Is that Warren Blackfoot up there?"

He's probably never called him anything but Wart, Bryce thought. Bryce couldn't bring himself to call him that, either. Warren Blackfoot suddenly had the respect of death.

"Yeah, I'm pretty sure it is."

"Oh, man. We gotta tell the sheriff. We can't just leave him there."

"You didn't hear anything I said."

"Yeah, I heard. Did you kill the little snot?" A car passed and Cody turned away from it.

"No."

"But you know who did."

"We gotta find out more about the legend."

"This isn't a freaking fairy tale. That kid's dead! And you know who did it!"

"Shut up about it!"

Cody grabbed Bryce's jacket and shoved him back. "You want me to shut up you better tell me why, because I don't want this on my back! I don't care if they know we found him because *I* didn't put him there!"

Bryce felt all his alarm bells going off at once. Why couldn't Cody just shut up and listen? He wanted to take his fist and mash Cody's nose to a pulp. In his head he could see himself doing it: ripping away the fingers that were gripping his jacket and breaking them back in one quick, violent motion; then crashing his knuckles into that disbelieving face. The image was so strong his muscles twitched violently, as if some better, more powerful instinct had reigned him in at the last second. He blinked the image away, unable to speak.

He shook his head. He wanted to cry, but he held it in.

"Meg. I think Meg did it."

Cody let go. But he didn't say anything.

"I don't know why. And I don't know how. *But she did it. And she did Bigfoot's eyes too.*"

"You're twisted. You are messed up royal!" Cody backed away. He shook his head.

"It's because of that legend, that Spirit. I know it is. She wouldn't do anything like that if . . . if something didn't make her."

"No, man. This is . . . I gotta tell the sheriff."

"You can't!"

"I have to!"

"You can't! Jason's in on it too. You saw the way they were last night. Jason did it too!"

Cody was walking backwards. He pointed a finger at Bryce and spat. He was shaking.

"You're twisted, man." Cody turned and ran. A car broke fast and skidded to avoid him. The driver swore as Cody tore up Katie Avenue.

Bryce watched him go. The snow fell.

Meg and Cody were his best friends. In the span of a few days he'd lost them both. He was alone.

The Stingray leaned against the snowbank beneath Cross Hill, nearly covered with snow itself.

How far would he get if he just rode out of town and kept going? Could he make Sedona without freezing or sliding off a cliff somewhere? What would he do if he made it? Could he just leave Meg and his dad? He closed his eyes and saw a thousand images, mostly dumb things like he and Trevor repacking the Stingray's bearings, Meg reading her latest *National Geographic* in the chair by the fireplace, the two of them hot-dogging figure eights on the lake in Schenectady's Central Park.

He walked toward Front Street feeling bruised and weary. But he wasn't giving up without a fight.

A T Piñon Rim Drugs, there was actually a line at the cash register and two people sipping coffee at the counter. It shouldn't have surprised Bryce. There were a number of cars parked along Front Street already, frustrating the post-Halloween cleanup and the final Helldorado Days preparations. Despite the snow, the streets of Piñon Rim were slowly filling up.

"Go ahead and pour yourself a cup," Jordan called from behind the register.

Bryce did and grabbed an empty stool near the Easton pictures. The boy with the ball stared back at him. Being right had never felt so creepy. He looked at the later picture of the Easton family minus Boyd, and then at the "Upstairs at the Lucky Slipper" photo. Rose Bowman smiled back, just happy to be plying her trade in the "boomtown," totally clueless to the steadily brewing horror around her.

The door chimes jangled.

Cody hesitated at the door, then walked in. His eyes were puffy and red.

" C A M E back for my shades." Cody slid onto the next stool "You didn't say anything?"

"Got all the way to the sheriff's and turned around." He stared at the napkin on the counter. "So what now?"

A beefy guy in a plaid wool coat grunted and slid the Sports section from a paper on the stool next to him. Bryce kept his voice low, nearly a whisper.

"Then you know?"

"There's something way wrong. I guess . . . I thought it would go away or something if I didn't mess with it. Jason . . . I don't know. Whatever's goin' on with your sister's double with him."

Bryce nodded. "Want coffee?"

"Stuff's gross, man."

Bryce pulled the shades from his jacket.

"Keep 'em." Cody slid out a brand-new pair of ski glasses. "I bought myself a present." He slipped them back.

"What's up with you two?" Bill Jordan ran a towel along the bar.

"Out for the snow," Cody said.

"Snow's gotta last all winter. Don't use it all up the first day." He topped off all the cups as he moved along the bar to the register, where a couple stood with postcards.

The guy near Cody took a last gulp, slapped a bill on the counter, and walked out, leaving his paper behind.

"See the pictures right in front of me," Bryce whispered, "the Eastons?"

Cody nodded. "They've been here all my life."

"Yeah, but they were just pictures on a wall. You probably never really looked at them. Now they're important."

Cody screwed up his face and stared a hole through them. He didn't see anything weird.

"Is this more perspective bull?"

"The kid with the ball"—the volume was creeping up, so he pulled it down—"Boyd Easton. The kid I saw."

"*Dreamed* you saw."

"I *did* see him, and I wasn't asleep. I know that now."

The man in the plaid coat who had been sitting near Cody stopped outside the front window. For a moment he looked straight at them. Then he moved on.

Jordan made change at the cash register, glancing their way and then out the window. Bryce remembered the first time he'd come in, the smiles Jordan had shared with the old-timers across the street when Aggie passed by.

"Anyway, forget it. I've been looking at these pictures a lot lately. Check out the one without Boyd."

"When did they take it?"

"Not too long after the first one."

"Can't be. The dad's a lot older."

"He's aged all right, but I don't think he's any older."

"What?"

"I know. It's hard to figure. If you look at each one alone, you have a sort of normal-looking family standing in front of a carriage. If you put the pictures together they're impossible."

"Mrs. Easton looks young. She probably was. But she looks a whole lot younger in the second picture. And I think that's just 'cause she's standing next to Mr. Easton, who suddenly looks a lot older."

Cody shook his head.

"Look. Use the older brother like sort of a reference point. His head's exactly even with the top of the carriage wheel in both pictures. I've grown a lot the past couple years. I'm sure you have too. These photos can't be more than a few months apart."

Cody shook his head. "I still don't get it. The dad's older; the mom's either younger or just looks younger next to him; and Shep hasn't gone either way. It doesn't make sense."

"That's the point. It only adds up if you can handle the idea that something made Mr. Easton age really fast."

"Like what?"

"I don't know. That's why I keep thinking it's got something to do with that legend. It's gotta be something totally *out there*. Like magic or something supernatural. And whatever it was, it started when Boyd died."

"Conversation's gettin' deep."

Hearing Jordan's voice was like sitting on a high-voltage wire; they nearly hit the ceiling.

Jordan flashed his gold teeth. "What's got you two goin' now?"

"When Boyd Easton got lost, how did he die? Did he starve or something?"

"Don't really know. Probably coyotes got him, or a cougar. They never found the body."

"They buried an empty casket?"

"Happens all the time when someone's missin' long enough. After a while folks gotta let go. Ceremony helps."

"How long was he missing?"

"Don't know exactly. But a little boy wouldn't last long out there alone."

"So the town just gave up?" Cody said.

"Givin' up and acceptin' facts is two very different things. Boyd was Katie Easton's favorite, and it was her decision to get on with things. You can't fault a mother's love. And you can't start healing 'less you close the wound."

Bryce went a little numb and felt himself drifting somehow. His dream flashed by. He saw Boyd at the mouth of the Wizard, silently watching as his own funeral unfolded below him. Bryce could feel cold wind on his own face as Shep looked up.

"Shep knew he was alive."

"And that sadness il'strates the point. Shep never stopped lookin' for his brother. Never could accept it. And you know what happened to *him*."

"No. He really knew! When he was at the funeral he saw Boyd up by the mine."

Jordan cocked his head as though he wasn't sure what he'd just heard. Cody was staring at Bryce slack-jawed.

Bryce shook his head. *"They found Shep where I found that kid. When?"* It was nearly a croak; the inside of his mouth had gone bone-dry.

"Not long after Boyd."

"How long did it take for the town to . . . you know, to die after Boyd got lost?"

"Well now, Rose Bowman, she'd already come in. Gold played out, things went sour pretty quick. Girl brought bad luck on the whole town, you know." Jordan chewed his lip; he seemed to be calculating the answer on the ceiling beams. "If you figure it from the day they lost Boyd, maybe a month, I guess."

"*A month?*" That suffocating feeling from the cave was coming back. It had been a month since Meg had gone into the cave alone.

"Town went up fast and went down even faster." The old man shrugged.

Bryce's stomach was doing a slow roll. He was pretty sure he'd already gotten the answer to his next question from the infamous "Upstairs at the Lucky Slipper" photo. But he needed to hear what Jordan had to say; suddenly that was very important.

"How did Rose Bowman die?"

"Took sick. Died in her sleep. By that time, the damage was done. No justice to that, is there? No justice at all in this world, I guess, 'less you make it yourself."

Bryce nodded and stood. He put down fifty cents and Jordan slid it back to him.

"Your money's no good here. You know that." Jordan winked.

There was a commotion outside. The window damped the sound, but a good, solid swear session was going on in the street. A tourist had parked next to a ladder, and the workman, a lanky, ferret-faced man with scraggly blond hair, had stepped down to tell him, in extremely colorful terms, he couldn't park there.

Bryce and Cody headed for the door.

As the driver, a bald man in sunglasses and an expensive-looking tan coat, opened his door and started to get out, the workman's boot lashed out, kicking the door right back on him. There was a sickening, wet *thump* like a hammer striking a melon, a sound made even worse when diminished by the Lucky Slipper's window. Scarlet fingers of blood ran down the car door. Bryce caught a quick, horrible glimpse of the driver's face, his eyes bulging, beyond terror or pain. Another worker leaned calmly against the ladder, his face utterly devoid of expression.

258

Cody froze. Bryce threw open the jangling door of the drugstore and screams from the driver's wife blew in like a summer storm. He pushed Cody out.

The ferret-faced workman wasn't through. Even as others ran to the driver's aid, the workman grabbed the man's damaged head and rammed it through the window of the open door. Beads of bright red glass showered the street.

Cody stared, a rabbit caught by headlights. Bryce shoved him forward.

"Walk! Just walk!"

Cody said something shapeless, nonsensical, as if he'd somehow forgotten how to form consonants. Bryce kept him moving forward down the boardwalk. Running footsteps and screams. Others walked nonchalantly by as the pulping blows continued.

The door to the Wizard's Palette opened. Andre smiled.

They kept walking. Their footsteps drummed the boardwalk. The man's wife kept screaming.

Cody's eyes were wide open as he jolted forward.

"It's gonna get worse," Bryce said. *"It's gonna bust all over again!"*

They made it to the end of the walkway and halfway down the steps before Cody hugged the rail and threw up.

T H E snow was still falling. The trails they'd made on Cross Hill were still visible, but barely. They walked on legs filled with sponge, barely feeling the road beneath them.

Cody chewed a handful of snow and spat it out.

"We could've helped that guy," he said.

"We'd've gotten too messed up to do anything else." Bryce shook his head. "He was dead when the door hit him."

A breeze sent sidewinders of snow drifting across the road.

"You know before, when you wanted to go to the sheriff? I wanted to smash your face in. I saw myself breaking your fingers and *really smashing your face in.*"

"I was a little crazed too."

"The thing is, I've been in fights before. I've gotten mad, but nothing like that. I never thought I could *really* kill somebody.

I came close last week with Matt Connors. I came a lot closer today. That guy at the drugstore . . . maybe it's the same with him."

"What do you mean?"

"Today he wanted to bash somebody's head in and he just did it. Maybe tomorrow I won't hold back either. Maybe a dozen other people'll get mad and do the same thing, maybe half the town will. And the rest will be like the other guy, just chewing his freaking cud like his friend's giving directions to Sedona."

"This is crazy." Cody looked straight ahead. He looked dazed. "I mean, look at the snow, man. This is a freaking great day. We should get the sleds out—"

"We can't think like that. We can't pretend it's okay."

"Be real, man. What can the two of us do about anything?"

"We gotta find out more about that legend."

"It's caveman stuff."

"But it's real! You saw what happened to Bigfoot—and Warren."

"No evil spirit did that!"

"Maybe it didn't, not by itself. Jordan called Rose Bowman something—a cattle-list, I think. He said cattle-lists don't do anything themselves, but they make things happen just by being there. Maybe that's what it does. Maybe the Spirit makes killers out of people. Your grandfather knows about it. Maybe he knows how to stop it."

"My folks—"

"Your folks know more than they want to tell. They think it's crazy, but they're wrong."

"They'll think I'm nuts."

"Man, we don't have a choice! Whatever happened then is happening now. I told you Meg went into that cave by herself just before I got sick."

Cody nodded.

"Just before it happened, an old Navajo woman told me to stop her. The woman had no freaking eyes at all, and she was walking down Sluice—alone."

"You've told me the weirdest stuff. Why didn't you tell me that?"

"Because I thought she was crazy. I thought you'd think I was if I told you. But that's the point. We've gotta find out everything we can, even if people think we're totally whacked. Do you know who she is?"

"Maybe. My grandfather talked about a blind woman on the reservation. A holy woman. I can't think of her name. But I saw something weird too. That day you showed me how they'd rebuilt the Lucky Slipper, I broke up two little kids fighting at school. They were fighting hard, real hard. One of 'em gave me a shot you wouldn't believe. *They were fighting over Meg.* And she was smiling about it. Like it was totally cool."

"Megan's the key," Bryce said. "When Dad and I found her that night she asked if we'd seen the Wizard. We thought she was asleep—you know, dreaming."

"She saw the Spirit," Cody said. His voice was soft and the color had gone out of his skin. Bryce couldn't help thinking, ironically, of the term *paleface.*

"Yeah. The Spirit's the Wizard—*the real Wizard.* And I think Boyd Easton saw it a hundred years ago. Back then, *he* was the key."

They had walked nearly to Bryce's bike, and it gave him the creeps to be this close to Cross Hill. He found himself staring at the lonely grave outside the fence.

"But they blamed Rose Bowman, and all along Boyd was the cattle-list thing. I mean, look at the graves up there. After he disappeared the place went nuts. They couldn't bury people fast enough. And Rose Bowman didn't just get sick and die, either."

"It's history."

"The same history that says the Lucky Slipper never burned down."

"Why would Bill Jordan lie?"

"I don't think he knows. He just knows things are great now, like everybody else here. They don't know jack about Boyd. And they don't know anything about the Spirit your grandfather talked about. That's why we gotta get the whole story and tell everybody."

Cody shivered. High on Cross Hill, Warren Blackfoot's grave looked grossly uneven where they'd dug into it.

"So what happened to Rose Bowman?" Cody said.

"I think that's the bad thing that happened at the Lucky Slipper. That's what they had to lie about.

"Remember those names I asked about in the cemetery—Del MacKenna and Lilleth Trenton?"

"Yeah."

"I wondered where I'd seen them before. Then I saw their names written under that photo in the drugstore—you know, 'Upstairs at the Lucky Slipper.' They're the two girls with Rose Bowman. Their tombstones say they died in a wildfire. I think they were murdered with Rose in the Lucky Slipper."

"They burned them?" Cody's voice was hushed. Suddenly it was like talking in church. *"Like witches?"*

Bryce nodded.

"This Wizard thing is smart. It probably used Rose on purpose, made the Christian people hate her. But it was Boyd from day one. *It knows who to pick.* I mean, the Wizard could've gotten me just as easy as Meg. But if I'd been the one, Meg would've known something was up right off. She'd've had it figured weeks ago and probably stopped it by now. She's such a freaking genius."

"Jason's another one, a whiz at everything."

Bryce balanced on the pedals. "It's up to the dummies to save the world," he said.

Cody saluted. "Here's to the dummies."

Cody looked across the road at the mine's screaming mouth. In town, a siren blared and died.

"I'll find out what my folks know. I'll get grounded for a week."

"We don't have a week. Jordan said everything blew a month after Boyd disappeared. It's been longer than that since Meg went into the cave alone."

Cody kicked snow across the road. They were stalling and

they both knew it. It was tough to separate. Wherever they were going now, they'd be going alone.

"I just thought of something," Cody said. "What if Meg isn't the key? What if the Spirit just wants people to think she is? You know, like it did with Rose Bowman."

There were shouts from town. They both turned to look. More trouble out of sight on Front Street.

"You saw the way she was last night. Anyway, if it was going to do that again, it'd pick somebody everybody knows."

"It was just a thought."

The wind and snow were picking up. Getting home would be hell. *But not nearly as bad as being there.*

Cody must have read his mind.

"Do you wanna go to my place instead?"

Bryce shook his head.

"Thanks, I'm okay."

He wasn't. He was scared to death. He pushed off and started the long ride back, thinking about Shep, hearing Shep's tortured breath as he bolted across the cemetery, feeling the cold burn in his throat as he ran full out up Harper's Peak.

Shep never gave up on Boyd. *And you know what happened to him.*

In the end it hadn't made a difference.

But it might with Meg. Meg hadn't disappeared; they still lived under the same roof. Maybe she still looked up to him, needed him.

Maybe.

22

B R Y C E did better on his return trip. He only fell once, when he had been pushing the speed. As long as they kept the roads somewhat clear, he could escape on the Stingray if he had to. It was good to know.

He rested at the top of the hill on Redman. Slimer looked like the world's biggest snowman. Frosty on steroids. One day after Halloween and the roof of the Big House was thick with snow. Smoke curled from the chimney. A bumper crop of icicles had already begun to hang over the porch as the snow on the skylight melted. The lights were off in his room and in Megan's.

A single trail led into the woods. Meg was still gone.

What was he going to do when she came back? What was he going to do anyway?

There were no footprints in the snow except for Meg's trail into the forest. It was past noon, but his dad and Cathleen hadn't been outside.

The skylights glowed. Of course, Trevor sometimes kept the lights on when the daylight wasn't quite up to it, and it was pretty gray now. The kitchen light was on, but Bryce didn't see anyone through the windows.

One set of tracks.

He tacked and backpedaled his way carefully down Redman, keeping one eye on Megan's trail where it disappeared into the shadows of the forest. He felt that cold pocket of dread in his chest.

What if she'd retraced her steps?

There was no movement at all from the house.

He skidded to a stop, climbed off, and pushed his bike to the top of the snowbank. He followed it over and left it where it lay as he walked slowly to the porch. Some of Meg's tracks were clearly visible now. A lot were pretty clean, but some were broken and uneven. She could have backtracked, but it would have been tough. She would've had to walk backward to line the treads up right. He could see her doing it though, could see Cathleen glancing out the window at some point and thinking it was odd but just like a little kid to play at matching her tracks in the fresh snow. Cathleen would go back to drying the dishes or reading the paper and forget all about it—until a shadow fell nearby or something shifted behind her. She would turn suddenly, and there would be Megan, not an eleven-year-old but the Megan he'd seen that night in his dream, a Megan who was tall and lithe with blue fire burning in her eyes, and a cleaver raised over her head.

Something moved past the kitchen window. Cathleen waved and Bryce let go of the breath he'd been holding since he'd climbed over the bank. He leapt up the porch steps, popped his boots off beside the mat, and ran into the house in his socks. He'd never dreamed seeing Cathleen would make him feel so good.

BRYCE sipped cappuccino by the living room window. The new coffee beans Cathleen used tasted a little bit like old tires, but it hardly mattered. The house smelled like cinnamon and fresh bread, but he wasn't hungry. His eyes were riveted to the end of Meg's trail. Snow was falling again.

"School day tomorrow," Cathleen said from the kitchen.

"Uh-huh. Dad been down yet?"

"No. He's been a worker bee. It's great he's so excited about painting again. I don't think any of us . . ." Her voice trailed off. She carried her cappuccino into the living room. She smiled without much behind it; when her eyes caught up with it, years seemed to melt away.

She glanced upstairs, a deep breath lifting her shoulders.

"He's hard to understand sometimes. I mean, I've worked

with artists a long time, but I've never figured out how they can do that, devote themselves like that."

Bryce shook his head.

"I only see him when he stumbles into bed, or at least I'm *aware* of him being there. That's if he lets himself out at all. A lot of times he spends the whole night in that studio."

"Don't you think that's weird? He never used to lock me out."

"I think it's great he's into it! I was starting to wonder what we'd do." Her face lit up, but it was such a quick transition that Bryce couldn't help seeing the bare nerve beneath it.

"How was your party?" she said too quickly.

"You didn't hear anything about Bigfoot? You know, Johnny Blackfoot? Meg didn't say anything?"

She shook her head.

"You haven't been outside, either. I mean, there aren't any tracks."

"I've been cleaning. Why? What's outside?"

Her tone had taken that same annoyed edge it had this morning when he'd asked about Meg's glasses. Bryce shifted uneasily.

"Snow. It's the first snow."

She laughed, but it carried even less weight than her smile had.

"My days of making snow angels are over. What happened last night?"

Bryce thought about making it sound less horrific. He wasn't sure how she'd take it. Finally, he just said it.

"Someone ripped out Johnny Blackfoot's eyes."

Cathleen looked at him blankly. He wasn't sure if he'd shocked the hell out of her or if she really hadn't understood. Then she just glanced out the window.

He felt every hair prick up on the back of his neck when she said, "Well, that's awful, isn't it?"

"Yeah," he said, horrified by the question in her voice.

"I'm not surprised something bad happened to him. Meg says he was a terrible boy."

"How does Meg know?"

266

"The kids at school told her some of the things he's done—always fighting, feeding aspirin to birds."

"Alka-Seltzer."

"Whatever. He's a bully. And that little brother of his is obnoxious too."

Bryce tried not to react, but it felt like a cold steel wire was twisting between the spools of bone in his back. There was a quick, convulsive pain and then a sort of numbness.

"Warren . . . is missing."

"Probably ran away, having a brother like Johnny Blackfoot. I've heard their father is an alcoholic too."

"Someone ripped Johnny Blackfoot's eyes out! I saw him after it happened. Meg did too. We all did. I've never seen anything like that."

Were her ears filled with mud? Bryce was shaking. He was near, so near, to blurting everything out: that he was convinced her precious little daughter, Meg, had done it, that maybe she'd killed Warren too. He wasn't sure what was stopping him. He looked quickly out the window.

The "what" was out there somewhere. His cheeks burned.

"That is terrible. I'm sure he wasn't far from deserving it, though."

Bryce shook his head. Was there a remote possibility someone might deserve that? He didn't think so.

"You've torn your jacket—and your pants."

He nodded, a part of him stepping back, watching this whole picture from a great distance. From where he stood, the picture was very wrong.

"Yeah." Then he added, with the numbness of habit, "They're not my good ones."

"You shouldn't ride your bike in the snow. I want you to take the bus with Meg while there's snow and ice on the ground."

"The snow's okay. I've got the hang of it now."

"Well don't expect me to sew them!"

A slug of foamy milk topped her cup and splattered to the floor. She ignored it and walked back to the kitchen.

Bryce's stomach hitched. It was suddenly, horribly obvious.

She knows all about Johnny and Warren Blackfoot. She knows all about Meg.

His throat felt lumpy and dry. Part of his dream rammed suddenly home, the last part: Shep was at the mouth of the Wizard mine staring down as the tragic sham of Boyd's funeral played out below. Shep knew his brother was alive: *he'd seen him.* And as the coffin was lowered and the mourners wept and prayed, one face raised up to his—*his mother's.*

Katie Easton had known all along. The mock funeral had been her idea. Jordan said it. Boyd's "death" removed any chance of suspicion. And Rose Bowman's relationship with Katie's husband made Rose all the more hateful to the town. That's why Katie had ignored it. *She was protecting her favorite the best way she could.*

And Cathleen would protect Meg the best way *she* could.

Jordan had nearly told him about Katie Easton the day Matt Connors had run him off the road. He would have if that kid hadn't spilled the coffee.

No. *Thrown the coffee.* It had seemed so random at the time, but maybe it wasn't random at all. Suddenly, the air around him weighed tons, as he began to realize the depth of the quicksand he was standing in.

One more gruesome image stung him: Shep Easton floating, facedown, in Sharpe's Creek. Which had Shep seen last, the Wizard . . . or his own mother?

What had possessed Bryce to come back here?

"Meg's been out there awhile," he said finally, because he had to say something. Wind whistled through the eaves. Outside, the snow was falling again, falling hard. How far would he get? Not very.

"Meg's upstairs," Cathleen said from the kitchen. "I was a little worried about you, though."

"She's here?" His voice was hoarse, barely more than a whisper. As his eyes moved up the stairs, he could see a corner of Meg's bedroom ceiling through her open door. The pocket of air became a cold fist squeezing his heart.

"I think she walked backwards all the way from the forest." Cathleen smiled from the kitchen door. "She acts so grown-up most of the time that sometimes I forget she's still a little girl. Funny, isn't it?"

Bryce wasn't laughing.

He climbed the stairs slowly, now very aware that Cathleen was between him and the back door.

He'd come home to face Meg. Well, here she was. Now what?

"Meg?"

He could see halfway into her room now. Her light was off, but there were books scattered over the bed as though she'd been reading. The room opened as he climbed. At last, he saw her at the window, a silhouette against the white forest beyond. He couldn't tell if she was facing him or the yard.

"Hi, Bryce." The voice was cheerful, and definitely Meg's. "What's up?"

The feeling of dread slid from his shoulders like a sopping wet coat. Meg was okay.

Of course she was okay. Man, what was he? Totally freaked? And Cathleen, Cathleen was just being weird. She wasn't out to get him. And Katie Easton didn't drown her eldest son. It was all ridiculous bull.

He wanted to hug her and laugh about all this psycho crud lurking in the dark corners of his twisted lump of a brain. He wanted to hear that stupid billygoat laugh of hers. Then he'd just call Cody and apologize for scaring the heck out of him. Tomorrow they'd go back to school and play British Bulldog in the snow. He'd still have to get over Connie Bowman, but, really, so what? Meg was all right and the world was spinning again.

Megan stepped away from the window and Bryce's heart stopped cold. He was back in the Bizzaro world.

She was wearing her favorite T-shirt, the pink one with the *Billboard* logo on the left side, a T-shirt that was way too small now. Her jeans, nearly shapeless the last time he'd noticed, were fighting hard to contain the curves beneath. Her blue eyes were bright and conspicuously unframed.

"You hardly ever talk to me anymore."

His jaw fell. His lips felt bee-stung and stupid.

"Where are your glasses?" he managed to say.

"You like me better without them, don't you? Everybody does."

"Meg." His skin tingled. He was drifting, a punctured balloon slowly dying. "What happened?"

"I outgrew them."

He shook his head. "What you have doesn't work that way."

"It works the way you work it. *Everything* works the way you work it."

He swallowed, but the elevator in his throat got caught between floors, and he nearly choked.

"If you want something bad enough, you can make it happen," she said.

She came toward him and the budding flesh jiggled beneath her shirt. His gut undulated and knotted; raw heat rose in his face. Her hand drifted up to his face and he saw another hand, a tiny blue one in the snow, matted with frozen blood and raw earth. He pushed hers away. There was a brief and awful sensation of touching something else entirely, something papery and dry, barely there at all.

Her eyes grew wide and for a split second a light seemed to flash inside them, but it was only the reflection from the window as she turned away. Her shoulders tremored.

He stepped back, his legs suddenly too weak to support him, and practically tumbled into the hall.

The door to Trevor's loft was open just enough to glimpse an enormous jumble of painted canvases. He heard a hoarse, rattling cough, and something hunched and gray moved toward him as he ran past.

The door slammed shut.

Bryce locked his own door and shoved the dresser against it. He wedged his chair against that. Then he sat at the foot of his bed and hugged his knees, a billion voices screaming in his head at once, jamming every circuit.

23

GORDON held his place in the big book and watched Trish type. While he'd spent his morning tracking leads, a man named Ben Walker had spent his turning a man's head to pulp.

Trish's eyebrows squared off, ready to tangle as she hammered out Walker's arrest report. She must have felt Gordon's eyes because she looked up at him and shook her head. Gordon went back to his reading. He didn't need ESP to read her mind. The jail was built for eight, *max.* Walker made six. Six men in the cells below charged with grievous assault or worse. Maybe he'd have Pat Phillips draw up a NO VACANCY sign and hang it outside—if he could find Pat Phillips. When it rained crud it poured; Pat's radio had gone dead, and Trish couldn't reach him.

Gordon had been through most of these books already. After he'd found Anaweh's bottle he'd pretty much cleaned out the library's section on Indian history. He hadn't seen any "Circle of the Harvest" mentioned, but he'd expected to see it by name. Now that he'd talked to Daniel Whitefeather and knew what it was, he could look for references to it. Suddenly, that was very important.

It didn't take long to find.

One book, *The First Americans—Their Legends and Lore,* was crammed full of campy illustrations. He'd once seen it advertised in a sports magazine next to an ad for silver-plated chess pieces depicting officers of the Civil War. It wasn't an in-depth treatment by any means, but one blurb under the heading "The First Arizonans" caught his eye:

Long before the Navajo, the Anasazi, master architects and
agriculturalists, flourished and then vanished from an area
of northern Arizona later deserted by the Navajo.

The story had not been deemed worthy of a campy drawing,
only a thumbnail sketch of a map. And smack-dab in the
center of that map was a tiny blue dot with just two words
beneath it: Piñon Rim.

. . . *an area of northern Arizona later deserted by the Navajo.*

And picked up dirt cheap by the white man. Who threw the
Navajo onto the reservation with all the wit and wisdom of
B'rer Fox flinging B'rer Rabbit out of harm's way.

Gordon had picked up more books at the library in Prescott.
As he skimmed through them, the knot that had been slowly
forming in the pit of his stomach since he'd left the reservation
twisted and pulled tight. They all said the same thing: the
Navajo and Anasazi communities flourished here and either
moved on or disintegrated entirely.

What they didn't mention was one bit of extremely relevant
history about the whites in Piñon Rim. That would never be
found alongside Indian lore, mainly because white and Indian
traditions had been hacked in twain by a lot of bad blood and
even worse government ink. The missing piece could be titled
The Remarkable Boom and Catastrophic Bust of Piñon Rim.

But those dots were easy enough to connect sitting, as Gordon was, smack-dab in the center of the map.

Gordon glanced up. No one was pressed to the glass watching him pore over the books with the big colorful pictures like
a Cub Scout. He'd taken Whitefeather's advice and plundered
the Piñon Rim Historical Society's book collection as well, but
for now he put those books to one side and opened Anaweh's
packet again.

It contained a U.S. Geological Survey map upon which Anaweh had drawn a square. That square defined roughly the same
region shown in the *First Americans* book.

Underneath was written:

Leave this area at once.
—Anaweh

J O H N Anaweh moved as quickly between the columns and their grisly momentos as the waist-deep pool would allow. The constant, mindless buffeting of the eels was taking its toll, whittling him down to raw nerves.

His lantern cast violent silhouettes of past battles, of broken weapons and shattered limbs. Petrified bones, splintered to razor sharpness, jutted from the gypsum pedestals. In death, the warriors had become weapons themselves.

The ceiling angled sharply down, and the current tugged him forward. Just past the silent carnage, the chamber ended in five vaulted tunnels.

Michael Buckhorn had passed through one of these tunnels on his way to the den of the Spirit. His death would have rendered him useless to the Spirit, an unworthy offering— exactly as Morning Sun intended.

But it hadn't ended there. And that left only one option: destroying the Spirit where it lived. These underground channels could lead anywhere. He had to find the right one.

Anaweh removed a bottle from his pack. He placed the medallion from Morning Sun's hogan inside and sealed it. It floated away as he watched.

The cricket-eaters, which he'd seen ravenously attack the water droplets that fell from the ceiling, gave it a wide berth. The bottle moved toward one of the passages, slowed, then stopped altogether.

There was a subtle shift in the current. Anaweh moved the light beam slowly across the mouths of the tunnels. The cool air grew colder. A breeze lapped the water's surface.

He slid his bow from the pack, fixed it, and drew an arrow. A small wave slapped his chest, and he felt something sharp at his back. Broken ribs jutted from a pedestal behind him. He stepped away, took aim at the bottle, then he lifted the point of his arrow to the center of the opening.

The tunnel slowly filled with blue light. The cricket-eaters jostled him, but it wasn't a search for food driving them. They swam past him, away from the tunnels, their translucent bodies streaking through the water like tracer bullets.

Anaweh fought the growing current, trying to steady the bow. The light in the tunnel grew stronger. Somewhere a siphon was opening, and the water was retreating.

A long shadow crawled the length of the tunnel, moving closer and closer to Anaweh. The water lapped the back of his knees, sending shockwaves up his spine. He pulled the bowstring until it sang.

From deep within the tunnel came a roar of water. The tide was rushing back. He braced himself as the shadow crossed the threshold. White foam gushed from the tunnels. He stood his ground and waited for his shot as the wave thundered toward him.

A girl stepped into his sights. His point wandered from its target on her throat for only an instant, but it was an instant too long. The wave lifted him, threw him backward.

There was a numbing impact; beneath the crash and hiss of the tidewater was a sound like snapping branches.

Anaweh's legs jerked above the receding tide. The girl was gone; in her place, a tall white shadow. Anaweh's bow floated out of reach in the suddenly quiet pool, a pool growing darker with each twitch of his limbs. He managed to raise one hand to his chest. Two new ribs had sprung between his own.

The tall white shadow drifted back into the tunnel. The bottle drifted slowly behind it, and then darkness swallowed everything.

CRACK!

Crack!

Deputy Pat Phillips woke to see a rectangle of snow-filled dusk. What the hell was he doing sitting in a cave? He was freezing. His head hurt and his joints ached. It was like he'd just come off a bad drunk. A hunting rifle lay across his lap.

Crack!

Crack!

There was a loud cheer, a huge crowd somewhere.

Railroad tracks ran beside him. A pegboard with numbered

274

brass tags was fixed to the wall. At least he knew where he was now. Miners had used that board to "brass in" and "brass out" each day. Even in its heyday the mine was treacherous. More than a time clock, a full board of tags told the shift boss everyone who'd made it in had made it out. But how the hell had he wound up at the entrance to the Wizard mine?

Crack!

The sound of gunshots knifed his temples. Stars flashed. For a moment, everything blurred.

He walked to the light. It had to be the quick-draw contest in town.

He looked down on the streets of Piñon Rim. But through his rifle scope he didn't see a crowd of tourists dressed in heavy coats cheering on latter-day gunslingers firing blanks; he saw kids in jeans and T-shirts climbing a huge mound of earth in the center of town.

The first kid up threw the others back.

It was a game of King of the Hill, the biggest darn version he'd ever seen. It was a game he'd never been good at. And it wasn't because he was small, either. He'd been taller than most as a kid. He just wasn't aggressive, that was all. It wasn't that he was a pansy or a momma's boy, like they'd said sometimes. He just wasn't violent like the others. He was just a good boy, that was why he couldn't play right. That was why they always threw him off and held him down and pounded him all those times. He was just a good boy. Not a pansy. *Not a wimp.*

Crack!

Crack!

There was a tall kid down there, towheaded and pale. Every time he got close, they pushed him back. And it wasn't just the kid on top doing it, either. *They were all doing it.* The towheaded kid wasn't doing anything about it. He just kept trying and kept getting thrown back.

"Come on. Do it. Fight back," Pat Phillips said, under his breath.

Finally, the boy sat down away from the rest. He started to cry.

275

"Don't cry, darn it," Phillips muttered. "Fight back, you little pansy. Get back and fight, you—"

Crack!

The kid was wailing. The other kids rained him with dirt clods.

"Get up and fight, darn it!"

One kid ran up next to him and plowed a dirt clod right into his face.

"Get up!" Pat Phillips snarled. "Get up and fight, you white-faced wimp!"

"HONESTLY, Agnetha. You probably scared him to death." Andre dropped another scoopful of pellets in the trough. The furnace erupted in blue-green sparks behind the glass.

Aggie Hudson sipped her brandy thoughtfully while the wind howled outside. Several shots were fired downstairs on Front Street. A bullhorn announced a new high score, and the crowd cheered as one more Sunday Afternoon Wyatt Earp loaded up and took his place before the sand-filled barrel.

She couldn't believe they were still going at it, snow and all. She shook her head.

"It was innocent enough—"

"Innocence is the one sin you've never been guilty of, my dear. He's in love with the girl, after all. And I'm sure he has a terrific crush on you, like every other man in this town."

"Why, Andre . . ."

"Did I say *every* man?" He smiled wryly. "Anyway, we're getting nowhere with this. He's probably fine, but if you think you've rocked his cradle too hard, the telephone is a marvelous healer." He pushed another sheet of slides across the coffee table. "In the meantime, take a look at these. I'm not going to say anything."

She moved the last one to the growing pile beside her, then set the new one on the light box.

"Ecchh!"

"Exactly. I think we can nix Reginald Whitney from this exhibit. Try these."

"Not bad. The two on the upper right would show well next to the Penmars."

"Mmm."

More shots were fired. The bullhorn blared. Andrew swirled his brandy and sank deep into his chair. He dropped another sheet of slides onto the coffee table and yawned. Outside, the sky was an even gray through the snow. They'd been at it since early afternoon. And Agnetha hadn't been into it from the beginning.

The downstairs chimes tinkled, and the door hissed shut.

"I'm back!"

"Ahh, dinner has arrived at last. In any case, your little friend has probably forgotten all about his visit to Aunt Aggie's chamber of horrors. He was here this morning, before that man was killed."

"What man?"

"What corner of the planet have you been on?"

"I've been in the studio. What happened? Who was killed?"

"A tourist. Right outside the pharmacy. One of the workmen went into a frenzy. Crushed the man's skull in front of his family."

Aggie's jaw dropped. "That's awful!"

"Yeah." Connie's head popped over the railing. "That's all anybody's talking about in town. That makes five dead people here in a month." She set three bags emblazoned with the Redrock Cafe logo on the coffee table and handed Aggie the change.

"Outta tiramisu."

"Too many damn tourists."

Snow pelted the small windows. Several shots went off in rapid succession. Over the cheering someone screamed. Suddenly guns seemed to be going off all over town.

"What are they *doing* out there?" Andre said.

They were at the windows in a heartbeat. By that time the end had begun. The three of them gaped through the ornate leaded bars upstairs at the Lucky Slipper.

On the snow-covered, darkening streets of Piñon Rim, people were running for their lives. Already, half a dozen bodies lay in attitudes of restless sleep. Gunshots and screams punctuated the cries of the broken and dying. Smoke rolled across the sky.

Pockets of onlookers simply watched, like cattle in a pasture. Now and again one in their midst would drop suddenly. The others stood unaffected.

"She's the one!"

The man stood wide-eyed, in the middle of the street, a burning stump of wood in his hand. He pointed the torch toward the windows where they stood. In an instant, he was joined by others. Some of them held rifles.

There was a soft *clink* as one tiny windowpane spiderwebbed beside Aggie.

Andre stepped back. He glanced incredulously at Aggie, then his eyes seemed to roll back into his head. He turned on his heels and fell through the coffee table, shot dead. Connie screamed.

Aggie blinked herself back into the world as the glass door downstairs flew back on its hinges and shattered.

The man in the street was Bill Jordan.

24

 B R Y C E sat against the bedframe and listened. His stomach growled.

When Cathleen called him down for supper around 6:00, he'd asked her to save him some. He'd said he had a history test to study for. She didn't push it. It was after 7:00 now, and the only thing he'd eaten all day was that Indian fried bread on Cross Hill.

He'd *heard* supper this evening. Mostly he'd heard the metallic conversation of dishes and silverware downstairs; there was very little said between Meg and her mom.

He needed to talk to Trevor. An occasional cough had broken from across the hall, but his dad hadn't left the studio. Maybe his dad was in the same boat he was. Maybe it was Meg and Cathleen against the two of them. He remembered running with him that night they'd searched for Meg, the night that started all this. There had been something strong there, something protective and good.

When he remembered that awful gray shadow moving between the jumble of canvases, slamming the studio door as Bryce had passed, a tremor raced through him.

He had to get through somehow. Cathleen was Megan's protector, a fortress erected around her precious little Meg. The fact that her precious little Meg had gone from child to adolescent in a matter of days hadn't phased her. And if that didn't, what would?

But there was still hope with his dad. Maybe there was some way out of this. Maybe his dad wasn't too far gone to side with him. Maybe he should just go downstairs and eat something

279

before hunger made him stupid. What would Meg do? Rip his eyes out?

That was a distinct possibility.

He'd left two messages, but his mom hadn't called back. He was sorry he'd written that stupid letter. It had been better not knowing where he stood. She didn't write back, she didn't call. She just didn't care. He was totally cut off.

The phone rang and he nearly hit the ceiling.

"Hello?"

"Bryce?" It was Cody. His voice was strained, barely more than a whisper.

"What?"

"We gotta get outta here fast. They told me the rest of the legend, but they still won't believe it. It's gonna drive everybody kill-crazy. It needs someone to start it off, then it's like British Bulldog: that one gets the next one, then those two get someone else. Man, you were right. Your sister's it!" There was a *click*, the sound of a far-off television commercial cutting in. Cody's voice was suddenly, desperately animated. "So that's how it is, dude. See you." A louder, final *click*.

Bryce listened to the dial tone for some time, that hollow feeling rising in his chest.

Your sister's it!

He should have gone to Cody's. Better yet, they both should have left town when they had the chance. All that bull he'd said about doing something. When it came right down to it, he'd been just as stupid as everybody else in town.

It happened so fast.

Town went up fast, and went down even faster.

Footsteps. Someone coming upstairs.

He sucked a breath that only made it halfway down to his lungs. He eased the chair away and slid open the top drawer of his dresser. His hunting knife from camp was buried in there. He ran his hand beneath his T-shirts until he gripped its leather sheath. The landing at the top of the stairway groaned. He slid the blade out and stepped back. The blade gleamed; little stars flashed from the nicks along the bright edge. The nicks had come from errant throws at trees, from striking pebbles in the ground during games of mumblety-peg—not from skinning, not from gutting. He'd never cut flesh with it. He'd never cut *anything* with it.

His breaths came short and shallow.

"Honey?" Cathleen said. "You ready for dinner?"

"Not hungry, thanks."

"It's porkchops. Done all crispy."

"Thanks, later. I've gotta finish this."

Another groan from the floor—this one closer—right outside his door.

"It's your favorite." She insisted.

"Thanks, yeah. I'm almost done with this."

"It's waiting."

Oh, God, it's waiting all right. The imitation deerhorn handle was slick with sweat. Fire exploded up Bryce's neck to his temples. His stomach growled. He would have smelled porkchops cooking. That she'd lie so poorly only made it worse. It meant she didn't care if he believed her or not. He was trapped and she knew it. His legs were beginning to go. The shakes began to spread upward. He fought to keep them out of his voice.

"I've gotta finish, thanks."

Silence. What would happen if she tried the door? When she felt the pressure against it the whole thing would be over. No more of this polite stuff. Then what? She'd rush him, wouldn't she? She'd have to—*they both would.* And he'd have to use the knife that had never cut anything. He'd have to shove it into them and keep shoving it into them until they were dead, because if he didn't they'd do worse to him, wouldn't they? *What would it feel like to kill someone? Could he do that?*

He tried to pull out some of that anger he'd felt when he was arguing with Cody. He could use it now, he needed it now, but it wouldn't come back. Maybe because he was onto it. More likely because whatever had given him that feeling in the first place wanted him dead now.

He wanted to walk away from this, just freaking walk away. Maybe he could. Maybe if he just moved the chair and the dresser away, just walked downstairs and played the game with them until he could eat something. He'd feel better then, stronger.

A heartbeat passed. "Bryce?"

"Uh-huh?"

"No more using the phone tonight, okay? There's a curfew on phone use—until you get your homework done."

He reached back and lifted the phone off the hook. He raised it to his ear. The silence from the earpiece was deadly. He laid it quietly back on the desk.

" W E ' R E experiencing difficulty with that line."

"It was okay before. I got a call . . ." Sara hooked the receiver under her chin and removed Cervantes from the counter with one graceful sweep of her arm. The rankness of unchanged litter box was an oily yellow presence. She checked the microwave clock. "I got a call from that line about an hour ago."

"We're running diagnostics. Is this an emergency?"

"Well . . . no. How long will it take to fix?"

"We won't know till we trace the problem, ma'am."

"Okay, thanks."

"Thank you for—"

Sara shifted Cervantes to her shoulder and hung up. He nestled comfortably.

Was it an emergency? Maybe it was.

The wrinkled pages of Bryce's letter were still in her hand, the residue of two weeks of free-flowing margaritas still in her bloodstream.

She bent and dropped the cat to the tile and nearly lost her balance. Her head ached. Cervantes lifted his tail and stiff-legged it out the kitchen door.

She checked the utility room. Cindy had definitely fallen behind in the changing department. Half a dozen little tootsie rolls in Cervantes's box. She cracked open the back door and slid the offending tray into the frigid night air. She couldn't deal with dirty litter after the flight from Puerto Vallarta. Cindy was a sweetheart for baby-sitting on short notice, but she just wasn't a cat person.

Sara made the rounds. No boogeyman waiting in the bedroom. Nothing out of place. In her den she tapped the fireplace control. Flames leapt across fresh mesquite logs; Cindy was a sweetheart all right. The litter smell began to dissipate. Thank God for roasting mesquite. The couch was soft and familiar. She dropped her shoes and slid her long legs out across it. Cervantes took the cue and landed himself between her waist and the back cushions. She stroked him absently as she reread Bryce's letter.

The letter was heavy with pubescent anguish. God, she still remembered what that was like, (it wasn't that long ago, was it?): the terrible realization that from this point on, nothing in life, not even love, would be gained without pain. Hadn't she made a promise then? Something about being there for her kids when it hit, the way her folks never were?

Michael's motives for having her drop everything and meet him in Puerto Vallarta were about as complicated as the recipe for mud. He'd caught her off guard—Michael, with his smooth hands and Mediterranean good looks. No, that was a lie. He'd caught her all right, but she wanted it as much as he did.

Timing is everything.

She laid the letter on her chest and stared at the heavy wooden beams above her. There were faces in the old wood, faces she'd traced again and again. There's a place in every home where you feel safe, where your mind opens and all thoughts, good and bad, flow freely. This was her place. The heart of her home.

That heart was suddenly beating fast.

There was something just beneath the surface of Bryce's letter that went beyond pubescent angst, something dark that made the back of her neck feel prickly and cold and set her mothering instinct on red alert. The faces etched in the grain above her could be warming and friendly; depending upon the lines her eyes followed at any given time, they could also be terrifying. Tonight she couldn't find the smiling ones.

The letter was dated over a week ago, the day she'd left with Michael.

And as bad as the letter was, Bryce's voice on the answering machine was worse.

He's afraid. But afraid of what?

She'd played the message three times before she called back. Then she'd erased it. She was a horrible mother. It wasn't any consolation at all that Trevor was a terrible husband—at least Trevor had the guts to tough it out and be there.

Maybe it *was* an emergency.

She was in her bedroom dialing his number before she knew it, before she had any plan at all.

"The number you have dialed is experiencing—"

Thanks a lot.

She calmed herself down. The computer voice on the line was a good sign; it meant they were doing something.

She scooted her Day-Timer off the counter and found Larry Brill's number.

The phone rang while she ran cold water into her sink. She set it down, tied back her long black hair, splashed her face, and toweled off while the phone rang on, a bee-sized buzz from her sink. Bryce stared back from the mirror.

"Hello?"

She scooped the remote and nearly dropped it.

"Larry?"

The return voice was hesitant.

"Sara?"

"Larry, hi. Sorry I haven't been in touch. I—"

" 'Sno prob, babe."

He's been drinking. Well, so have I.

"Been . . . oh, outta touch myself."

"Larry. What's happening with Trevor? I can't get through."

A long pause. The remote wasn't always so great. She repeated the question.

"Same as me, babe. Livin' the good life."

There was a long pause. She wasn't sure if he was finished or not.

"When did you see—"

"Same as me. Gotta go, babe."

She dialed again. It was busy.

284

After one of the fastest and coldest showers she'd ever taken, she tried both numbers again. The same computerized voice message answered both numbers now.

Sara dialed the operator. This time it was an emergency. When the operator asked her for specifics she hung up and made two more phone calls, one to America West Airlines and the other to Hertz at Sky Harbor Airport in Phoenix. On her way out, she tried Bryce and Larry one more time each, then she called Cindy.

Before she left she retrieved the litter box, dumped the old, and poured in fresh. She kissed Cervantes good-bye.

B R Y C E shifted the pack between himself and the foot of the bed to give his back some support. He'd changed into his best jeans and snowpants and laid his good ski jacket, hat, and gloves on the bed. The others were torn—no use messing with them. He wouldn't be coming back.

There was a cough from the studio. Silence from downstairs. But Megan and Cathleen were there all right. He could feel them, a cold dread crawling up the stairs and between the floorboards where he sat. The stepsister from hell and her mom.

He stood and flipped off the light, holding the switch as he did it, not wanting a click. There was a moment of panic before his eyes adjusted to the darkness, but the rest of the house was bound to be dark when he left, especially the hallway. He didn't want any surprises.

Snow drifted silently past the window. The plows wouldn't be back this way till morning, if they came at all. If snow covered the ice, he'd kill himself on the Stingray. Wherever he intended to go, he'd have to walk. And he'd probably freeze to death before he got anywhere. This wasn't good. This was definitely not good.

And he was tired. So tired. Leaning back against his backpack, he pulled his jacket over his shoulders. He wrapped his fingers around the handle of his hunting knife. His head nodded; he jerked it back. He couldn't sleep now. He had to listen for Cathleen and Meg to go to their rooms. He had to listen for his chance.

Little by little, his chin sunk to his chest. He didn't lift it this time . . .

I T was November 1, 1894. An early snow choked the streets, but that didn't tame the spirit of Boomtown Piñon Rim. A pistol discharged twice in quick succession; the rounds whistled harmlessly into the night.

Drunks weaved through town oblivious to the cold, singing at the top of their lungs, cursing, and dodging traffic as best they could. Horses shivered, their coats not yet thick enough to warm them. They were caught worse off than their human masters by the freak storm. They puffed steam and kicked white bursts of snow as the coach wheels cut ravines through the streets behind them. The coach drivers had bright and wary eyes; they kept their weapons close at hand. Piñon Rim had become a very dangerous place to be.

Raucous piano music and laughter poured from the tenderloin parlors on Front Street, and the Lucky Slipper was the biggest and loudest of them all.

On Cross Hill, parlor music gave way to a hundred plus earnest human voices singing "Rock of Ages" in unison. The singers stood in their pews with tears on their cheeks, their eyes every bit as bright as those of the coach drivers', every bit as bright and wild as any in town. But the light in their eyes was one of revelation, not of drunkenness or fear or the madness that was sweeping through their town. It was God's own light, not the blight of sinners.

As the last strains of "Rock of Ages" died, "Amazing Grace" began. Ending the town meeting with such devotions was not the custom, but a decision of righteousness had been reached tonight.

The town elders stood stiffly before their chairs. One chair among them was conspicuously vacant.

Below Cross Hill, six men walked toward town. They carried Spencer rifles and Colt Dragoon pistols. One also carried a sledgehammer, and a rope strung with pine wedges was slung over his shoulder. Another carried a large tin of kerosene.

A driver pulling his team onto Katie Avenue had to swing wide to avoid them. He cut off his curse before it could crawl halfway up his throat, and thanked his dumb luck and slow tongue when he saw their eyes.

They regarded him as a pack of wolves might a flea on a field mouse. He pulled his team as far to the side as safety allowed and looked straight ahead. He clicked his tongue and drove his team quickly away.

The six walked on, the streets becoming silent and still as they passed.

A drunk careened off the Front Street boardwalk and found himself face-to-face with six preachers. He smiled and blinked them into focus, and two Spencers swung his way. He simultaneously vomited and shit his pants. He held his hands and the bottle straight out to his sides as they passed. His pants and the snow at his feet were steaming, his whole body shaking. Two steps past him, one of the six turned, put his Colt to the man's head, and blew his brains across Katie Avenue.

The piano played on through shouts and laughter at the Lucky Slipper. "Amazing Grace" could still be heard in the lulls. The batwing doorway cast crazy dancing shadows across the street.

Now the rest of Pinon Rim was still, quiet as the tomb it was soon to become. The Lucky Slipper had been caught laughing in church.

The six walked slowly up the steps, in double file like pallbearers, their guns at the ready.

As the doors swung wide, they opened fire.

Laughter exploded into shrieks. Blood and glass showered the room. The bartender swung a shotgun from beneath the counter. He got off two loads: the first blew a batwing off its hinges. The other splintered a post near the man with the sledgehammer, shredding his coat sleeve but leaving him unharmed. A hail of fire and spinning glass ripped the bartender in half before he could reload.

The Lucky Slipper doves ran screaming for the stairway. One

struck a table with her hip and fell. A .44 slug tore most of her neck away. Her head dropped loosely to her chest.

The six emptied their guns, reloaded, and emptied them again. Two men at a far corner of the room raised their hands over their heads. When three slugs nailed one of them to the wall, the other dove beneath the wreckage of a table and popped up a beat later with a Colt of his own. Before one of the Spencers splintered a tabletop through his heart, he fired once, drilling one gunman—the one who had earlier dispatched the drunk in the street—and nicking his right lung. The gunman would die two days later, but it was the only injury the six would receive. In less than forty-five seconds it was over.

From upstairs came the cries of the ladies.

The six reloaded. One stepped outside to cover the upstairs windows. There was little chance of escape through those windows: they were built decoratively enough, but their purpose was to deny the opportunistic an alternative to paying. Still, people did amazing things when pressed. The other five climbed the stairway to the brothel. Halfway up, the gunman who had been hit collapsed. The others, their faces dotted with powder and blood, went on. At least one of the women had been hit squarely, leaving bright red fans of blood waist-high on the pink fleur-de-lys wallpaper.

The man with the sledgehammer unknotted his rope and kicked the loose wedges down the hall. The first door forced open was the only one they'd need, though they did the rest as well. Rose Bowman, beautiful even now with her eyes wide with fear, her blouse slick with blood, cradled Del MacKenna in her arms. Del was dead, and her left arm was gone beneath the elbow.

The man with the sledgehammer had never known Rose, although he supposed he could have—just like anyone else who could pay for it. He'd been awed by her looks. It was a shame, he thought now. He swung a rooster tail of kerosene toward her, splashing her blouse and Del's dead face. Rose shrieked, a shriek like he'd never heard before.

He slammed the door and pounded the wedges into place beneath it. He poured more kerosene over the threshold and down the hall while the other doors were secured. He set the can in the middle of the hallway.

Shrieks and cries for mercy came from every room, from men as well as women. Men screamed pretty much the same as women when it came right down to it, he guessed, but that sound coming from Rose's door, that was something awful, something he'd never forget.

He could almost believe, as he shattered a lamp and watched flames leap toward the doors, that Rose Bowman really was the devil, just like the elders said.

T H E back door slammed. Bryce heard it echoing from his dream.

Had someone screamed? There was nothing. Silence.

Then footsteps across the den and up the stairs. Light footsteps, not heavy enough to make the stairway groan. They paused outside his door. His heart fluttered in his chest like a bat in a small cage.

The footsteps proceeded down the hallway to Meg's room. Her door shut.

He took a deep breath and sank back against his bed. His back was sore from sleeping sitting up. His right arm had fallen asleep. It was 12:00. He'd been asleep (helpless) for three hours! She could have killed him. But she hadn't.

She'd gone out, but where?

He stood carefully, not wanting to make the floorboards creak, and found that his arm wasn't the only thing that had gone south for the evening: his entire right leg was pins and needles.

The snow was still falling, heavier now. And there was something else. An orange glow above the trees. He walked quietly to the window and gaped toward town. The glow flickered. Black smoke against the clouds.

Piñon Rim was on fire.

S E C O N D S after he'd finished talking to Sara Rojo, Larry Brill had forgotten the entire conversation. He groped for the hook with the receiver, forgot he was holding something, and let the receiver clatter to the floor.

The sound startled him. He glanced around, having lost the sense that something important had taken place. Then he was back at work.

He sniffed as that puzzling but now familiar stale odor wafted by. It retreated as he applied more linseed oil to his palette. The hand that held his brush was thin, hairless, and gray but for the clusters of liver spots which, lately, had made his entire arm look like a tube-shaped relief map of world populations. The very same shirt that had bound his shoulders annoyingly only days ago was now two sizes too big. That had given him a start this morning, as had the sight of the shriveled head and neck that poked turtlelike from his undershirt. But he never fretted any of these things for long.

Heck if the paintings ain't good.

And he had lots of them.

They cramped the studio. Some were stacked up and down the staircase, others propped neatly against the furniture. His kitchen was so packed with canvases that he couldn't use it, which was okay since he wasn't hungry. Assignments came steadily in, but he was way ahead—two or three lifetimes ahead—and he'd lost track. A year ago the Rothgar series alone would have kept him going for months. He'd finished that entire series in less than a week. Now he created his own adventures.

Just pumpin' 'em out.

He worked five paintings at a time. The latest quintet encircled him like the monoliths of Stonehenge. He painted sitting down, swiveling his stool from one to the next, scraping the excess from this one with a palette knife, adding to another, changing his mind completely on a third and wiping a section clean with a rag soaked in turpentine.

Rothgar the Warrior ripped through the rough fabric of Larry Brill's canvases. They were like the unfinished Michelangelo sculptures, each granite-hard muscle possessing a powerful vitality all its own. Rothgar battling the Viking Dreadnoughts. Rothgar battling the Dragon of the Black Sea. Rothgar battling hosts of unspeakably evil-looking creatures. His best work ever.

The lights dimmed and brightened. Then they dimmed and stayed put, just a notch or two below comfort. Larry stood, only now acknowledging the pain creeping along his spine.

Well, he'd been at it a long time. His chair wasn't exactly ergodynamic. He slowly stretched his stiff muscles and adjusted the lights.

The lights were dim again before he'd settled back on the stool. He stood—or tried to. Cold lightning struck his back. He doubled over and let out a scream that was more a high-pitched wheeze.

Jeez, was that him?

He never did right himself, not completely. He reached for the light switch and the hand before him was like a doll's hand fashioned from old cornhusks. He pulled it back, shocked and confused, his breath rattling in his lungs like a mouse in a paper bag. That smell, cloying and musty, was everywhere now. The light had died to a dim tunnel of yellow-brown.

Downstairs, something rammed into the kitchen door so hard that the loft floor vibrated. Larry pulled in a rattling breath. It struck again. He hunched at the top of the stairs, clutching the rail for balance. A window burst, and shards of glass exploded across the tile. He peered through a thickening haze into the den, barely able to move, suddenly terrified of falling.

The shadowy figure of a large man stood squarely in the center of the den, surrounded by the best damn paintings Larry Brill had ever done. He held a woodman's axe in his hands.

"Who are you?" Larry croaked.

The man just stood there. Larry's fading eyesight flickered to give him one last clear view. He saw a man with a pink face who was the size of a mountain. His chin was shiny with sweat and drool. It registered with Larry that he had seen this man before, at the lumberyard where Larry had once purchased a load of one-by-twos and quarter rounds to build his own stretcher bars. The man had been friendly enough; he'd asked him what he was going to build. That was the extent of their conversation. Now he was standing here in Larry's den with an axe, his eyes sparkling and gleeful. A churlish grin cut that wide pink face ear to ear as the man raised the axe to his shoulder.

The sight hammered Larry.

The axe shattered the first five paintings it touched in one effortless swing. A chuckle bubbled out of the big man. He swung again and again.

Larry Brill shrieked, forgot where he was, forgot how difficult even small movements had become. His life's work, his small mark on the cold granite face of this planet, was being erased before his eyes.

His foot moved out over the first step. It took his balance with it. His knee seized up like a dry piston. He pitched out over the stairway, his right arm and leg catching the banister at the same time; they snapped off at the joints like balsa wood.

He had one last sickening sensation of pain and collapse as his chest struck the bottom steps and flattened, then his head shattered against the floor.

C O D Y sat behind the pool table with his father's shotgun across his lap. His mouth was nearly dry as he chewed another wad of gum. Upstairs, little kids were tearing the place apart. They'd be down here soon enough. He pried open the end of a 10-gauge shell and emptied the pellets into his hand.

His parents had been nearly comatose when the end had come. They'd let it happen. But he wouldn't. He spat out the gum, rolled in the pellets, and stuffed the lumpy wad as far as he could down the muzzle. He loaded it and ran it back to its place in the rack. The gun was long and unwieldy, and it only held one shell. It was too clumsy to take with him, but if they tried to use it they'd regret it.

Two sets of tiny legs ran past the cellar window. He wasn't sure how many kids were still outside. Once they'd bashed open the front door they'd poured in like ants, but so far they'd left the cellar alone.

As soon as he'd hung up the phone with Bryce, Jason was on it. And then the phone didn't work anymore.

Then *they* came.

The cellar window was small; it would take time to squeeze through. If a bunch of brats were waiting outside they'd hack him to pieces before he made it halfway out. Better off fighting his way through the kitchen.

Something hammered the cellar door.

Cody took a cuestick from the rack, spun off the thin end, and threw it aside. The door shuddered, then splintered. He snatched the cue ball from the table. The first one through the door got the ball. After that he'd use the stick.

He raised the ball to his ear as the door flew back. Jason came through first. The moment he could have thrown it came and went. The cellar window shattered, and he turned that way and threw.

He recognized little Peter Meuller's face framed for an instant in the empty window. A white blur hurtled toward it like a meteor, then half of Peter's face shifted straight up. His body slid through the window like a ragdoll till it caught on something in the frame. Blood sheeted down the wall.

Time froze on the horror. Cody literally blanked for a second, and in that time Jason had the shotgun on him.

Cody's heart tore loose. He swallowed hard.

"Don't do it! Ja—"

Jason squeezed the trigger. There was a staggering, hollow boom that rang the cellar like a brass bell, and everything above Jason's hands disappeared in a cloud of pink mist.

A scream curdled the air. The kids closest to Jason's body stood at odd angles, broken dolls gaping at him from ruined faces. The scream split the night again, and Cody barely recognized it as his own.

He leapt past them, cracking them out of his path with the cuestick. Fresh troops rushed the gap, swinging kitchen knives, bats, pokers, anything they could carry. He ripped through them, crying and laughing like a madman. He was hit, kicked, and stabbed but didn't feel a bit of it.

A kid ran at him swinging a gas can, but Cody swatted his hand away and the gas splashed over the stove. He bulled his

293

way through the door and into the frozen night as they shrieked and batted at him. Flames raced across the kitchen.

Five adults stood outside in the snow-covered yard, watching their kids murder as though it were Gymboree.

"You stupid idiots!"

One parent turned to him and smiled. Cody swung the stick and it snapped across the man's face. He went down in a heap. The others watched.

Then Cody was running for the trees. He was free. The snow fell windlessly as he ran. He heard an explosion behind him, and he knew everything that had gone before was gone forever. It had been the press of a button, a laser flash.

All gone. Hyperspace.

Trees blurred past him. He was running at warp speed. Press a button and *blip,* you appear in another sector of the universe. That's how it worked. He'd pressed the button and escaped.

The light was patchy in the forest, casting odd, ghostly patterns of blue, white, and black. He ran on clumsily now, feeling a cold burning in his side. As numb as he was to the pain, the effort to escape had been enormous; his batteries were drained. The heavy snow clutched at his feet, pulling him down as he labored on. His jaw hung open as he ran, gobbling in the cold night air the way a shark gobbles blue water. He was moving forward to survive, but his lungs were barely able to keep up. He took a breath with every uneven, twisting step. His arms jounced at his sides. His grip on the broken cue loosened, but he caught it again.

Dark spots spattered the snow as he ran. His breathing was raspy and oddly doubled somehow; a second, smaller breath for every one he took. Something was way wrong: he should be able to run faster, farther than this, he always could before.

The cold burning in his side came to a needle point. His cry was hoarse, windless. He pushed on, not feeling his legs. The trees spun around him, stopped, and spun again.

Just ahead a patch of snow seemed to pull itself straight up from the forest floor. He could still see the shadowy shapes of the trees behind the white patch as it rose high above him. In its center, something twitched and turned to face him. His brain shrieked at his legs to move, but the message never got there. He saw white teeth and long, dagger-tipped fingers. *The Spirit had come for him.* His throat opened to scream and the apparition was gone.

Megan Willems stood in its place.

Cody put everything he had into the swing. The cue whistled toward her head. There was a snapping sound and the cue thumped into the snow behind her. White-hot pain shivered from his elbow to his spine. She released his broken elbow and just as quickly caught his throat. His other hand moved weakly to fend her off, but there was no strength, no air.

She slammed him backward into the snow and sat on his stomach. Her face was a shiny moon above him. It winked out, then came back.

She smiled. Silver-blue light danced in her eyes.

"That was good," she said, "give me more." She reached back into the snow and he knew she was going for the cuestick. His frozen fingers tried to find her eyes, but she simply pushed them away with her cheek and held them against her shoulder. The movement made a rasping sound, and her skin felt like old, rotted newspapers. The cuestick was poised above him. He could see the sharp jags where the end had broken off.

"How do you like your home, Cody?"

He gritted his teeth, his whole body tremored. He saw his house destroyed as his parents watched; he saw Jason disintegrating in a cloud of pink mist.

She plunged the stick through his heart.

25

SARA's shoes made little wisp noises across the carpet as she walked through the cavernous America West terminal at Sky Harbor.

She'd had two more drinks on the plane, which was probably a mistake but she needed *something*.

Was she crazy? What was she doing in Phoenix in the middle of the night?

A silver-haired man in a cheap blue suit leered from his bar stool as she went by. She took pains not to make eye contact, but she could feel his eyes contacting her every curve. She silently repeated her question. She wondered how obvious it was that she'd had a few. Men could spot a tipsy female at a thousand paces, no matter how old or how blind they might seem to be.

The terminal wasn't empty by any means. At a decent hour it would probably be packed with snowbirds escaping the cold nether regions. This wasn't a decent hour and there were still quite a few. Dark blue Chicago Bears caps whizzed by, as did real fur coats, which released a heady scent of sweat and old game. Everyone escaping the Frozen North for the Valley of the Sun.

And why had she come to Phoenix? To head north. Go figure.

She popped a Tic-Tac as she approached the car rental booths. It wouldn't do to rent a car reeking of booze, would it?

The girl in the yellow blazer smiled. There was as much synthetic in that smile as in the jacket. The eyes behind it were passable, maybe even pretty with a more deft application of makeup. *Woman, you are nasty tonight.*

No, she corrected herself. You're scared stiff.

The business was finished in an instant. A possibility of snow near Sedona. There were chains in the trunk, but they wouldn't be necessary.

She made one more fruitless try at calling Trevor and Larry. Then she hurried into the clear, star-filled night.

T H E only sound in the rest of the house was an occasional dry, rasping cough from the studio.

The cough seemed weaker as the night wore on. Bryce hoped that it was his imagination. He slid his window up slowly, stopping and waiting at every squeak. He'd still have the storm window to deal with. If he detached it from the inside he'd break it, and then he'd have to jump and run for it. The last thing he wanted to do was chance a sprain. He had a long, long ride once he left the house. The window would be a last resort.

And he wasn't going anywhere until he talked to his dad.

He was glad now for the few hours of sleep he'd gotten. His head had cleared and he wasn't as likely to drift off. He wondered how Cody was doing. If Cody had any sort of lead at all, nobody could outrun him, no way. Bryce held tightly to that.

He pulled on his jacket, folded and stuffed his gloves and a roll-up hat in his pockets, and slid on his pack. He did these things deliberately, acutely aware of the texture and color of each, the thin rushing sounds the fabrics made in his hands.

He looked back at the falling snow and the rusty glow beyond the forest. Then he freed the dresser and walked it slowly from the door. He picked up the knife. Breaths were coming fast and shallow. Cold sweat beaded on his temples. His arms were wet beneath the down jacket.

His hand stretched for the knob, a robot's limb telescoping toward a possible bomb. He made cold contact, pushing the knob in as it turned to avoid the click; and then the door was open.

Across the hall, a ribbon of white light rimmed the studio door. The house was dark.

The knife seemed to float on its own just above his hip. It was a thing capable of killing, though it had never served that purpose. It was also a red flag. If Megan or Cathleen saw it, they would try to kill him. It was that simple.

He felt light-headed. He fought it, fought the part of him that just wanted things safe and sane again. There was no safe and no sane. He gripped the killing thing tightly in his hand.

The studio wasn't locked.

The door stopped on something a few inches inside. It gave enough for him to squeeze by. He eased the door shut behind him and stood there gaping at an undulating cyclorama of dark, rain-drenched canyons and slate-colored skies. From floor to ceiling, one gigantic canvas weaved through the entire room.

He began walking, spellbound. He saw a city carved into the rock of the cliffs, ancient people in rich dress running through the streets. Bryce recognized the bell-like red-rock formations above the city. It was a view he remembered from looking east from the top of Cross Hill. But the mountains in the painting were sharper and more rugged, and taller somehow. Then he realized why: the area was covered by foothills now. What was this—Arizona a million years ago?

Bryce followed the painting as it curved back to the far wall. He saw men tending fields of tall corn. Many had stopped their work to stare at the angry skies.

The detail was staggering. You could see the worried lines in their faces, *could feel their terror*.

He saw the same area now from a slightly different view, looking north toward Sedona. Trevor had somehow melded both views into one continuous scene.

Snow had fallen in a treacherously deep blanket, one meant to smother, not comfort. There was no sign of life.

The skin prickled down the back of Bryce's neck. He should get out now, turn and run while he could. But he kept walking around the canvas. He couldn't take his eyes off it.

Looking south now. Desert, awesome in its sheer starkness, dry and lifeless as concrete. The city was gone. He kept walking.

Rainfall. A river now flowed, disappearing below the surface. Men were hunting wild pigs and deer. Another city rose from the valley floor. Wide rivers of green cornstalks wound through the canyons.

Another rain, another snow, another desert. He kept walking. It was the same scene over and over again. And yet it wasn't. He followed the next curve *and saw Piñon Rim.*

It was Front Street, when the Wizard had pumped gold and life was good; the heyday of Rose Bowman and the Lucky Slipper. The realism was frightening. Rich carriages cruised the street. Men tipped their hats. A man dressed in a black suit with a gold watch chain (Was that Percival Easton? Yes, it was) stood, one hand on the batwing door of the Slipper, as he called to someone just out of sight inside.

Bryce kept walking. He no longer saw the rough tooth of the canvas beneath the painting: *he no longer saw a painting.* The scene before him was real, the people in it alive, their motion merely suspended. He had become a time-traveling ghost, a ghost suddenly cursed with all the answers but helpless to act on any of them.

He turned another corner and stood on the walkway directly across from the Slipper.

It was nighttime. Snow had fallen, and the upper floor of the Lucky Slipper was in flames. *Was he hearing the screams?* He was. And music. A choir singing somewhere in the distance.

Easton had left his carriage in the middle of the street. It had since been dragged to one side, leaving deep ruts in the snow, as the bucket brigade attacked the flames. Where was Easton?

Bryce searched the faces in the brigade and those of the many who stood, disinterested and unconcerned, to one side. He knew those faces, or ones like them. He'd seen them when the man got his head crushed in front of the drugstore. People who stood and watched.

A group of men dressed like preachers tended to one of their own who lay injured in the street. The nearby snow was flecked black with his blood. Two of the preacher men were gesturing up to the second floor. Bryce followed their eyes, realizing now that he was witnessing the end of his own nightmare.

The second-floor windows glowed yellow, the fiery view plates of a furnace. In one of them was a man's face, his mouth a black shadow of a scream. *It was Percy Easton.* He'd defied the elders, run in behind the assassins, and tried to rescue Rose Bowman, the luckless woman whom the Wizard had cruelly chosen as its pariah and scapegoat.

The windowpanes had blasted out with the heat. The ornate framework that remained might as well have been prison bars. Easton's scorched hands clutched the frame.

"God . . ."

The sound of his own voice frightened Bryce as much as anything he'd seen. But the painting continued on.

He stood in the yard of the Big House. Roughly half of this scene was painted. The house and yard faded into a skeleton of gray washes and sienna sketch lines. Snow blanketed the roof except where the skylight broke through. The front door was open. His Stingray lay against the snowbank. It was covered with snow. Its broken chain lay half-coiled beside it like a frozen snake.

A rasping cough made every joint in Bryce's body snap straight. It could have come from anywhere.

The mirrored wall reflected the horrific tableau, reflected his own fright, magnified it. His father was nowhere to be seen.

"Dad?"

Another cough. A pile of rags shifted near the table. It pulled itself together and rose from the floor.

Bryce's heart and lungs froze in his chest. A pair of watery yellow eyes peered out from a living skull.

His father stared past him, through him, to the painting. His fingers, as knotted and twisted as old roots, selected a brush, squeezed color from a large tube, mixed in oil, squeezed out another line of color, mixed that. His father moved to the canvas. A thick, sweet smell like rotted leather rose as he passed. More of the house began to appear on the canvas with eerie precision.

"Dad?"

To connect that word with what stood before him made

Bryce's stomach twist. But the connection was there. *This was his father.*

What was left of Trevor Willems took no notice of Bryce. It swirled a brush against the mesh liner in the cleaning jar, squeezed the tip with a rag, tossed the rag, and chose another color.

Bryce turned and ran. Tears reduced the painting to a rainbow as he flew past the murders of Rose Bowman and Percival Easton, past the rise and fall of so many who had gone before. He slammed the door behind him.

Megan stood in the hallway, her eyes glowing blue in the darkness. And suddenly, his fist was hurtling toward her face. He struck her square on the mouth. When she turned back to him, her lips were split and blood was splattered on her T-shirt.

He didn't see the back of her hand coming at him, didn't even feel it connect. He only knew he was flying backward. His pack took the first hit from the wall, then his arms and head slapped it so hard that plaster fell. His knife whisked down the hallway. Bright lights exploded. The hallway turned on end, then righted itself.

She was on him in an instant. Her fists balled his jacket against his throat. Her bloody face was all he could see.

Was this it then? Maybe it was. He didn't care anymore.

Her tongue flicked out, assessing the damage to her lips. Her ruined, beautiful mouth smiled, and more blood stained her shirt.

"Yeah, I bleed. Did you think I wouldn't? It's still me, Bryce."

Suddenly he was spinning out of control. His hip shivered the banister. He began to topple over, but she pulled him back.

"It's me. It's Meg. Little sis. You know." Her voice was small, a little kid's voice again. The horrible blue lights in her eyes were sharp, pinpricks in a blackout curtain.

"No you aren't. Meg's dead."

Her lips worked slowly. Her eyes moved over his face.

He closed his eyes. He couldn't stand seeing hers anymore, and still the pinpricks of light burned through. He turned his face away.

Her fingers released him, and he walked to the stairs, barely feeling his legs and feet.

From the den a dozen small faces turned up to his. *Meg's friends. Isn't that nice.* If there had been any feeling at all left inside him, he would have been terrified.

As it was, he just kept walking downstairs. Their faces were sullen, immobile; if Meg's eyes glowed with a sort of supernatural intelligence, the lack of any brains at all radiated from theirs.

What had happened here? Could he have stopped it? Sure he could have—that day Megan saw the Wizard in that stupid cave. He knew that. He could have been there when she needed him, but he wasn't.

Cathleen stood just outside the kitchen, waiting for her precious Megan to make the call.

"There's nowhere to go," Meg said.

"Yeah."

He kept walking.

"I've got friends now. I'm grown up. *I can see.*"

"You don't see *anything*."

Outside, the snow was falling. The Stingray's chain was indeed broken. Meg had probably snapped it with her pinkie. He couldn't have used the bike anyway—too much snow. Ha-ha.

He trudged across the yard and climbed over the bank to the road. And then he was running, running toward a town that might not even be there, and the tears began to flow. He cried like a little kid, like a freaking baby, until the tears froze on his cheeks and there was no voice left.

26

S A R A Rojo whistled through chattering teeth. She'd needed the chains *and* the four-wheel drive, thank you very much. When she got back to Phoenix she'd take that polyester scarf and strangle her with it.

The heater worked just fine, but the last hundred drivers had been chain smokers. It was a fight between defrosting to see and breathing—not an easy balance to maintain. But she was doing pretty well for someone half-asleep driving on an unfamiliar, snow-covered mountain road in the dead of night.

She'd made one bad decision just north of Camp Verde: instead of going farther north and cutting back through Sedona, she had chosen this mountainous route. It looked great on paper—a hell of a lot shorter, and it even connected with Sluice Road just west of Piñon Rim. And Sluice Road connected with Redman, and Redman was where Bryce and Trevor lived, and the leg bone's connected to the . . .

What am I doing out here?

The only problem was that on the map not only was the line for this road wavy, which meant it was a lot longer than it looked, but it was also dotted, one of those drive-at-your-own-risk kind of lines. Fire the navigator.

She had a death-grip on the wheel. Her eyes were three cups of coffee wide. At least the last traces of alcohol were gone. She'd left them at a rest stop called Sunset Point.

She'd hit snow five miles back and the road hadn't been clear since. In fact, it was getting steadily worse. And she hadn't passed anyone else, which meant getting stuck out here could be getting stuck for life. She tried not to dwell on that.

A warm glow lit the treetops ahead. If that was Piñon Rim, it was damn well lit for a ghost town.

H E L L in a handcart.

That's where Piñon Rim had gone.

Tom Gordon crouched against a smoldering BMW to reload, and watched the sheriff's station collapse in a hurricane of sparks and flame.

He'd defended the station for a while—until Trish took one in the head. That had pretty much done it for him. After that, he'd collected all the ordnance he could carry and freed the inmates.

The driver hadn't made it out of the Beamer. He/she/it was just another piece of blackened wreckage welded to the seat frame. The *whole town* was blackened wreckage.

When the first firebugs struck, the firemen did their job like champs. Then the frenzy hit and they took to the streets with their axes.

A bullet whistled overhead and a section of the boardwalk exploded behind him as Gordon dropped to the snow. He duck walked over the body of a fireman, his riot gun cocked, the skin on his face tight from the heat. Most of the buildings were still burning. On Front Street, the Lucky Slipper had miraculously gone out on its own; the first floor was practically untouched, but everything above that was gone.

A torn banner rolled through the street and plastered itself against a snowbank. As Gordon crawled past it to cover he read, WELCOME TO HELL. Another bullet sliced the air; a chunk of wood hissed into the snow.

That sniper wasn't on any roof. Gordon saw the next muzzle flash at the entrance to the Wizard mine. The bullet ripped a hole the size of his fist through a Honda Civic.

Gordon propped his gun over the hood and rapid-fired. He wasn't going to drop anyone from this distance, but he'd keep the so-and-so pinned. He ducked and ran to the next cover, firing as he went. Snow kicked behind him, shots from town this time.

There was nowhere to go.

Someone groaned. A man lurched into the street ahead and, just as quickly, jerked backward into the air. He hit the ground twitching.

Gordon's legs pumped. The cold air bit his lungs.

A plow had veered off Sluice and rammed a tree early on in the mayhem. A vicious snarl of burning cars had built up behind it. Clouds of oily smoke pumped into the night. He sprinted for the plow. If he could get the thing turned around, the smoke could cover his escape.

Then he'd floor it and keep it floored until he was outside Anaweh's magic rectangle, and God help anyone that so much as spit in his direction along the way.

S A R A flicked off the engine and took a deep breath in the sudden silence.

Bryce was right, there wasn't another house like this one anywhere. Its skylights blazed like hot knives, throwing long church windows across the snow-covered yard.

Maybe it was more cheerful in daylight.

So, how do we do this—just walk in? *Hi, Ex-husband! Hi, Kitty. Just happened to be in the next state and thought I'd drop by.*

Two-thirty in the morning.

She laid her head on the steering wheel and closed her eyes. She blinked herself back into the world.

Gotta do it. You're not here for those two anyway.

She shouldered the door and crunched out into the snow. For the first time since she'd started the trip, she smelled something other than stale cigarettes. Mesquite smoke was coming from the fireplace, but there was something else in the air, something even sweeter, cloying. The glow in the west flickered. A radio newsman had been her companion on the drive here. He hadn't said anything about a fire in Piñon Rim. Actually, he hadn't mentioned Piñon Rim at all.

The garage was closed; the snow was deep and smooth in the driveway. Trevor might never leave the house once he got going, but what about Cathleen? She had to shop, after all.

Sara crunched around to the porch. There were small footprints, lots of them. Megan must have had a party. Bryce's

(Trevor's) old Stingray was half-buried in the snowbank. Seeing it made her feel vaguely homesick.

She bit her lip. This wasn't her home. *This wasn't her anything*.

It was strange for Bryce to leave it out like that. It had always had its own place near the back door at their house in Schenectady.

Something lay in the snow next to it.

She stooped to retrieve the broken gear chain, and a silent alarm went off. *Bryce wouldn't have left this in the snow*. Absentminded as Trevor was, he wouldn't either; *they love that stupid bike*.

She carried the chain with her and laid it safely on the porch swing. She wiped the grease from her gloves with snow, held her breath, and knocked.

Her eyes settled on the little footprints again. So many of them. They'd come up the road; they'd left toward the forest. It was snowing, but the tracks were still sharp. What sort of parents would let their kids walk way out here at night, let alone allow them to wander into the forest?

One larger set of footprints led away from the others—toward the road.

"Sara?"

She turned so fast a nerve sang in her neck.

"Kitty?"

Cathleen smiled. "Well, this is unexpected."

"Sorry to just be here like this. Did you know your phone's out?"

"No. I didn't. I was just having coffee. It's no use trying to sleep when Trevor gets on a kick."

"I know."

"I guess you . . . Would you like a cup? Come on in."

"Thanks, yeah." She smiled so wide she thought her cheeks would crack. "That'd be great. I had some business in Sedona." It was lame but better than the truth.

"We're a long drive from Sedona."

"Tell me about it."

She followed Cathleen inside. It hadn't been nearly as excruciating as she'd expected.

TREVOR painted faster than ever, swept along by the momentum of finishing.

The Big House was the final scene. It was nighttime, but the meadow was well lit. The Stingray still lay against the snowbank, but its chain was no longer in the snow beside it. A woman lay on her back on the porch as if asleep. The swing had been thrown violently back and hung tenuously above the porch rail.

Trevor cleaned his brushes thoroughly. He would need pure color for the finale. For the light, he selected cadmium yellow and cadmium red. On the far end of his palette he squeezed out three long slugs of raw umber and a smaller one of burnt sienna; he'd wet these down with turpentine and linseed oil for the smoke.

There would be lots of smoke. Under his worktable sat five one-gallon cans of premium unleaded.

IT was just one more body in the snow. Gordon had seen plenty in town. There was no good reason to stop for this one, but stop he did. He had a gut feeling about it, and right now gut feelings were all Tom Gordon had to go on.

He pulled the shotgun over and eased the door open. The body moved.

He raised the muzzle waist-high and walked slowly toward it.

Bryce Willems raised his frozen face from the snow.

THE cab was warm and Bryce's face and limbs needled with blood coming back too quickly.

"The town's burning up, isn't it?" he said. It hurt to talk. His voice was like old cornstalks in the wind.

"Yeah."

"What are you going to do?"

Gordon shook his head. "Town's gone. A friend told me what would happen. I didn't believe him."

Bryce closed his eyes. He'd skipped school to find out about this place, and he'd avoided the sheriff on purpose. After the run-in with Connors, Jordan had practically begged him to see the sheriff and he'd gone to Aggie's instead. He found Warren Blackfoot's body on Cross Hill and he *still* wouldn't see the sheriff. If he'd done it any one of those times . . .

"Is he alive?"

"I don't know."

"Where is he?"

"In a cave somewhere out there."

Bryce sat back heavily against the seat. He'd made it all the way to Connie's house to warn her. The house was deserted. He'd been on his way to Cody's when his strength had left him entirely. At that point, he'd resigned himself to the fact there was no escape. Sleeping in the snow and never waking up would have been just fine. The cave at Sharpe's Creek was the last place in the world he wanted to go, and now it might be the last place he would go. He took a deep breath.

"I know where he's trying to go. I can show you."

Gordon slowed the car. He studied the muddy face beside him. The eyes were humorless and steady.

"Tell me what you know."

" T A K E the chair by the fire. You must be freezing."

"Thanks. Listen, I'm sure Bryce is asleep, but I'd like to see him." Sara turned her head slowly. The nerve she'd pinched was loosening up a little.

"He is, but I know he'll want to see you—and Trevor will too."

Sara doubted that last bit. She could tell by Cathleen's hesitation that Cathleen also doubted it—or wanted to.

The fire felt good. The crackle was peaceful, hypnotic.

Cathleen still hadn't checked the phone. Sara was pretty sure if someone walked in at 2:30 A.M. saying her phone was out she'd have that receiver in her hand.

Here she was, Trevor's ex, barging in from out-of-state in the middle of the night and expecting normal reactions. Miss Kitty had to be totally off-balance at this point. She was handling it pretty well all in all.

"Would you like a cappuccino?"

"Whatever you've got going there would be great."

"The couch opens into a queen-size bed. It's really comfortable."

She hadn't even thought about that. Just where was she planning on sleeping tonight? What an imposition this was. She'd talk to Bryce and then go sleep in the car. She yawned so hard her tonsils hurt.

Forget that, it was freezing out there. She'd sleep right here in this chair; imposition or not, she wasn't sure she could get up.

Cathleen hadn't gone to wake Bryce yet. She hadn't checked the phone, either. If she didn't soon, Sara'd check it herself or go crazy. *Chill out.* She's trying to make you comfortable, she's getting coffee, she's being a hostess for Christ's sake.

Sara stared at the fire. Her eyelids drooped.

CATHLEEN finished her business in the kitchen. She'd been careful, painfully careful, sliding the carving knife from the wood block.

She and Meg had spent the early evening making the kitchen knives razor-sharp. Megan had said they would need them that way and she'd been right. Meg was always right.

Cathleen walked softly into the den. She stood behind Sara and angled the knife slightly upward. There was no wooden brace in the center of the chair, only padding behind Sara's beating heart.

THE painting was finished. Trevor Willems stood before his creation and stared into the mirror.

The reflection put him smack-dab in the center of his own painting. He was part of his own creation, *and his creation was perfect*. Well, not quite perfect—there was one last thing to do.

He was prepared; he'd already doused the rags and laid them at the foot of his masterpiece. Creation was really a form of destruction, wasn't it?

He lit the match.

S A R A drifted.

There was snow everywhere, snow like she'd never seen before! She was running, dancing through it to her house. Her parents laughed from the doorway, their arms opened wide.

But the snow was sticky and thick as taffy. It tugged at her shoes, pulled them off. She pushed herself forward barefoot, but the snow dragged her back, began to pull her under. Her parents—

A flash of heat and light. It wasn't her parents anymore—it was Bryce. And he was screaming!

Another flash of heat and light stung her awake. A huge ball of flame whooshed down the stairs, baking the air, baking her lungs.

Sara's initial horror that Bryce was somewhere up there in those flames was eclipsed by the flash of a knife through the air. She stumbled backward and the blade sliced her jacket. She kicked the chair and Cathleen tumbled over it.

Sara bolted upstairs. Wallpaper blistered and cracked beside her bright yellow flames rolled down the hallway. The air was too hot to breathe. She screamed for Bryce and choked.

Cathleen pounded up the stairs behind her. She slashed through the top of Sara's boot; white-hot pain bit Sara's calf. Sara spun, lashed out, and connected, and Cathleen tumbled, screaming, onto the burning carpet.

The second floor was an inferno.

Sara had made it into the hall, but the heat forced her back again. She cried. She couldn't see a thing up there. Her hair crisped over her forehead. Her legs fried where her pants touched them, her calf felt branded.

Cathleen leapt up the stairs. Her eyes were wide, insane. Her cheek had bubbled up and turned black, a chunk of smoking carpet still embedded there. She swung the knife and Sara kicked her. Cathleen wheeled, somehow caught Sara's leg, and they both tumbled downstairs.

Sara's jacket caught fire. She ripped it off as she ran for the door. Cathleen labored at her side.

Sara made it out first. She ducked and the blade chipped her scalp. Blood sluiced down the back of her neck and spattered her shoulders. She swept the air with her forearm and blocked Cathleen's charge, but the force of the lunge threw them both into the porch swing. It flew out over the rail and lodged there. They slid beneath it. The knife whispered out into the snow.

Cathleen threw her weight on top. The window blazed behind her. Her fingers closed around Sara's throat. She dug in and squeezed.

Sara's strength ebbed as the blood flow to her brain began to dry up. She tore at Cathleen's hands but couldn't break their grip. When her nails found the burnt flesh of Cathleen's cheek, she scratched it to bloody ribbons. Cathleen shrieked as blood poured from the gaping wounds. She squeezed harder.

Sara dropped her hands to the porch in a last effort to find purchase, to pull herself up. Her arms swept a final wide arc, *and she touched something:* the gear chain had fallen beside her.

The window blew. Hot glass sizzled into the snow, into Cathleen's hair. She screeched, her grip loosened.

It was just enough.

Sara swung the frozen chain with everything she had. It ratchetted around Cathleen's neck and whipped Sara's fingers. She caught it, twisting her wrist till it nearly popped.

Cathleen released her hold on Sara completely. She dug at the chain, trying to work her fingers beneath it, but the links bit deep. Her eyes bulged in an effort to see what had gone so terribly wrong with her throat.

Sara's wrist ached and still she twisted. She managed to get her other hand on the chain and pulled even tighter. Flames roared through the open window.

Cathleen bucked against her, her feet lashing out in every direction. Her throat began to balloon. She made a strangling, cawing sound.

Sara's jaw was bruised from gritting her teeth. It was like twisting a pumped inner tube: she could feel the pressure build to the breaking point. Her own throat was ragged.

''You killed my son! *So you just die. You hear me? You . . . just . . . die!''*

Flames leapt across the ceiling of the porch and boiled down the post. Burning debris landed around them, on them. Sara gave the chain one last yank, then released it.

Cathleen's mouth flew wide open. A spray of blood stung Sara's eyes, and she rolled away. Cathleen stood straight up, wind rasping through her broken pipes, her fingers tearing at her temples, as every last valve and knuckle of plumbing in her head blew at once.

Sara dragged herself down the steps and into the snow. She crawled to safety in the middle of the yard. Her throat and calf thumped pain with every heartbeat.

Cathleen crumpled to the deck. As the fire raged around her, she lay on the porch, peaceful at last. Sara had one last glimpse of Cathleen as the porch collapsed, taking her away to Hell.

T H E Big House was a smoldering ruin as they topped the hill on Redman.

"I'm sorry," Gordon said.

Bryce shook his head. Finally, the words came out in a rasping monotone. "Nothing left in there anyway."

A white Subaru was parked nearby. They'd seen quite a few cars abandoned on Sluice. All were battered. Most had mosaics of glass beads for windows, and many were burning. This one looked new. It was pointed toward town; the driver hadn't been trying to escape.

"Rental plates," Gordon said. He drove past, one hand on the shotgun, and pulled over. Pointed tracks led from the car to the house, a woman's boots. Bryce threw open his door and jumped out.

"Hold it! You don't know who's out there!"

Bryce swallowed hard, his heart crashing against his ribs. He spun back. His eyes were wide.

"It's my mom!"

"What?" Gordon's knees popped and groaned as he lumbered after him through the deep snow. His earlier run had cost him plenty.

"My *real* mom. I know it is. We gotta find her!"

The boot tracks led back out of the house. In the middle of the yard they were met by dozens of other, littler ones. The snow there was cratered, and there were signs of a struggle. A bloody furrow had been gouged deep into the forest. Bryce's throat seemed to freeze. He could barely talk as it was.

"They got her," he rasped. *"Meg's little army."*

Gordon yelled, "Wait up!" He shouldered the shotgun and chased Bryce down, shaking the frozen batteries in his flashlight as he ran. Finally, the beam came on.

"We gotta stay together here. You ever fire a gun?"

"Yeah."

Gordon slid one from his jacket and handed it to him. It was heavy and solid, and it gleamed like the polished chrome handles on a coffin. The idea of cutting someone had been tough enough. This was a genuine killing machine. There was a peculiar sense of passage in taking it.

"You're deputized. Let's go."

Eddies of wind swirled snow through the flashlight beam. The air was heavy with a thick, musty smell, and Bryce noticed a palpable vibration, as though a strong electrical current was flowing through the forest. The deeper in they went, the stronger it was. Gordon felt it too. Finally he aimed the light into the trees. He winced.

Countless eyes stared back from high in the branches; unblinking stars in a dead universe. The birds hadn't heard about more bugs down the road; they hadn't migrated away at all. They'd stayed right where they were, where they always would be.

Just past the boulder where Bryce and Trevor had found Meg, the ground tipped down fast, and the snow made the hillside treacherous. They zigzagged down from tree to tree. At the edge of the ravine they stopped, their bodies aching, their frozen breath pumping in white clouds around them.

Across the creek, the Wizard's cave was a silver-blue eye. The camouflage had been ripped away; no need to hide, *Meg and her Wizard ran the game now*. Just seeing the entrance made Bryce's lungs seize up. He could feel the walls of that tomb closing around him, *and this time Meg would be waiting inside*. If he'd come here with her a month ago, if he'd only kept that one promise, they'd be safe and warm in their beds now; the shove that sent this mad wheel spinning would never have happened. He couldn't help wondering if Shep Easton had broken a similar promise.

Gordon's voice came as if through a dense fog.

"If you wanna stay up here and keep an eye out, that's okay."

Bryce shook his head.

"They've got my mom."

"Okay, then. Let's go."

They struggled down past the boulders to the creekbed. Lights flared over the water like tracers as they ran along the bank. When, at last, they stood before the glowing maw of the cave, Bryce saw reflections of deep water, the silver plane of the surface miles above his head. He blinked the image away. The gun he'd been given was solid and oddly reassuring in his hand, but would it do any good against whatever was in there? And what if he had to shoot Meg? *Could he do it?* He'd been holding the knife when he hit her—he hadn't used it.

Gordon must have read his thoughts. His face, scarred by gunfire and lit blue by the cave's eerie light, should have been frightening. His eyes belied that. Even with all they'd seen, they were gentle now.

"If the Indians are right, it could be your sister or us. Can you handle that?"

Bryce nodded.

"The guns'll be loud inside. They'll surprise you if you're not ready. Make sure the safety's out and try not to shoot my butt off."

Gordon nearly filled the entrance as he hunched inside. Bryce might as well have crawled into a coffin and closed the lid. He fought the urge to run back out and keep running as they passed the first bend.

At the back wall, the floor dropped away into the light.

"That was underwater," Bryce whispered. "Meg came back here alone. She must have gone under. She was soaked when we found her."

"Brave kid."

"Yeah."

Gordon crouched low and peered over the edge. He slid the shotgun carefully to Bryce.

"If something grabs me, empty the thing on whatever sticks its head out."

Slowly, Gordon eased himself into the hole. When he stood on firm ground, he nodded.

"We're clear."

Bryce handed him the shotgun and followed him down.

This passage was narrower than the first. Light poured from a gash in the ceiling farther on, giving the wet rock a mirrored finish. The walls were dotted with dark holes.

Bryce felt an odd tremor as they made their way through the chamber, as though something were moving just behind the walls.

Suddenly, water thundered into the chamber.

The impact swept Bryce off his feet, and he fought his way forward to the light, barely able to keep the gun over his head. Gordon boosted him through the hole in the ceiling and Bryce splashed into another chamber.

If he'd had any wind left, he would've screamed it out.

A small skeleton sat beside the hole. Its tiny fingers clutched the tattered remnants of a leather ball.

Gordon pulled himself up and out. He grimaced at the find.

"Boyd Easton," Bryce said, when a good breath finally came. "He found this place a hundred years ago. This time it was Meg."

They stood in the center of a wide chamber. The walls were filled with tunnels. Only one tunnel was lit and they ran to it.

"It's leading us."

"*Meg* is."

Water ran behind these walls too. Bryce could hear it. The sides of the cave were pitted, but the ceiling was smooth. If this one flooded, they'd have no place to go. Bryce took a deep breath of the cold damp air. A metallic, bitter taste filled his mouth. They plunged ahead.

The tunnel curved. The light grew brighter. The floor gave way to a narrow ledge; deep water flowed beside it.

Gordon raised the shotgun and motioned for Bryce to stop.

And then Bryce heard the voices too.

They moved forward carefully, their backs flat to the wall. Bryce's finger twitched against the trigger. Gordon raised his hand and Bryce held his breath.

The sheriff pulled himself around the bend and straightened. He motioned Bryce forward.

Kids, maybe twenty of them, stood silently along the ledge. They wore twisted, leathery masks, corded and lined with deep grooves. At least that's what Bryce thought until he moved closer.

He'd seen pictures of mummies in Meg's *National Geographics*; this looked worse.

Gordon did little more than brush one of them as he tried to inch by and the whole row toppled. They burst to dust as they struck the ledge. Their collapse left a fetid green cloud in the chamber.

Laughter echoed through the passage. Gordon shook his head.

As cold as it was, Bryce had grown a second skin of sweat.

As they walked forward, the voices grew louder and the tunnel opened. They stood, speechless, at the doorway to a gigantic ballroom.

Through the flat, harsh light, they saw well-dressed people and long tables piled high with food. Paintings and sculptures lined the walls. A huge ice sculpture of a wizard stood behind the last table. Champagne poured, glasses clinked.

Color leeched into the ghostly blue light and there they were. But where were they?

Most of these people were strangers, many of whom were fairly exotic, a nationality Bryce couldn't place. But the others . . .

Larry Brill stuffed a small potato heaped with egg and caviar into his mouth. Champagne slopped to the floor from his glass. Even in a tux, Larry was a pig. Bill Jordan held a tray of hors d'oeuvre aloft as he glided between the guests, no trace of a limp now.

There were other faces Bryce had seen only in sepia tones before: Katie Easton chatted with Lill Trenton and Del Mac-

Kenna, who were arm in arm with two guys sporting handlebar moustaches. Shep and Boyd Easton sat with a group of other kids off to one side.

Gordon and Bryce had gone in after a monster and found Brigadoon.

"Dad!"

His father strolled through the crowd, not the living skeleton Bryce had last seen, but tall and strong. *Trevor was safe. He was okay.* That thing in the studio, whatever it was, was gone. Bryce ran to him.

"Glad you finally made it!"

Trevor smiled, and Bryce couldn't help noticing his teeth. All that coffee had left them stained, but now they were white as a new sink, and the gray was gone from his hair. Like everybody else here, he looked great, better than ever.

His father walked past him. Aggie Hudson, barely contained in black chiffon, slipped her arm beneath Trevor's.

"They can't see you."

A gorgeous girl in a red dress walked toward him. It took Bryce a heartbeat to recognize Megan. She looked like she'd just left a senior prom. That cold wire was twisting its way down Bryce's spine again.

A movement at the ice sculpture caught his eye. In its center was another, smaller one—a baby wizard or something. He could swear the little one had twitched.

"You're invited," Meg said. "Your friend's invited too."

He'd forgotten all about the sheriff.

Gordon stood just inside the entrance to the ballroom. He made no gesture either of appreciation or disapproval. He was staring dead ahead.

Bryce took a long, hard look around him. Trevor had just said something that made Aggie laugh. Two guys who looked like college students from the twenties looked up from their card game and smiled, and he recognized the codgers from Coop's. Cathleen held Boyd Easton on her lap now. The fact that Aggie was all over her husband didn't seem to bother her in the least. Everybody was happy.

Meg smiled.

"It's great, isn't it? If you want something, the Wizard gives it to you, *for free.*"

"*Where's my mom?*"

"Uhmm . . ." She glanced casually around the room. "Sara's here . . . somewhere."

"What about Rose and Connie? *What about Cody?*"

Her eyes narrowed. For a split second, the room seemed to pulse. The eerie blue light dashed along the walls and was gone.

"Not everybody wants it bad enough." Her smile sent a peculiar current through him. Her eyes were deep somehow, deep and as blue as the sky he'd seen that first morning after the storm. He knew he shouldn't be looking at them, but there was something in her eyes drawing him in, *draining him*. She ran the tip of her tongue along her lips, wetting them as she moved toward him.

Bryce's feet were lead blocks at the ends of his tired legs. He stepped slowly back and nearly fell. Behind him, deep water flowed sluggishly through a wide crack in the stone floor.

"Put that down. It's a *mean* thing. You don't need to be mean here."

The gun was level with her heart. His finger was still on the trigger. It had to move back a centimeter at most and the killing machine would go off.

"I tried to tell you about this place, about the party." Her eyes flashed the way they had back in the hallway, but he couldn't turn away this time. They were wide and beautiful. Pinpricks of light burned deep within them.

"Nobody dies here. Everybody's happy. *The party goes on forever!*"

He wanted to believe it. He wanted to believe that his father really was here, strong and alive again; that Meg would still be his little sister; that Sara would be with them. They'd all be together. *He could almost believe that life would be perfect then.*

GORDON gripped the shotgun. He was seeing an incredible banquet set in the middle of a cave, and apparently Bryce was seeing it too. But Gordon wasn't buying it. He'd seen the town go nuts. He'd seen Piñon Rim die, and many of these people with it. But here he was, and here they were.

Whatever was causing him to see this madness—Whitefeather's Spirit, whatever—this couldn't be happening.

But if this wasn't, what was?

Moments after they'd stepped into the cavern he'd begun reciting the Miranda card in his head. It was simple, direct, something he could concentrate on. He repeated it over and over. Gradually, his thoughts began to clear.

The scene began a slow fade to blue. The bluer it got, the harder he concentrated. The laughter was explosive. The costumes were colorful and bright. People rushed here and there, more food was brought in. The scene came back. But for a second there . . .

Near the center of the floor was a sculpture of some sort covered with a black veil. He shut out everything else and focused on that. He started the Miranda card again:

You have the right to remain silent. Anything you say can and will be used against you in a court of law. You have the right . . .

Gradually the veil faded, and another form appeared in its place. Lights flashed, swirling around the room and stinging his eyes.

The banquet was gone, the *sculpture* unveiled.

His jaw dropped. It was a woman tied to a post. *Bryce's mom—it had to be.* She was screaming her lungs out, but Bryce couldn't hear her. He stood a few feet away at the edge of the river, talking calmly to what looked like a whirling ball of light. While Gordon had been dreaming he'd let Bryce walk square into a trap.

The ball exploded, a million needles of blinding light fanned out. Gordon couldn't see to aim. In a flash, the light pulled in on itself and began to solidify once more. Gordon made out what seemed to be long, tapering limbs. Something nearly shapeless churned and rolled in its belly. The creature swept toward Bryce, a black gash of a mouth opened across its eyeless face.

Gordon whipped the shotgun up and something hot struck him in the gut. The shotgun flipped out of his hands. His own blood arced across the floor as he flew back into the passageway. He heard the shot an instant later.

His stomach was torn wide open. He nearly blacked out from nausea and pain. *What hit him? An elephant gun?* A gut shot. Why couldn't it have been his heart or his head?

A fistful of limestone blasted away near his hand. His shotgun was at the bottom of the river; he dragged himself along the ledge and pulled out his Beretta.

He leaned toward the cavern, holding in the coils of his own intestines. He tried yelling at Bryce to use the gun or grab cover, but he barely made a sound.

The shots had come from somewhere high, about ten o'clock. He fired two quick rounds that way and pulled back in agony from the motion.

He'd seen khaki up there, a *uniform* behind the rocks. Pat Phillips? It made sense. Par for this course. His head floated. He turned and vomited.

Needles of light cascaded off the rocks, and a wind whirled up from nowhere. It howled through the cavern. Bryce's little sister stood at the center of the light now, where the creature had been. Bryce was still talking to her, oblivious to it all. He'd had the gun on her, but now it drifted down to his side.

Gordon lifted the Beretta. It took the strength of Hercules to do it. He aimed at the center of her back.

The blue light flared, went white and then black.

The gun fell beside him and went off. His head dropped to his chest, his eyes staring at the scarlet clouds billowing in the water next to him. He didn't see the clouds, and he never saw the small bottle float by.

A s Meg leaned forward to kiss Bryce, something exploded. A shockwave rippled the ballroom; blue light filtered through. Bryce shook his head.

Meg in the prom dress had vanished and in her place was Meg the way she'd looked in the hallway: years younger, her shirt and arms spattered with blood, her lips split wide and swollen.

Behind her, the sculpture within a sculpture twitched, and

suddenly Bryce saw those little kids disintegrating in the hall, blowing up like puffballs; he saw Warren Blackfoot's small, blue hand jutting from a makeshift grave, *and he saw his mother's bloody footprints in the snow.*

"What's wrong?" she said.

Meg changed again. She was little now. She wore her old caving suit and her glasses. She moved toward him and he brought the gun to her heart.

"Get my mom!"

"Put that stupid gun down. *It can't do anything!"*

More explosions, barely there at all, as if a battle was being waged in some far-off land. The room seemed to ripple in sympathy.

"You can bleed, Meg. *I know I can hurt you."*

"You don't know anything! I invited you here!" Meg was seventeen again, back in her red formal. *"I invited you."*

"I wanna see Sara, *now!"*

"We don't need her, Bryce!" She shook her head. He thought he saw tears in her eyes.

Bryce held the gun with both hands. It was hot, and his hands were shaking and sweating rivers. If he pulled the trigger, Meg's chest would explode like a ripe melon.

"I've got friends now. Everybody likes me! And I'll never go blind here, Bryce! *The Wizard made that go away."*

"It made the whole town go away! Don't you get it? Your friends are dead! Your Wizard killed them! This is a graveyard!"

"The Wizard can give us whatever we want! I'm all grown up!"

"You're not grown up—you're old! It sucked your life out!"

Another explosion. Closer this time. And then, over all else, he heard his name. *Sara was screaming his name.* Suddenly, the image of the banquet was like a threadbare cloth tearing before his eyes, and blue light poured from billions of holes.

Sara was only a few yards away! She was screaming!

The gun whipped out of his hands.

"Fine," Meg snarled. "Have it your way." He threw his hand up to protect himself, but her hand was lightning-fast.

Something else was faster.

She screamed so loud he thought his ears would burst. Her

face was a mask of pain and rage. An arrow had ripped through her forearm. She spun away and the whole world seemed to spin with her. Wind whistled through the cavern. Spears of blue light darted in every direction. Gunshots pounded the air. A calcite pedestal shattered inches from his shoulder.

"Get down!"

An Indian man with long silver hair stood in the river. His next arrow was pointed directly at Bryce's head. Bryce dropped as it sang over him. It found its mark on a ledge high above Bryce. A man tumbled from his perch and splashed into the river, his rifle following him down.

The wind sent the river washing over the cavern floor. Bryce leapt for his gun and rescued it before the wave took it away. Megan's screams joined with Sara's in the wind. He couldn't see them. He couldn't see anything. Bursts of light pierced his eyes. The freezing wind whipped him.

It was as though he were being swallowed whole by the blinding light, absorbed into it. The feeling drained like blood from his limbs; he drifted. Then a tall shadow broke through.

The Indian man stood before him.

"This will guide you!" He pressed a silver medallion into Bryce's palm.

"My mother!"

"There's no time. Go now!"

The Indian man was gone. It was as though he had never been. The cold silver pulsed in Bryce's hand. He felt it move softly against his fingers, as if drawn by a magnet. He began to walk blindly forward, then to run.

Screams and laughter. The wind buffeted him. He saw faces in the swirling bursts of light and dark. He saw Percival Easton, his scorched, bleeding hands clutching the ornate framework that trapped him. He saw Shep standing above Sharpe's Creek, turning back too late to ward off the blow that would send him plunging to his death. He saw Rose Bowman, her face slick with kerosene, screaming as the flames leapt toward her.

And he saw his mother. Sara had come for him at last. And if he failed now, she would be just one more victim of this hideous cycle, another reaped and scattered by the Harvest.

The wind slowed, then died altogether. The light flickered and the voices went silent. He found himself in another passage. The walls here were slimy and close, very close. Blue and white diamonds raced along them. He had that feeling of being on the bottom of a deep pool, seeing the surface high above, and knowing he couldn't reach it. He heard water everywhere, rushing over and around him.

He held the gun straight out as he ran, clicking the safety in and out. The tunnel veered sharply dead ahead.

A long and narrow shadow knifed across the turn. Meg's shadow. *She was waiting for him.*

He slowed to a walk.

"Meg?" he practically croaked.

"Bryce?" she said, mimicking him.

His throat was dry as salt.

She didn't move. The light grew brighter behind her.

The bend in the tunnel was less than ten feet away. Her shadow remained where it was, rigid. The medallion pulsed in sync with the light.

He put his back to the wall and inched forward. The cave yawned open. The smooth wall reflected the light, amplified it. He pulled the gun to his chest. Her shadow was two steps away. He took a deep breath and clenched his teeth. He would have to do it this time. He'd have to pull the trigger.

He stepped into her shadow and screamed.

Megan's flesh had shriveled down to the bone. Her eyes were crescents of yellow parchment. They turned his way and stopped. One last breath whistled in her throat.

Behind her body, the light brightened, drew into itself.

He raised the gun to its throbbing center.

"I'm okay, Bryce. I'm really okay." Meg's voice had come from the light. It was small again. A little kid's voice.

"Look at me. *I'm better than I ever was.*"

Bryce froze. The Wizard sat at the back of the cave, formless and white. Blue light swirled beneath its transparent skin.

Megan was curled inside it. She was alive.

Cold light burned in her eyes as she turned to face him.

"That was a phase, like a cocoon. *This is forever!*"

She peaked her fingertips, thrust them forward, and a thin membrane began to tear. Blue light flooded out.

"You can be forever too. *Come and be with me.*"

She opened her arms wide as she pushed through.

He saw her skating backward in Central Park, laughing at him over her shoulder. Then he saw her grinning down at him from her room in the Big House.

He gripped the medallion in his hand, and he could feel its cold roughness where the circle was broken.

"Meg . . ."

Bryce leaned into the light and slid his arm around her shoulders. He placed the gun to her chest and closed his eyes. He kept pulling the trigger long after it ceased to matter, long after her screams had stopped ringing in his ears.

27

W H E N he found his way back to the cavern at last, his mother hugged him so tight he thought she'd never let go, and that would have been just fine with him.

Sadly, they laid Gordon to rest where he'd fallen. The Indian man never reappeared, and though Bryce had gripped for dear life the medallion he'd been given, by the time he'd returned it was gone.

He doesn't know how long he and Sara followed the underground river in total darkness, not sure if their next footsteps would bring them closer to escape or hurl them to their deaths. It could have been hours, it might have been days. After a time, the river disappeared beneath the stone. It was there that they saw the first bit of daylight and followed it. When they finally emerged, they stood near the top of Harper's Peak, in the mouth of the Wizard mine. It wasn't until that moment that he cried.

There's a dream he still has some winter nights at his new home in Santa Fe, and when a cold wind rattles his bedroom window he'll wake, covered in sweat, those images, forgotten by day, suddenly remembered.

In his dream there's a bright light, the sun glaring off the snow, and the smell of smoke. He can see the cemetery on Cross Hill and just outside the fence, the grave of Rose Bowman, no longer lonely. A blackened post has been sunk at its foot, and chained to it is something charred and hideously disfigured. A wealth of silver and turquoise jewelry hangs from its throat, and, placed carefully on a stone before it, is a thin gold chain with a single, small heart.

By morning, the images are gone.

There's a photo of Meg on his desk. It's her Confirmation picture and she's wearing her glasses.

Some mornings he'll hear the screen door slam, and he'll glance out his window half-expecting to see her racing to the bus stop. But it's always just Cervantes chasing something imaginary through the backyard.

3-el